# Elster's Folly

# Elster's Folly

## A Novel

# Mrs. Henry Wood

**MINT EDITIONS**

*Elster's Folly: A Novel* was first published in 1866.

This edition published by Mint Editions 2021.

ISBN 9781513281131 | E-ISBN 9781513286150

Published by Mint Editions®

minteditionbooks.com

Publishing Director: Jennifer Newens
Design & Production: Rachel Lopez Metzger
Project Manager: Micaela Clark
Typesetting: Westchester Publishing Services

# Contents

I. By the Early Train      7

II. Willy Gum      19

III. Anne Ashton      28

IV. The Countess-Dowager      38

V. Jealousy      47

VI. At the Bridge      57

VII. Listeners      68

VIII. The Wager Boats      78

IX. Waiting for Dinner      87

X. Mr. Pike's Visit      97

XI. The Inquest      105

XII. Later in the Day      113

XIII. Fever      122

XIV. Another Patient      132

XV. Val's Dilemma      141

XVI. Between the Two      151

XVII. An Agreeable Wedding      162

XVIII. The Stranger      174

XIX. A Chance Meeting 182

XX. The Stranger Again 191

XXI. Secret Care 205

XXII. Asking the Rector 214

XXIII. Mr. Carr at Work 224

XXIV. Somebody Else at Work 234

XXV. At Hartledon 242

XXVI. Under the Trees 252

XXVII. A Tête-à-Tête Breakfast 263

XXVIII. Once more 273

XXIX. Cross-questioning Mr. Carr 283

XXX. Maude's Disobedience 293

XXXI. The Sword Slipped 301

XXXII. In the Park 311

XXXIII. Coming Home 321

XXXIV. Mr. Pike on the Wing 330

XXXV. The Shed Razed 339

XXXVI. The Dowager's Alarm 346

XXXVII. A Painful Scene 356

XXXVIII. Explanations 365

# I

## By the Early Train

The ascending sun threw its slanting rays abroad on a glorious August morning, and the little world below began to awaken into life—the life of another day of sanguine pleasure or of fretting care.

Not on many fairer scenes did those sunbeams shed their radiance than on one existing in the heart of England; but almost any landscape will look beautiful in the early light of a summer's morning. The county, one of the midlands, was justly celebrated for its scenery; its rich woods and smiling plains, its river and gentler streams. The harvest was nearly gathered in—it had been a late season—but a few fields of golden grain, in process of reaping, gave their warm tints to the landscape. In no part of the country had the beauties of nature been bestowed more lavishly than on this, the village of Calne, situated about seven miles from the county town.

It was an aristocratic village, on the whole. The fine seat of the Earl of Hartledon, rising near it, had caused a few families of note to settle there, and the nest of white villas gave the place a prosperous and picturesque appearance. But it contained a full proportion of the poor or labouring class; and these people were falling very much into the habit of writing the village "Cawn," in accordance with its pronunciation. Phonetic spelling was more in their line than Johnson's Dictionary. Of what may be called the middle class the village held few, if any: there were the gentry, the small shopkeepers, and the poor.

Calne had recently been exalted into importance. A year or two before this bright August morning some good genius had brought a railway to it—a railway and a station, with all its accompanying work and bustle. Many trains passed it in the course of the day; for it was in the direct line of route from the county town, Garchester, to London, and the traffic was increasing. People wondered what travellers had done, and what sort of a round they traversed, before this direct line was made.

The village itself lay somewhat in a hollow, the ground rising to a gentle eminence on either side. On the one eminence, to the west, was situated the station; on the other, eastward, rose the large stone mansion, Hartledon House. The railway took a slight *détour* outside Calne, and was a conspicuous feature to any who chose to look at it; for the line had been raised above the village hollow to correspond with the height at either end.

Six o'clock was close at hand, and the station began to show signs of life. The station-master came out of his cottage, and opened one or two doors on the platform. He had held the office scarcely a year yet; and had come a stranger to Calne. Sitting down in his little bureau of a place, on the door of which was inscribed "Station-master—Private," he began sorting papers on the desk before him. A few minutes, and the clock struck six; upon which he went out to the platform. It was an open station, as these small stations generally are, the small waiting-rooms and offices on either side scarcely obstructing the view of the country, and the station-master looked far out in the distance, towards the east, beyond the low-lying village houses, shading his eyes with his hand from the dazzling sun.

"Her's late this morning."

The interruption came from the surly porter, who stood by, and referred to the expected train, which ought to have been in some minutes before. According to the precise time, as laid down in the way-bills, it should reach Calne seven minutes before six.

"They have a heavy load, perhaps," remarked the station-master.

The train was chiefly for goods; a slow train, taking no one knew how many hours to travel from London. It would bring passengers also; but very few availed themselves of it. Now and then it happened that the station at Calne was opened for nothing; the train just slackened its speed and went on, leaving neither goods nor anything else behind it. Sometimes it took a few early travellers from Calne to Garchester; especially on Wednesdays and Saturdays, Garchester market-days; but it rarely left passengers at Calne.

"Did you hear the news, Mr. Markham?" asked the porter.

"What news?" returned the station-master.

"I heard it last night. Jim come into the Elster Arms with it, and *he'd* heard it at Garchester. We are going to have two more sets o' telegraph wires here. I wonder how much more work they'll give us to do?"

"So you were at the Elster Arms again last night, Jones?" remarked the station-master, his tone reproving, whilst he passed over in silence Mr. Jones's item of news.

"I wasn't in above an hour," grumbled the man.

"Well, it is your own look-out, Jones. I have said what I could to you at odd times; but I believe it has only tried your patience; so I'll say no more."

"Has my wife been here again complaining?" asked the man, raising his face in anger.

"No; I have not seen your wife, except at church, these two months. But I know what public-houses are to you, and I was thinking of your little children."

"Ugh!" growled the man, apparently not gratified at the reminder of his flock; "there's a peck o' *them* surely! Here she comes!"

The last sentence was spoken in a different tone; one of relief, either at getting rid of the subject, or at the arrival of the train. It was about opposite to Hartledon when he caught sight of it, and it came on with a shrill whistle, skirting the village it towered above; a long line of covered waggons with a passenger carriage or two attached to them. Slackening its pace gradually, but not in time, it shot past the station, and had to back into it again.

The guard came out of his box and opened the door of one of the carriages—a dirty-looking second-class compartment; the other was a third-class; and a gentleman leaped out. A tall, slender man of about four-and-twenty; a man evidently of birth and breeding. He wore a light summer overcoat on his well-cut clothes, and had a most attractive face.

"Is there any law against putting on a first-class carriage to this night-train?" he asked the guard in a pleasing voice.

"Well, sir, we never get first-class passengers by it," replied the man; "or hardly any passengers at all, for the matter of that. We are too long on the road for passengers to come by us."

"It might happen, though," returned the traveller, significantly. "At any rate, I suppose there's no law against your carriages being clean, whatever their class. Look at that one."

He pointed to the one he had just left, as he walked up to the station-master. The guard looked cross, and gave the carriage door a slam.

"Was a portmanteau left here last night by the last train from London?" inquired the traveller of the station-master.

"No, sir; nothing was left here. At least, I think not. Any name on it, sir?"

"Elster."

A quick glance from the station-master's eyes met the answer. Elster was the name of the family at Hartledon. He wondered whether this could be one of them, or whether the name was merely a coincidence.

"There was no portmanteau left, was there, Jones?" asked the station-master.

"There couldn't have been," returned the porter, touching his cap to the stranger. "I wasn't on last night; Jim was; but it would have been put in the office for sure; and there's not a ghost of a thing in it this morning."

"It must have been taken on to Garchester," remarked the traveller; and, turning to the guard, he gave him directions to look after it, and despatch it back again by the first train, slipping at the same time a gratuity into his hand.

The guard touched his hat humbly; he now knew who the gentleman was. And he went into inward repentance for slamming the carriage-door, as he got into his box, and the engine and train puffed on.

"You'll send it up as soon as it comes," said the traveller to the station-master.

"Where to, sir?"

The stranger raised his eyes in slight surprise, and pointed to the house in the distance. He had assumed that he was known.

"To Hartledon."

Then he *was* one of the family! The station-master touched his hat. Mr. Jones, in the background, touched his, and for the first time the traveller's eye fell upon him as he was turning to leave the platform.

"Why, Jones! It's never you?"

"Yes, it is, sir." But Mr. Jones looked abashed as he acknowledged himself. And it may be observed that his language, when addressing this gentleman, was a slight improvement upon the homely phraseology of his everyday life.

"But—you are surely not working here!—a porter!"

"My business fell through, sir," returned the man. "I'm here till I can turn myself round, sir, and get into it again."

"What caused it to fall through?" asked the traveller; a kindly sympathy in his fine blue eyes.

Mr. Jones shuffled upon one foot. He would not have given the true answer—"Drinking"—for the world.

"There's such opposition started up in the place, sir; folks would draw your heart's blood from you if they could. And then I've such a lot of mouths to feed. I can't think what the plague such a tribe of children come for. Nobody wants 'em."

The traveller laughed; but put no further questions. Remembering somewhat of Mr. Jones's propensity in the old days, he thought perhaps something besides children and opposition had had to do with the downfall. He stood for a moment looking at the station which had not been completed when he last saw it—and a very pretty station it was, surrounded by its gay flowerbeds—and then went down the road.

"I suppose he is one of the Hartledon family, Jones?" said the station-master, looking after him.

"He's the earl's brother," replied Mr. Jones, relapsing into sulkiness. "There's only them two left; t'other died. Wonder if they be coming to Hartledon again? Calne haven't seemed the same since they left it."

"Which is this one?"

"He can't be anybody but himself," retorted Mr. Jones, irascibly, deeming the question superfluous. "There be but the two left, I say— the earl and him; everybody knows him for the Honourable Percival Elster. The other son, George, died; leastways, was murdered."

"Murdered!" echoed the station-master aghast.

"I don't see that it could be called much else but murder," was Mr. Jones's answer. "He went out with my lord's gamekeepers one night and got shot in a poaching fray. 'Twas never known for certain who fired the shot, but I think I could put my finger on the man if I tried. Much good *that* would do, though! There's no proof."

"What are you saying, Jones?" cried the station-master, staring at his subordinate, and perhaps wondering whether he had already that morning paid a visit to the tap of the Elster Arms.

"I'm saying nothing that half the place didn't say at the time, Mr. Markham. *You* hadn't come here then, Mr. Elster—he was the Honourable George—went out one night with the keepers when warm work was expected, and got shot for his pains. He lived some weeks, but they couldn't cure him. It was in the late lord's time. *He* died soon after, and the place has been deserted ever since."

"And who do you suppose fired the shot?"

"Don't know that it 'ud be safe to say," rejoined the man. "He might give my neck a twist some dark night if he heard on't. He's the blackest sheep we've got in Calne, sir."

"I suppose you mean Pike," said the station-master. "He has the character for being that, I believe. I've seen no harm in the man myself."

"Well, it was Pike," said the porter. "That is, some of us suspected him. And that's how Mr. George Elster came by his death. And this one, Mr. Percival, shot up into notice, as being the only one left, except Lord Elster."

"And who's Lord Elster?" asked the station-master, not remembering to have heard the title before.

Mr. Jones received the question with proper contempt. Having been familiar with Hartledon and its inmates all his life, he had as little compassion for those who were not so, as he would have had for a man who did not understand that Garchester was in England.

"The present Earl of Hartledon," said he, shortly. "In his father's lifetime—and the old lord lived to see Mr. George buried—he was Lord Elster. Not one of my tribe of brats but could tell that any Lord Elster must be the eldest son of the Earl of Hartledon," he concluded with a fling at his superior.

"Ah, well, I have had other things to do since I came here besides inquiring into titles and folks that don't concern me," remarked the station-master. "What a good-looking man he is!"

The praise applied to Mr. Elster, after whom he was throwing a parting look. Jones gave an ungracious assent, and turned into the shed where the lamps were kept, to begin his morning's work.

All the world would have been ready to echo the station-master's words as to the good looks of Percival Elster, known universally amidst his friends as Val Elster; for these good looks did not lie so much in actual beauty—which one lauds, and another denies, according to its style—as in the singularly pleasant expression of countenance; a gift that finds its weight with all.

He possessed a bright face; his complexion was fair and fresh, his eyes were blue and smiling, his features were good; and as he walked down the road, and momentarily lifted his hat to push his light hair— as much of a golden colour as hair ever is—from his brow, and gave a cordial "good-day" to those who met him on their way to work— few strangers but would have given him a second look of admiration. A physiognomist might have found fault with the face; and, whilst admitting its sweet expression, would have condemned it for its utter want of resolution. What of that? The inability to say "no" to any sort of persuasion, whether for good or ill; in short, a total absence of what may be called moral courage; had been from his childhood Val Elster's besetting sin.

There was a joke against little Val when he was a boy of seven. Some playmates had insisted upon his walking into a pond, and standing there. Poor Val, quite unable to say "no," walked in, and was nearly drowned for his pains. It had been a joke against him then; how many such "jokes" could have been brought against him since he grew up, Val himself could alone tell. As the child had been, so was the man. The scrapes his irresolution brought him into he did not care to glance at; and whilst only too well aware of his one lamentable deficiency, he was equally aware that he was powerless to stand against it.

People, in speaking of this, called it "Elster's Folly." His extreme sensitiveness as to the feelings of other people, whether equals or inferiors, was, in a degree, one of the causes of this yielding nature; and he would almost rather have died than offer any one a personal offence, an insulting word or look. There are such characters in the world; none can deny that they are amiable; but, oh, how unfit to battle with life!

Mr. Elster walked slowly through the village on his way to Hartledon, whose inmates he would presently take by surprise. It was about twenty months since he had been there. He had left Hartledon at the close of the last winter but one; an appointment having been obtained for him as an *attaché* to the Paris embassy. Ten months of service, and some scrape he fell into caused him (a good deal of private interest was brought to bear in the matter) to be removed to Vienna; but he had not remained there very long. He seemed to have a propensity for getting into trouble, or rather an inability to keep out of it. Latterly he had been staying in London with his brother.

His thoughts wandered to the past as he looked at the chimneys of Hartledon—all he could see of it—from the low-lying ground. He remembered the happy time when they had been children in it; five of them—the three boys and the two girls—he himself the youngest and the pet. His eldest sister, Margaret, had been the first to leave it. She married Sir James Cooper, and went with him to his remote home in Scotland, where she was still. The second to go was Laura, who married Captain Level, and accompanied him to India. Then he, Val, a young man in his teens, went out into the world, and did all sorts of harm in it in an unintentional sort of way; for Percival Elster never did wrong by premeditation. Next came the death of his mother. He was called home from a sojourn in Scotland—where his stay had been prolonged from the result of an accident—to bid her farewell. Then he was at home for a year or more, making love to charming Anne Ashton. The next move was his departure for Paris; close upon which, within a fortnight, occurred the calamity to his brother George. He came back from Paris to see him in London, whither George had been conveyed for medical advice, and there then seemed a chance of his recovery; but it was not borne out, and the ill-fated young man died. Lord Hartledon's death was the next. He had an incurable complaint, and his death followed close upon his son's. Lord Elster became Earl of Hartledon; and he, Val, heir-presumptive. Heir-presumptive! Val Elster was heir to all sorts of follies, but—

"Good morning to your lordship!"

The speaker was a man in a smock-frock, passing with a reaping-hook on his shoulder. Mr. Elster's sunny face and cheery voice gave back the salutation with tenfold heartiness, smiling at the title. Half the peasantry had been used to addressing the brothers so, indiscriminately; they were all lords to them.

The interruption awoke Mr. Elster from his thoughts, and he marched gaily on down the middle of the road, noting its familiar features. The small shops were on his right hand, the line of rails behind them. A few white villas lay scattered on his left, and beyond them, but not to be seen from this village street, wound the river; both running parallel with the village lying between them. Soon the houses ceased; it was a small place at best; and after an open space came the church. It lay on his right, a little way back from the road, and surrounded by a large churchyard. Almost opposite, on the other side of the road, but much further back, was a handsome modern white house; its delightful gardens sloping almost to the river. This was the residence of the Rector, Dr. Ashton, a wealthy man and a church dignitary, prebendary and sub-dean of Garchester Cathedral. Percival Elster looked at it yearningly, if haply he might see there the face of one he loved well; but the blinds were drawn, and the inmates were no doubt steeped in repose.

"If she only knew I was here!" he fondly aspirated.

On again a few steps, and a slight turn in the road brought him to a small red-brick house on the same side as the church, with green shutters attached to its lower windows. It lay in the midst of a garden well stocked with vegetables, fruit, and the more ordinary and brighter garden-flowers. A straight path led to the well-kept house-door, its paint fresh and green, and its brass-plate as bright as rubbing could make it. Mr. Elster could not read the inscription on the plate from where he was, but he knew it by heart: "Jabez Gum, Parish Clerk." And there was a smaller plate indicating other offices held by Jabez Gum.

"I wonder if Jabez is as shadowy as ever?" thought Mr. Elster, as he walked on.

One more feature, and that is the last you shall hear of until Hartledon is reached. Close to the clerk's garden, on a piece of waste land, stood a small wooden building, no better than a shed.

It had once been a stable, but so long as Percival Elster could remember, it was nothing but a receptacle for schoolboys playing at hide-and-seek. Many a time had he hidden there. Something different in this shed now caught his eye; the former doorway had been boarded up, and a long iron tube, like a thin chimney, ascended from its roof.

"Who on earth has been adding that to it?" exclaimed Mr. Elster.

A little way onward, and he came to the lodge-gates of Hartledon. The house was on the same side as the Rectory, its park stretching eastward, its grounds, far more beautiful and extensive than those of the Rectory, descending to the river. As he went in at the smaller side-gate, he turned his gaze on the familiar road he had quitted, and most distinctly saw a wreath of smoke ascending from the pipe above the shed. Could it be a chimney, after all?

The woman of the lodge, hearing footsteps, came to her door with hasty words.

"Now then! What makes you so late this morning? Didn't I—" And there she stopped in horror; transfixed; for she was face to face with Mr. Elster.

"Law, sir! *You!* Mercy be good to us!"

He laughed. In her consternation she could only suppose he had dropped from the clouds. Giving her a pleasant greeting, he drew her attention to the appearance that was puzzling him. The woman came out and looked at it.

"*Is* it a chimney, Mrs. Capper?"

"Well, yes, sir, it be. Pike have put it in. He come here, nobody knew how or when, he put himself into the old shed, and has never left it again."

"Who is 'Pike'?"

"It's hard to say, sir; a many would give a deal to know. He lay in the shed a bit at first, as it were, all open. Then he boarded up that front doorway, opened a door at the back, cut out a square hole for a window, and stuck that chimney in the roof. And there he's lived ever since, and nobody interferes with him. His name's Pike, and that's all that's known. I should think my lord will see to it when he comes."

"Does he work for his living?"

"Never does a stroke o' work for nobody, sir. And how he lives is just one o' them mysteries that can't be dived into. He's a poacher, a snarer, and a robber of the fishponds—any one of 'em when he gets the chance; leastways it's said so; and he looks just like a wild man o' the woods; wilder than any Robison Crusoe! And he—but you might not like me to mention that, sir."

"Mention anything," replied Mr. Elster. "Go on."

"Well, sir, it's said by some that his was the shot that killed Mr. George," she returned, dropping her voice; and Percival Elster started.

"Who is he?" he exclaimed.

"He is not known to a soul. He came here a stranger."

"But—he was not here when I left home. And I left it, you may remember, only a few days before that night."

"He must have come here at that very time, sir; just as you left."

"But what grounds were there for supposing that he—that he—I think you must be mistaken, Mrs. Capper. Lord Hartledon, I am sure, knows nothing of this suspicion."

"I never heard nothing about grounds, sir," simply replied the woman. "I suppose folks fastened it on him because he's a loose character: and his face is all covered with hair, like a howl."

He almost laughed again as he turned away, dismissing the suspicion she had hinted at as unworthy a moment's credit. The broad gravel-walk through this portion of the park was very short, and the large greystone house was soon reached. Not to the stately front entrance did he bend his steps, but to a small side entrance, which he found open. Pursuing his way down sundry passages, he came to what used to be called the "west kitchen;" and there sat three women at breakfast.

"Well, Mirrable! I thought I should find you up."

The two servants seated opposite stared with open mouths; neither knew him: the one he had addressed as Mirrable turned at the salutation, screamed, and dropped the teapot. She was a thin, active woman, of forty years, with dark eyes, a bunch of black drooping ringlets between her cap and her thin cheeks, a ready tongue and a pleasant manner. Mirrable had been upper maid at Hartledon for years and years, and was privileged.

"Mr. Percival! Is it your ghost, sir?"

"I think it's myself, Mirrable."

"My goodness! But, sir, how did you get here?"

"You may well ask. I ought to have been here last night, but got out at some obscure junction to obtain a light for my cigar, and the train went on without me. I sat on a bench for a few hours, and came on by the goods train this morning."

Mirrable awoke from her astonishment, sent the two girls flying, one here, one there, to prepare rooms for Mr. Elster, and busied herself arranging the best breakfast she could extemporise. Val Elster sat on a table whilst he talked to her. In the old days, he and his brothers, little fellows, had used to carry their troubles to Mirrable; and he was just as much at home with her now as he would have been with his mother.

"Did Capper see you as you came by, sir? Wouldn't she be struck!"

"Nearly into stone," he laughed.

Mirrable disappeared for a minute or two, and came back with a silver coffee-pot in her hand. The name of the lodge-keeper had brought to his remembrance the unpleasant hint she mentioned, and he spoke of it impulsively—as he did most things.

"Mirrable, what man is it they call Pike, who has taken possession of that old shed?"

"I'm sure I don't know, sir," answered Mirrable, after a pause, which Mr. Elster thought was involuntary; for she was busy at the moment rubbing the coffee-pot with some wash-leather, her head and face bent over it, as she stood with her back to him. He slipped off the table, and went up to her.

"I saw smoke rising from the shed, and asked Capper what it meant, and she told me about this man Pike. Pike! It's a curious name."

Mirrable rubbed away, never answering.

"Capper said he had been suspected of firing the shot that killed my brother," he continued, in low tones. "Did *you* ever hear of such a hint, Mirrable?"

Mirrable darted off to the fireplace, and began stirring the milk lest it should boil over. Her face was almost buried in the saucepan, or Mr. Elster might have seen the sudden change that came over it; the thin cheeks that had flushed crimson, and now were deadly white. Lifting the saucepan on to the hob, she turned to Mr. Elster.

"Don't you believe any such nonsense, sir," she said, in tones of strange emphasis. "It was no more Pike than it was me. The man keeps himself to himself, and troubles nobody; and for that very reason idle folk carp at him, like the mischief-making idiots they are!"

"I thought there was nothing in it," remarked Mr. Elster.

"I'm *sure* there isn't," said Mirrable, conclusively. "Would you like some broiled ham, sir?"

"I should like anything good and substantial, for I'm as hungry as a hunter. But, Mirrable, you don't ask what has brought me here so suddenly."

The tone was significant, and Mirrable looked at him. There was a spice of mischief in his laughing blue eyes.

"I come on a mission to you; an avant-courier from his lordship, to charge you to have all things in readiness. To-morrow you will receive a houseful of company; more than Hartledon will hold."

Mirrable looked aghast. "It is one of your jokes, Mr. Val!"

"Indeed, it is the truth. My brother will be down with a trainful; and desires that everything shall be ready for their reception."

"My patience!" gasped Mirrable. "And the servants, sir?"

"Most of them will be here to-night. The Countess-Dowager of Kirton is coming as Hartledon's mistress for the time being."

"Oh!" said Mirrable, who had once had the honour of seeing the Countess-Dowager of Kirton. And the monosyllable was so significant that Val Elster drew down the corners of his mouth.

"I don't like the Countess-Dowager, sir," remarked Mirrable in her freedom.

"I can't bear her," returned Val Elster.

# II

## Willy Gum

Had Percival Elster lingered ever so short a time near the clerk's house that morning he would have met that functionary himself; for in less than a minute after he had passed out of sight Jabez Gum's door opened, and Jabez Gum glided out of it.

It is a term chiefly applied to ghosts; but Mr. Gum was a great deal more like a ghost than like a man. He was remarkably tall and thin; a very shadow; with a white shadow of a face, and a nose that might have served as a model for a mask in a carnival of guys. A sharp nose, twice the length and half the breadth of any ordinary nose—a very ferret of a nose; its sharp tip standing straight out into the air. People said, with such a nose Mr. Gum ought to have a great deal of curiosity. And they were right; he *had* a great deal in a quiet way.

A most respectable man was Mr. Gum, and he prided himself upon it. Mr. Gum—more often called Clerk Gum in the village—had never done a wrong thing in his life, or fallen into a scrape. He had been altogether a pattern to Calne in general, and to its black sheep in particular. Dr. Ashton himself could not have had less brought against him than Clerk Gum; and it would just have broken Mr. Gum's heart had his good name been tarnished in ever so slight a degree. Perhaps no man living had been born with a larger share of self-esteem than Jabez Gum. Clerk of the parish longer than Dr. Ashton had been its Rector, Jabez Gum had lived at his ease in a pecuniary point of view. It was one of those parishes (I think few of them remain now) where the clerk's emoluments are large. He also held other offices; was an agent for one or two companies, and was looked upon as an exceedingly substantial man for his station in life. Perhaps he was less so than people imagined. The old saying is all too true: "Nobody knows where the shoe pinches but he who wears it."

Jabez Gum had his thorn, as a great many more of us have ours, if the outside world only knew it. And Jabez, at odd moments, when the thorn pierced him very sharply, had been wont to compare his condition to St. Paul's, and to wonder whether the pricks inflicted on that holy man could have bled as his own did. He meant no irreverence when he thought this; neither do I in writing it. We are generally wounded in the most vulnerable spot about us, and Jabez Gum made no exception to the rule. He had been assailed in his cherished respectability, his self-esteem. Assailed and *scarred*. How broad and deep the scar was Jabez never told the world, which as a rule does not sympathise with such scars, but turns aside in its cruel indifference. The world had almost forgotten the scar now, and supposed Clerk Gum had done the same. It was all over and done with years ago.

Jabez Gum's wife—to whom you will shortly have the honour of an introduction, but she is in her bedroom just now—had borne him one child, and only one. How this boy was loved, how tenderly reared, let Calne tell you. Mrs. Gum had to endure no inconsiderable amount of ridicule at the time from her gossiping friends, who gave Willy sundry endearing names, applied in derision. Certainly, if any mother ever was bound up in a child, Mrs. Gum was in hers. The boy was well brought up. A good education was given him; and at the age of sixteen he went to London and to fortune. The one was looked upon as a natural sequence to the other. Some friend of Jabez Gum's had interested himself to procure the lad's admission into one of the great banks as a junior clerk. He might rise in time to be cashier, manager, even partner; who knew? Who knew indeed? And Clerk Gum congratulated himself, and was more respectable than ever.

Better that Willy Gum had remained at Calne! And yet, and again— who knew? When the propensity for ill-doing exists it is sure to come out, no matter where. There were some people in Calne who could have told Clerk Gum, even then, that Willy, for his age, was tolerably fast and forward. Mrs. Gum had heard of one or two things that had caused her hair to rise on end with horror; ay, and with apprehension; but, foolish mother that she was, not a syllable did she breathe to the clerk; and no one else ventured to tell him.

She talked to Willy with many sighs and tears; implored him to be a good boy and enter on good courses, not on bad ones that would break her heart. Willy, the little scapegrace, was willing to promise anything. He laughed and made light of it; it wasn't his fault if folks told stories about him; she couldn't be so foolish as to give ear to them. London? Oh, he should be all right in London! One or two fellows here were rather fast, there was no denying it; and they drew him with them; they were older than he, and ought to have known better. Once away from Calne, they could have no more influence over him, and he should be all right.

MRS. HENRY WOOD

She believed him; putting faith in the plausible words. Oh, what trust can be so pure, and at the same time so foolish, as that placed by a mother in a beloved son! Mrs. Gum had never known but one idol on earth; he who now stood before her, lightly laughing at her fears, making his own tale good. She leaned forward and laid her hands upon his shoulders and kissed him with that impassioned fervour that some mothers could tell of, and whispered that she would trust him wholly.

Mr. Willy extricated himself with as little impatience as he could help: these embraces were not to his taste. And yet the boy did love his mother. She was not at all a wise woman, or a clever one; rather silly, indeed, in many things; but she was fond of him. At this period he was young-looking for his age, slight, and rather undersized, with an exceedingly light complexion, a wishy-washy sort of face with no colour in it, unmeaning light eyes, white eyebrows, and ragged-looking light hair with a tawny shade upon it.

Willy Gum departed for London, and entered on his engagement in the great banking-house of Goldsworthy and Co.

How he went on in it Calne could not get to learn, though it was moderately inquisitive upon the point. His father and mother heard from him occasionally; and once the clerk took a sudden and rather mysterious journey to London, where he stayed for a whole week. Rumour said—I wonder where such rumours first have their rise—that Willy Gum had fallen into some trouble, and the clerk had had to buy him out of it at the cost of a mint of money. The clerk, however, did not confirm this; and one thing was indisputable: Willy retained his place in the banking-house. Some people looked on this fact as a complete refutation of the rumour.

Then came a lull. Nothing was heard of Willy; that is, nothing beyond the reports of Mrs. Gum to her gossips when letters arrived: he was well, and getting on well. It was only the lull that precedes a storm; and a storm indeed burst on quiet Calne. Willy Gum had robbed the bank and disappeared.

In the first dreadful moment, perhaps the only one who did *not* disbelieve it was Clerk Gum. Other people said there must be some mistake: it could not be. Kind old Lord Hartledon came down in his carriage to the clerk's house—he was too ill to walk—and sat with the clerk and the weeping mother, and said he was sure it could not be so bad as was reported. The next morning saw handbills—great, staring, large-typed handbills—offering a reward for the discovery of William Gum, posted all over Calne.

Once more Clerk Gum went to London. What he did there no one knew. One thing only was certain—he did not find Willy or any trace of him. The defalcation was very nearly eight hundred pounds; and even if Mr. Gum could have refunded that large sum, he might not do so, said Calne, for of course the bank would not compound a felony. He came back looking ten years older; his tall, thin form more shadowy, his nose longer and sharper. Not a soul ventured to say a syllable to him, even of condolence. He told Lord Hartledon and his Rector that no tidings whatever could be gleaned of his unhappy son; the boy had disappeared, and might be dead for all they knew to the contrary.

So the handbills wore themselves out on the walls, serving no purpose, until Lord Hartledon ordered them to be removed; and Mrs. Gum lived in tears, and audibly wished herself dead. She had not seen her boy since he quitted Calne, considerably more than two years before, and he was now nearly nineteen. A few days' holiday had been accorded him by the banking-house each Christmas; but the first Christmas Willy wrote word that he had accepted an invitation to go home with a brother-clerk; the second Christmas he said he could not obtain leave of absence—which Mrs. Gum afterwards found was untrue; so that Willy Gum had not been at Calne since he left it. And whenever his mother thought of him—and that was every hour of the day and night—it was always as the fair, young, light-haired boy, who seemed to her little more than a child.

A year or so of uncertainty, of suspense, of wailing, and then came a letter from Willy, cautiously sent. It was not addressed directly to Mrs. Gum, to whom it was written, but to one of Willy's acquaintances in London, who enclosed it in an envelope and forwarded it on.

Such a letter! To read it one might have thought Mr. William Gum had gone out under the most favourable auspices. He was in Australia; had gone up to seek his fortune at the gold-diggings, and was making money rapidly. In a short time he should refund with interest the little sum he had borrowed from Goldsworthy and Co., and which was really not taken with any ill intention, but was more an accident than anything else. After that, he should accumulate money on his own score, and—all things being made straight at home—return and settle down, a rich man for life. And she—his mother—might rely on his keeping his word. At present he was at Melbourne; to which place he and his mates had come to bring their acquired gold, and to take a bit of a spree after their recent hard work. He was very jolly, and after a week's holiday they should go back again. And he hoped his father had overlooked the past; and he remained ever her affectionate son, William Gum.

The effect of this letter upon Mrs. Gum was as though a dense cloud had suddenly lifted from the world, and given place to a flood of sunshine. We estimate things by comparison. Mrs. Gum was by nature disposed to look on the dark side of things, and she had for the whole year past been indulging the most dread pictures of Willy and his fate that any woman's mind ever conceived. To hear that he was in life, and well, and making money rapidly, was the sweetest news, the greatest relief she could ever experience in this world.

Clerk Gum—relieved also, no doubt—received the tidings in a more sober spirit; almost as if he did not dare to believe in them. The man's heart had been well-nigh broken with the blow that fell upon him, and nothing could ever heal it thoroughly again. He read the letter in silence; read it twice over; and when his wife broke out into a series of rapt congratulations, and reproached him mildly for not appearing to think it true, he rather cynically inquired what then, if true, became of her dreams.

For Mrs. Gum was a dreamer. She was one of those who are now and again visited by strange dreams, significant of the future. Poor Mrs. Gum carried these dreams to an excess; that is, she was always having them and always talking about them. It had been no wonder, with her mind in so miserable a state regarding her son, that her dreams in that first twelve-month had generally been of him and generally bad. The above question, put by her husband, somewhat puzzled her. Her dreams *had* foreshadowed great evil still to Willy; and her dreams had never been wrong yet.

But, in the enjoyment of positive good, who thinks of dreams? No one. And Mrs. Gum's grew a shade brighter, and hope again took possession of her heart.

Two years rolled on, during which they heard twice from Willy; satisfactory letters still, in a way. Both testified to his "jolly" state: he was growing rich, though not quite so rapidly as he had anticipated; a fellow had to spend so much! Every day he expected to pick up a nugget which would crown his fortune. He complained in these letters that he did not hear from home; not once had news reached him; had his father and mother abandoned him?

The question brought forth a gush of tears from Mrs. Gum, and a sharp abuse of the post-office. The clerk took the news philosophically, remarking that the wonder would have been had Willy received the letters, seeing that he seemed to move about incessantly from place to place.

Close upon this came another letter, written apparently in haste. Willy's "fortune" had turned into reality at last; he was coming home with more gold than he could count; had taken his berth in the good ship *Morning Star*, and should come off at once to Calne, when the ship reached Liverpool. There was a line written inside the envelope, as though he had forgotten to include it in the letter: "I have had one from you at last; the first you wrote, it seems. Thank dad for what he has done for me. I'll make it all square with him when I get home."

This had reference to a fact which Calne did not know. In that unhappy second visit of Clerk Gum's to London, he *did* succeed in appeasing the wrath of Goldsworthy and Co., and paid in every farthing of the money. How far he might have accomplished this but for being backed by the urgent influence of old Lord Hartledon, was a question. One thing was in his favour: the firm had not taken any steps whatever in the matter, and those handbills circulated at Calne were the result of a misapprehension on the part of an officious local police-officer. Things had gone too far for Goldsworthys graciously to condone the offence—and Clerk Gum paid in his savings of years. This was the fact written by Mrs. Gum to her son, which had called forth the line in the envelope.

Alas! those were the last tidings ever received from Willy Gum. Whilst Mrs. Gum lived in a state of ecstacy, showing the letter to her neighbours and making loving preparations for his reception, the time for the arrival of the *Morning Star* at Liverpool drew on, and passed, and the ship did not arrive.

A time of anxious suspense to all who had relations on board—for it was supposed she had foundered at sea—and tidings came to them. An awful tale; a tale of mutiny and wrong and bloodshed. Some of the loose characters on board the ship—and she was bringing home such—had risen in disorder within a month of their sailing from Melbourne; had killed the captain, the chief officer, and some of the passengers and crew.

The ringleader was a man named Gordon; who had incited the rest to the crime, and killed the captain with his own hand. Obtaining command of the ship, they put her about, and commenced a piratical raid. One vessel they succeeded in disarming, despoiling, and then leaving her to her fate. But the next vessel they attacked proved a more formidable enemy, and there was a hand-to-hand struggle for the mastery, and for life or death. The *Morning Star* was sunk, with the greater portion of her living freight. A few, only some four or five, were saved by the other ship, and conveyed to England.

It was by them the dark tale was brought. The second officer of the *Morning Star* was one of them; he had been compelled to dissemble and to appear to serve the mutinous band; the others were innocent passengers, whose lives had not been taken. All agreed in one thing: that Gordon, the ringleader, had in all probability escaped. He had put off from the *Morning Star*, when she was sinking, in one of her best boats; he and some of his lawless helpmates, with a bag of biscuit, a cask of water, and a few bottles that probably contained rum. Whether they succeeded in reaching a port or in getting picked up, was a question; but it was assumed they had done so.

The owners of the *Morning Star*, half paralyzed at the news of so daring and unusual an outrage, offered the large reward of five hundred pounds for the capture of George Gordon; and Government increased the offer by two hundred, making it seven in all.

Overwhelming tidings for Clerk Gum and his wife! A brief season of agonized suspense ensued for the poor mother; of hopes and fears as to whether Willy was amongst the remnant saved; and then hope died away, for he did not come.

Once more, for the last time, Clerk Gum took a journey, not to London, but to Liverpool. He succeeded in seeing the officer who had been saved; but he could give him no information. He knew the names of the first-class passengers, but only a few of the second-class; and in that class Willy had most likely sailed.

The clerk described his son; and the officer thought he remembered him: he had a good deal of gold on board, he said. One of the passengers spoke more positively. Yes, by Clerk Gum's description, he was sure Willy Gum had been his fellow-passenger in the second cabin, though he did not recollect whether he had heard his name. It seemed, looking back, that the passengers had hardly had time to become acquainted with each other's names, he added. He was sure it was the young man; of very light complexion, ready and rather loose (if Mr. Gum would excuse his saying so) in speech. He had made thoroughly good hauls of gold at the last, and was going home to spend it. He was the second killed, poor fellow; had risen up with a volley of oaths (excuses begged again) to defend the captain, and was struck down and killed.

Poor Jabez Gum gasped. *Killed?* was the gentleman *sure?* Quite sure; and, moreover, he saw his body thrown overboard with the rest of the dead. And the money—the gold? Jabez asked, when he had somewhat recovered himself. The passenger laughed—not at the poor father, but at the worse than useless question; gold and everything else on board the *Morning Star* had gone down with her to the bottom of the sea.

A species of savage impulse rose in the clerk's mind, replacing his first emotion of grief; an impulse that might almost have led him to murder the villain Gordon, could he have come across him. Was there a chance that the man would be taken? he asked. Every chance, if he dared show his face in England, the passenger answered. A reward of seven hundred pounds was an inducement to the survivors to keep their eyes open; and they'd do it, besides, without any reward. Moreover—if Gordon had escaped, his comrades in the boat had escaped with him. They were lawless men like himself, every one of them, and they would be sure to betray him when they found what a price was set upon his capture.

Clerk Gum returned home, bearing to his wife and Calne the final tidings which crushed out all hope. Mrs. Gum sank into a state of wild despair. At first it almost seemed to threaten loss of reason. Her son had been her sole idol, and the idol was shattered. But to witness unreasonably violent grief in others always has a counteracting effect on our own, and Mr. Gum soothed his sorrow and brought philosophy to his aid.

"Look you," said he, one day, sharply to his wife, when she was crying and moaning, "there's two sides to every calamity,—a bright and a dark 'un;" for Mr. Gum was not in the habit of treating his wife, in the privacy of their domestic circle, to the quality-speech kept for the world. "He is gone, and we can't help it; we'd have welcomed him home if we could, and killed the fatted calf, but it was God's will that it shouldn't be. There may be a blessing in it, after all. Who knows but he might have broke out again, and brought upon us what he did before, or worse? For my part, I should never have been without the fear; night and morning it would always have stood before me; not to be driven away. As it is, I am at rest."

She—the wife—took her apron from her eyes and looked at him with a sort of amazed anger.

"Gum! do you forget that he had left off his evil ways, and was coming home to be a comfort to us?"

"No, I don't forget it," returned Mr. Gum. "But who was to say that the mood would last? He might have got through his gold, however much it was, and then—. As it is, Nance Gum, we can sleep quiet in our beds, free from *that* fear."

Clerk Gum was not, on the whole, a model of suavity in the domestic fold. The first blow that had fallen upon him seemed to have affected his temper; and his helpmate knew from experience that whenever he called her "Nance" his mood was at its worst.

Suppressing a sob, she spoke reproachfully.

"It's my firm belief, Gum, and has been all along, that you cared more for your good name among men than you did for the boy."

"Perhaps I did," he answered, by way of retort. "At any rate, it might have been better for him in the long run if we—both you and me—hadn't cared for him quite so foolishly in his childhood; we spared the rod and we spoiled the child. That's over, and—"

"It's *all* over," interrupted Mrs. Gum; "over for ever in this world. Gum, you are very hard-hearted."

"And," he continued, with composure, "we may hope now to live down in time the blow he brought upon us, and hold up our heads again in the face of Calne. We couldn't have done that while he lived."

"We couldn't?"

"No. Just dry up your useless tears, Nancy; and try to think that all's for the best."

But, metaphorically speaking, Mrs. Gum could not dry her tears. Nearly two years had elapsed since the fatal event; and though she no longer openly lamented, filling Calne with her cries and her faint but heartfelt prayers for vengeance on the head of the cruel monster, George Gordon, as she used to do at first, she had sunk into a despairing state of mind that was by no means desirable: a startled, timid, superstitious woman, frightened at every shadow.

# III

## ANNE ASHTON

Jabez Gum came out of his house in the bright summer morning, missing Mr. Elster by one minute only. He went round to a small shed at the back of the house and brought forth sundry garden-tools. The whole garden was kept in order by himself, and no one had finer fruit and vegetables than Clerk Gum. Hartledon might have been proud of them, and Dr. Ashton sometimes accepted a dish with pleasure.

In his present attire: dark trousers, and a short close jacket buttoned up round him and generally worn when gardening, the worthy man might decidedly have been taken for an animated lamp-post by any stranger who happened to come that way. He was applying himself this morning, first to the nailing of sundry choice fruit-trees against the wall that ran down one side of his garden—a wall that had been built by the clerk himself in happier days; and next, to plucking some green walnuts for his wife to pickle. As he stood on tip-toe, his long thin body and long thin arms stretched up to the walnut-tree, he might have made the fortune of any travelling caravan that could have hired him. The few people who passed him greeted him with a "Good morning," but he rarely turned his head in answering them. Clerk Gum had grown somewhat taciturn of late years.

The time went on. The clock struck a quarter-past seven, and Jabez Gum, as he heard it, left the walnut-tree, walked to the gate, and leaned over it; his face turned in the direction of the village. It was not the wooden gate generally attached to smaller houses in rustic localities, but a very pretty iron one; everything about the clerk's house being of a superior order. Apparently, he was looking out for some one in displeasure; and, indeed, he had not stood there a minute, when a girl came flying down the road, and pushed the gate and the clerk back together.

Mr. Gum directed her attention to the church clock. "Do you see the time, Rebecca Jones?"

Had the pages of the church-register been visible as well as the clock, Miss Rebecca Jones's age might have been seen to be fifteen; but, in knowledge of the world and in impudence, she was considerably older.

"Just gone seven and a quarter," answered she, making a feint of shading her eyes with her hands, though the sun was behind her.

"And what business have you to come at seven and a quarter? Half-past six is your time; and, if you can't keep it, your missis shall get those that can."

"Why can't my missis let me stop at night and clear up the work?" returned the girl. "She sends me away at six o'clock, as soon as I've washed the tea-things, and oftentimes earlier than that. It stands to reason I can't get through the work of a morning."

"You could do so quite well if you came to time," said the clerk, turning away to his walnut-tree. "Why don't you?"

"I overslept myself this morning. Father never called me afore he went out. No doubt he had a drop too much last night."

She went flying up the gravel-path as she spoke. Her father was the man Jones whom you saw at the railway station; her step-mother (for her own mother was dead) was Mrs. Gum's cousin.

She was a sort of stray sheep, this girl, in the eyes of Calne, not belonging very much to any one; her father habitually neglected her, her step-mother had twice turned her out of doors. Some three or four months ago, when Mrs. Gum was changing her servant, she had consented to try this girl. Jabez Gum knew nothing of the arrangement until it was concluded, and disapproved of it. Altogether, it did not work satisfactorily: Miss Jones was careless, idle, and impudent; her step-mother was dissatisfied because she was not taken into the house; and Clerk Gum threatened every day, and his wife very often, to dismiss her.

It was only within a year or two that they had not kept an indoor servant; and the fact of their not doing so now puzzled the gossips of Calne. The clerk's emoluments were the same as ever; there was no Willy to encroach on them now; and the work of the house required a good servant. However, it pleased Mrs. Gum to have one in only by day; and who was to interfere with her if the clerk did not?

Jabez Gum worked on for some little time after eight o'clock, the breakfast-hour. He rather wondered he was not called to it, and registered a mental vow to discharge Miss Becky. Presently he went indoors, put his head into a small sitting-room on the left, and found the room empty, but the breakfast laid. The kitchen was behind it, and Jabez Gum stalked on down the passage, and went into it. On the other side of the passage was the best sitting-room, and a very small room at the back of it, which Jabez used as an office, and where he kept sundry account-books.

"Where's your missis?" asked he of the maid, who was on her knees toasting bread.

"Not down yet," was the short response.

"Not down yet!" repeated Jabez in surprise, for Mrs. Gum was generally down by seven. "You've got that door open again, Rebecca. How many more times am I to tell you I won't have it?"

"It's the smoke," said Rebecca. "This chimbley always smokes when it's first lighted."

"The chimney doesn't smoke, and you know that you are telling a falsehood. What do you want with it open? You'll have that wild man darting in upon you some morning. How will you like that?"

"I'm not afeard of him," was the answer, as Rebecca got up from her knees. "He couldn't eat me."

"But you know how timid your mistress is," returned the clerk, in a voice of extreme anger. "How dare you, girl, be insolent?"

He shut the door as he spoke—one that opened from the kitchen to the back garden—and bolted it. Washing his hands, and drying them with a round towel, he went upstairs, and found Mrs. Gum—as he had now and then found her of late—in a fit of prostration. She was a little woman, with a light complexion, and insipid, unmeaning face—some such a face as Willy's had been—and her hair, worn in neat bands under her cap, was the colour of tow.

"I couldn't help it, Gum," she began, as she stood before the glass, her trembling fingers trying to fasten her black alpaca gown—for she had never left off mourning for their son. "It's past eight, I know; but I've had such an upset this morning as never was, and I *couldn't* dress myself. I've had a shocking dream."

"Drat your dreams!" cried Mr. Gum, very much wanting his breakfast.

"Ah, Gum, don't! Those morning dreams, when they're vivid as this was, are not sent for ridicule. Pike was in it; and you know I can't *bear* him to be in my dreams. They are always bad when he is in them."

"If you wanted your breakfast as much as I want mine, you'd let Pike alone," retorted the clerk.

"I thought he was mixed up in some business with Lord Hartledon. I don't know what it was, but the dream was full of horror. It seemed that Lord Hartledon was dead or dying; whether he'd been killed or not, I can't say; but an awful dread was upon me of seeing him dead. A voice called out, 'Don't let him come to Calne!' and in the fright I awoke. I can't remember what part Pike played in the dream," she continued, "only the impression remained that he was in it."

"Perhaps he killed Lord Hartledon?" cried Gum, mockingly.

"No; not in the dream. Pike did not seem to be mixed up in it for ill. The ill was all on Lord Hartledon; but it was not Pike brought it upon him. Who it was, I couldn't see; but it was not Pike."

Clerk Gum looked down at his wife in scornful pity. He wondered sometimes, in his phlegmatic reasoning, why women were created such fools.

"Look here, Mrs. G. I thought those dreams of yours were pretty nearly dreamed out—there have been enough of 'em. How any woman, short of a born idiot, can stand there and confess herself so frightened by a dream as to be unable to get up and go about her duties, is beyond me."

"But, Gum, you don't let me finish. I woke up with the horror, I tell you—"

"What horror?" interrupted the clerk, angrily. "What did it consist of? I can't see the horror."

"Nor can I, very clearly," acknowledged Mrs. Gum; "but I know it was there. I woke up with the very words in my ears, 'Don't let him come to Calne!' and I started out of bed in terror for Lord Hartledon, lest he *should* come. We are only half awake, you know, at these moments. I pulled the curtain aside and looked out. Gum, if ever I thought to drop in my life, I thought it then. There was but one person to be seen in the road—and it was Lord Hartledon."

"Oh!" said Mr. Gum, cynically, after a moment of natural surprise. "Come out of his vault for a morning walk past your window, Mrs. G.!"

"Vault! I mean young Lord Hartledon, Gum."

Mr. Gum was a little taken back. They had been so much in the habit of calling the new Lord Hartledon, Lord Elster—who had not lived at Calne since he came into the title—that he had thought of the old lord when his wife was speaking.

"He was up there, just by the turning of the road, going on to Hartledon. Gum, I nearly dropped, I say. The next minute he was out of sight; then I rubbed my eyes and pinched my arms to make sure I was awake."

"And whether you saw a ghost, or whether you didn't," came the mocking retort.

"It was no ghost, Gum; it was Lord Hartledon himself."

"Nonsense! It was just as much one as the other. The fact is, you hadn't quite woke up out of that fine dream of yours, and you saw double. It was just as much young Hartledon as it was me."

"I never saw a ghost yet, and I don't fear I ever shall, Gum. I tell you it was Lord Hartledon. And if harm doesn't befall him at Calne, as shadowed forth in my dream, never believe me again."

"There, that's enough," peremptorily cried the clerk; knowing, if once Mrs. Gum took up any idea with a dream for its basis, how impossible it was to turn her. "Is the key of that kitchen door found yet?"

"No: it never will be, Gum. I've told you so before. My belief is, and always has been, that Rebecca let it drop by accident into the waste bucket."

"*My* belief is, that Rebecca made away with it for her own purposes," said the clerk. "I caught her just now with the door wide open. She's trying to make acquaintance with the man Pike; that's what she's at."

"Oh, Gum!"

"Yes; it's all very well to say 'Oh, Gum!' but if you were below-stairs looking after her, instead of dreaming up here, it might be better for everyone. Let me once be certain about it, and off she goes the next hour. A fine thing 'twould be some day for us to find her head smothered in the kitchen purgatory, and the silver spoons gone; as will be the case if any loose characters get in."

He was descending the stairs as he spoke the last sentence, delivered in loud tones, probably for the benefit of Miss Rebecca Jones. And lest the intelligent Protestant reader should fear he is being introduced to unorthodox regions, it may be as well to mention that the "purgatory" in Mr. Jabez Gum's kitchen consisted of an excavation, two feet square, under the hearth, covered with a grating through which the ashes and the small cinders fell; thereby enabling the economical housewife to throw the larger ones on the fire again. Such wells or "purgatories," as they are called, are common enough in the old-fashioned kitchens of certain English districts.

Mrs. Gum, ready now, had been about to follow her husband; but his suggestion—that the girl was watching an opportunity to make acquaintance with their undesirable neighbour, Pike—struck her motionless.

It seemed that she could never see this man without a shiver, or overcome the fright experienced when she first met him. It was on a dark autumn night. She was coming through the garden when she discerned, or thought she discerned, a light in the abandoned shed. Thinking of fire, she hastily crossed the stile that divided their garden from the waste land, and ran to it. There she was confronted by what she took to be a bear—but a bear that could talk; for he gruffly asked her who she was and what she wanted. A black-haired, black-browed man, with a pipe between his teeth, and one sinewy arm bared to the elbow.

How Mrs. Gum tore away and tumbled over the stile in her terror, and got home again, she never knew. She supposed it to be a tramp, who had taken shelter there for the night; but finding to her dismay that the tramp stayed on, she had never overcome her fright from that hour to this.

Neither did her husband like the proximity of such a gentleman. They caused securer bolts to be put on their doors—for fastenings in small country places are not much thought about, people around being proverbially honest. They also had their shutters altered. The shutters to the windows, back and front, had holes in them in the form of a heart, such as you may have sometimes noticed. Before the wild-looking man—whose name came to be known as Pike—had been in possession of the shed a fortnight, Jabez Gum had the holes in his shutters filled-in and painted over. An additional security, said the neighbours: but poor timid Mrs. Gum could not overcome that first fright, and the very mention of the man set her trembling and quaking.

Nothing more was said of the dream or the apparition, real or fancied, of Lord Hartledon: Clerk Gum did not encourage the familiar handling of such topics in everyday life. He breakfasted, devoted an hour to his own business in the little office, and then put on his coat to go out. It was Friday morning. On that day and on Wednesdays the church was open for baptisms, and it was the clerk's custom to go over at ten o'clock and apprize the Rector of any notices he might have had.

Passing in at the iron gates, the large white house rose before him, beyond the wide lawn. It had been built by Dr. Ashton at his own expense. The old Rectory was a tumbledown, inconvenient place, always in dilapidation, for as soon as one part of it was repaired another fell through; and the Rector opened his heart and his purse, both large and generous, and built a new one. Mr. Gum was making his way unannounced to the Rector's study, according to custom, when a door on the opposite side of the hall opened, and Dr. Ashton came out. He was a pleasant-looking man, with dark hair and eyes, his countenance one of keen intellect; and though only of middle height, there was something stately, grand, imposing in his whole appearance.

"Is that you, Jabez?"

Connected with each other for so many years—a connection which had begun when both were young—the Rector and Mrs. Ashton had never called him anything but Jabez. With other people he was Gum, or Mr. Gum, or Clerk Gum: Jabez with them. He, Jabez, was the older man of the two by six or seven years, for the Rector was not more than forty-five. The clerk crossed the hall, its tessellated flags gleaming under the colours thrown in by the stained windows, and entered the drawing-room, a noble apartment looking on to the lawn in front. Mrs. Ashton, a tall, delicate-looking woman, with a gentle face, was standing before a painting just come home and hung up; to look at which the Rector and his wife had gone into the room.

It was the portrait of a sweet-looking girl with a sunny countenance. The features were of the delicate contour of Mrs. Ashton's; the rich brown hair, the soft brown eyes, and the intellectual expression of the face resembled the doctor's. Altogether, face and portrait were positively charming; one of those faces you must love at first sight, without waiting to question whether or not they are beautiful.

"Is it a good likeness, Jabez?" asked the Rector, whilst Mrs. Ashton made room for him with a smile of greeting.

"As like as two peas, sir," responded Jabez, when he had taken a long look. "What a face it is! Oftentimes it comes across my mind when I am not thinking of anything but business; and I'm always the better for it."

"Why, Jabez, this is the first time you have seen it."

"Ah, ma'am, you know I mean the original. There's two baptisms to-day, sir," he added, turning away; "two, and one churching. Mrs. Luttrell and her child, and the poor little baby whose mother died."

"Mrs. Luttrell!" repeated the Rector. "It's soon for her, is it not?"

"They want to go away to the seaside," replied the clerk. "What about that notice, sir?"

"I'll see to it before Sunday, Jabez. Any news?"

"No, sir; not that I've heard of. My wife wanted to persuade me she saw—"

At this moment a white-haired old serving-man entered the room with a note, claiming the Rector's attention. "The man's to take back the answer, sir, if you please."

"Wait then, Simon."

Old Simon stood aside, and the clerk, turning to Mrs. Ashton, continued his unfinished sentence.

"She wanted to persuade me she saw young Lord Hartledon pass at six o'clock this morning. A very likely tale that, ma'am."

"Perhaps she dreamt it, Jabez," said Mrs. Ashton, quietly.

Jabez chuckled; but what he would have answered was interrupted by the old servant.

"It's Mr. Elster that's come; not Lord Hartledon."

"Mr. Elster! How do you know, Simon?" asked Mrs. Ashton.

"The gardener mentioned it, ma'am, when he came in just now," was the servant's reply. "He said he saw Mr. Elster walk past this morning, as if he had just come by the luggage-train. I'm not sure but he spoke to him."

"The answer is 'No,' Simon," interposed the Rector, alluding to the note he had been reading. "But you can send word that I'll come in some time to-day."

"Charles, did you hear what Simon said—that Mr. Elster has come down?" asked Mrs. Ashton.

"Yes, I heard it," replied the doctor; and there was a hard dry tone in his voice, as if the news were not altogether palatable to him. "It must have been Percival Elster your wife saw, Jabez; not Lord Hartledon."

Jabez had been arriving at the same conclusion. "They used to be much alike in height and figure," he observed; "it was easy to mistake the one for the other. Then that's all this morning, sir?"

"There is nothing more, Jabez."

In a room whose large French window opened to flowerbeds on the side of the house, bending over a table on which sundry maps were spread, her face very close to them, sat at this moment a young lady. It was the same face you have just seen in the portrait—that of Dr. and Mrs. Ashton's only daughter. The wondrously sunny expression of countenance, blended with strange sweetness, was even more conspicuous than in the portrait. But what perhaps struck a beholder most, when looking at Miss Ashton for the first time, was a nameless grace and refinement that distinguished her whole appearance. She was of middle height, not more; slender; her head well set upon her shoulders. This was her own room; the schoolroom of her girlhood, the sitting-room she had been allowed to call her own since then. Books, work, music, a drawing-easel, and various other items, presenting a rather untidy collection, met the eye. This morning it was particularly untidy. The charts covered the table; one of them lay on the carpet; and a pot of mignonette had been overturned inside the open window scattering some of the mould. She was very busy; the open sleeves of her lilac-muslin dress were thrown back, and her delicate hands were putting the finishing touches in pencil to a plan she had been copying, from one of the maps. A few minutes more, and the pencil was thrown down in relief.

"I won't colour it this morning; it must be quite an hour and a half since I began; but the worst is done, and that's worth a king's ransom." In the escape from work, the innocent gaiety of her heart, she broke into a song, and began waltzing round the room. Barely had she passed the open window, her back turned to it, when a gentleman came up, looked in, stepped softly over the threshold, and imprisoned her by the waist.

"Be quiet, Arthur. Pick up that mignonette-pot you threw down, sir."

"My darling!" came in a low, heartfelt whisper. And Miss Ashton, with a faint cry, turned to see her engaged lover, Val Elster.

She stood before him, literally unable to speak in her great astonishment, the red roses going and coming in her delicate cheeks, the rich brown eyes, that might have been too brilliant but for their exceeding sweetness, raised questioningly to his. Mr. Elster folded her in his arms as if he would never release her again, and kissed the shrinking face repeatedly.

"Oh, Percival, Percival! Don't! Let me go."

He did so at last, and held her before him, her eyelids drooping now, to gaze at the face he loved so well—yes, loved fervently and well, in spite of his follies and sins. Her heart was beating wildly with its own rapture: for her the world had suddenly grown brighter.

"But when did you arrive?" she whispered, scarcely knowing how to utter the words in her excessive happiness.

He took her upon his arm and began to pace the room with her while he explained. There was an attempt at excuse for his prolonged absence—for Val Elster had returned from his duties in Vienna in May, and it was now August, and he had lingered through the intervening time in London, enjoying himself—but that was soon glossed over; and he told her how his brother was coming down on the morrow with a houseful of guests, and he, Val, had offered to go before them with the necessary instructions. He did not say *why* he had offered to do this; that his debts had become so pressing he was afraid to show himself longer in London. Such facts were not for the ear of that fair girl, who trusted him as the truest man she knew under heaven.

MRS. HENRY WOOD

"What have you been doing, Anne?"

He pointed to the maps, and Miss Ashton laughed.

"Mrs. Graves was here yesterday; she is very clever, you know; and when something was being said about the course of ships out of England, I made some dreadful mistakes. She took me up sharply, and papa looked at me sharply—and the result is, I have to do a heap of maps. Please tell me if it's right, Percival?"

She held up her pencilled work of the morning. He was laughing.

"What mistakes did you make, Anne?"

"I am not sure but I said something about an Indiaman, leaving the London Docks, having to pass Scarborough," she returned demurely. "It was quite as bad."

"Do you remember, Anne, being punished for persisting, in spite of the slate on the wall and your nursery-governess, that the Mediterranean lay between Scotland and Ireland? Miss Jevons wanted to give you bread and water for three days. How's that prig Graves?" he added rather abruptly.

Anne Ashton laughed, blushing slightly. "He is just as you left him; very painstaking and efficient in the parish, and all that, but, oh, so stupid in some things! Is the map right?"

"Yes, it's right. I'll help you with the rest. If Dr. Ashton—"

"Why, Val! Is it you? I heard Lord Hartledon had come down."

Percival Elster turned. A lad of seventeen had come bounding in at the window. It was Dr. Ashton's eldest living son, Arthur. Anne was twenty-one. A son, who would have been nineteen now, had died; and there was another, John, two years younger than Arthur.

"How are you, Arthur, boy?" cried Val. "Edward hasn't come. Who told you he had?"

"Mother Gum. I have just met her."

"She told you wrong. He will be down to-morrow. Is that Dr. Ashton?"

Attracted perhaps by the voices, Dr. and Mrs. Ashton, who were then out on the lawn, came round to the window. Percival Elster grasped a hand of each, and after a minute or two's studied coldness, the doctor thawed. It was next to impossible to resist the genial manner, the winning attractions of the young man to his face. But Dr. Ashton could not approve of his line of conduct; and had sore doubts whether he had done right in allowing him to become the betrothed of his dearly-loved daughter.

# IV

## The Countess-Dowager

The guests had arrived, and Hartledon was alive with bustle and lights. The first link in the chain, whose fetters were to bind more than one victim, had been forged. Link upon link; a heavy, despairing burden no hand could lift; a burden which would have to be borne for the most part in dread secrecy and silence.

Mirrable had exerted herself to good purpose, and Mirrable was capable of it when occasion needed. Help had been procured from Calne, and on the Friday evening several of the Hartledon servants arrived from the town-house. "None but a young man would have put us to such a rout," quoth Mirrable, in her privileged freedom; "my lord and lady would have sent a week's notice at least." But when Lord Hartledon arrived on the Saturday evening with his guests, Mirrable was ready for them.

She stood at the entrance to receive them, in her black-silk gown and lace cap, its broad white-satin strings falling on either side the bunch of black ringlets that shaded her thin face. Who, to look at her quick, sharp countenance, with its practical sense, her active frame, her ready speech, her general capability, would believe her to be sister to that silly, dreaming Mrs. Gum? But it was so. Lord Hartledon, kind, affable, unaffected as ever was his brother Percival, shook hands with her heartily in the eyes of his guests before he said a word of welcome to them; and one of those guests, a remarkably broad woman, with a red face, a wide snub nose, and a front of light flaxen hair, who had stepped into the house leaning on her host's arm—having, in fact, taken it unasked, and seemed to be assuming a great deal of authority—turned round to stare at Mirrable, and screwed her little light eyes together for a better view.

"Who is she, Hartledon?"

"Mrs. Mirrable," answered his lordship rather shortly. "I think you must have seen her before. She has been Hartledon's mistress since my mother died," he rather pointedly added, for he saw incipient defiance in the old lady's countenance.

"Oh, Hartledon's head servant; the housekeeper, I presume," cried she, as majestically as her harsh voice allowed her to speak. "Perhaps you'll tell her who I am, Hartledon; and that I have undertaken to preside here for a little while."

"I believe Mrs. Mirrable knows you, ma'am," spoke up Percival Elster, for Lord Hartledon had turned away, and was lost amongst his guests. "You have seen the Countess-Dowager of Kirton, Mirrable?"

The countess-dowager faced round upon the speaker sharply.

"Oh, it's *you*, Val Elster? Who asked you to interfere? I'll see the rooms, Mirrable, and the arrangements you have made. Maude, where are you? Come with me."

A tall, stately girl, with handsome features, raven hair and eyes, and a brilliant colour, extricated herself from the crowd. It was Lady Maude Kirton. Mirrable went first; the countess-dowager followed, talking volubly; and Maude brought up the rear. Other servants came forward to see to the rest of the guests.

The most remarkable quality observable in the countess-dowager, apart from her great breadth, was her restlessness. She seemed never still for an instant; her legs had a fidgety, nervous movement in them, and in moments of excitement, which were not infrequent, she was given to executing a sort of war-dance. Old she was not; but her peculiar graces of person, her rotund form, her badly-made front of flaxen curls, which was rarely in its place, made her appear so. A bold, scheming, unscrupulous, vulgar-minded woman, who had never considered other people's feelings in her life, whether equals or inferiors. In her day she must have been rather tall—nearly as tall as that elegant Maude who followed her; but her astounding width caused her now to appear short. She went looking into the different rooms as shown to her by Mirrable, and chose the best for herself and her daughter.

"Three en suite. Yes, that will be the thing, Mirrable. Lady Maude will take the inner one, I will occupy this, and my maid the outer. Very good. Now you may order the luggage up."

"But my lady," objected Mirrable, "these are the best rooms in the house; and each has a separate entrance, as you perceive. With so many guests to provide for, your maid cannot have one of these rooms."

"What?" cried the countess-dowager. "My maid not have one of these rooms? You insolent woman! Do you know that I am come here with my nephew, Lord Hartledon, to be mistress of this house, and of every one in it? You'd better mind *your* behaviour, for I can tell you that I shall look pretty sharply after it."

"Then," said Mirrable, who never allowed herself to be put out by any earthly thing, and rarely argued against the stream, "as your ladyship has come here as sole mistress, perhaps you will yourself apportion the rooms to the guests."

"Let them apportion them for themselves," cried the countess-dowager. "These three are mine; others manage as they can. It's Hartledon's fault. I told him not to invite a heap of people. You and I shall get on together very well, I've no doubt, Mirrable," she continued in a false, fawning voice; for she was remarkably alive at all times to her own interests. "Am I to understand that you are the housekeeper?"

"I am acting as housekeeper at present," was Mirrable's answer. "When my lord went to town, after my lady's death, the housekeeper went also, and has remained there. I have taken her place. Lord Elster—Lord Hartledon, I mean—has not lived yet at Hartledon, and we have had no establishment."

"Then who are you?"

"I was maid to Lady Hartledon for many years. Her ladyship treated me more as a friend at the last; and the young gentlemen always did so."

"*Very* good," cried the untrue voice. "And, now, Mirrable, you can go down and send up some tea for myself and Lady Maude. What time do we dine?"

"Mr. Elster ordered it for eight o'clock."

"And what business had *he* to take orders upon himself?" and the pale little eyes flashed with anger. "Who's Val Elster, that he should interfere? I sent word by the servants that we wouldn't dine till nine."

"Mr. Elster is in his own house, madam; and—"

"In his own house!" raved Lady Kirton. "It's no house of his; it's his brother's. And I wish I was his brother for a day only; I'd let Mr. Val know what presumption comes to. Can't dinner be delayed?"

"I'm afraid not, my lady."

"Ugh!" snapped the countess-dowager. "Send up tea at once; and let it be strong, with a great deal of green in it. And some rolled bread-and-butter, and a little well-buttered toast."

Mirrable departed with the commands, more inclined to laugh at the selfish old woman than to be angry. She remembered the countess-dowager arriving on an unexpected visit some three or four years before, and finding the old Lord Hartledon away and his wife ill in bed. She remained three days, completely upsetting the house; so completely upsetting the invalid Lady Hartledon, that the latter was glad to lend her a sum of money to get rid of her.

Truth to say, Lady Kirton had never been a welcome guest at Hartledon; had been shunned, in fact, and kept away by all sorts of *ruses*. The only other visit she had paid the family, in Mirrable's remembrance, was to the town-house, when the children were young. Poor little Val had been taught by his nurse to look upon her as a "bogey;" went about in terror of her; and her ladyship detecting the feeling, administered sly pinches whenever they met. Perhaps neither of them had completely overcome the antagonism from that time to this.

A scrambling sort of life had been Lady Kirton's. The wife of a very poor and improvident Irish peer, who had died early, leaving her badly provided for, her days had been one long scramble to make both ends meet and avoid creditors. Now in Ireland, now on the Continent, now coming out for a few brief weeks of fashionable life, and now on the wing to some place of safety, had she dodged about, and become utterly unscrupulous.

There was a whole troop of children, who had been allowed to go to the good or the bad very much in their own way, with little help or hindrance from their mother. All the daughters were married now, excepting Maude, mostly to German barons and French counts. One had espoused a marquis—native country not clearly indicated; one an Italian duke: but the marquis lived somewhere over in Algeria in a small lodging, and the Duke condescended to sing an occasional song on the Italian stage.

It was all one to Lady Kirton. They had taken their own way, and she washed her hands of them as easily as though they had never belonged to her. Had they been able to supply her with an occasional bank-note, or welcome her on a protracted visit, they had been her well-beloved and most estimable daughters.

Of the younger sons, all were dispersed; the dowager neither knew nor cared where. Now and again a piteous begging-letter would come from one or the other, which she railed at and scolded over, and bade Maude answer. Her eldest son, Lord Kirton, had married some four or five years ago, and since then the countess-dowager's lines had been harder than ever. Before that event she could go to the place in Ireland whenever she liked (circumstances permitting), and stay as long as she liked; but that was over now. For the young Lady Kirton, who on her own score spent all the money her husband could scrape together, and more, had taken an inveterate dislike to her mother-in-law, and would not tolerate her.

Never, since she was thus thrown upon her own resources, had the countess-dowager's lucky star been in the ascendant as it had been this season, for she contrived to fasten herself upon the young Lord Hartledon, and secure a firm footing in his town-house. She called him her nephew—"My nephew Hartledon;" but that was a little improvement upon the actual relationship, for she and the late Lady Hartledon had been cousins only. She invited herself for a week's sojourn in May, and had never gone away again; and it was now August. She had come down with him, *sans cérémonie*, to Hartledon; had told him (as a great favour) that she would look after his house and guests during her stay, as his mother would have done. Easy, careless, good-natured Hartledon acquiesced, and took it all as a matter of course. To him she was ever all sweetness and suavity.

None knew better on which side her bread was buttered than the countess-dowager. She liked it buttered on both sides, and generally contrived to get it.

She had come down to Hartledon House with one fixed determination—that she did not quit it until the Lady Maude was its mistress. For a long while Maude had been her sole hope. Her other daughters had married according to their fancy—and what had come of it?—but Maude was different. Maude had great beauty; and Maude, truth to say, was almost as selfishly alive to her own interest as her mother. *She* should marry well, and so be in a position to shelter the poor, homeless, wandering dowager. Had she chosen from the whole batch of peers, not one could have been found more eligible than he whom fortune seemed to have turned up for her purpose—Lord Hartledon; and before the countess-dowager had been one week his guest in London she began her scheming.

Lady Maude was nothing loth. Young, beautiful, vain, selfish, she yet possessed a woman's susceptible heart; though surrounded with luxury, dress, pomp, show, which are said to deaden the feelings, and in some measure do deaden them, Lady Maude insensibly managed to fall in love, as deeply as ever did an obscure damsel of romance. She had first met him two years before, when he was Viscount Elster; had liked him then. Their relationship sanctioned their being now much together, and the Lady Maude lost her heart to him.

Would it bring forth fruit, this scheming of the countess-dowager's, and Maude's own love? In her wildest hopes the old woman never dreamed of what that fruit would be; or, unscrupulous as she was by habit, unfeeling by nature, she might have carried away Maude from Hartledon within the hour of their arrival.

Of the three parties more immediately concerned, the only innocent one—innocent of any intentions—was Lord Hartledon. He liked Maude very well as a cousin, but otherwise he did not care for her. They might succeed—at least, had circumstances gone on well, they might have succeeded—in winning him at last; but it would not have been from love. His present feeling towards Maude was one of indifference; and of marriage at all he had not begun to think.

Val Elster, on the contrary, regarded Maude with warm admiration. Her beauty had charms for him, and he had been oftener at her side but for the watchful countess-dowager. It would have been horrible had Maude fallen in love with the wrong brother, and the old lady grew to hate him for the fear, as well as on her own score. The feeling of dislike, begun in Val's childhood, had ripened in the last month or two to almost open warfare. He was always in the way. Many a time when Lord Hartledon might have enjoyed a *tête-à-tête* with Maude, Val Elster was there to spoil it.

But the culminating point had arrived one day, when Val, half laughingly, half seriously, told the dowager, who had been provoking him almost beyond endurance, that she might spare her angling in regard to Maude, for Hartledon would never bite. But that he took his pleasant face beyond her reach, it might have suffered, for her fingers were held out alarmingly.

From that time she took another little scheme into her hands—that of getting Percival Elster out of his brother's favour and his brother's house. Val, on his part, seriously advised his brother *not* to allow the Kirtons to come to Hartledon; and this reached the ears of the dowager. You may be sure it did not tend to soothe her. Lord Hartledon only laughed at Val, saying they might come if they liked; what did it matter?

But, strange to say, Val Elster was as a very reed in the hands of the old woman. Let her once get hold of him, and she could turn him any way she pleased. He felt afraid of her, and bent to her will. The feeling may have had its rise partly in the fear instilled into his boyhood, partly in the yielding nature of his disposition. However that might be, it was a fact; and Val could no more have openly opposed the resolute, sharp-tongued old woman to her face than he could have changed his nature. He rarely called her anything but "ma'am," as their nurse had taught him and his brothers and sisters to do in those long-past years.

Before eight o'clock the guests had all assembled in the drawing-room, except the countess-dowager and Maude. Lord Hartledon was going about amongst them, talking to one and another of the beauties of this, his late father's place; scarcely yet thought of as his own. He was a tall slender man; in figure very much resembling Percival, but not in face: the one was dark, the other fair. There was also the same indolent sort of movement, a certain languid air discernible in both; proclaiming the undoubted fact, that both were idle in disposition and given to ennui. There the resemblance ended. Lord Hartledon had nothing of the irresolution of Percival Elster, but was sufficiently decisive in character, prompt in action.

A noble room, this they were in, as many of the rooms were in the fine old mansion. Lord Hartledon opened the inner door, and took them into another, to show them the portrait of his brother George—a fine young man also, with a fair, pleasing countenance.

"He is like Elster; not like you, Hartledon," cried a young man, whose name was Carteret.

"*Was*, you mean, Carteret," corrected Lord Hartledon, in tones of sad regret. "There was a great family resemblance between us all, I believe."

"He died from an accident, did he not?" said Mr. O'Moore, an Irishman, who liked to be called "The O'Moore."

"Yes."

Percival Elster turned to his brother, and spoke in low tones. "Edward, was any particular person suspected of having fired the shot?"

"None. A set of loose, lawless characters were out that night, and—"

"What are you all looking at here?"

The interruption came from Lady Kirton, who was sailing into the room with Maude. A striking contrast the one presented to the other. Maude in pink silk and a pink wreath, her haughty face raised in pride, her dark eyes flashing, radiantly beautiful. The old dowager, broad as she was high, her face rouged, her short snub nose always carried in the air, her light eyes unmeaning, her flaxen eyebrows heavy, her flaxen curls crowned by a pea-green turban. Her choice attire was generally composed, as to-day, of some cheap, flimsy, gauzy material bright in colour. This evening it was orange lace, all flounces and frills, with a lace scarf; and she generally had innumerable ends of quilted net flying about her skirts, not unlike tails. It was certain she did not spend much money upon her own attire; and how she procured the costly dresses for Maude the latter appeared in was ever a mystery. You can hardly fancy the bedecked old figure that she made. The O'Moore nearly laughed out, as he civilly turned to answer her question.

"We were looking at this portrait, Lady Kirton."

"And saying how much he was like Val," put in young Carteret, between whom and the dowager warfare also existed. "Val, which was the elder?"

"George was."

"Then his death made you heir-presumptive," cried the thoughtless young man, speaking impulsively.

"Heir-presumptive to what?" asked the dowager snapping at the words.

"To Hartledon."

"*He* heir to Hartledon! Don't trouble yourself, young man, to imagine that Val Elster's ever likely to come into Hartledon. Do you want to shoot his lordship, as *he* was shot?"

The uncalled-for retort, the strangely intemperate tones, the quick passionate fling of the hand towards the portrait astonished young Carteret not a little. Others were surprised also; and not one present but stared at the speaker. But she said no more. The pea-green turban and flaxen curls were nodding ominously; and that was all.

The animus to Val Elster was very marked. Lord Hartledon glanced at his brother with a smile, and led the way back to the other drawing-room. At that moment the butler announced dinner; the party filed across the hall to the fine old dining-room, and began finding their seats.

"I shall sit there, Val. You can take a chair at the side."

Val did look surprised at this. He was about to take the foot of his brother's table, as usual; and there was the pea-green turban standing over him, waiting to usurp it. It would have been quite beyond Val Elster, in his sensitiveness, to tell her she should not have it; but he did feel annoyed. He was sweet-tempered, however. Moreover, he was a gentleman, and only waited to make one remark.

"I fear you will not like this place, ma'am. Won't it look odd to see a lady at the bottom of the table?"

"I have promised my dear nephew to act as mistress, and to see after his guests; and I don't choose to sit at the side under those circumstances." But she had looked at Lord Hartledon, and hesitated before she spoke. Perhaps she thought his lordship would resign the head of the table to her, and take the foot himself. If so, she was mistaken.

"You will be more comfortable at the side, Lady Kirton," cried Lord Hartledon, when he discovered what the bustle was about.

"Not at all, Hartledon; not at all."

"But I like my brother to face me, ma'am. It is his accustomed place."

Remonstrance was useless. The dowager nodded her pea-green turban, and firmly seated herself. Val Elster dexterously found a seat next Lady Maude; and a gay gleam of triumph shot out of his deep-blue eyes as he glanced at the dowager. It was not the seat she would have wished him to take; but to interfere again might have imperilled her own place. Maude laughed. She did not care for Val—rather despised him in her heart; but he was the most attractive man present, and she liked admiration.

Another link in the chain! For how many, many days and years, dating from that evening, did that awful old woman take a seat, at intervals, at Lord Hartledon's table, and assume it as a right!

# V

## JEALOUSY

The rain poured down on the Monday morning; and Lord Hartledon stood at the window of the countess-dowager's sitting-room—one she had unceremoniously adopted for her own private use—smoking a cigar, and watching the clouds. Any cigar but his would have been consigned to the other side the door. Mr. Elster had only shown (by mere accident) the end of his cigar-case, and the dowager immediately demanded what he meant by displaying that article in the presence of ladies. A few minutes afterwards Lord Hartledon entered, smoking, and was allowed to enjoy his cigar with impunity. Good-tempered Val's delicate lips broke into a silent smile as he marked the contrast.

He lounged on the sofa, doing nothing, in his idle fashion; Lord Hartledon continued to watch the clouds. On the previous Saturday night the gentlemen had entered into an argument about boating: the result was that a match on the river was arranged, and some bets were pending on it. It had been fixed to come off this day, Monday; but if the rain continued to come down, it must be postponed; for the ladies, who had been promised the treat, would not venture out to see it.

"It has come on purpose," grumbled Lord Hartledon. "Yesterday was as fine and bright as it could be, the glass standing at set fair; and now, just because this boating was to come off, the rain peppers down!"

The rain excepted, it was a fair vision that he looked out upon. The room faced the back of the house, and beyond the lovely grounds green slopes extended to the river, tolerably wide here, winding peacefully in its course. The distant landscape was almost like a scene from fairyland.

The restless dowager—in a nondescript head-dress this morning, adorned with an upright tuft of red feathers and voluminous skirts of brown net, a jacket and flounces to match—betook herself to the side of Lord Hartledon.

"Where d'you get the boats?" she asked.

"They are kept lower down, at the boat-house," he replied, puffing at his cigar. "You can't see it from here; it's beyond Dr. Ashton's; lots of 'em; any number to be had for the hiring. Talking of Dr. Ashton, they will dine here to-day, ma'am."

"Who will?" asked Lady Kirton.

"The doctor, Mrs. Ashton—if she's well enough—and Miss Ashton."

"Who are they, my dear nephew?"

"Why, don't you know? Dr. Ashton preached to you yesterday. He is Rector of Calne; you must have heard of Dr. Ashton. They will be calling this morning, I expect."

"And you have invited them to dinner! Well, one must do the civil to this sort of people."

Lord Hartledon burst into a laugh. "You won't say 'this sort of people' when you see the Ashtons, Lady Kirton. They are quite as good as we are. Dr. Ashton has refused a bishopric, and Anne is the sweetest girl ever created."

Lady Maude, who was drawing, and exchanging a desultory sentence once in a way with Val, suddenly looked up. Her colour had heightened, though it was brilliant at all times.

"Are you speaking of my maid?" she said—and it might be that she had not attended to the conversation, and asked in ignorance, not in scorn. "Her name is Anne."

"I was speaking of Anne Ashton," said Lord Hartledon.

"Allow me to beg Anne Ashton's pardon," returned Lady Maude; her tone this time unmistakably mocking. "Anne is so common a name amongst servants."

"I don't care whether it is common amongst servants or uncommon," spoke Lord Hartledon rather hotly, as though he would resent the covert sneer. "It is Anne Ashton's; and I love the name for her sake. But I think it a pretty name; and should, if she did not bear it; prettier than yours, Maude."

"And pray who *is* Anne Ashton?" demanded the countess-dowager, with as much hauteur as so queer an old figure and face could put on, whilst Maude bent over her employment with white lips.

"She is Dr. Ashton's daughter," spoke Lord Hartledon, shortly. "My father valued him above all men. He loved Anne too—loved her dearly; and—though I don't know whether it is quite fair to Anne to let this out—the probable future connection between the families was most welcome to him. Next to my father, we boys reverenced the doctor; he was our tutor, in a measure, when we were staying at Hartledon; at least, tutor to poor George and Val; they used to read with him."

"And you would hint at some alliance between you and this Anne Ashton!" cried the countess-dowager, in a fume; for she thought she saw a fear that the great prize might slip through her fingers. "What sort of an alliance, I should like to ask? Be careful what you say, Hartledon; you may injure the young woman."

"I'll take care I don't injure Anne Ashton," returned Lord Hartledon, enjoying her temper. "As to an alliance with her—my earnest wish is, as it was my father's, that time may bring it about. Val there knows I wish it."

Val glanced at his brother by way of answer. He had taken no part in the discussion; his slight lips were drawn down, as he balanced a pair of scissors on his forefinger, and he looked less good-tempered than usual.

"Has she red hair and sky-blue eyes, and a doll's face? Does she sit in the pew under the reading-desk with three other dolls?" asked the foaming dowager.

Lord Hartledon turned and stared at the speaker in wonder—what could be so exciting her?

"She has soft brown hair and eyes, and a sweet gentle face; she is a graceful, elegant, attractive girl," said he, curtly. "She sat alone yesterday; for Arthur was in another part of the church, and Mrs. Ashton was not there. Mrs. Ashton is not in good health, she tells me, and cannot always come. The Rector's pew is the one with green curtains."

"Oh, *that* vulgar-looking girl!" exclaimed Maude, her unjust words— and she knew them to be unjust—trembling on her lips. "The Grand Sultan might exalt her to be his chief wife, but he could never make a lady of her, or get her to look like one."

"Be quiet, Maude," cried the countess-dowager, who, with all her own mistakes, had the sense to see that this sort of disparagement would only recoil upon them with interest, and who did not like the expression of Lord Hartledon's face. "You talk as if you had seen this Mrs. Ashton, Hartledon, since your return."

"I should not be many hours at Hartledon without seeing Mrs. Ashton," he answered. "That's where I was yesterday afternoon, ma'am, when you were so kindly anxious in your inquiries as to what had become of me. I dare say I was absent an unconscionable time. I never know how it passes, once I am with Anne."

"We represent Love as blind, you know," spoke Maude, in her desperation, unable to steady her pallid lips. "You apparently do not see it, Lord Hartledon, but the young woman is the very essence of vulgarity."

A pause followed the speech. The countess-dowager turned towards her daughter in a blazing rage, and Val Elster quitted the room.

"Maude," said Lord Hartledon, "I am sorry to tell you that you have put your foot in it."

"Thank you," panted Lady Maude, in her agitation. "For giving my opinion of your Anne Ashton?"

"Precisely. You have driven Val away in suppressed indignation."

"Is Val of the Anne Ashton faction, that the truth should tell upon him, as well as upon you?" she returned, striving to maintain an assumption of sarcastic coldness.

"It is upon him that the words will tell. Anne is engaged to him."

"Is it true? Is Val really engaged to her?" cried the countess-dowager in an ecstacy of relief, lifting her snub nose and painted cheeks, whilst a glad light came into Maude's eyes again. "I did hear he was engaged to some girl; but such reports of younger sons go for nothing."

"Val was engaged to her before he went abroad. Whether he will get her or not, is another thing."

"To hear you talk, Hartledon, one might have supposed you cared for the girl yourself," cried Lady Kirton; but her brow was smooth again, and her tone soft as honey. "You should be more cautious."

"Cautious! Why so? I love and respect Anne beyond any girl on earth. But that Val hastened to make hay when the sun shone, whilst I fell asleep under the hedge, I don't know but I might have proposed to her myself," he added, with a laugh. "However, it shall not be my fault if Val does not win her."

The countess-dowager said no more. She was worldly-wise in her way, and thought it best to leave well alone. Sailing out of the room she left them alone together: as she was fond of doing.

"Is it not rather—rather beneath an Elster to marry an obscure country clergyman's daughter?" began Lady Maude, a strange bitterness filling her heart.

"I tell you, Maude, the Ashtons are our equals in all ways. He is a proud old doctor of divinity—not old, however—of irreproachable family and large private fortune."

"You spoke of him as a tutor?"

"A tutor! Oh, I said he was in a measure our tutor when we were young. I meant in training us—in training us to good; and he allowed George and Val to read with him, and directed their studies: all for love, and out of the friendship he and my father bore each other. Dr. Ashton a paid tutor!" exclaimed Lord Hartledon, laughing at the notion.

"Dr. Ashton an obscure country clergyman! And even if he were, who is Val, that he should set himself up?"

"He is the Honourable Val Elster."

"Very honourable! Val is an unlucky dog of a spendthrift; that's what Val is. See how many times he has been set up on his legs!—and has always come down again. He had that place in the Government my father got him. He was attaché in Paris; subsequently in Vienna; he has had ever so many chances, and drops through all. One can't help loving Val; he is an attractive, sweet-tempered, good-natured fellow; but he was certainly born under an unlucky star. Elster's folly!"

"Val will drop through more chances yet," remarked Lady Maude. "I pity Miss Ashton, if she means to wait for him."

"Means to! She loves him passionately—devotedly. She would wait for him all her life, and think it happiness only to see him once in a way."

"As an astronomer looks at a star through a telescope," laughed Maude; "and Val is not worth the devotion."

"Val is not a bad fellow in the main; quite the contrary, Maude. Of course we all know his besetting sin—irresolution. A child might sway him, either for good or ill. The very best thing that could happen to Val would be his marriage with Anne. She is sensible and judicious; and I think Val could not fail to keep straight under her influence. If Dr. Ashton could only be brought to see the matter in this light!"

"Can he not?"

"He thinks—and I don't say he has not reason—that Val should show some proof of stability before his marriage, instead of waiting until after it. The doctor has not gone to the extent of parting them, or of suspending the engagement; but he is prepared to be strict and exacting as to Mr. Val's line of conduct; and I fancy the suspicion that it would be so has kept Val away from Calne."

"What will be done?"

"I hardly know. Val does not make a confidant of me, and I can't get to the bottom of how he is situated. Debts I am sure he has; but whether—"

"Val always had plenty of those," interrupted Maude.

"True. When my father died, three parts of Val's inheritance went to pay off debts nobody knew he had contracted. The worst is, he glides into these difficulties unwittingly, led and swayed by others. We don't say Elster's sin, or Elster's crimes; we say Elster's folly. I don't believe Val ever in his life did a bad thing of deliberate intention. Designing people get hold of him—fast fellows who are going headlong down-hill themselves—and Val, unable to say 'No,' is drawn here and drawn there, and tumbles with them into a quagmire, and perhaps has to pay his friends' costs, as well as his own, before he can get out of it. Do you believe in luck, Maude?"

"In luck?" answered Maude, raising her eyes at the abrupt question. "I don't know."

"I believe in it. I believe that some are born under a lucky star, and others under an unlucky one. Val is one of the latter. He is always unlucky. Set him up, and down he comes again. I don't think I ever knew Val lucky in my life. Look at his nearly blowing his arm off that time in Scotland! You will laugh at me, I dare say; but a thought crosses me at odd moments that his ill-luck will prevail still, in the matter of Miss Ashton. Not if I can help it, however; I'll do my best, for Anne's sake."

"You seem to think very much of her yourself," cried Lady Maude, her cheeks crimsoning with an angry flush.

"I do—as Val's future wife. I love Anne Ashton better than any one else in the world. We all loved her. So would you if you knew her. In my mother's last illness Anne was a greater comfort to her than Laura."

"Should you ever think of a wife on your own score, she may not like this warm praise of Miss Anne Ashton," said Lady Maude, assiduously drawing, her hot face bent down to within an inch of the cardboard.

"Not like it? She wouldn't be such an idiot, I hope, as to dislike it. Is not Anne going to be my brother's wife? Did you suppose I spoke of Anne in that way?—you must have been dreaming, Maude."

Maude hoped she had been. The young man took his cigar from his mouth, ran a penknife through the end, and began smoking again.

"That time is far enough off, Maude. *I* am not going to tie myself up with a wife, or to think of one either, for many a long year to come."

Her heart beat with a painful throbbing. "Why not?"

"No danger. My wild oats are not sown yet, any more than Val's; only you don't hear of them, because I have money to back me, and he has not. I must find a girl I should like to make my wife before that event comes off, Maude; and I have not found her yet."

Lady Maude damaged her landscape. She sketched in a tree where a chimney ought to have been, and laid the fault upon her pencil.

"It has been real sport, Maude, ever since I came home from knocking about abroad, to hear and see the old ladies. They think I am to be caught with a bait; and that bait is each one's own enchanting daughter. Let them angle, an they please—it does no harm. They are amused, and I am none the worse. I enjoy a laugh sometimes, while I take care of myself; as I have need to do, or I might find myself the victim of some detestable breach-of-promise affair, and have to stand damages. But for Anne Ashton, Val would have had his head in that Westminster-noose a score of times; and the wonder is that he has kept out of it. No, thank you, my ladies; I am not a marrying man."

"Why do you tell me this?" asked Lady Maude, a sick faintness stealing over her face and heart.

"You are one of ourselves, and I tell you anything. It will be fun for you, Maude, if you'll open your eyes and look on. There are some in the house now who—" He stopped and laughed.

"I would rather not hear this!" she cried passionately. "Don't tell me."

Lord Hartledon looked at her, begged her pardon, and quitted the room with his cigar. Lady Maude, black as night, dashed her pencil on to the cardboard, and scored her sketch all over with ugly black lines. Her face itself looked ugly then.

"Why did he say this to me?" she asked of her fevered heart. "Was it said with a purpose? Has he found out that I *love* him? that my shallow old mother is one of the subtlest of the anglers? and that—"

"What on earth are you at with your drawing, Maude?"

"Oh, I have grown sick of the sketch. I am not in a drawing mood to-day, mamma."

"And how fierce you were looking," pursued the countess-dowager, who had darted in at rather an inopportune moment for Maude— darting in on people at such moments being her habit. "And that was the sketch Hartledon asked you to do for him from the old painting!"

"He may do it himself, if he wants it done."

"Where is Hartledon?"

"I don't know. Gone out somewhere."

"Has he offended you, or vexed you?"

"Well, he did vex me. He has just been assuring me with the coolest air that he should never marry; or, at least, not for years and years to come. He told me to notice what a heap of girls were after him— or their mothers for them—and the fun he had over it, not being a marrying man."

"Is that all? You need not have put yourself in a fatigue, and spoilt your drawing. Lord Hartledon shall be your husband before six months are over—or reproach me ever afterwards with being a false prophetess and a bungling manager."

Maude's brow cleared. She had almost childlike confidence in the tact of her unscrupulous mother.

But how the morning's conversation altogether rankled in her heart, none save herself could tell: ay, and in that of the dowager. Although Anne Ashton was the betrothed of Percival Elster, and Lord Hartledon's freely-avowed love for her was evidently that of a brother, and he had said he should do all he could to promote the marriage, the strongest jealousy had taken possession of Lady Maude's heart. She already hated Anne Ashton with a fierce and bitter hatred. She turned sick with envy when, in the morning visit that was that day paid by the Ashtons, she saw that Anne was really what Lord Hartledon had described her—one of the sweetest, most lovable, most charming of girls; almost without her equal in the world for grace and goodness and beauty. She turned more sick with envy when, at dinner afterwards, to which the Ashtons came, Lord Hartledon devoted himself to them, almost to the neglect of his other guests, lingering much with Anne.

The countess-dowager marked it also, and was furious. Nothing could be urged against them; they were unexceptionable. The doctor, a chatty, straightforward, energetic man, of great intellect and learning, and emphatically a gentleman; his wife attracting by her unobtrusive gentleness; his daughter by her grace and modest self-possession. Whatever Maude Kirton might do, she could never, for very shame, again attempt to disparage them. Surely there was no just reason for the hatred which took possession of Maude's heart; a hatred that could never be plucked out again.

But Maude knew how to dissemble. It pleased her to affect a sudden and violent friendship for Anne.

"Hartledon told me how much I should like you," she whispered, as they sat together on the sofa after dinner, to which Maude had drawn her. "He said I should find you the dearest girl I ever met; and I do so. May I call you 'Anne'?"

Not for a moment did Miss Ashton answer. Truth to say, far from reciprocating the sudden fancy boasted of by Maude, she had taken an unaccountable dislike to her. Something of falsity in the tone, of sudden *hardiesse* in the handsome black eyes, acted upon Anne as an instinctive warning.

"As you please, Lady Maude."

"Thank you so much. Hartledon whispered to me the secret about you and Val—Percival, I mean. Shall you accomplish the task, think you?"

"What task?"

"That of turning him from his evil ways."

"His evil ways?" repeated Anne, in a surprised indignation she did not care to check. "I do not understand you, Lady Maude."

"Pardon me, my dear Anne: it was hazardous so to speak *to you*. I ought to have said his thoughtless ways. Quant à moi, je ne vois pas la différence. Do you understand French?"

Miss Ashton looked at her, really not knowing what this style of conversation might mean. Maude continued; she had a habit of putting forth a sting on occasion, or what she hoped might be a sting.

"You are staring at the superfluous question. Of course it is one in these *French* days, when everyone speaks it. What was I saying? Oh, about Percival. Should he ever have the luck to marry, meaning the income, he will make a docile husband; but his wife will have to keep him under her finger and thumb; she must be master as well as mistress, for his own sake."

"I think Mr. Elster would not care to be so spoken of," said Miss Ashton, her face beginning to glow.

"You devoted girl! It is you who don't care to hear it. Take care, Anne; too much love is not good for gaining the mastership; and I have heard that you are—shall I say it?—*éperdue*."

Anne, in spite of her calm good sense, was actually provoked to a retort in kind, and felt terribly vexed with herself for it afterwards. "A rumour of the same sort has been breathed as to the Lady Maude Kirton's regard for Lord Hartledon."

"Has it?" returned Lady Maude, with a cool tone and a glowing face. "You are angry with me without reason. Have I not offered to swear to you an eternal friendship?"

Anne shook her head, and her lips parted with a curious expression. "I do not swear so lightly, Lady Maude."

"What if I were to avow to you that it is true?—that I do love Lord Hartledon, deeply as it is known you love his brother," she added, dropping her voice—"would you believe me?"

Anne looked at the speaker's face, but could read nothing. Was she in jest or earnest?

"No, I would not believe you," she said, with a smile. "If you did love him, you would not proclaim it."

"Exactly. I was jesting. What is Lord Hartledon to me?—save that we are cousins, and passably good friends. I must avow one thing, that I like him better than I do his brother."

"For that no avowal is necessary," said Anne; "the fact is sufficiently evident."

"You are right, Anne;" and for once Maude spoke earnestly. "I do *not* like Percival Elster. But I will always be civil to him for your sweet sake."

"Why do you dislike him?—if I may ask it. Have you any particular reason for doing so?"

"I have no reason in the world. He is a good-natured, gentlemanly fellow; and I know no ill of him, except that he is always getting into scrapes, and dropping, as I hear, a lot of money. But if he got out of his last guinea, and went almost in rags, it would be nothing to me; so *that's* not it. One does take antipathies; I dare say you do, Miss Ashton. What a blessing Hartledon did not die in that fever he caught last year! Val would have inherited. What a mercy!"

"That he lived? or that Val is not Lord Hartledon?"

"Both. But I believe I meant that Val is not reigning."

"You think he would not have made a worthy inheritor?"

"A worthy inheritor? Oh, I was not glancing at that phase of the question. Here he comes! I will give up my seat to him."

It is possible Lady Maude expected some pretty phrases of affection; begging her to keep it. If so, she was mistaken. Anne Ashton was one of those essentially quiet, self-possessed girls in society, whose manners seem almost to border on apathy. She did not say "Do go," or "Don't go." She was perfectly passive; and Maude moved away half ashamed of herself, and feeling, in spite of her jealousy and her prejudice, that if ever there was a ladylike girl upon earth, it was Anne Ashton.

"How do you like her, Anne?" asked Val Elster, dropping into the vacant place.

"Not much."

"Don't you? She is very handsome."

"Very handsome indeed. Quite beautiful. But still I don't like her."

"You would like her if you knew her. She has a rare spirit, only the old dowager keeps it down."

"I don't think she much likes you, Val."

"She is welcome to dislike me," returned Val Elster.

# VI

## AT THE BRIDGE

The famous boat-race was postponed. Some of the competitors had discovered they should be the better for a few days' training, and the contest was fixed for the following Monday.

Not a day of the intervening week but sundry small cockle-shells—things the ladies had already begun to designate as the "wager-boats," each containing a gentleman occupant, exercising his arms on a pair of sculls—might be seen any hour passing and repassing on the water; and the green slopes of Hartledon, which here formed the bank of the river, grew to be tenanted with fair occupants. Of course they had their favourites, these ladies, and their little bets of gloves on them.

As the day for the contest drew near the interest became really exciting; and on the Saturday morning there was quite a crowd on the banks. The whole week, since Monday, had been most beautiful—calm, warm, lovely. Percival Elster, in his rather idle fashion, was not going to join in the contest: there were enough without him, he said.

He was standing now, talking to Anne. His face wore a sad expression, as she glanced up at him from beneath the white feather of her rather large-brimmed straw hat. Anne had been a great deal at Hartledon that week, and was as interested in the race as any of them, wearing Lord Hartledon's colours.

"How did you hear it, Anne?" he was asking.

"Mamma told me. She came into my room just now, and said there had been words."

"Well, it's true. The doctor took me to task exactly as he used to do when I was a boy. He said my course of life was sinful; and I rather fired up at that. Idle and useless it may be, but sinful it is not: and I said so. He explained that he meant that, and persisted in his assertion—that an idle, aimless, profitless life was a sinful one. Do you know the rest?"

"No," she faltered.

"He said he would give me to the end of the year. And if I were then still pursuing my present frivolous course of life, doing no good to myself or to anyone else, he should cancel the engagement. My darling, I see how this pains you."

She was suppressing her tears with difficulty. "Papa will be sure to keep his word, Percival. He is so resolute when he thinks he is right."

"The worst is, it's true. I do fall into all sorts of scrapes, and I have got out of money, and I do idle my time away," acknowledged the young man in his candour. "And all the while, Anne, I am thinking and hoping to do right. If ever I get set on my legs again, *won't* I keep on them!"

"But how many times have you said so before!" she whispered.

"Half the follies for which I am now paying were committed when I was but a boy," he said. "One of the men now visiting here, Dawkes, persuaded me to put my name to a bill for him for fifteen hundred pounds, and I had to pay it. It hampered me for years; and in the end I know I must have paid it twice over. I might have pleaded that I was under age when he got my signature, but it would have been scarcely honourable to do so."

"And you never profited by the transaction?"

"Never by a sixpence. It was done for Dawkes's accommodation, not mine. He ought to have paid it, you say? My dear, he is a man of straw, and never had fifteen hundred pounds of his own in his life."

"Does Lord Hartledon know of this? I wonder he has him here."

"I did not mention it at the time; and the thing's past and done with. I only tell you now to give you an idea of the nature of my embarrassments and scrapes. Not one in ten has really been incurred for myself: they only fall upon me. One must buy experience."

Terribly vexed was that sweet face, an almost painful sadness upon the generally sunny features.

"I will never give you up, Anne," he continued, with emotion. "I told the doctor so. I would rather give up life. And you know that your love is mine."

"But my duty is theirs. And if it came to a contest—Oh, Percival! you know, you know which would have to give place. Papa is so resolute in right."

"It's a shame that fortune should be so unequally divided!" cried the young man, resentfully. "Here's Edward with an income of thirty thousand a year, and I, his own brother, only a year or two younger, can't boast a fourth part as many hundreds!"

"Oh, Val! your father left you better off than that!"

"But so much of it went, Anne," was the gloomy answer. "I never understood the claims that came in against me, for my part. Edward had no debts to speak of; but then look at his allowance."

"He was the eldest son," she gently said.

"I know that. I am not wishing myself in Edward's place, or he out of it. I heartily wish him health and a long life to wear his honours; it is no fault of his that he should be rolling in riches, and I a martyr to poverty. Still, one can't help feeling at odd moments, when the shoe's pinching awfully, that the system is not altogether a just one."

"Was that a sincere wish, Val Elster?"

Val wheeled round on Lady Maude, from whom the question came. She had stolen up to them unperceived, and stood there in her radiant beauty, her magnificent dark eyes and her glowing cheeks set off by a little coquettish black-velvet hat.

"A sincere wish—that my brother should live long to enjoy his honours!" echoed Val, in a surprised tone. "Indeed it is. I hope he will live to a green old age, and leave goodly sons to succeed him."

Maude laughed. A brighter hue stole into her face, a softer shade to her eyes: she saw herself, as in a vision, the goodly mother of those goodly sons.

"Are you going to wear *that*?" she asked, touching the knot of ribbon in Miss Ashton's hands with her petulant fingers. "They are Lord Hartledon's colours."

"I shall wear it on Monday. Lord Hartledon gave it to me."

A rash avowal. The competitors, in a sort of joke, had each given away one knot of his own colours. Lady Maude had had three given to her; but she was looking for another worth them all—from Lord Hartledon. And now—it was given, it appeared, to Anne Ashton! For her very life she could not have helped the passionate taunt that escaped from her, not in words, but in tone:

"To *you*!"

"Kissing goes by favour," broke from the delicate lips of Val Elster, and Lady Maude could have struck him for the significant, saucy expression of his violet-blue eyes. "Edward loves Anne better than he ever loved his sisters; and for any other love—*that's* still far enough from his heart, Maude."

She had recovered herself instantly; cried out "Yes" to those in the distance, as if she heard a call, and went away humming a tune.

"Val, she loves your brother," whispered Anne.

"Do you think so? I do sometimes; and again I'm puzzled. She acts well if she does. The other day I told Edward she was in love with him: he laughed at me, and said I was dreaming; that if she had any love for him, it was cousin's love. What's more, Anne, he would prefer not to receive any other; so Maude need not look after him: it will be labour lost. Here comes that restless old dowager down upon us! I shall leave you to her, Anne. I never dare say my soul's my own in the presence of that woman."

Val strolled away as he spoke. He was not at ease that day, and the sharp, meddling old woman would have been intolerable. It was all very well to put a good face on matters to Anne, but he was in more perplexity than he cared to confess to. It seemed to him that he would rather die than give up Anne: and yet—in the straightforward, practical good sense of Dr. Ashton, he had a formidable adversary to deal with.

He suddenly found an arm inserted within his own, and saw it was his brother. Walking together thus, there was a great resemblance between them.

They were of the same height, much the same build; both were very good-looking men, but Percival had the nicer features; and he was fair, and his brother dark.

"What is this, Val, about a dispute with the doctor?" began Lord Hartledon.

"It was not a dispute," returned Val. "There were a few words, and I was hasty. However, I begged his pardon, and we parted good friends."

"Under a flag of truce, eh?"

"Something of that sort."

"Something of that sort!" repeated Lord Hartledon. "Don't you think, Val, it would be to your advantage if you trusted me more thoroughly than you do? Tell me the whole truth of your position, and let me see what can be done for you."

"There's not much to tell," returned Val, in his stupidity. Even with his brother his ultra-sensitiveness clung to him; and he could no more have confessed the extent of his troubles than he could have taken wing that moment and soared away into the air. Val Elster was one of those who trust to things "coming right" with time.

"I have been talking to the doctor, Val. I called in just now to see Mrs. Ashton, and he spoke to me about you."

"Very kind of him, I'm sure!" retorted Val. "It is just this, Edward. He is vexed at what he calls my idle ways, and waste of time: as if I need plod on, like a city clerk, six days a week and no holidays! I know I must do something before I can win Anne; and I will do it: but the doctor need not begin to cry out about cancelling the engagement."

"How much do you owe, Val?"

"I can't tell."

Lord Hartledon thought this an evasion. But it was true. Val Elster knew he owed a great deal more than he could pay; but how much it might be on the whole, he had but a very faint idea.

"Well, Val, I have told the doctor I shall look into matters, and I hope to do it efficiently, for Anne's sake. I suppose the best thing will be to try and get you an appointment again."

"Oh, Edward, if you would! And you know you have the ear of the ministry."

"I dare say it can be managed. But this will be of little use if you are still to remain an embarrassed man. I hear you were afraid of arrest in London."

"Who told you that?"

"Dawkes."

"Dawkes! Then, Edward—" Val Elster stopped. In his vexation, he was about to retaliate on Captain Dawkes by a little revelation on the score of *his* affairs, certain things that might not have redounded to that gallant officer's credit. But he arrested the words in time: he was of a kindly nature, not fond of returning ill for ill. With all his follies, Val Elster could not remember to have committed an evil act in all his life, save one. And that one he had still the pleasure of paying for pretty deeply.

"Dawkes knows nothing of my affairs except from hearsay, Edward. I was once intimate with the man; but he served me a shabby trick, and that ended the friendship. I don't like him."

"I dare say what he said was not true," said Lord Hartledon kindly. "You might as well make a confidant of me. However, I have not time to talk to-day. We will go into the matter, Val, after Monday, when this race has come off, and see what arrangement can be made for you. There's only one thing bothers me."

"What's that?"

"The danger that it may be a wasted arrangement. If you are only set up on your legs to come down again, as you have before, it will be so much waste of time and money; so much loss, to me, of temper. Don't you see, Val?"

Percival Elster stopped in his walk, and withdrew his arm from his brother's; his face and voice full of emotion.

"Edward, I have learnt a lesson. What it has cost me I hardly yet know: but it is *learnt*. On my sacred word of honour, in the solemn presence of Heaven, I assert it, that I will never put my hand to another bill, whatever may be the temptation. I have overcome, in this respect at least, my sin."

"Your sin?"

"My nature's great sin; the besetting sin that has clung to me through life; the unfortunate sin that is my bane to this hour—cowardly irresolution."

"All right, Val; I see you mean well now. We'll talk of these matters next week. Instead of Elster's Folly, let it become Elster's Wisdom."

Lord Hartledon wrung his brother's hand and turned away. His eyes fell on Miss Ashton, and he went straight up to her. Putting the young lady's arm within his own, without word or ceremony, he took her off to a distance: and old Lady Kirton's skirts went round in a dance as she saw it.

"I am about to take him in hand, Anne, and set him going again: I have promised Dr. Ashton. We must get him a snug berth; one that even the doctor won't object to, and set him straight in other matters. If he has mortgaged his patrimony, it shall be redeemed. And, Anne, I think—I do think—he may be trusted to keep straight for the future."

Her soft sweet eyes sparkled with pleasure, and her lips parted with a sunny smile. Lord Hartledon took her hand within his own as it lay on his arm, and the furious old dowager saw it all from the distance.

"Don't say as much as this to him, Anne: I only tell you. Val is so sanguine, that it may be better not to tell him all beforehand. And I want, of course, first of all, to get a true list of—that is, a true statement of facts," he broke off, not caring to speak the word "debts" to that delicate girl before him. "He is my only brother; my father left him to me, for he knew what Val was; and I'll do my best for him. I'd do it for Val's own sake, apart from the charge. And, Anne, once Val is on his legs with an income, snug and comfortable, I shall recommend him to marry without delay; for, after all, you will be his greatest safeguard."

A blush suffused her face, and Lord Hartledon smiled.

Down came the countess-dowager.

"Here's that old dowager calling to me. She never lets me alone. Val sent me into a fit of laughter yesterday, saying she had designs on me for Maude. Poor deluded woman! Yes, ma'am, I hear. What is it?"

Mr. Elster went strolling along on the banks of the river, towards Calne; not with any particular purpose, but in his restless uneasiness. He had a tender conscience, and his past follies were pressing on it heavily. Of one thing he felt sure—that he was more deeply involved than Hartledon or anyone else suspected, perhaps even himself. The way was charming in fine weather, though less pleasant in winter. It was by no means a frequented road, and belonged of right to Lord Hartledon only; but it was open to all. Few chose it when they could traverse the more ordinary way. The narrow path on the green plain, sheltered by trees, wound in and out, now on the banks of the river, now hidden amidst a portion of the wood. Altogether it was a wild and lonely pathway; not one that a timid nature would choose on a dark night. You might sit in the wood, which lay to the left, a whole day through, and never see a soul.

One part of the walk was especially beautiful. A green hollow, where the turf was soft as moss; open to the river on the right, with a glimpse of the lovely scenery beyond; and on the left, the clustering trees of the wood. Yet further, through a break in the trees, might be seen a view of the houses of Calne. A little stream, or rivulet, trickled from the wood, and a rustic bridge—more for ornament than use, for a man with long legs could stride the stream well—was thrown over it. Val had reached thus far, when he saw someone standing on the bridge, his arms on the parapet, apparently in a brown study.

A dark, wild-looking man, whose face, at the first glimpse, seemed all hair. There was certainly a profusion of it; eyebrows, beard, whiskers, all heavy, and black as night. He was attired in loose fustian clothes with a red handkerchief wound round his throat, and a low slouching hat—one of those called wide-awake—partially concealed his features. By his side stood another man in plain, dark, rather seedy clothes, the coat outrageously long. He wore a cloth hat, whose brim hid his face, and he was smoking a cigar. Both men were slightly built and under middle height. This one was adorned with red whiskers.

The moment Mr. Elster set eyes on the dark one, he felt that he saw the man Pike before him. It happened that he had not met him during these few days of his sojourn; but some of the men staying at Hartledon had, and had said what a loose specimen he appeared to be. The other was a stranger, and did not look like a countryman at all.

Mr. Elster saw them both give a sharp look at him as he approached; and then they spoke together. Both stepped off the bridge, as though deferring to him, and stood aside as they watched him cross over, Pike touching his wide-awake.

"Good-day, my lord."

Val nodded by way of answer, and continued his stroll onwards. In the look he had taken at Pike, it struck him he had seen the face before: something in the countenance seemed familiar to his memory. And to his surprise he saw that the man was young.

The supposed reminiscence did not trouble him: he was too pre-occupied with thoughts of his own affairs to have leisure for Mr. Pike's. A short bit of road, and this rude, sheltered part of the way terminated in more open ground, where three paths diverged: one to the front of Hartledon; one to some cottages, and on through the wood to the high-road; and one towards the Rectory and Calne. Rural paths still, all of them; and the last was provided with a bench or two. Val Elster strolled on almost to the Rectory, and then turned back: he had no errand at Calne, and the Rectory he would rather keep out of just now. When he reached the little bridge Pike was on it alone; the other had disappeared. As before, he stepped off to make way for Mr. Elster.

"I beg pardon, sir, for addressing you just now as Lord Hartledon."

The salutation took Val by surprise; and though the voice seemed muffled, as though the man purposely mouthed his words, the accent and language were superior to anything he might have expected from one of Mr. Pike's appearance and reputed character.

"No matter," said Val, courteous even to Pike, in his kindly nature. "You mistook me for my brother. Many do."

"Not I," returned the man, assuming a freedom and a roughness at variance with his evident intelligence. "I know you for the Honourable Percival Elster."

"Ah," said Mr. Elster, a slight curiosity stirring his mind, but not sufficient to induce him to follow it up.

"But I like to do a good turn if I can," pursued Pike; "and I think, sir, I did one to you in calling you Lord Hartledon."

Val Elster had been passing on. He turned and looked at the man.

"Are you in any little temporary difficulty, might I ask?" continued Pike. "No offense, sir; princes have been in such before now."

Val Elster was so supremely conscious, especially in that reflective hour, of being in a "little difficulty" that might prove more than temporary, that he could only stare at the questioner and wait for more.

"No offence again, if I'm wrong," resumed Pike; "but if that man you saw here on the bridge is not looking after the Honourable Mr. Elster, I'm a fool."

"Why do you think this?" inquired Val, too fully aware that the fact was a likely one to attempt any reproof or disavowal.

"I'll tell you," said Pike; "I've said I don't mind doing a good turn when I can. The man arrived here this morning by the slow six train from London. He went into the Stag and had his breakfast, and has been covertly dodging about ever since. He inquired his way to Hartledon. The landlord of the Stag asked him what he wanted there, and got for answer that his brother was one of the grooms in my lord's service. Bosh! He went up, sneaking under the hedges and along by-ways, and took a view of the house, standing a good hour behind a tree while he did it. I was watching him."

It instantly struck Percival Elster, by one of those flashes of conviction that are no less sure than subtle, that Mr. Pike's interest in this watching arose from a fear that the stranger might have been looking after *him*. Pike continued:

"After he had taken his fill of waiting, he came dodging down this way, and I got into conversation with him. He wanted to know who I was. A poor devil out of work, I told him; a soldier once, but maimed and good for little now. We got chatty. I let him think he might trust me, and he began asking no end of questions about Mr. Elster: whether he went out much, what were his hours for going out, which road he mostly took in his walks, and how he could know him from his brother the earl; he had heard they were alike. The hound was puzzled; he had seen a dozen swells come out of Hartledon, any one of which might be Mr. Elster; but I found he had the description pretty accurate. Whilst we were talking, who should come into view but yourself! 'This is him!' cried he. 'Not a bit of it,' said I, carelessly; 'that's my lord.' Now you know, sir, why I saluted you as Lord Hartledon."

"Where is he now?" asked Percival Elster, feeling that he owed his present state of liberty to this lawless man.

Pike pointed to the narrow path in the wood, leading to the high-road. "I filled him up with the belief that the way beyond this bridge up to Hartledon was private, and he might be taken up for trespassing if he attempted to follow it; so he went off that way to watch the front. If the fellow hasn't a writ in his pocket, or something worse, call me a simpleton. You are all right, sir, as long as he takes you for Lord Hartledon."

But there was little chance the fellow could long take him for Lord Hartledon, and Percival Elster felt himself attacked with a shiver. He knew it to be worse than a writ; it was an arrest. An arrest is not a pleasant affair for any one; but a strong opinion—a certainty—seized upon Val's mind that this would bring forth Dr. Ashton's veto of separation from Anne.

"I thank you for what you have done," frankly spoke Mr. Elster.

"It's nothing, sir. He'll be dodging about after his prey; but I'll dodge about too, and thwart his game if I can, though I have to swear that Lord Hartledon's not himself. What's an oath, more or less, to me?"

"Where have I seen you before?" asked Val.

"Hard to say," returned Pike. "I have knocked about in many parts in my time."

"Are you from this neighbourhood?"

"Never was in these parts at all till a year or so ago. It's not two years yet."

"What are you doing here?"

"What I can. A bit of work when I can get it given to me. I went tramping the country after I left the regiment—"

"Then you have been a soldier?" interrupted Mr. Elster.

"Yes, sir. In tramping the country I came upon this place: I crept into a shed, and was there for some days; rheumatism took hold of me, and I couldn't move. It was something to find I had a roof of any sort over my head, and was let lie in it unmolested: and when I got better I stayed on."

"And have adopted it as your own, putting a window and a chimney into it! But do you know that Lord Hartledon may not choose to retain you as a tenant?"

"If Lord Hartledon should think of ousting me, I would ask Mr. Elster to intercede, in requital for the good turn I've done him this day," was the bold answer.

Mr. Elster laughed. "What is your name?"

"Tom Pike."

"I hear a great deal said of you, Pike, that's not pleasant; that you are a poacher, and a—"

"Let them that say so prove it," interrupted Pike, his dark brows contracting.

"But how do you manage to live?"

"That's my business, and not Calne's. At any rate, Mr. Elster, I don't steal."

"I heard a worse hint dropped of you than any I have mentioned," continued Val, after a pause.

"Tell it out, sir. Let's have the whole catalogue at once."

"That the night my brother, Mr. Elster, was shot, you were out with the poachers."

"I dare say you heard that I shot him, for I know it has been said," fiercely cried the man. "It's a black lie!—and the time may come when I shall ram it down Calne's throat. I swear that I never fired a shot that night; I swear that I no more had a hand in Mr. Elster's death than you had. Will you believe me, sir?"

The accents of truth are rarely to be mistaken, and Val was certain he heard them now. So far, he believed the man; and from that moment dismissed the doubt from his mind, if indeed he had not dismissed it before.

"Do you know who did fire the shot?"

"I do not; I was not out at all that night. Calne pitched upon me, because there was no one else in particular to pitch upon. A dozen poachers were in the fray, most of them with guns; little wonder the random shot from one should have found a mark. I know nothing more certain than that, so help—"

"That will do," interrupted Mr. Elster, arresting what might be coming; for he disliked strong language. "I believe you fully, Pike. What part of the country were you born in?"

"London. Born and bred in it."

"That I do not believe," he said frankly. "Your accent is not that of a Londoner."

"As you will, sir," returned Pike. "My mother was from Devonshire; but I was born and bred in London. I recognized that one with the writ for a fellow cockney at once; and for what he was, too—a sheriffs officer. Shouldn't be surprised but I knew him for one years ago."

Val Elster dropped a coin into the man's hand, and bade him good morning. Pike touched his wide-awake, and reiterated his intention of "dodging the enemy." But, as Mr. Elster cautiously pursued his way, the face he had just quitted continued to haunt him. It was not like any face he had ever seen, as far as he could remember; nevertheless ever and anon some reminiscence seemed to start out of it and vibrate upon a chord in his memory.

# VII

## Listeners

It was a somewhat singular coincidence, noted after the terrible event, now looming in the distance, had taken place, and when people began to weigh the various circumstances surrounding it, that Monday, the second day fixed for the boat-race, should be another day of rain. As though Heaven would have interposed to prevent it! said the thoughtful and romantic.

A steady, pouring rain; putting a stop again to the race for that day. The competitors might have been willing to face the elements themselves, but could not subject the fair spectators to the infliction. There was some inward discontent, and a great deal of outward grumbling; it did no good, and the race was put off until the next day.

Val Elster still retained his liberty. Very chary indeed had he been of showing himself outside the door on Saturday, once he was safely within it. Neither had any misfortune befallen Lord Hartledon. That unconscious victim must have contrived, in all innocence, to "dodge" the gentleman who was looking out for him, for they did not meet.

On the Sunday it happened that neither of the brothers went to church. Lord Hartledon, on awaking in the morning, found he had a sore throat, and would not get up. Val did not dare show himself out of doors. Not from fear of arrest that day, but lest any officious meddler should point him out as the real Simon Pure, Percival Elster. But for these circumstances, the man with the writ could hardly have remained under the delusion, as he appeared at church himself.

"Which is Lord Hartledon?" he whispered to his neighbour on the free benches, when the party from the great house had entered, and settled themselves in their pews.

"I don't see him. He has not come to-day."

"Which is Mr. Elster?"

"He has not come, either." So for that day recognition was escaped.

It was not to be so on the next. The rain, as I have said, came down, putting off the boat-race, and keeping Hartledon's guests indoors all the morning; but late in the afternoon some unlucky star put it into Lord

Hartledon's head to go down to the Rectory. His throat was better—almost well again; and he was not a man to coddle himself unnecessarily.

He paid his visit, stayed talking a considerable time with Mrs. Ashton, whose company he liked, and took his departure about six o'clock. "You and Anne might almost walk up with me," he remarked to the doctor as he shook hands; for the Rector and Miss Ashton were to dine at Hartledon that day. It was to have been the crowning festival to the boat-race—the race which now had not taken place.

Lord Hartledon looked up at the skies, and found he had no occasion to open his umbrella, for the rain had ceased. Sundry bright rays in the west seemed to give hope that the morrow would be fair; and, rejoicing in this cheering prospect, he crossed the broad Rectory lawn. As he went through the gate some one laid a hand upon his shoulder.

"The Honourable Percival Elster, I believe?"

Lord Hartledon looked at the intruder. A seedy man, with a long coat and red whiskers, who held out something to him.

"Who are you?" he asked, releasing his shoulder by a sharp movement.

"I'm sorry to do it, sir; but you know we are only the agent of others in these affairs. You are my prisoner, sir."

"Indeed!" said Lord Hartledon, taking the matter coolly. "You have got hold of the wrong man for once. I am not Mr. Percival Elster."

The capturer laughed: a very civil laugh. "It won't do, sir; we often have that trick tried on us."

"But I tell you I am *not* Mr. Elster," he reiterated, speaking this time with some anger. "I am Lord Hartledon."

He of the loose coat shook his head. He had his hand again on the supposed Mr. Elster's arm, and told him he must go with him.

"You cannot take me; you cannot arrest a peer. This is simply ridiculous," continued Lord Hartledon, almost laughing at the real absurdity of the thing. "Any child in Calne could tell you who I am."

"As well make no words over it, sir. It's only waste of time."

"You have a warrant—as I understand—to arrest Mr. Percival Elster?"

"Yes, sir, I have. The man that was looking for you in London got taken ill, and couldn't come down, so our folks sent me. 'You'll know him by his good looks,' said they; 'an aristocrat every inch of him.' Don't give me trouble, sir."

"Well now—I am not Percival Elster: I am his brother, Lord Hartledon. You cannot take one brother for another; and, what's more, you had better not try to do it. Stay! Look here."

He pulled out his card-case, and showed his cards—"Earl of Hartledon." He exhibited a couple of letters that happened to be about him—"The Right Honble. the Earl of Hartledon." It was of no use.

"I've known that dodge tried before too," said his obstinate capturer.

Lord Hartledon was growing more angry. He saw some proof must be tendered before he could regain his liberty. Jabez Gum happened to be standing at his gate opposite, and he called to him.

"Will you be so kind as to tell this man who I am, Mr. Gum. He is mistaking me for some one else."

"This is the Earl of Hartledon," said Jabez, promptly.

A moment's hesitation on the officer's part; but he felt too sure of his man to believe this. "I'll take the risk," said he, stolidly. "Where's the good of your holding out, Mr. Elster?"

"Come this way, then!" cried Lord Hartledon, beginning to lose his temper. "And if you carry this too far, my man, I'll have you punished."

He went striding up to the Rectory. Had he taken a moment for consideration, he might have turned away, rather than expose this misfortune of Val's there. The doctor came into the hall, and was recognized as the Rector, and there was some little commotion; Anne's white face looking on from a distance. The man was convinced, and took his departure, considerably crestfallen.

"What is the amount?" called the doctor, sternly.

"Not very much, *this*, sir. It's under three hundred."

Which was as much as to say there was more behind it. Dr. Ashton mentally washed his hands of Percival Elster as a future son-in-law.

The first intimation that ill-starred gentleman received of the untoward turn affairs were taking was from the Rector himself.

Mr. Percival Elster had been chuckling over that opportune sore throat, as a means of keeping his brother indoors; and it never occurred to him that Lord Hartledon would venture out at all on the Monday. Being a man with his wits about him, it had not failed to occur to his mind that there was a possibility of Lord Hartledon's being arrested in place of himself; but so long as Hartledon kept indoors the danger was averted. Had Percival Elster seen his brother go out he might have plucked up courage to tell him the state of affairs.

But he did not see him. Lounging idly—what else had he, a poor prisoner, to do?—in the sunny society of Maude Kirton and other attractive girls, Mr. Elster was unconscious of the movements of the household in general. He was in his own room dressing for dinner when the truth burst upon him.

Dr. Ashton was a straightforward; practical man—it has been already stated—who went direct to the point at once in any matters of difficulty. He arrived at Hartledon a few minutes before the dinner-hour, found Mr. Elster was yet in his dressing-room, and went there to him.

The news, the cool, scornful anger of the Rector, the keen question—"Was he mad?" burst upon the unhappy Val like a clap of thunder. He was standing in his shirt-sleeves, ready to go down, all but his coat and waistcoat, his hair-brushes in the uplifted hands. Hands and brushes had been arrested midway in the shock. The calm clerical man; all the more terrible then because of his calmness; standing there with his cold stinging words, and his unhappy culprit facing him, conscious of his heinous sins—the worst sin of all: that of being found out.

"Others have done so much before me, sir, and have not made the less good men," spoke Val, in his desperation.

Dr. Ashton could not help admiring the man, as he stood there in his physical beauty. In spite of his inward anger, his condemnation, his disappointment—and they were all very great—the good looks of Percival Elster struck him forcibly with a sort of annoyance: why should these men be so outwardly fair, so inwardly frail? Those good looks had told upon his daughter's heart; and they all loved *her*, and could not bear to cause her pain. Tall, supple, graceful, strong, towering nearly a head above the doctor, he stood, his pleasing features full of the best sort of attraction, his violet eyes rather wider open than usual, the waves of his silken hair smooth and bright. "If he were only half as fair in conduct as in looks!" muttered the grieved divine.

But those violet eyes, usually beaming with kindness, suddenly changed their present expression of depreciation to one of rage. Dr. Ashton gave a pretty accurate description of how the crisis had been brought to his knowledge—that Lord Hartledon had come to the Rectory, with his mistaken assailant, to be identified; and Percival Elster's anger was turned against his brother. Never in all his life had he been in so great a passion; and having to suppress its signs in the presence of the Rector only made the fuel burn more fiercely. To ruin him with the doctor by going *there* with the news! Anywhere else—anywhere but the Rectory!

Hedges, the butler, interrupted the conference. Dinner was waiting. Lord Hartledon looked at Val as the two entered the room, and was rather surprised at the furious gaze of reproach that was cast back on him.

Miss Ashton was not there. No, of course not! It needed not Val's glance around to be assured of that. Of course they were to be separated from that hour; the fiat was already gone forth. And Mr. Val Elster felt so savage that he could have struck his brother. He heard Dr. Ashton's reply to an inquiry—that Mrs. Ashton was feeling unusually poorly, and Anne remained at home with her—but he looked upon it as an evasion. Not a word did he speak during dinner: not a word, save what was forced from him by common courtesy, spoke he after the ladies had left the room; he only drank a great deal of wine.

A very unusual circumstance for Val Elster. With all his weak resolution, his yielding nature, drinking was a fault he was scarcely ever seduced into. Not above two or three times in his life could he remember to have exceeded the bounds of strict, temperate sobriety. The fact was, he was in wrath with himself: all his past follies were pressing upon him with bitter condemnation. He was just in that frame of mind when an object to vent our fury upon becomes a sort of necessity; and Mr. Elster's was vented on his brother.

He was waiting at boiling-point for the opportunity to "have it out" with him: and it soon came. As the gentlemen left the dining-room— and in these present days they do not, as a rule, sit long, especially when the host is a young man—Percival Elster touched his brother to detain him, and shut the door on the heels of the rest.

Lord Hartledon was surprised. Val's attack was so savage. He was talking off his superfluous wrath, and the wine he had taken did not tend to cool his heat. Lord Hartledon, vexed at the injustice, lost his temper; and for once there was a quarrel, sharp and loud, between the brothers. It did not last long; in its very midst they parted; throwing cutting words one at the other. Lord Hartledon quitted the room, to join his guests; Val Elster strode outside the window to cool his brain.

But now, look at the obstinate pride of those two foolish men! They were angry with each other in temper, but not in heart. In Percival Elster's conscience there was an underlying conviction that his brother had acted only in thoughtless impulse when he carried the misfortune to the Rectory; whilst Lord Hartledon was even then full of plans for serving Val, and considered he had more need to help him than ever. A day or two given to the indulgence of their anger, and they would be firmer friends than ever.

　　　　　　　　　　　　　　　　　　　MRS. HENRY WOOD

The large French window of the dining-room, opening to the ground, was flung back by Val Elster; and he stepped forth into the cool night, which was beautifully fine. The room looked towards the river. The velvet lawn, wet with the day's rain, lay calm and silent under the bright stars; the flowers, clustering around far and wide, gave out their sweet and heavy night perfume. Not an instant had he been outside when he became conscious that some figure was gliding towards him—was almost close to him; and he recognised Mr. Pike. Yes, that worthy gentleman appeared to be only then arriving on his evening visit: in point of fact, he had been glued ear and eye to the window during the quarrel.

"What do you want?" demanded Mr. Elster.

"Well, I came up here hoping to get a word with you, sir," replied the man in his rough, abrupt manner, more in character with his appearance and lawless reputation than with his accent and unmistakable intelligence. "There was a nasty accident a few hours ago: that shark came across his lordship."

"I know he did," savagely spoke Val. "The result of your informing him that I was Lord Hartledon."

"I did it for the best, Mr. Elster. He'd have nabbed you that very time, but for my putting him off the scent as I did."

"Yes, yes, I am aware you did it for the best, and I suppose it turned out to be so," quickly replied Val, some of his native kindliness resuming its sway. "It's an unfortunate affair altogether, and that's the best that can be said of it."

"What I came up here for was to tell you he was gone."

"Who is gone?"

"The shark."

"Gone!"

"He went off by the seven train. Lord Hartledon told him he'd communicate with his principals and see that the affair was arranged. It satisfied the man, and he went away by the next train—which happened to be the seven-o'clock one."

"How do you know this?" asked Mr. Elster.

"This way," was the answer. "I was hovering about outside that shed of mine, and I saw the encounter at the parson's gate—for that's where it took place. The first thing the fellow did when it was all over was to bolt across the road, and accuse me of purposely misleading him. 'Not a bit of it,' said I; 'if I did mislead you, it was unintentional, for I took the one who came over the bridge on Saturday to be Lord Hartledon, safe as eggs. But they have been down here only a week,' I went on, 'and I suppose I don't know 'em apart yet.' I can't say whether he believed me; I think he did; he's a soft sort of chap. It was all right, he said: the earl had passed his word to him that it should be made so without his arresting Mr. Elster, and he was off to London at once."

"And he has gone?"

Mr. Pike nodded significantly. "I watched him go; dodged him up to the station and saw him off."

Then this one danger was over! Val might breathe freely again.

"And I thought you would like to know the coast was clear; so I came up to tell you," concluded Pike.

"Thank you for your trouble," said Mr. Elster. "I shall not forget it."

"You'll remember it, perhaps, if a question arises touching that shed," spoke the man. "I may need a word sometime with Lord Hartledon."

"I'll remember it, Pike. Here, wait a moment. Is Thomas Pike your real name?"

"Well, I conclude it is. Pike was the name of my father and mother. As to Thomas—not knowing where I was christened, I can't go and look at the register; but they never called me anything but Tom. Did you wish to know particularly?"

There was a tone of mockery in the man's answer, not altogether acceptable to his hearer; and he let him go without further hindrance. But the man turned back in an instant of his own accord.

"I dare say you are wanting to know why I did you this little turn, Mr. Elster. I have been caught in corners myself before now; and if I can help anybody to get out of them without trouble to myself, I'm willing to do it. And to circumvent these law-sharks comes home to my spirit as wholesome refreshment."

Mr. Pike finally departed. He took the lonely way, and only struck into the high-road opposite his own domicile, the shed. Passing round it, he hovered at its rude door—the one he had himself made, along with the ruder window—and then, treading softly, he stepped to the low stile in the hedge, which had for years made the boundary between the waste land on which the shed stood and Clerk Gum's garden. Here he halted a minute, looking all ways. Then he stepped over the stile, crouched down amongst Mr. Gum's cabbages, got under shelter of the hedge, and so stole onwards, until he came to an anchor at the kitchen-window, and laid his ear to the shutter, just as it had recently been laid against the glass in the dining-room of my Lord Hartledon.

That he had a propensity for prying into the private affairs of his neighbours near and distant, there could be little doubt about. Mr. Pike, however, was not destined on this one occasion to reap any substantial reward. The kitchen appeared to be wrapped in perfect silence. Satisfying himself as to this, he next took off his heavy shoes, stole past the back door, and so round the clerk's house to the front. Very softly indeed went he, creeping by the wall, and emerging at last round the angle, by the window of the best parlour. Here, most excessively to Mr. Pike's consternation, he came upon a lady doing exactly what he had come to do—namely, stealthily listening at the window to anything there might be to hear inside.

The shrill scream she gave when she found her face in contact with the wild intruder, might have been heard over at Dr. Ashton's. Clerk Gum, who had been quietly writing in his office, came out in haste, and recognized Mrs. Jones, the wife of the surly porter at the station, and step-mother to the troublesome young servant, Rebecca. Pike had totally disappeared.

Mrs. Jones, partly through fright, partly in anger arising from a long-standing grievance, avowed the truth boldly: she had been listening at the parlour-shutters ever since she went out of the house ten minutes ago, and had been set upon by that wolf Pike.

"Set upon!" exclaimed the clerk, looking swiftly in all directions for the offender.

"I don't know what else you can call it, when a highway robber—a murderer, if all tales be true—steals round upon you without warning, and glares his eyes into yours," shrieked Mrs. Jones wrathfully. "And if he wasn't barefoot, Gum, my eyes strangely deceived me. I'd have you and Nancy take care of your throats."

She turned into the house, to the best parlour, where the clerk's wife was sitting with a visitor, Mirrable. Mrs. Gum, when she found what the commotion had been about, gave a sharp cry of terror, and shook from head to foot.

"On our premises! Close to our house! That dreadful man! Oh, Lydia, don't you think you were mistaken?"

"Mistaken!" retorted Mrs. Jones. "That wild face isn't one to be mistaken: I should like to see its fellow in Calne. Why Lord Hartledon don't have him taken up on suspicion of that murder, is odd to me."

"You'd better hold your tongue about that suspicion," interposed Mirrable. "I have cautioned you before, *I* shouldn't like to breathe a word against a desperate man; I should go about in fear that he might hear of it, and revenge himself."

In came the clerk. "I don't see a sign of any one about," he said; "and I'm sure whoever it was could not have had time to get away. You must have been mistaken, Mrs. Jones."

"Mistaken in what, pray?"

"That any man was there. You got confused, and fancied it, perhaps. As to Pike, he'd never dare come on my premises, whether by night or day. What were you doing at the window?"

"Listening," defiantly replied Mrs. Jones. "And now I'll just tell out what I've had in my head this long while, Mr. Gum, and know the reason of Nancy's slighting me in the way she does. What secret has she and Mary Mirrable got between them?"

"Secret?" repeated the clerk, whilst his wife gave a faint cry, and Mirrable turned her calm face on Mrs. Jones. "Have they a secret?"

"Yes, they have," raved Mrs. Jones, giving vent to her long pent-up emotion. "If they haven't, I'm blind and deaf. If I have come into your house once during the past year and found Mrs. Mirrable in it, and the two sitting and whispering, I've come ten times. This evening I came in at dusk; I turned the handle of the door and peeped into the best parlour, and there they were, nose and knees together, starting away from each other as soon as they saw me, Nance giving one of her faint cries, and the two making believe to have been talking of the weather. It's always so. And I want to know what secret they have got hold of, and whether I'm poison, that I can't be trusted with it."

Jabez Gum slowly turned his eyes on the two in question. His wife lifted her hands in deprecation at the idea that she should have a secret: Mirrable was laughing.

"Nancy's secret to-night, when you interrupted us, was telling me of a dream she had regarding Lord Hartledon, and of how she mistook Mr. Elster for him the morning he came down," cried the latter. "And if you have really been listening at the shutters since you went out, Mrs. Jones, you should by this time know how to pickle walnuts in the new way: for I declare that is all our conversation has been about since. You always were suspicious, you know, and you always will be."

"Look here, Mrs. Jones," said the clerk, decisively; "I don't choose to have my shutters listened at: it might give the house a bad name, for quarrelling, or something of that sort. So I'll trouble you not to repeat what you have done to-night, or I shall forbid your coming here. A secret, indeed!"

"Yes, a secret!" persisted Mrs. Jones. "And if I don't come at what it is one of these days, my name's not Lydia Jones. And I'll tell you why. It strikes me—I may be wrong—but it strikes me it concerns me and my husband and my household, which some folks are ever ready to interfere with. I'll take myself off now; and I would recommend you, as a parting warning, to denounce Pike to the police for an attempt at housebreaking, before you're both murdered in your bed. That'll be the end on't."

She went away, and Clerk Gum wished he could denounce *her* to the police. Mirrable laughed again; and Mrs. Gum, cowardly and timid, fell back in her chair as one seized with ague.

Beyond giving an occasional dole to Mrs. Jones for her children—and to tell the truth, she clothed them all, or they would have gone in rags—Mirrable had shaken her cousin off long ago: which of course did not tend to soothe the naturally jealous spirit of Mrs. Jones. At Hartledon House she was not welcomed, and could not go there; but she watched for the visits of Mirrable at the clerk's, and was certain to intrude on those occasions.

"I'll find it out!" she repeated to herself, as she went storming through the garden-gate; "I'll find it out. And as to that poacher, he'd better bring his black face near mine again!"

# VIII

## The Wager Boats

Tuesday morning rose, bright and propitious: a contrast to the two previous days arranged for the boat-race. All was pleasure, bustle, excitement at Hartledon: but the coolness that had arisen between the brothers was noticed by some of the guests. Neither of them was disposed to take the first step towards reconciliation: and, indeed, a little incident that occurred that morning led to another ill word between them. An account that had been standing for more than two years was sent in to Lord Hartledon's steward; it was for some harness, a saddle, a silver-mounted whip, and a few trifles of that sort, supplied by a small tradesman in the village. Lord Hartledon protested there was nothing of the sort owing; but upon inquiry the debtor proved to be Mr. Percival Elster. Lord Hartledon, vexed that any one in the neighbourhood should have waited so long for his money, said a sharp word on the score to Percival; and the latter retorted as sharply that it was no business of his. Again Val was angry with himself, and thus gave vent to his temper. The fact was, he had completely forgotten the trifling debt, and was as vexed as Hartledon that it should have been allowed to remain unpaid: but the man had not sent him any reminder whilst he was away.

"Pay it to-day, Marris," cried Lord Hartledon to his steward. "I won't have this sort of thing at Calne."

His tone was one of irritation—or it sounded so to the ears of his conscious brother, and Val bit his lips. After that, throughout the morning, they maintained a studied silence towards each other; and this was observed, but was not commented on. Val was unusually quiet altogether: he was saying to himself that he was sullen.

The starting-hour for the race was three o'clock; but long before that time the scene was sufficiently animated, not to say exciting. It was a most lovely afternoon. Not a trace remained of the previous day's rain; and the river—wide just there, as it took the sweeping curve of the point—was dotted with these little wager boats. Their owners for the time being, in their white boating-costume, each displaying his colours, were in highest spirits; and the fair gazers gathered on the banks were anxious as to the result. The favourite was Lord Hartledon—by long odds, as Mr. Shute grumbled. Had his lordship been known not to possess the smallest chance, nine of those fair girls out of ten would, nevertheless, have betted upon him. Some of them were hoping to play for a deeper stake than a pair of gloves. A staff, from which fluttered a gay little flag, had been driven into the ground, exactly opposite the house; it was the starting and the winning point. At a certain distance up the river, near to the mill, a boat was moored in mid-stream: this they would row round, and come back again.

At three o'clock they were to take the boats; and, allowing for time being wasted in the start, might be in again and the race won in three-quarters-of-an-hour. But, as is often the case, the time was not adhered to; one hindrance after another occurred; there was a great deal of laughing and joking, forgetting of things, and of getting into order; and at a quarter to four they were not off. But all were ready at last, and most of the rowers were each in his little cockle-shell. Lord Hartledon lingered yet in the midst of the group of ladies, all clustered together at one spot, who were keeping him with their many comments and questions. Each wore the colours of her favourite: the crimson and purple predominating, for they were those of their host. Lady Kirton displayed her loyalty in a conspicuous manner. She had an old crimson gauze skirt on, once a ball-dress, with ends of purple ribbon floating from it and fluttering in the wind; and a purple head-dress with a crimson feather. Maude, in a spirit of perversity, displayed a blue shoulder-knot, timidly offered to her by a young Oxford man who was staying there, Mr. Shute; and Anne Ashton wore the colours given her by Lord Hartledon.

"I can't stay; you'd keep me here all day: don't you see they are waiting for me?" he laughingly cried, extricating himself from the throng. "Why, Anne, my dear, is it you? How is it I did not see you before? Are you here alone?"

She had not long joined the crowd, having come up late from the Rectory, and had been standing outside, for she never put herself forward anywhere. Lord Hartledon drew her arm within his own for a moment and took her apart.

"Arthur came up with me: I don't know where he is now. Mamma was afraid to venture, fearing the grass might be damp."

"And the Rector *of course* would not countenance us by coming," said Lord Hartledon, with a laugh. "I remember his prejudices against boating of old."

"He is coming to dinner."

"As you all are; Arthur also to-day. I made the doctor promise that. A jolly banquet we'll have, too, and toast the winner. Anne, I just wanted to say this to you; Val is in an awful rage with me for letting that matter get to the ears of your father, and I am not pleased with him; so altogether we are just now treating each other to a dose of sullenness, and when we do speak it's to growl like two amiable bears; but it shall make no difference to what I said last week. All shall be made smooth, even to the satisfaction of your father. You may trust me."

He ran off from her, stepped into the skiff, and was taking the sculls, when he uttered a sudden exclamation, leaped out again, and began to run with all speed towards the house.

"What is it? Where are you going?" asked the O'Moore, who was the appointed steward.

"I have forgotten—" *What*, they did not catch; the word was lost on the air.

"It is bad luck to turn back," called out Maude. "You won't win."

He was already half-way to the house. A couple of minutes after entering it he reappeared again, and came flying down the slopes at full speed. Suddenly his foot slipped, and he fell to the ground. The only one who saw the accident was Mr. O'Moore; the general attention at that moment being concentrated upon the river. He hastened back. Hartledon was then gathering himself up, but slowly.

"No damage," said he; "only a bit of a wrench to the foot. Give me your arm for a minute, O'Moore. This ground must be slippery from yesterday's rain."

Mr. O'Moore held out his arm, and Hartledon took it. "The ground is not slippery, Hart; it's as dry as a bone."

"Then what caused me to slip?"

"The rate you were coming at. Had you not better give up the contest, and rest?"

"Nonsense! My foot will be all right in the skiff. Let us get on; they'll all be out of patience."

When it was seen that something was amiss with him, that he leaned rather heavily on the O'Moore, eager steps pressed round him. Lord Hartledon laughed, making light of it; he had been so clumsy as to stumble, and had twisted his ankle a little. It was nothing.

"Stay on shore and give it a rest," cried one, as he stepped once more into the little boat. "I am sure you are hurt."

"Not I. It will have rest in the boat. Anne," he said, looking up at her with his pleasant smile, "do you wear my colours still?"

She touched the knot on her bosom, and smiled back to him, her tone full of earnestness. "I would wear them always."

And the countess-dowager, in her bedecked flounces and crimson feather, looked as if she would like to throw the knot and its wearer into the river, in the wake of the wager boats. After one or two false starts, they got off at last.

"Do you think it seemly, this flirtation of yours with Lord Hartledon?"

Anne turned in amazement. The face of the old dowager was close to her; the snub nose and rouged cheeks and false flaxen front looked ready to eat her up.

"I have no flirtation with Lord Hartledon, Lady Kirton; or he with me. When I was a child, and he a great boy, years older, he loved me and petted me as a little sister: I think he does the same still."

"My daughter tells me you are counting upon one of the two. If I say to you, do not be too sanguine of either, I speak as a friend; as your mother might speak. Lord Hartledon is already appropriated; and Val Elster is not worth appropriating."

Was she mad? Anne Ashton looked at her, really doubting it. No, she was only vulgar-minded, and selfish, and utterly impervious to all sense of shame in her scheming. Instinctively Anne moved a pace further off.

"I do not think Lord Hartledon is appropriated yet," spoke Anne, in a little spirit of mischievous retaliation. "That some amongst his present guests would be glad to appropriate him may be likely enough; but what if he is not willing to be appropriated? He said to Mr. Elster, last week, that they were wasting their time."

"Who's Mr. Elster?" cried the angry dowager. "What right has he to be at Hartledon, poking his nose into everything that does not concern him?—what right has he, I ask?"

"The right of being Lord Hartledon's brother," carelessly replied Anne.

"It is a right he had best not presume upon," rejoined Lady Kirton. "Brothers are brothers as children; but the tie widens as they grow up and launch out into their different spheres. There's not a man of all Hartledon's guests but has more right to be here than Val Elster."

"Yet they are brothers still."

"Brothers! I'll take care that Val Elster presumes no more upon the tie when Maude reigns at—"

For once the countess-dowager caught up her words. She had said more than she had meant to say. Anne Ashton's calm sweet eyes were bent upon her, waiting for more.

"It is true," she said, giving a shake to the purple tails, and taking a sudden resolution, "Maude is to be his wife; but I ought not to have let it slip out. It was unintentional; and I throw myself on your honour, Miss Ashton."

"But it is not true?" asked Anne, somewhat perplexed.

"It *is* true. Hartledon has his own reasons for keeping it quiet at present; but—you'll see when the time comes. Should I take upon myself so much rule here, but that it is to be Maude's future home?"

"I don't believe it," cried Anne, as the old story-teller sailed off. "That she loves him, and that her mother is anxious to secure him, is evident; but he is truthful and open, and would never conceal it. No, no, Lady Maude! you are cherishing a false hope. You are very beautiful, but you are not worthy of him; and I should not like you for my sister-in-law at all. That dreadful old countess-dowager! How she dislikes Val, and how rude she is! I'll try not to come in her way again after to-day, as long as they are at Hartledon."

"What are you thinking of, Anne?"

"Oh, not much," she answered, with a soft blush, for the questioner was Mr. Elster. "Do you think your brother has hurt himself much, Val?"

"I didn't know he had hurt himself at all," returned Val rather coolly, who had been on the river at the time in somebody's skiff, and saw nothing of the occurrence. "What has he done?"

"He slipped down on the slopes and twisted his ankle. I suppose they will be coming back soon."

"I suppose they will," was the answer. Val seemed in an ungracious mood. He and Mr. O'Moore and young Carteret were the only three who had remained behind. Anne asked Val why he did not go and look on; and he answered, because he didn't want to.

It was getting on for five o'clock when the boats were discerned returning. How they clustered on the banks, watching the excited rowers, some pale with their exertions, others in a white heat! Captain Dawkes was first, and was doing all he could to keep so; but when only a boat's length from the winning-post another shot past him, and won by half a length. It was the young Oxonian, Mr. Shute—though indeed it does not much matter who it was, save that it was not Lord Hartledon.

"Strike your colours, ladies, you that sport the crimson and purple!" called out a laughing voice from one of the skiffs. "Oxford blue wins."

Lord Hartledon arrived last. He did not get up for some minutes after the rest were in. In short, he was distanced.

"Hart has hurt his arm as well as his foot," observed one of the others, as he came alongside. "That's why he got distanced."

"No, it was not," dissented Lord Hartledon, looking up from his skiff at the crowd of fair faces bent down upon him. "My arm is all right; it only gave me a few twinges when I first started. My oar fouled, and I could not get right again; so, finding I had lost too much ground, I gave up the contest. Anne, had I known I should disgrace my colours, I would not have given them to *you*."

"Miss Ashton loses, and Maude wins!" cried the countess-dowager, executing a little dance of triumph. "Maude is the only one who wears the Oxford blue."

It was true. The young Oxonian was a retiring and timid man, and none had voluntarily assumed his colours. But no one heeded the countess-dowager.

"You are like a child, Hartledon, denying that your arm's damaged!" exclaimed Captain Dawkes. "I know it is: I could see it by the way you struck your oar all along."

What feeling is it in man that prompts him to disclaim physical pain?—make light of personal injury? Lord Hartledon's ankle was swelling, at the bottom of the boat; and without the slightest doubt his arm *was* paining him, although perhaps at the moment not very considerably. But he maintained his own assertions, and protested his arm was as sound as the best arm present. "I could go over the work again with pleasure," cried he.

"Nonsense, Hart! You could not."

"And I *will* go over it," he added, warming with the opposition. "Who'll try his strength with me? There's plenty of time before dinner."

"I will," eagerly spoke young Carteret, who had been, as was remarked, one of those on land, and was wild to be handling the oars. "If Dawkes will let me have his skiff, I'll bet you ten to five you are distanced again, Hartledon."

Perhaps Lord Hartledon had not thought his challenge would be taken seriously. But when he saw the eager, joyous look of the boy Carteret—he was not yet nineteen—the flushed pleasure of the beardless face, he would not have retracted it for the world. He was just as good-natured as Percival Elster.

"Dawkes will let you have his skiff, Carteret."

Captain Dawkes was exceedingly glad to be rid of it. Good boatman though he was, he rarely cared to spend his strength superfluously, when nothing was to be gained by it, and had no fancy to row his skiff back to its moorings, as most of the others were already doing with theirs. He leaped out.

"Any one but you, Hartledon, would be glad to come out of that tilting thing, and enjoy a rest, and get your face cool," cried the countess-dowager.

"I dare say they might, ma'am. I'm afraid I am given to obstinacy; always was. Be quick, Carteret."

Mr. Carteret was hastily stripping himself of his coat, and any odds and ends of attire he deemed superfluous. "One moment, Hartledon; only one moment," came the joyous response.

"And you'll come home with your arm and your ankle like your colours, Hartledon—crimson and purple," screamed the dowager. "And you'll be laid up, and go on perhaps to locked jaw; and then you'll expect me to nurse you!"

"I shall expect nothing of the sort, ma'am, I pledge you my word; I'll nurse myself. All ready, Carteret?"

"All ready. Same point as before, Hart?"

"Same point: round the boat and home again."

"And it's ten sovs. to five, Hart?"

"All right. You'll lose, Carteret."

Carteret laughed. He saw the five sovereigns as surely in his possession as he saw the sculls in his hands. There was no trouble with the start this time, and they were off at once.

Lord Hartledon took the lead. He was spurring his strength to the uttermost: perhaps out of bravado; that he might show them nothing was the matter with his arm. But Mr. Carteret gained on him; and as they turned the point and went out of sight, the young man's boat was the foremost.

The race had been kept—as the sporting men amongst them styled it—dark. Not an inkling of it had been suffered to get abroad, or, as Lord Hartledon had observed, they should have the banks swarming. The consequence was, that not more than half-a-dozen curious idlers had assembled: those were on the opposite side, and had now gone down with the boats to Calne. No spectators, either on the river or the shore, attended this lesser contest: Lord Hartledon and Mr. Carteret had it all to themselves.

And meanwhile, during the time Lord Hartledon had remained at rest in his skiff under the winning flag, Percival Elster never addressed one word to him. There he stood, on the edge of the bank; but not a syllable spoke he, good, bad, or indifferent.

Miss Ashton was looking for her brother, and might just as well have looked for a needle in a bottle of hay. Arthur was off somewhere.

"You need not go home yet, Anne," said Val.

"I must. I have to dress for dinner. It is all to be very smart to-night, you know," she said, with a merry laugh.

"With Shute in the post of honour. Who'd have thought that awkward, quiet fellow would win? I will see you home, Anne, if you must go."

Miss Ashton coloured vividly with embarrassment. In the present state of affairs, she did not know whether that might be permitted: poor Val was out of favour at the Rectory. He detected the feeling, and it tended to vex him more and more.

"Nonsense, Anne! The veto has not yet been interposed, and they can't kill you for allowing my escort. Stay here if you like: if you go, I shall see you home."

It was quite imperative that she should go, for dinner at Hartledon was that evening fixed for seven o'clock, and there would be little enough time to dress and return again. They set out, walking side by side. Anne told him of what Lord Hartledon had said to her that day; and Val coloured with shame at the sullenness he had displayed, and his heart went into a glow of repentance. Had he met his brother then, he had clasped his hand, and poured forth his contrition.

He met some one else instead, almost immediately. It was Dr. Ashton, coming for Anne. Percival was not wanted now: was not invited to continue his escort. A cold, civil word or two passed, and Val struck across the grove into the high-road, and returned to Hartledon.

He was about to turn in at the lodge-gates with his usual greeting to Mrs. Capper when his attention was caught by a figure coming down the avenue. A man in a long coat, his face ornamented with red whiskers. It required no second glance for recognition. Whiskers and coat proclaimed their owner at once; and if ever Val Elster's heart leaped into his mouth, it certainly leaped then.

He went on, instead of turning in; quietly, as if he were only a stranger enjoying an evening stroll up the road; but the moment he was past the gates he set off at breakneck speed, not heeding where. That the man was there to arrest him, he felt as sure as he had ever felt of anything in this world; and in his perplexity he began accusing every one of treachery, Lord Hartledon and Pike in particular.

The river at the back in this part took a sweeping curve, the road kept straight; so that to arrive at a given point, the one would be more quickly traversed than the other. On and on went Val Elster; and as soon as an opening allowed, he struck into the brushwood on the right, intending to make his way back by the river to Hartledon.

But not yet. Not until the shades of night should fall on the earth: he would have a better chance of getting away from that shark in the darkness than by daylight. He propped his back against a tree and waited, hating himself all the time for his cowardice. With all his scrapes and dilemmas, he had never been reduced to this sort of hiding.

And his pursuer had struck into the wood after him, passed straight through it, though with some little doubt and difficulty, and was already by the river-side, getting there just as Lord Hartledon was passing in his skiff. Long as this may have seemed in telling, it took only a short time to accomplish; still Lord Hartledon had not made quick way, or he would have been further on his course in the race.

Would the sun ever set?—daylight ever pass? Val thought *not*, in his impatience; and he ventured out of his shelter very soon, and saw for his reward—the long coat and red whiskers by the river-side, their owner conversing with a man. Val went further away, keeping the direction of the stream: the brushwood might no longer be safe. He did not think they had seen him: the man he dreaded had his back to him, the other his face. And that other was Pike.

# IX

## Waiting for Dinner

Dinner at Hartledon had been ordered for seven o'clock. It was beyond that hour when Dr. Ashton arrived, for he had been detained—a clergyman's time is not always under his own control. Anne and Arthur were with him, but not Mrs. Ashton. He came in, ready with an apology for his tardiness, but found he need not offer it; neither Lord Hartledon nor his brother having yet appeared.

"Hartledon and that boy Carteret have not returned home yet," said the countess-dowager, in her fiercest tones, for she liked her dinner more than any other earthly thing, and could not brook being kept waiting for it. "And when they do come, they'll keep us another half-hour dressing."

"I beg your ladyship's pardon—they have come," interposed Captain Dawkes. "Carteret was going into his room as I came out of mine."

"Time they were," grumbled the dowager. "They were not in five minutes ago, for I sent to ask."

"Which of the two won the race?" inquired Lady Maude of Captain Dawkes.

"I don't think Carteret did," he replied, laughing. "He seemed as sulky as a bear, and growled out that there had been no race, for Hartledon had played him a trick."

"What did he mean?"

"Goodness knows."

"I hope Hartledon upset him," charitably interrupted the dowager. "A ducking would do that boy good; he is too forward by half."

There was more waiting. The countess-dowager flounced about in her pink satin gown; but it did not bring the loiterers any the sooner. Lady Maude—perverse still, but beautiful—talked in whispers to the hero of the day, Mr. Shute; wearing a blue-silk robe and a blue wreath in her hair. Anne, adhering to the colours of Lord Hartledon, though he had been defeated, was in a rich, glistening white silk, with natural flowers, red and purple, on its body, and the same in her hair. Her sweet face was sunny again, her eyes were sparkling: a word dropped by Dr. Ashton had given her a hope that, perhaps, Percival Elster might be forgiven sometime.

He was the first of the culprits to make his appearance. The dowager attacked him of course. What did he mean by keeping dinner waiting?

Val replied that he was late in coming home; he had been out. As to keeping dinner waiting, it seemed that Lord Hartledon was doing that: he didn't suppose they'd have waited for him.

He spoke tartly, as if not on good terms with himself or the world. Anne Ashton, near to whom he had drawn, looked up at him with a charming smile.

"Things may brighten, Percival," she softly breathed.

"It's to be hoped they will," gloomily returned Val. "They look dark enough just now."

"What have you done to your face?" she whispered.

"To my face? Nothing that I know of."

"The forehead is red, as if it had been bruised, or slightly grazed."

Val put his hand up to his forehead. "I did feel something when I washed just now," he remarked slowly, as though doubting whether anything was wrong or not. "It must have been done—when I—struck against that tree," he added, apparently taxing his recollection.

"How was that?"

"I was running in the dusk, and did not notice the branch of a tree in my way. It's nothing, Anne, and will soon go off."

Mr. Carteret came in, looking just as Val Elster had done—out of sorts. Questions were showered upon him as to the fate of the race; but the dowager's voice was heard above all.

"This is a pretty time to make your appearance, sir! Where's Lord Hartledon?"

"In his room, I suppose. Hartledon never came," he added in sulky tones, as he turned from her to the rest. "I rowed on, and on, thinking how nicely I was distancing him, and got down, the mischief knows where. Miles, nearly, I must have gone."

"But why did you pass the turning-point?" asked one.

"There was no turning-point," returned Mr. Carteret; "some confounded meddler must have unmoored the boat as soon as the first race was over, and I, like an idiot, rowed on, looking for it. All at once it came into my mind what a way I must have gone, and I turned and waited. And might have waited till now," he added, "for Hart never came."

"Then his arm must have failed him," exclaimed Captain Dawkes. "I thought it was all wrong."

"It wasn't right, for I soon shot past him," returned young Carteret. "But Hart knew the spot where the boat ought to have been, though I didn't; what he did, I suppose, was to clear round it just as though it had been there, and come in home again. It will be an awful shame if he takes an unfair advantage of it, and claims the race."

"Hartledon never took an unfair advantage in his life," spoke up Val Elster, in clear, decisive tones. "You need not be afraid, Carteret. I dare say his arm failed him."

"Well, he might have hallooed when he found it failing, and not have suffered me to row all that way for nothing," retorted young Carteret. "Not a trace could I see of him as I came back; he had hastened home, I expect, to shut himself up in his room with his damaged arm and foot."

"I'll see what he's doing there," said Val.

He went out; but returned immediately.

"We are all under a mistake," was his greeting. "Hartledon has not returned yet. His servant is in his room waiting for him."

"Then what do you mean by telling stories?" demanded the countess-dowager, turning sharply on Mr. Carteret.

"Good Heavens, ma'am! you need not begin upon me!" returned young Carteret. "I have told no stories. I said Hart let me go on, and never came on himself; if that's a story, I'll swallow Dawkes's skiff and the sculls too."

"You said he was in his room. You know you did."

"I said I supposed so. It's usual for a man to go there, I believe, to get ready for dinner," added young Carteret, always ripe for a wordy war, in his antipathy to the countess-dowager.

"*You* said he had come in;" and the angry woman faced round on Captain Dawkes. "You saw them going into their rooms, you said. Which was it—you did, or you didn't?"

"I did see Carteret make his appearance; and assumed that Lord Hartledon had gone on to his room," replied the captain, suppressing a laugh. "I am sorry to have misled your ladyship. I dare say Hart was about the house somewhere."

"Then why doesn't he appear?" stormed the dowager. "Pretty behaviour this, to keep us all waiting dinner. I shall tell him so. Val Elster, ring for Hedges."

Val rang the bell. "Has Lord Hartledon come in?" he asked, when the butler appeared.

"No, sir."

"And dinner's spoiling, isn't it, Hedges?" broke in the dowager.

"It won't be any the better for waiting, my lady."

"No. I must exercise my privilege and order it served. At once, Hedges, do you hear? If Hartledon grumbles, I shall tell him it serves him right."

"But where can Hartledon be?" cried Captain Dawkes.

"That's what I am wondering," said Val. "He can't be on the river all this time; Carteret would have seen him in coming home."

A strangely grave shade, looking almost like a prevision of evil, arose to Dr. Ashton's face. "I trust nothing has happened to him," he exclaimed. "Where did you part company with him, Mr. Carteret?"

"That's more than I can tell you, sir. You must have seen—at least—no, you were not there; but those looking on must have seen me get ahead of him within view of the starting-point; soon after that I lost sight of him. The river winds, you know; and of course I thought he was coming on behind me. Very daft of me, not to divine that the boat had been removed!"

"Do you think he passed the mill?"

"The mill?"

"That place where the river forms what might almost be called a miniature harbour. A mill is built there which the stream serves. You could not fail to see it."

"I remember now. Yes, I saw the mill. What of it?"

"Did Lord Hartledon pass it?"

"How should I know!" cried the boy. "I had lost sight of him ages before that."

"The current is extremely rapid there," observed Dr. Ashton. "If he found his arm failing, he might strike down to the mill and land there; and his ankle may be keeping him a prisoner."

"And that's what it is!" exclaimed Val.

They were crossing the hall to the dining-room. Without the slightest ceremony, the countess-dowager pushed herself foremost and advanced to the head of the table.

"I shall occupy this seat in my nephew's absence," said she. "Dr. Ashton, will you be so good as to take the foot? There's no one else."

"Nay, madam; though Lord Hartledon may not be here, Mr. Elster is."

She had actually forgotten Val; and would have liked to ignore him now that he was recalled to remembrance; but that might not be. As much contempt as could be expressed in her face was there, as she turned her snub nose and small round eyes defiantly upon that unoffending younger brother.

"I was going to request you to take it, sir," said Percival, in low tones, to Dr. Ashton. "I shall go off in the pony-carriage for Edward. He must think we are neglecting him."

"Very well. I hate these rowing matches," heartily added the Rector.

"What a curious old fish that parson must be!" exclaimed young Carteret to his next neighbour. "He says he doesn't like boating."

It happened to be Arthur Ashton, and the lad's brow lowered. "You are speaking of my father," he said. "But I'll tell you why he does not like it. He had a brother once, a good deal older than himself; they had no father, and Arthur—that was the elder—was very fond of him: there were only those two. He took him out in a boat one day, and there was an accident: the eldest was drowned, the little one saved. Do you wonder that my father has dreaded boating ever since? He seems to have the same sort of dread of it that a child who has been frightened by its nurse has of the dark."

"By Jove! that was a go, though!" was the sympathising comment of Mr. Carteret.

The doctor said grace, and dinner proceeded. It was not half over when Mr. Elster came in, in his light overcoat. Walking straight up to the table, he stood by it, his face wearing a blank, perplexed look. A momentary silence of expectation, and then many tongues spoke together.

"Where's your brother? Where's Lord Hartledon? Has he not come?"

"I don't know where he is," answered Val. "I was in hopes he had reached home before me, but I find he has not. I can't make it out at all."

"Did he land at the mill?" asked Dr. Ashton.

"Yes, he must have done so, for the skiff is moored there."

"Then he's all right," cried the doctor; and there was a strangely-marked sound of relief in his tones.

"Oh, he is all right," confidently asserted Percival. "The only question is, where he can be. The miller was out this afternoon, and left his place locked up; so that Hartledon could not get in, and had nothing for it but to start home with his lameness, or sit down on the bank until some one found him."

"He must have set off to walk."

"I should think so. But where has he walked to?" added Val. "I drove slowly home, looking on either side of the road, but could see nothing of him."

"What should bring him on the side of the road?" demanded the dowager. "Do you think he would turn tramp, and take his seat on a heap of stones? Where do you get your ideas from?"

"From common sense, ma'am. If he set out to walk, and his foot failed him half-way, there'd be nothing for it but to sit down and wait. But he is *not* on the road: that is the curious part of the business."

"Would he come the other way?"

"Hardly. It is so much further by the river than by the road."

"You may depend upon it that is what he has done," said Dr. Ashton. "He might think he should meet some of you that way, and get an arm to help him."

"I declare I never thought of that," exclaimed Val, his face brightening. "There he is, no doubt; perched somewhere between this and the mill, like patience on a monument, unable to put foot to the ground."

He turned away. Some of the men offered to accompany him: but he declined their help, and begged them to go on with their dinner, saying he would take sufficient servants with him, even though they had to carry Hartledon.

So Mr. Elster went, taking servants and lanterns; for in some parts of this road the trees overhung, and rendered it dark. But they could not find Lord Hartledon. They searched, and shouted, and waved their lanterns: all in vain. Very much perplexed indeed did Val Elster look when he got back again.

"Where in the world can he have gone to?" angrily questioned the countess-dowager; and she glared from her seat at the head of the table on the offender Val, as she asked it. "I must say all this is most unseemly, and Hartledon ought to be brought to his senses for causing it. I suppose he has taken himself off to a surgeon's."

It was possible, but unlikely, as none knew better than Val Elster. To get to the surgeon's he would have to pass his own house, and would be more likely to go in, and send for Mr. Hillary, than walk on with a disabled foot. Besides, if he had gone to the surgeon's, he would not stay there all this time. "I don't know what to do," said Percival Elster; and there was the same blank, perplexed look on his face that was observed the first time he came in. "I don't much like the appearance of things."

"Why, you don't think anything's wrong with him!" exclaimed young Carteret, starting-up with an alarmed face. "He's safe to turn up, isn't he?"

MRS. HENRY WOOD

"Of course he will turn up," answered Val, in a dreamy tone. "Only this uncertainty, as to where to look for him, is not pleasant."

Dr. Ashton motioned Val to his side. "Are you fearing an accident?" he asked in low tones.

"No, sir."

"I am. That current by the mill is so fearfully strong; and if your brother had not the use of his one arm—and the boat was drawn onwards, beyond his control—and upset—"

Dr. Ashton paused. Val Elster looked rather surprised.

"How could it upset, sir? The skiffs are as safe as this floor. I don't fear that in the least: what I do fear is that Edward may be in some out-of-the-way nook, insensible from pain, and won't be found until daylight. Fancy, a whole night out of doors, in that state! He might be half-dead with cold by the morning."

Dr. Ashton shook his head in dissent. His dislike of boating seemed just now to be rising into horror.

"What are you going to do now, Elster?" inquired Captain Dawkes.

"Go to the mill again, I think, and find out if any one saw Hartledon leave the skiff, and which way he took. One of the servants can run down to Hillary's the while."

Dr. Ashton rose, bowing for permission to Lady Kirton; and the gentlemen with one accord rose with him, the same purpose in the mind of all—that of more effectually scouring the ground between the mill and Hartledon. The countess-dowager felt that she should like to box the ears of every one of them. The idea of danger in connection with Lord Hartledon had not yet penetrated to her brain.

At this moment, before they had left the room, there arose a strange wild sound from without—almost an unearthly sound—that seemed to come from several voices, and to be bearing round the house from the river-path. Mrs. O'Moore put down her knife and fork, and rose up with a startled cry.

"There's nothing to be alarmed at," said the dowager. "It is those Irish harvesters. I know their horrid voices, and dare say they are riotously drunk. Hartledon ought to put them in prison for it."

The sounds died away into silence. Mrs. O'Moore took her hands from her eyes, where they had been pressed. "Don't you know what it is, Lady Kirton? It is the Irish death-wail!"

It rose again, louder than before, for those from whom it came were nearing the house—a horribly wailing sound, ringing out in the silence of the night. Mrs. O'Moore crouched into her chair again, and hid her terrified face. She was not Irish, and had never heard that sound but once, and that was when her child died.

"She is right," cried her husband, the O'Moore; "that is the death-wail. Hark! it is for a chieftain; they mourn the loss of one high in the land. And—they are coming here! Oh, Elster! can DEATH have overtaken your brother?"

The gentlemen had stood spell-bound, listening to the sound, their faces a mixture of surprise and credulity. At the words they rushed out with one accord, and the women stole after them with trembling steps and blanched lips.

"If ever I saw such behaviour in all my existence!" irascibly spoke the countess-dowager, who was left alone in her glory. "The death-wail, indeed! The woman's a fool. I'll get those Irishmen transported, if I can."

In the hall the servants were gathered, cowering almost as the ladies did. Their master had flown down the hall-steps, and the labourers were coming steadily up to it, bearing something in procession. Dr. Ashton came back as quickly as he had gone out, extending his arms before him.

"Ladies, I pray you go in," he urged, in strange agitation. "You must not meet these—these Irishmen. Go back to the dining-room, I entreat you, and remain in it."

But the curiosity of women—who can suppress it? They were as though they heard not, and were pressing on to the door, when Val Elster dashed in with a white face.

"Back, all of you! You must not stay here. This is no place or sight for you. Anne," he added, seizing Miss Ashton's hand in peremptory entreaty, "you at least know how to be calm. Get them away, and keep them out of the hall."

"Tell me the worst," she implored. "I will indeed try to be calm. Who is it those men are bringing here?"

"My dear brother—my dead brother. Madam," he continued to the countess-dowager, who had now come out, dinner-napkin in hand, her curls all awry, "you must not come here. Go back to the dining-room, all of you."

"Not come here! Go back to the dining-room!" echoed the outraged dowager. "Don't take quite so much upon yourself, Val Elster. The house is Lord Hartledon's, and I am a free agent in it."

A shriek—an agonized shriek—broke from Lady Maude. In her suspense she had stolen out unperceived, and lifted the covering of the

MRS. HENRY WOOD

rude bier, now resting on the steps. The rays of the hall-lamp fell on the face, and Maude, in her anguish, with a succession of hysterical sobs, came shivering back to sink down at her mother's feet.

"Oh, my love—my love! Dead! dead!"

The only one who heard the words was Anne Ashton. The countess-dowager caught the last.

"Who is dead? What is this mystery?" she asked, unceremoniously lifting her satin dress, with the intention of going out to see, and her head began to nod—perhaps with apprehension—as if she had the palsy. "You want to force us away. No, thank you; not until I've come to the bottom of this."

"Let us tell them," cried young Carteret, in his boyish impulse, "and then perhaps they will go. An accident has happened to Lord Hartledon, ma'am, and these men have brought him home."

"He—*he's* not dead?" asked the old woman, in changed tones.

Alas! poor Lord Hartledon was indeed dead. The Irish labourers, in passing near the mill, had detected the body in the water; rescued it, and brought it home.

The countess-dowager's grief commenced rather turbulently. She talked and shrieked, and danced round, exactly as if she had been a wild Indian. It was so intensely ludicrous, that the occupants of the hall gazed in silence.

"Here to-day, and gone to-morrow!" she sobbed. "Oh—o—o—o—o—o—oh!"

"Nay," cried young Carteret, "here to-day, and gone *now*. Poor fellow! it is awful."

"And you have done it!" she cried, turning her grief upon the astonished boy. "You! What business had you to allure him off again in that miserable boat, once he had got home?"

"Don't trample me down, please," he indignantly returned; "I am as cut up as you can be. Hedges, hadn't you better get Lady Kirton's maid here? I think she is going mad."

"And now the house is without a master," she bemoaned, returning to her own griefs and troubles, "and I have all the arrangements thrown upon myself."

"The house is not without a master," said young Carteret, who seemed inclined to have the last word. "If one master has gone from it, poor fellow! there's another to replace him; and he is at your elbow now."

He at her elbow was Val Elster. Lady Kirton gathered in the sense of the words, and gave a cry; a prolonged cry of absolute dismay.

"*He* can't be its master."

"I should say he *is*, ma'am. At any rate he is now Lord Hartledon."

She looked from one to the other in helpless doubt. It was a contingency that had never so much as occurred to her. Had she wanted confirmation, the next moment brought it to her from the lips of the butler.

"Hedges," called out Percival sternly, in his embarrassment and grief, "open the dining-room door. We *must* get the hall cleared."

"The door is open, my lord."

"*He* Lord Hartledon!" shrieked the countess-dowager, "why, I was going to recommend his brother to ship him off to Canada for life."

It was altogether an unseemly scene at such a time. But almost everything the Countess-Dowager of Kirton did was unseemly.

# X

## Mr. Pike's Visit

Percival Elster was in truth Earl of Hartledon. By one of those unexpected calamities, which are often inexplicable—and which most certainly was so as yet in the present instance—a promising young life had been snapped asunder, and another reigned in his place. In one short hour Val Elster, who had scarcely cross or coin to call his own, had been going in danger of arrest from one moment to another, had become a peer of the realm and a man of wealth.

As they laid the body down in a small room opening from the hall, and his late companions and guests crowded around in awe-struck silence, there was one amidst them who could not control his grief and emotion. It was poor Val. Pushing aside the others, never heeding them in his bitter sorrow, he burst into passionate sobs as he leaned over the corpse. And none of them thought the worse of Val for it.

"Oh, Percival! how did it happen?"

The speaker was Dr. Ashton. Little less affected himself, he clasped the young man's hand in token of heartfelt sympathy.

"I cannot think *how* it could have happened," replied Percival, when able to control his feelings sufficiently to speak. "It seems awfully strange to me—mysteriously so."

"If he found himself going wrong, why didn't he shout out?" asked young Carteret, with a rueful face. "I couldn't have helped hearing him."

It was a question that was passing through the minds of all; was being whispered about. How could it have happened? The body presented the usual appearance of death from drowning; but close to the left temple was a wound, and the face was otherwise disfigured. It must have been done, they thought, by coming into contact with something or other in the water; perhaps the skiff itself. Arm and ankle were both much swollen.

Nothing was certainly known as yet of Lord Hartledon from the time Mr. Carteret parted company with him, to the time when the body was found. It appeared that these Irish labourers were going home from their work, singing as they went, their road lying past the mill, when they were spoken to by the miller's boy. He stood on the species of estrade which the miller had placed there for his own convenience, bending down as far as his young head and shoulders could reach, and peering into the water attentively. "I think I see some'at in the stream," quoth he, and the men stopped; and after a short time, proceeded to search. It proved to be the dead body of Lord Hartledon, caught amongst the reeds.

It was rather a curious coincidence that Percival Elster and his servants in the last search should have heard the voices of the labourers singing in the distance. But they were too far off on their return to Hartledon to be within hearing when the men found the body.

The news spread; people came up from far and near, and Hartledon was besieged. Mr. Hillary, the surgeon, gave it as his opinion that the wound on the temple, no doubt caused before death, had rendered Lord Hartledon insensible, and unable to extricate himself from the water. The mill and cottage were built on what might be called an arm of the river. Lord Hartledon had no business there at all; but the current was very strong; and if, as was too probable, he had become almost disabled, he might have drifted to it without being able to help himself; or he might have been making for it, intending to land and rest in the cottage until help could be summoned to convey him home. How he got into the water was not known. Once in the water, the blow was easy enough to receive; he might have struck against the estrade.

There is almost sure to be some miserable coincidence in these cases to render them doubly unfortunate. For three weeks past, as the miller testified—a respectable man named Floyd—his mill had not been deserted; some one, man, boy, or woman, had always been there. On this afternoon it was closed, mill and cottage too, and all were away. What might have been simply a slight accident, had help been at hand, had terminated in an awful death for the want of it.

It was eleven o'clock before anything like order was restored at Hartledon, and the house left in quiet. The last person to quit it was Dr. Ashton. Hedges, the butler, had been showing him out, and was standing for a minute on the steps looking after him, and perhaps to cool, with a little fresh air, his perplexed brow—for the man was a faithful retainer, and the affair had shocked him in no common degree—when he was accosted by Pike, who emerged stealthily from behind one of the outer pillars, where he seemed to have been sheltering.

"Why, what have you been doing there?" exclaimed the butler.

"Mr. Hedges, I've been waiting here—hiding, if you like to call it so," was the answer; and it should be observed that the man's manner, quite unlike his usual rough, devil-may-care tone, was characterized by singular respect and earnestness. To hear him, and not see him, you might think you were listening to some staid and respectable friend of the family. "I have been standing there this hour past, keeping behind the pillar while other folk went in and out, and waiting my time to speak to you."

"To me?" repeated Hedges.

"Yes, sir. I want you to grant me a favour; and I hope you'll pardon my boldness in asking it."

Hedges did not know what to make of this. It was the first time he had enjoyed the honour of a personal interview with Mr. Pike; and the contrast between that gentleman's popular reputation and his present tone and manner struck the butler as exceedingly singular. But that the butler was in a very softened mood, feeling full of subdued charity towards all the world, he might not have condescended to parley with the man.

"What is the favour?" he inquired.

"I want you to let me in to see the poor young earl—what's left of him."

"Let you in to see the earl!" echoed Hedges in surprise. "I never heard such a bold request."

"It is bold. I've already said so, and asked you to pardon it."

"What can you want that for? It can't be for nothing but curiosity; and—"

"It's not curiosity," interrupted Pike, with an emphasis that told upon his hearer. "I have a different motive, sir; and a good motive. If I were at liberty to tell it—which I'm not—you'd let me in without another word. Lots of people have been seeing him, I suppose."

"Indeed they have not. Why should they? It is a bold thing for *you* to come and ask it."

"Did he come by his death fairly?" whispered the man.

"Good heavens!" exclaimed the butler, stepping back aghast. "I don't think you know what you are talking about. Who would harm Lord Hartledon?"

"Let me see him," implored the man. "It can't hurt him or anybody else. Only just for a minute, sir, in your presence. And if it's ever in my power to do you a good turn, Mr. Hedges, I'll do it. It doesn't seem likely now; but the mouse gnawed the lion's net, you know, and set him free."

Whether it was the strange impressiveness with which the request was proffered, or that the softened mood of Hedges rendered him incapable of contention, certain it was that he granted it; and most likely would wonder at himself for it all his after-life. Crossing the hall with silent tread, and taking up a candle as he went, he led the way to the room; Mr. Pike stepping after him with a tread equally silent.

"Take your hat off," peremptorily whispered the butler; for that worthy had entered the room with it on. "Is that the way to—"

"Hedges!"

Hedges was struck with consternation at the call, for it was that of his new master. He had not bargained for this; supposing that he had gone to his room for the night. However he might have been foolishly won over to accede to the man's strange request, it was not to be supposed it would be approved of by Lord Hartledon. The butler hesitated. He did not care to betray Pike, neither did he care to leave Pike alone.

"Hedges!" came the call again, louder and quicker.

"Yes, sir—my lord?" and Hedges squeezed out at the door without opening it much—which was rather a difficulty, for he was a portly man, with a red, honest sort of face—leaving Pike and the light inside. Lord Hartledon—as we must unfortunately call him now—was standing in the hall.

"Has Dr. Ashton gone?"

"Yes, my lord."

"Did he leave that address?"

Hedges knew to what his master alluded: an address that was wanted in connection with certain official proceedings that must now take place. Hedges replied that Dr. Ashton had not left it with him.

"Then he must have forgotten it. He said he would write it down in pencil. Send over to the Rectory the first thing in the morning. And, Hedges—"

At this moment a slight noise was heard within the room like the sound of an extinguisher falling; as, in fact, it was. Lord Hartledon turned towards it.

"Who is there, Hedges?"

"I—it's no one in particular, sir—my lord."

What with the butler's bewilderment on the sudden change of masters, and what with his consciousness of the presence of his visitor, he was unusually confused. Lord Hartledon noticed it. It instantly occurred to him that one of the ladies, or perhaps one of the women-servants, had been admitted to the room; and he did not consider it a proper sight for any of them.

"Who is it?" he demanded, somewhat peremptorily.

So Hedges had to confess what had taken place, and that he had allowed the man to enter.

"Pike! Why, what can he want?" exclaimed Lord Hartledon in surprise. And he turned to the room.

The moment the butler left him alone Mr. Pike's first proceeding had been to cover his head again with his wide-awake, which he had evidently removed with reluctance, and might have refused to remove at all had it been consistent with policy; his second was to snatch up the candle, bend over the dead face, and examine it minutely both with eye and hand.

"There *is* a wound, then, and it's true what they are saying. I thought it might have been gossip," he muttered, as he pushed the soft dark hair from the temple. "Any more suspicious marks?" he resumed, taking a rapid view of the hands and head. "No; nothing but what he'd be likely to get in the water: but—I'll swear *that* might have been the blow of a human hand. 'Twould stun, if it wouldn't kill; and then, held under the water—"

At this moment Mr. Pike and his comments were interrupted, and he drew back from the table on which the body was lying; but not before Lord Hartledon had seen him touching the face of the dead.

"What are you doing?" came the stern demand.

"I wasn't harming him," was the answer; and Mr. Pike seemed to have suddenly returned to his roughness. "It's a nasty accident to have happened; and I don't like *this*."

He pointed to the temple as he spoke. Lord Hartledon's usually good-natured brow—at present a brow of deep sorrow—contracted with displeasure.

"It is an awful accident," he replied. "But I asked what you were doing here?"

"I thought I'd like to look upon him, sir; and the butler let me in. I wish I'd been a bit nearer the place at the time: I'd have saved him, or got drowned myself. Not much fear of that, though. I'm a rat for the water. Was that done fairly?" pointing again to the temple.

"What do you mean?" exclaimed Val.

"Well—it might be, or it might not. One who has led the roving life I have, and been in all sorts of scenes, bred in the slums of London too, looks on the suspicious side of these things. And there mostly is one in all of 'em."

Val was moved to anger. "How dare you hint at so infamous a suspicion, Pike? If—"

"No offence, my lord," interrupted Pike—"and it's my lord that you are now. Thoughts may be free in this room; but I am not going to spread suspicion outside. I say, though that *might* have been an accident, it might have been done by an enemy."

"Did you do it?" retorted Lord Hartledon in his displeasure.

Pike gave a short laugh.

"I did not. I had no cause to harm him. What I'm thinking was, whether anybody else had. He was mistaken for another yesterday," continued Pike, dropping his voice. "Some men in his lordship's place might have showed fight then: even blows."

Percival made no immediate rejoinder. He was gazing at Pike just as fixedly as the latter gazed at him. Did the man wish to insinuate that the unwelcome visitor had again mistaken the one brother for the other, and the result had been a struggle between them, ending in this? The idea rushed into his mind, and a dark flush overspread his face.

"You have no grounds for thinking that man—you know who I mean—attacked my brother a second time?"

"No, I have no grounds for it," shortly answered Pike.

"He was near to the spot at the time; I saw him there," continued Lord Hartledon, speaking apparently to himself; whilst the flush, painfully red and dark, was increasing rather than diminishing.

"I know you did," returned Pike.

The tone grated on Lord Hartledon's ear. It implied that the man might become familiar, if not checked; and, with all his good-natured affability, he was not one to permit it; besides, his position was changed, and he could not help feeling that it was. "Necessity makes us acquainted with strange bedfellows," says the very true proverb; and what might have been borne yesterday would not be borne to-day.

"Let me understand you," he said, and there was a stern decision in his tone and manner that surprised Pike. "Have you any reason whatever to suspect that man of having injured, or attempted to injure my brother?"

"*I*'ve not," answered Pike. "I never saw him nearer to the mill yesterday than he was when he looked at us. I don't think he went nearer. My lord, if I knew anything against the man, I'd tell it out, and be glad. I hate the whole tribe. *He* wouldn't make the mistake again," added Pike, half-contemptuously. "He knew which was his lordship fast enough to-day, and which wasn't."

"Then what did you mean by insinuating that the blow on the temple was the result of violence?"

"I didn't say it was: I said it might have been. I don't know a thing, as connected with this business, against a mortal soul. It's true, my lord."

"Perhaps, then, you will leave this room," said Lord Hartledon.

"I'm going. And many thanks to your lordship for not having turned me from it before, and for letting me have my say. Thanks to *you*, sir," he added, as he went out of the room and passed Hedges, who was waiting in the hall.

Hedges closed the door after him, and turned to receive a reprimand from his new master.

"Before you admit such men as that into the most sacred chamber the house at present contains, you will ask my permission, Hedges."

Hedges attempted to excuse himself. "He was so very earnest, my lord; he declared to me he had a good motive in wanting to come in. At these times, when one's heart is almost broken with a sudden blow, one is apt to be soft and yielding. What with that feeling upon me, and what with the fright he gave me—"

"What fright did he give you?" interrupted Val.

"Well, my lord, he—he asked me whether his lordship had come fairly by his death."

"How dare you repeat the insinuation?" broke forth Lord Hartledon, with more temper than Hedges had ever seen him display. "The very idea is absurd; it is wicked; it is unpardonable. My brother had not an enemy in the world. Take care not to repeat it again. Do you hear?"

He turned away from the astonished man, went into the room he had called sacred, and closed the door. Hedges wondered whether the hitherto sweet-tempered, easy-mannered younger brother had changed his nature with his inheritance.

As the days went on, few, if any, further particulars were elicited as to the cause of accident. That the unfortunate Lord Hartledon had become partly, if not wholly, disabled, so as to be incapable of managing even the little skiff, had been drifted by the current towards the mills, and there upset, was assumed by all to have been the true history of the case. There appeared no reason to doubt that it was so. The inquest was held on the Thursday.

And on that same morning the new Lord Hartledon received a proof of the kindness of his brother. A letter arrived from Messrs. Kedge and Reck, addressed to Edward Earl of Hartledon. By it Percival found—there was no one else to open it now—that his brother had written to them early on the Tuesday morning, taking the debt upon himself; and they now wrote to say they accepted his responsibility, and had withdrawn the officer from Calne. Alas! Val Elster could have dismissed him himself now.

He sat with bent head and drooping eyelids. None, save himself, knew how bitter were the feelings within him, or the remorse that was his portion for having behaved unkindly to his brother within the last few hours of life. He had rebelled at his state of debt becoming known to Dr. Ashton; he had feared to lose Anne: it seemed to him now, that he would live under the doctor's displeasure for ever, would never see Anne again, could he recall his brother. Oh, these unavailing regrets! Will they rise up to face us at the Last Day?

With a suppressed exclaimation that was like a cry of pain, as if he would throw from him these reflections and could not, Lord Hartledon drew a sheet of paper before him and wrote a note to the lawyers. He briefly stated what had taken place; that his brother was dead from an accident, and he had inherited, and should take speedy measures for the discharge of any liabilities there might be against him: and he requested, as a favour, that the letter written to them by his brother might be preserved and returned to him: he should wish to keep it as the last lines his hand had traced.

# XI

## The Inquest

On this day, Thursday, the inquest was held. Most of the gay crowd staying at Hartledon had taken flight; Mr. Carteret, and one or two more, whose testimony might be wished for, remaining. The coroner and jury assembled in the afternoon, in a large boarded apartment called the steward's room. Lord Hartledon was present with Dr. Ashton and other friends: they were naturally anxious to hear the evidence that could be collected, and gather any light that might be thrown upon the accident. The doors were not closed to the public, and a crowd, gentle and simple, pressed in.

The surgeon spoke to the supposed cause of death—drowning: the miller spoke to his house and mill having been that afternoon shut up. He and his wife went over in their spring-cart to Garchester, and left the place locked up, he said. The coroner asked whether it was his custom to lock up his place when he went out; he replied that it was, when they went out together; but that event rarely happened. Upon his return at dusk, he found the little skiff loose in the stream, and secured it. It was his servant-boy, David Ripper, who called his attention to it first of all. He saw nothing of Lord Hartledon, and had not very long secured the skiff when Mr. Percival Elster came up in the pony-carriage, asking if his brother was there. He looked at the skiff, and said it was the one his lordship had been in. Mr. Elster said he supposed his brother was walking home, and he should drive slowly back and look out for him. Later Mr. Elster returned: he had several servants with him then and lanterns; they had come out to look for Lord Hartledon, but could not find him. It was only just after they had gone away again that the Irish harvest-men came up and found the body.

This was the substance of the miller's evidence; it was all he knew: and the next witness called was the boy David Ripper, popularly styled in the neighbourhood young Rip, in contradistinction to his father, a day-labourer. He was an urchin of ten or twelve, with a red, round face; quite ludicrous from its present expression of terrified consternation. The coroner sharply inquired what he was frightened at; and the boy burst into a roar by way of answer. He didn't know nothing, and hadn't seen nothing, and it wasn't him that drowned his lordship; and he couldn't tell more if they hanged him for it.

The miller interposed. The boy was one of the idlest young vagabonds he had ever had the luck to be troubled with; and he thought it exceedingly likely he had been off that afternoon and not near the mill at all. He had ordered him to take two sacks into Calne; but when he reached home he found the sacks untouched, lying where he had placed them outside. Mr. Ripper had no doubt been playing truant on his own account.

"Where did you pass Tuesday afternoon during your master's absence?" sternly demanded the coroner. "Take your hands from your face and answer me, boy."

David Ripper obeyed in the best manner he was capable of, considering his agitation. "I dun know now where I was," he said. "I was about."

"About where?"

Mr. Ripper apparently could not say where. He thought he was "setting his bird-trap" in the stubble-field; and he see a partridge, and watched where it scudded to; but he wasn't nigh the mill the whole time.

"Did you see anything of Lord Hartledon when he was in the skiff?"

"I never saw him," he sobbed. "I wasn't nigh the mill at all, and never saw him nor the skiff."

"What time did you get back to the mill?" asked the coroner.

He didn't know what time it was; his master and missis had come home.

This was true, Mr. Floyd said. They had been back some little time before Ripper showed himself. The first intimation he received of that truant's presence was when he drew his attention to the loose skiff.

"How came you to see the skiff?" sharply asked the coroner.

Ripper spoke up with trembling lips. He was waiting outside after he came up, and afraid to go in lest his master should beat him for not taking the sacks, which went clean out of his mind, they did, and then he saw the little boat; upon which he called out and told his master.

"And it was also you who first saw the body in the water," observed the coroner, regarding the reluctant witness curiously. "How came you to see that? Were you looking for something of the sort?"

The witness shivered. He didn't know how he come to see it. He was on the strade, not looking for nothing, when he saw some'at dark among the reeds, and told the harvesters when they come by. They said it was a man, got him out, and then found it was his lordship.

There was only one peculiarity about the boy's evidence—his manner. All he said was feasible enough; indeed, what would be most likely to happen under the circumstances. But whence arose his terror? Had he been of a timid temperament, it might have been natural; but the miller had spoken the truth—he was audacious and hardy. Only upon one or two, however, did the manner leave any impression. Pike, who made one of the crowd in the inquest-room, was one of these. His experience of human nature was tolerably keen, and he felt sure the boy was keeping something behind that he did not dare to tell. The coroner and jury were not so clear-sighted, and dismissed him with the remark that he was a "little fool."

"Call George Gorton," said the coroner, looking at his notes.

Very much to Lord Hartledon's surprise—perhaps somewhat to his annoyance—the man answering to this name was the one who had originally come to Calne on a special mission to himself. Some feeling caused him to turn from the man whilst he gave his evidence, a thing easily done in the crowded room.

It appeared that amidst the stirring excitement in the neighbourhood on the Tuesday night when the death became known, this stranger happened to avow in the public-house which he made his quarters that he had seen Lord Hartledon in his skiff just before the event must have happened. The information was reported, and the man received a summons to appear before the coroner.

And it may be as well to remark now, that his second appearance was owing to a little cowardice on his own part. He had felt perfectly satisfied at the time with the promise given him by Lord Hartledon to see the debt paid—given also in the presence of the Rector—and took his departure in the train, just as Pike had subsequently told Mr. Elster. But ere he had gone two stages on his journey, he began to think he might have been too precipitate, and to ask himself whether his employers would not tell him so when he appeared before them, unbacked by any guarantee from Lord Hartledon; for this, by a strange oversight, he had omitted to ask for. He halted at once, and went back by the next return train. The following day, Tuesday, he spent looking after Lord Hartledon, but, as it happened, did not meet him.

The man—a dissipated young man, now that his hat was off—came forward in his long coat, his red hair and whiskers. But it seemed that he had really very little information to give. He was on the banks of the river when Lord Hartledon passed in the skiff, and noticed how strangely he was rowing, one arm apparently lying useless. What part of the river was this, the coroner asked; and the witness avowed that he could not describe it. He was a stranger, never there but that once; all he knew was, that it was higher up, beyond Hartledon House. What might he have been doing there, demanded the coroner. Only strolling about, was the answer. What was his business at Calne? came the next question; and as it was put, the witness caught the eye of the new Lord Hartledon through an opening in the crowd. His business, the witness replied to the coroner, was his own business, and did not concern the public, and he respectfully declined to state it. He presumed Calne was a free place like other places, where a stranger might spend a few days without question, if he pleased.

Pike chuckled at this: incipient resistance to authority cheered that lawless man's heart. He had stood throughout, in the shadow of the crowd, just within the door, attentively watching the witnesses as they gave their evidence: but he was not prepared for what was to come next.

Did the witness see any other spectators on the bank? continued the coroner. Only one, was the answer: a man called Pike, or some such name. Pike was watching the little boat on the river when he got up to him; he remarked to Pike that his lordship's arm seemed tired; and he and Pike had walked back to Calne together.

Pike would have got away had he been able, but the coroner whispered to an officer. For one single moment Mr. Pike seemed inclined to show fight; he began struggling, not gently, to reach the door; the next he gave it up, and resigned himself to his fate. There was a little hubbub, in the midst of which a slip of paper with a pencilled line from Lord Hartledon, was handed to the coroner.

"*Press this point, whether they returned to Calne at once and together.*"

"George Gorton," cried the coroner, as he crushed the paper in his hand, "at what hour did you return to Calne?"

"I went at once. As soon as the little boat was out of sight."

"Went alone?"

"No, sir. I and the man Pike walked together. I've said so already."

"What made you go together?"

"Nothing in particular. We were both going back, I suppose, and strolled along talking."

It appeared to be all that the witness had to tell, and Mr. Pike came forward perforce. As he stood there, his elegant wide-awake bent in his hand, he looked more like the wild man of the woods he had been compared to, than a civilized being. Rough, rude, and abrupt were his tones as he spoke, and he bent his face and eyes downwards whilst he answered. It was in those eyes that lay the look which had struck Mr. Elster as being familiar to him. He persisted in giving his name as Tom, not Thomas.

But if the stranger in the long coat had little evidence to give, Pike had even less. He had been in the woods that afternoon and sauntered to the bank of the river just as Lord Hartledon passed in the skiff; but he had taken very little notice of him. It was only when the last witness, who came up at the moment, remarked upon the queer manner in which his lordship held his arm, that he saw it was lying idle.

Not a thing more could he or would he tell. It was all he knew, he said, and would swear it was all. He went back to Calne with the last witness, and never saw his lordship again alive.

It did appear to be all, just as it did in the matter of the other man. The coroner inquired whether he had seen any one else on the banks or near them, and Pike replied that he had not set eyes on another soul, which Percival knew to be false, for he had seen *him*. He was told to put his signature to his evidence, which the clerk had taken down, and affixed a cross.

"Can't you write?" asked the coroner.

Pike shook his head negatively. "Never learnt," he curtly said. And Percival believed that to be an untruth equally with the other. He could not help thinking that the avowal of their immediate return might also be false: it was just as possible that one or other, or both, had followed the course of the boat.

Mr. Carteret was examined. He could tell no more than he had already told. They started together, but he had soon got beyond his lordship, and had never seen him again alive. There was nothing more to be gleaned or gathered. Not the smallest suspicion of foul play, or of its being anything but a most unfortunate accident, was entertained for a moment by any one who heard the evidence, and the verdict of the jury was to that effect: Accidental Death.

As the crowd pressed out of the inquest-room, jostling one another in the gloom of the evening, and went their several ways, Lord Hartledon found himself close to Gorton, his coat flapping as he walked. The man was looking round for Pike: but Mr. Pike, the instant his forced evidence was given, had slunk away from the gaze of his fellow-men to ensconce himself in his solitary shed. To all appearance Lord Hartledon had overtaken Gorton by accident: the man turned aside in obedience to a signal, and halted. They could not see much of each other's faces in the twilight.

"I wish to ask you a question," said Percival in low, impressive, and not unkindly tones. "Did you speak with my brother, Lord Hartledon, at all on Tuesday?"

"No, my lord, I did not," was the ready answer. "I was trying to get to see his lordship, but did not."

"What did you want with him? What brought you back to Calne?"

"I wanted to get from him a guarantee for—for what your lordship knows of; which he had omitted to give, and I had not thought to ask for," civilly replied the man. "I was looking about for his lordship on the Tuesday morning, but did not get to see him. In the afternoon, when the boat-race was over, I made bold to call at Hartledon, but the servants said his lordship wasn't in. As I came away, I saw him, as I thought, pass the lodge and go up the road, and I cut after him, but couldn't overtake him, and at last lost sight of him. I struck into a tangled sort of pathway through the gorse, or whatever it's called down here, and it brought me out near the river. His lordship was just sculling down, and then I knew it was some one else had gone by the lodge, and not him. Perhaps it was your lordship?"

"You knew it was Lord Hartledon in the boat? I mean, you recognized him? You did not mistake him for me?"

"I knew him, my lord. If I'd been a bit nearer the lodge, I shouldn't have been likely to mistake even your lordship for him."

Lord Hartledon was gazing into the man's face still; never once had his eyes been removed from it.

"You did not see Lord Hartledon later?"

"I never saw him all day but that once when he passed in the skiff."

"You did not follow him, then?"

"Of what use?" debated the man. "I couldn't call out my business from the banks, and didn't know his lordship was going to land lower down. I went straight back to Calne, my lord, walking with that man Pike—who is a rum fellow, and has a history behind him, unless I'm mistaken; but it's no business of mine. I made my mind up to another night of it in Calne, thinking I'd get to Hartledon early next morning before his lordship had time to go out; and I was sitting comfortably with a pipe and a glass of beer, when news came of the accident."

Lord Hartledon believed the man to be telling the truth; and a weight—the source of which he did not stay to analyse—was lifted from his mind. But he asked another question.

"Why are you still in Calne?"

"I waited for orders. After his lordship died I couldn't go away without them—carrying with me nothing but the word of a dead man. The orders came this morning, safe enough; but I had the summons served on me then to attend the inquest, and had to stay for it. I'm going away now, my lord, by the first train."

Lord Hartledon was satisfied, and nodded his head. As he turned back he met Dr. Ashton.

"I was looking for you, Lord Hartledon. If you require any assistance or information in the various arrangements that now devolve upon you, I shall be happy to render both. There will be a good deal to do one way or another; more, I dare say, than your inexperience has the least idea of. You will have your solicitor at hand, of course; but if you want me, you know where to find me."

The Rector's words were courteous, but the tone was not warm, and the title "Lord Hartledon" grated on Val's ear. In his impulse he grasped the speaker's hand, pouring forth a heartfelt prayer.

"Oh, Dr. Ashton, will you not forgive me? The horrible trouble I brought upon myself is over now. I don't rejoice in it under the circumstances, Heaven knows; I only speak of the fact. Let me come to your house again! Forgive me for the past."

"In one sense the trouble is over, because the debts that were a formidable embarrassment to Mr. Elster are as nothing to Lord Hartledon," was the reply. "But let me assure you of one thing: that your being Lord Hartledon will not make the slightest difference to my decision not to give you my daughter, unless your line of conduct shall change."

"It is changed. Dr. Ashton, on my word of honour, I will never be guilty of carelessness again. One thing will be my safeguard, though all else should fail—the fact that I passed my word for this to my dear brother not many hours before his death. For my sake, for Anne's sake, you will forgive me!"

Was it possible to resist the persuasive tones, the earnestness of the honest, dark-blue eyes? If ever Percival Elster was to make an effort for good, and succeed, it must be now. The doctor knew it; and he knew that Anne's happiness was at stake. But he did not thaw immediately.

"You know, Lord Hartledon—"

"Call me Val, as you used to do," came the pleading interruption; and Dr. Ashton smiled in spite of himself.

"Percival, you know it is against my nature to be harsh or unforgiving; just as I believe it contrary to your nature to be guilty of deliberate wrong. If you will only be true to yourself, I would rather have you for my son-in-law than any other man in England; as I would have had when you were Val Elster. Do you note my words? *true to yourself.*"

"As I will be from henceforth," whispered Val, earnest tears rising to his eyes.

And as he would have been but for his besetting sin.

# XII

## LATER IN THE DAY

It happened that Clerk Gum had business on hand the day of the inquest, which obliged him to go to Garchester. He reached home after dark; and the first thing he saw was his wife, in what he was pleased to call a state of semi-idiocy. The tea-things were laid on the table, and substantial refreshment in the shape of cold meat, and a plate of muffins ready for toasting, all for the clerk's regalement. But Mrs. Gum herself sat on a low chair by the fire, her eyes swollen with crying.

"What's the matter now?" was the clerk's first question.

"Oh, Gum, I told you you ought not to have gone off to-day. You might have stayed for the inquest."

"Much good I should do the inquest, or the inquest do me," retorted the clerk. "Has Becky gone?"

"Long ago. Gum, that dream's coming round. I said it would. I *told* you there was ill in store for Lord Hartledon; and that Pike was mixed up in it, and Mr. Elster also in some way. If you'd only listen to me—"

The clerk, who had been brushing his hat and shaking the dust from his outer coat—for he was a careful man with his clothes, and always well-dressed—brought down his hand upon the table with some temper.

"Just stop that. I've heard enough of that dream, and of all your dreams. Confounded folly! Haven't I trouble and worry enough upon my mind, without your worrying me every time I come in about your idiotic dreams?"

"Well," returned Mrs. Gum, "if the dream's nothing, I'd like to ask why they had Pike up to-day before them all?"

"Who had him up?" asked the clerk, after a pause. "Had him up where?"

"Before the people sitting on the body of Lord Hartledon. Lydia Jones brought me the news just now. 'They had Pike the poacher up,' says she. 'He was up before the jury, and had to confess to it.' 'Confess to what,' said I. 'Why, that he was about in the woods when my lord met his end,' said she; 'and it's to know how my lord did meet it, and whether the poacher mightn't have dealt that blow on his temple and robbed him after it.' Gum—"

"There's no suspicion of foul play, is there?" interrupted the clerk, in strangely subdued tones.

"Not that I know of, except in Lydia's temper," answered Mrs. Gum. "But I don't like to hear he was up there at all."

"Lydia Jones is a foul-tongued woman, capable of swearing away any man's life. Is Pike in custody?"

"Not yet. They've let him off for the present. Oh, Gum, often and often do I wish my days were ended!"

"Often and often do I wish I'd a quiet house to come to, and not be bothered with dreams," was the scornful retort. "Suppose you toast the muffins."

She gave a sigh or two, put her cap straight, smoothed her ragged hair, and meekly rose to obey. The clerk was carefully folding up the outer coat, for it was one he wore only on high-days, when he felt something in the pocket—a small parcel.

"I'd almost forgotten this," he exclaimed, taking it out. "Thanks to you, Nance! What with your dreams and other worryings I can't think of my proper business."

"What is it?" she asked.

"A deed Dr. Ashton's lawyer got me to bring and save his clerk a journey—if you must know. I'll take it over at once, while the tea's brewing."

As Jabez Gum passed through his own gate he looked towards Mr. Pike's dwelling; it was only natural he should do so after the recent conversation; and he saw that worthy gentleman come stealing across the waste ground, with his usual cautious step. Although not given to exchanging courtesies with his neighbour, the clerk walked briskly towards him now, and waited at the hurdles which divided the waste ground from the road.

"I hear you were prowling about the mill when Lord Hartledon met with his accident," began the clerk, in low, condemning tones.

"And what if I was," asked Pike, leaning his arms on the hurdles and facing the clerk. "Near the mill I wasn't; about the woods and river I was; and I saw him pass down in the sculling boat with his disabled arm. What of it, I ask?"

Pike's tone, though short, was civil enough. The forced appearance before the coroner and public had disturbed his equanimity in no slight degree, and taken for the present all insolence out of him.

"Should any doubt get afloat that his lordship's death might not have been accidental, your presence at the spot would tell against you."

"No, it wouldn't. I left the spot before the accident could have happened; and I came back to Calne with a witness. As to the death having been something worse than accident, not a soul in the place has dreamt of such a thing except me."

"Except you! What do you mean?"

Pike leaned more over the hurdles, so as to bring his disreputable face closer to Mr. Gum, who slightly recoiled as he caught the low whisper.

"I don't think the death was accidental. I believe his lordship was just put out of the way quietly."

"Heaven forbid!" exclaimed the shocked clerk. "By whom? By you?" he added, in his bewilderment.

"No," returned the man. "If I'd done it, I shouldn't talk about it."

"What do you mean?" cried Mr. Gum.

"I mean that I have my suspicions; and good suspicions they are. Many a man has been hung on less. I am not going to tell them; perhaps not ever. I shall wait and keep my eyes open, and bring them, if I can, to certainties. Time enough to talk then, or keep silent, as circumstances may dictate."

"And you tell me you were not near the place at the time of the accident?"

"*I* wasn't," replied Mr. Pike, with emphasis.

"Who was?"

"That's my secret. And as I've a little matter of business on hand to-night, I don't care to be further delayed, if it's all the same to you, neighbour. And instead of your accusing me of prowling about the mill again, perhaps you'll just give a thought occasionally to what I have now said, keeping it to yourself. I'm not afraid of your spreading it in Calne; for it might bring a hornets' nest about your head, and about some other heads that you wouldn't like to injure."

With the last words Mr. Pike crossed the hurdles and went off in the direction of Hartledon. It was a light night, and the clerk stood and stared after him. To say that Jabez Gum in his astonishment was uncertain whether he stood on his head or his heels, would be saying little; and how much of these assertions he might believe, and what mischief Mr. Pike might be going after to-night, he knew not. Drawing a long sigh, which did not sound very much like a sigh of relief, he at length turned off to Dr. Ashton's, and the man disappeared.

We must follow Pike. He went stealthily up the road past Hartledon, keeping in the shade of the hedge, and shrinking into it when he saw any one coming. Striking off when he neared the mill, he approached it cautiously, and halted amidst some trees, whence he had a view of the mill-door.

He was waiting for the boy, David Ripper. Fully convinced by the lad's manner at the inquest that he had not told all he knew, but was keeping something back in fear, Mr. Pike, for reasons of his own, resolved to come at it if he could. He knew that the boy would be at work later than usual that night, having been hindered in the afternoon.

Imagine yourself standing with your back to the river, reader, and take a view of the premises as they face you. The cottage is a square building, and has four good rooms on the ground floor. The miller's thrifty wife generally locked all these rooms up if she went out, and carried the keys away in her pocket. The parlour window was an ordinary sash-window, with outside shutters; the kitchen window a small casement, protected by a fixed net-work of strong wire. No one could get in or out, even when the casement was open, without tearing this wire away, which would not be a difficult matter to accomplish. On the left of the cottage, but to your right as you face it, stands the mill, to which you ascend by steps. It communicates inside with the upper floor of the cottage, which is used as a store-room for corn; and from this store-room a flight of stairs descends to the kitchen below. Another flight of stairs from this store-room communicated with the open passage leading from the back-door to the stable. This is all that need be said: and you may think it superfluous to have described it at all: but it is not so.

The boy Ripper at length came forth. With a shuddering avoidance of the water he came tearing along as one running from a ghost, and was darting past the trees, when he found himself detained by an arm of great strength. Mr. Pike clapped his other hand upon the boy's mouth, stifling a howl of terror.

"Do you see this, Rip?" cried he.

Rip did see it. It was a pistol held rather inconveniently close to the boy's breast. Rip dearly loved his life; but it nearly went out of him then with fear.

"Now," said Pike, "I've come up to know about this business of Lord Hartledon's, and I will know it, or leave you as dead as he is. And I'll have you took up for murder, into the bargain," he rather illogically continued, "as an accessory to the fact."

David Ripper was in a state of horror; all idea of concealment gone out of him. "I couldn't help it," he gasped. "I couldn't get out to him; I was locked up in the mill. Don't shoot me."

"I'll spare you on one condition," decided Pike. "Disclose the whole of this from first to last, and then we may part friends. But try to palm off one lie upon me, and I'll riddle you through. To begin with: what brought you locked up in the mill?"

It was a wicked tale of a wicked young jail-bird, as Mr. Pike (probably the worse jail-bird by far of the two) phrased it. Master Ripper had purposely caused himself to be locked in the mill, his object being to supply himself with as much corn as he could carry about him for the benefit of his rabbits and pigeons and other live stock at home. He had done it twice before, he avowed, in dread of the pistol, and had got away safe through the square hole in the passage at the foot of the back staircase, whence he had dropped to the ground. To his consternation on this occasion, however, he had found the door at the foot of the stairs bolted, as it never had been before, and he could not get to the passage. So he was a prisoner all the afternoon, and had exercised his legs between the store-room and kitchen, both of which were open to him.

If ever a man showed virtuous indignation at a sinner's confession, Mr. Pike showed it now. "That's how you were about in the stubble-field setting your traps, you young villain! I saw the coroner look at you. And now about Lord Hartledon. What did you see?"

Master Ripper rubbed the perspiration from his face as he went on with his tale. Pike listened with all the ears he possessed and said not a word, beyond sundry rough exclamations, until the tale was done.

"You awful young dog! You saw all that from the kitchen-window, and never tried to get out of it!"

"I *couldn't* get out of it," pleaded the boy. "It's got a wire-net before it, and I couldn't break that."

"You are strong enough to break it ten times over," retorted Pike.

"But then master would ha' known I'd been in the mill!" cried the boy, a gleam of cunning in his eyes.

"Ugh," grunted Pike. "And you saw exactly what you've told me?"

"I saw it and heard the cries."

"Did he see you?"

"No; I was afeard to show myself. When master come home, the first thing he did was t' unlock that there staircase door, and I got out without his seeing me—"

"Where did you hide the grain you were loaded with?" demanded Pike.

"I'd emptied it out again in the store-room," returned the boy. "I told master there were a loose skiff out there, and he come out and secured it. Them harvesters come up next and got him out of the water."

"Yes, you could see fast enough what you were looking for! Well, young Rip," continued Mr. Pike, consolingly, "you stand about as rich a chance of being hanged as ever you'll stand in all your born days. If you'd jumped through that wire you'd have saved my lord, and he'd have made it right for you with old Floyd. I'd advise you to keep a silent tongue in your head, if you want to save your neck."

"I was keeping it, till you come and made me tell with that there pistol," howled the boy. "You won't go and split on me?" he asked, with trembling lips.

"I won't split on you about the grain," graciously promised Pike. "It's no business of mine. As to the other matter—well, I'll not say anything about that; at any rate, yet awhile. You keep it a secret; so will I."

Without another word, Pike extended his hand as a signal that the culprit was at liberty to depart; and he did so as fast as his legs would carry him. Pike then returned the pistol to his pocket and took his way back to Calne in a thoughtful and particularly ungenial mood. There was a doubt within him whether the boy had disclosed the truth, even to him.

Perhaps on no one—with the exception of Percival—did the death of Lord Hartledon leave its effects as it did on Lady Kirton and her daughter Maude. To the one it brought embarrassment; to the other, what seemed very like a broken heart. The countess-dowager's tactics must change as by magic. She had to transfer the affection and consideration evinced for Edward Lord Hartledon to his brother; and to do it easily and naturally. She had to obliterate from the mind of the latter her overbearing dislike to him, cause her insults to be remembered no more. A difficult task, even for her, wily woman as she was.

How was it to be done? For three long hours the night after Lord Hartledon's death, she lay awake, thinking out her plans; perhaps for the first time in her life, for obtuse natures do not lie awake. The death had affected her only as regarded her own interests; she could feel for none and regret none in her utter selfishness. One was fallen, but another had risen up. "Le roi est mort: vive le roi!"

On the day following the death she had sought an interview with Percival. Never a woman evinced better tact than she. There was no violent change in her manner, no apologies for the past, or display of sudden affection. She spoke quietly and sensibly of passing topics: the death, and what could have led to it; the immediate business on hand, some of the changes it entailed in the future. "I'll stay with you still, Percival," she said, "and look after things a bit for you, as I have been doing for your brother. It is an awful shock, and we must all have time to get over it. If I had only foreseen this, how I might have spared my temper and poor Maude's feelings!"

She looked out of the corner of her eye at the young man; but he betrayed no curiosity to hear more, and she went on unasked.

"You know, Val, for a portionless girl, as Maude is, it was a great blow to me when I found her fixing her heart upon a younger son. How cross and unjust it made me I couldn't conceal: mothers are mothers. I wanted her to take a fancy to Hartledon, dear fellow, and I suppose she could not, and it rendered me cross; and I know I worried her and worried my own temper, till at times I was not conscious of what I said. Poor Maude! she did not rebel openly, but I could see her struggles. Only a week ago, when Hartledon was talking about his marrying sometime, and hinting that she might care fox him if she tried, she scored her beautiful drawing all over with ugly marks; ran the pencil through it—"

"But why do you tell me this now?" asked Val.

"Hartledon—dear me! I wonder how long I shall be getting accustomed to your name?—there's only you and me and Maude left now of the family," cried the dowager; "and if I speak of such things, it is in fulness of heart. And now about these letters: do you care how they are worded?"

"I don't seem to care about anything," listlessly answered the young man. "As to the letters, I think I'd rather write them myself, Lady Kirton."

"Indeed you shall not have any trouble of that sort to-day. *I'll* write the letters, and you may indulge yourself in doing nothing."

He yielded in his unstable nature. She spoke of business letters, and it was better that he should write them; he wished to write them; but she carried her point, and his will yielded to hers. Would it be a type of the future?—would he yield to her in other things in defiance of his better judgment? Alas! alas!

She picked up her skirts and left him, and went sailing upstairs to her daughter's room. Maude was sitting shivering in a shawl, though the day was hot.

"I've paved the way," nodded the old woman, in meaning tones. "And there's one fortunate thing about Val: he is so truthful himself, one may take him in with his eyes open."

Maude turned *her* eyes upon her mother: very languid and unspeculative eyes just then.

"I gave him a hint, Maude, that you had been unable to bring yourself to like Hartledon, but had fixed your mind on a younger son. Later, we'll let him suspect who the younger son was."

The words aroused Maude; she started up and stood staring at her mother, her eyes dilating with a sort of horror; her pale cheeks slowly turning crimson.

"I don't understand," she gasped; "I *hope* I don't understand. You— you do not mean that I am to try to like Val Elster?"

"Now, Maude, no heroics. I'll not see *you* make a fool of yourself as your sisters have done. He's not Val Elster any longer; he is Lord Hartledon: better-looking than ever his brother was, and will make a better husband, for he'll be more easily led."

"I would not marry Val for the whole world," she said, with strong emotion. "I dislike him; I hate him; I never could be a wife to Val Elster."

"We'll see," said the dowager, pushing up her front, of which she had just caught sight in a glass.

"Thank Heaven, there's no fear of it!" resumed Maude, collecting her senses, and sitting down again with a relieved sigh; "he is to marry Anne Ashton. Thank Heaven that he loves her!"

"Anne Ashton!" scornfully returned the countess-dowager. "She might have been tolerated when he was Val Elster, not now he is Lord Hartledon. What notions you have, Maude!"

Maude burst into tears. "Mamma, I think it is fearfully indecent for you to begin upon these things already! It only happened last night, and—and it sounds quite horrible."

"When one has to live as I do, one has to do many things decent and indecent," retorted the countess-dowager sharply. "He has had his hint, and you've got yours: and you are no true girl if you suffer yourself now to be triumphed over by Anne Ashton."

Maude cried on silently, thinking how cruel fate was to have taken one brother and spared the other. Who—save Anne Ashton—would have missed Val Elster; while Lord Hartledon—at least he had made the life of one heart. A poor bruised heart now; never, never to be made quite whole again.

Thus the dowager, in her blindness, began her plans. In her blindness! If we could only foresee the ending of some of the unholy schemes that many of us are apt to weave, we might be more willing to leave them humbly in a higher Hand than ours. Do they ever bring forth good, these plans, born of our evil passions—hatred, malice, utter selfishness? I think not. They may seem to succeed triumphantly, but—watch the triumph to the end.

# XIII

## FEVER

The dews of an October evening were falling upon Calne, as Lord Hartledon walked from the railway-station. Just as unexpectedly as he had arrived the morning you first saw him, when he was only Val Elster, had he arrived now. By the merest accident one of the Hartledon servants happened to be at the station when the train arrived, and took charge of his master's luggage.

"All well at home, James?"

"All quite well, my lord."

Several weeks had elapsed since his brother's death, and Lord Hartledon had spent them in London. He went up on business the week after the funeral, and did not return again. In one respect he had no inducement to return; for the Ashtons, including Anne, were on a visit in Wales. They were at home now, as he knew well; and perhaps that had brought him down.

He went in unannounced, finding his way to the inner drawing-room. A large fire blazed in the grate, and Lady Maude sat by it so intent in thought as not to observe his entrance. She wore a black crêpe dress, with a little white trimming on its low body and sleeves. The firelight played on her beautiful features; and her eyelashes glistened as if with tears: she was thinner and paler; he saw it at once. The countess-dowager kept to Hartledon and showed no intention of moving from it: she and her daughter had been there alone all these weeks.

"How are you, Maude?"

She looked round and started up, backing from him with a face of alarm. Ah, was it *instinct* caused her so to receive him? What, or who, was she thinking of; holding her hands before her with that face of horror?

"Maude, have I so startled you?"

"Percival! I beg your pardon. I believe I was thinking of—of your brother, and I really did not know you in the uncertain light. We don't have the rooms lighted early," she added, with a little laugh.

He took her hands in his. Now that she knew him, and the alarm was over, she seemed really pleased to see him: the dark eyes were raised to his with a frank smile.

"May I take a cousin's greeting, Maude?"

Without waiting for yes or no, he stooped and took the kiss. Maude flung his hands away. He should have left out the "cousin," or not have taken the kiss.

He went and stood with his elbow on the mantelpiece, soberly, as if he had only kissed a sister. Maude sat down again.

"Why did you not send us word you were coming?" she asked.

"There was no necessity for it. And I only made my mind up this morning."

"What a long time you have been away! I thought you went for a week."

"I did not get my business over very quickly; and waited afterwards to see Thomas Carr, who was out of town. The Ashtons were away, you know; so I had no inducement to hurry back again."

"Very complimentary to *her*. Who's Thomas Carr?" asked Maude.

"A barrister; the greatest friend I possess in this world. We were at college together, and he used to keep me straight."

"Keep you straight! Val!"

"It's quite true. I went to him in all my scrapes and troubles. He is the most honourable, upright, straightforward man I know; and, as such, possesses a talent for serving—"

"Hartledon! Is it *you*?"

The interruption came from the dowager. She and the butler came in together, both looking equally astonished at the appearance of Lord Hartledon. The former said dinner was served.

"Will you let me sit down in this coat?" asked Val.

The countess-dowager would willingly have allowed him to sit down without any. Her welcome was demonstrative; her display of affection quite warm, and she called him "Val," tenderly. He escaped for a minute to his room, washed his hands, brushed his hair, and was down again, and taking the head of his own table.

It was pleasant to have him there—a welcome change from Hartledon's recent monotony; and even Maude, with her boasted dislike, felt prejudice melting away. Boasted dislike, not real, it had been. None could dislike Percival. He was not Edward, and it was him Maude had loved. Percival she never would love, but she might learn to like him. As he sat near her, in his plain black morning attire, courteous, genuinely sweet-tempered, his good looks conspicuous, a smile on his delicate, refined, but vacillating lips, and his honest dark-blue eyes bent upon her in kindness, Maude for the first time admitted a vision of the possible future, together with a dim consciousness that it might not be intolerable. Half the world, of her age and sex, would have deemed it indeed a triumph to be made the wife of that attractive man.

He had cautiously stood aside for Lady Kirton to take the head of the table; but the dowager had positively refused, and subsided into the chair at the foot. She did not fill it in dear Edward's time, she said; neither should she in dear Val's; he had come home to occupy his own place. And oh, thank goodness he was come! She and Maude had been so lonely and miserable, growing thinner daily from sheer *ennui*. So she faced Lord Hartledon at the end of the table, her flaxen curls surmounted by an array of black plumes, and looking very like a substantial female mute.

"What an awful thing that is about the Rectory!" exclaimed she, when they were more than half through dinner.

Lord Hartledon looked up quietly. "What is the matter at the Rectory?"

"Fever has broken out."

"Is that all!" he exclaimed, some amusement on his face. "I thought it must have taken fire."

"A fever's worse than a fire."

"Do you think so?"

"*Think so!* " echoed the dowager. "You can run away from a fire; but a fever may take you before you are aware of it. Every soul in the Rectory may die; it may spread to the parish; it may spread here. I have kept tar burning outside the house the last two days."

"You are not serious, Lady Kirton!"

"I am serious. I wouldn't catch a fever for the whole world. I should die of fright before it had time to kill me. Besides—I have Maude to guard. You were forgetting her."

"There's no danger at all. One of the servants became ill after they returned home, and it proved to be fever. I don't suppose it will spread."

"How did *you* hear about it?"

"From Miss Ashton. She mentioned it in her last letter to me."

"I didn't know you corresponded with her," cried the dowager, her tones rather shrill.

"Not correspond with Miss Ashton!" he repeated. "Of course I do."

The old dowager had a fit of choking: something had gone the wrong way, she said. Lord Hartledon resumed.

"It is an awful shame of those seaside lodging-house people! Did you hear the particulars, Maude? After the Ashtons concluded their visit in Wales, they went for a fortnight to the seaside, on their way home, taking lodgings. Some days after they had been settled in the rooms they discovered that some fever was in the house; a family who occupied another set of apartments being ill with it, and had been ill before the Ashtons went in. Dr. Ashton told the landlady what he thought of her conduct, and then they left the house for home. But Mrs. Ashton's maid, Matilda, had already taken it."

"Did Miss Ashton give you these particulars?" asked Maude, toying with a late rose that lay beside her plate.

"Yes. I should feel inclined to prosecute the woman, were I Dr. Ashton, for having been so wickedly inconsiderate. But I hope Matilda is better, and that the alarm will end with her. It is four days since I had Anne's letter."

"Then, Lord Hartledon, I can tell you the alarm's worse, and another has taken it, and the parish is up in arms," said the countess-dowager, tartly. "It has proved to be fever of a most malignant type, and not a soul but Hillary the surgeon goes near the Rectory, You must not venture within half-a-mile of it. Dr. Ashton was so careless as to occupy his pulpit on Sunday; but, thank goodness, I did not venture to church, or allow Maude to go. Your Miss Ashton will be having it next."

"Of course they have advice from Garchester?" he exclaimed.

"How should I know? My opinion is that the parson himself might be prosecuted for bringing the fever into a healthy neighbourhood. Port, Hedges! One has need of a double portion of tonics in a time like this."

The countess-dowager's alarms were not feigned—no, nor exaggerated. She had an intense, selfish fear of any sort of illness; she had a worse fear of death. In any time of public epidemic her terrors would have been almost ludicrous in their absurdity but that they were so real. And she "fortified" herself against infection by eating and drinking more than ever.

Nothing else was said: she shunned allusion to it when she could: and presently she and Maude left the dining-room. "You won't be long, Hartledon?" she observed, sweetly, as she passed him. Val only bowed in answer, closed the door upon them, and rang for Hedges.

"Is there much alarm regarding this fever at the Rectory?" he asked of the butler.

"Not very much, I think, my lord. A few are timid about it; as is always the case. One of the other servants has taken it; but Mr. Hillary told me when he was here this morning that he hoped it would not spread beyond the Rectory."

"Was Hillary here this morning? Nobody's ill?" asked Lord Hartledon, quickly.

"No one at all, my lord. The countess-dowager sent for him, to ask what her diet had better be, and how she could guard against infection more effectually than she was doing. She did not allow him to come in, but spoke to him from one of the upper windows, with a cloak and respirator on."

Lord Hartledon looked at his butler; the man was suppressing a grim smile.

"Nonsense, Hedges!"

"It's quite true, my lord. Mrs. Mirrable says she has five bowls of disinfectant in their rooms."

Lord Hartledon broke into a laugh, not suppressed.

"And in the courtyard, looking towards the Rectory, as may be said, there's several pitch-pots alight night and day," added Hedges. "We have had a host of people up, wanting to know if the place is on fire."

"What a joke!" cried Val—who was not yet beyond the age to enjoy such jokes. "Hedges," he resumed, in a more confidential tone, "no strangers have been here inquiring for me, I suppose?"

He alluded to creditors, or people acting for them. To a careless man, as Val had been, it was a difficult matter to know whether all his debts were paid or not. He had settled what he remembered; but there might be others. Hedges understood; and his voice fell to the same low tone: he had been pretty cognizant of the embarrassments of Mr. Percival Elster.

"Nobody at all, my lord. They wouldn't have got much information out of me, if they had come."

Lord Hartledon laughed. "Things are changed now, Hedges, and they may have as much information as they choose. Bring me coffee here; make haste."

Coffee was brought, and he went out as soon as he had taken it, following the road to the Rectory. It was a calm, still night, the moon tolerably bright; not a breath of wind stirred the air, warm and oppressive for October; not by any means the sort of night doctors covet when fever is in the atmosphere.

He turned in at the Rectory-gates, and was crossing to the house, when a rustling of leaves in a shrubbery path caused him to look over the dwarf laurels, and there stood Anne. He was at her side in an instant. She had nothing on her head, as though she had just come forth from the rooms for a breath of air. As indeed was the case.

"My darling!"

"I heard you had come," she whispered, as he held both her hands in his, and her heart bounded with an exquisite flutter of delight.

"How did you hear that?" he said, placing her hand within his arm, that he might pace the walk with her.

"Papa heard it. Some one had seen you walking home from the train: I think it was Mr. Hillary. But, Percival, ought you to have come here?" she added in alarm. "This is infected ground, you know."

"Not for me. I have no more fear of fever than I have of moonstroke. Anne, I hope *you* will not take it," he gravely added.

"I hope not, either. Like you, I have no fear of it. I am so glad Arthur is away. Was it not wrong of that landlady to let her rooms to us when she had fever in them?"

"Infamously wrong," said Lord Hartledon warmly.

"She excused herself afterwards by saying, that as the people who had the fever were in quite a different part of the house from ours, she thought there could be no danger. Papa was so angry. He told her he was sorry the law did not take cognizance of such an offence. We had been a week in the house before we knew of it."

"How did you find it out?"

"The lady who was ill with it died, and Matilda saw the coffin going up the back stairs. She questioned the servants of the house, and one of them told her all about it then, bit by bit. Another lady was lying ill, and a third was recovering. The landlady, by way of excuse, said the greatest wrong had been done to herself, for these ladies had brought the fever into her house, and brought it deliberately. Fever had broken out in their own home, some long way off, and they ran away from it, and took her apartments, saying nothing; which was true, we found."

"Two wrongs don't make a right," observed Lord Hartledon. "Their bringing the fever into her house was no justification for receiving you into it when it was there. It's the way of the world, Anne: one wrong leading to others. Is Matilda getting over it?"

"I hardly know. She is not out of danger; but Mr. Hillary has hopes of her. One of the other servants has taken it, and is worse than Matilda. Mr. Hillary has been with her three times to-day, and is coming again. She was ill when I last wrote to you, Val; but we did not know it."

"Which of them is it?" he asked.

"The dairymaid; a stout girl, who has never had a day's illness before. I don't suppose you know her. There was some trouble with her. She would not take any medicine; would not do anything she ought to have done, and the consequence is that the fever has got dangerously ahead. I am sure she is very ill."

"I hope it will not spread beyond the Rectory."

"Oh, Val, that is our one great hope," she said, turning her earnest face to him in the moonlight. "We are taking all possible precautions. None of us are going beyond the grounds, except papa, and we do not receive any one here. I don't know what papa will say to your coming."

He smiled. "But you can't keep all the world away!"

"We do—very nearly. Mr. Hillary comes, and Dr. Beamish from Garchester, and one or two people have been here on business. If any one calls at the gate, they are not asked in; and I don't suppose they would come in if asked. Jabez Gum's the most obstinate. He comes in just as usual."

"Lady Kirton is in an awful fright," said Val, in an amused tone.

"Oh, I have heard of it," cried Anne, clasping her hands in laughter. "She is burning tar outside the house; and she spoke to Mr. Hillary this morning through the window muffled up in a cloak and respirator. What a strange old thing she is!"

Val shrugged his shoulders. "I don't think she means badly *au fond*; and she has no home, poor creature."

"Is that why she remains at Hartledon?"

"I suppose so. Reigning at Hartledon must be something like a glimpse of Paradise to her. She won't quit it in a hurry."

"I wonder you like to have her there."

"I know I shall never have courage to tell her to go," was the candid and characteristic answer. "I was afraid of her as a boy, and I'm not sure but I'm afraid of her still."

"I don't like her—I don't like either of them," said Anne in a low tone.

"Don't you like Maude?"

"No. I am sure she is not true. To my mind there is something very false about them both."

"I think you are wrong, Anne; certainly as regards Maude."

Miss Ashton did not press her opinion: they were his relatives. "But I should have pitied poor Edward had he lived and married her," she said, following out her thoughts.

"I was mistaken when I thought Maude cared for Edward," observed Lord Hartledon. "I'm sure I did think it. I used to tell Edward so; but a day or two after he died I found I was wrong. The dowager had been urging Maude to like him, and she could not, and it made her miserable."

"Did Maude tell you this?" inquired Anne; her radiant eyes full of surprise.

"Not Maude: she never said a word to me upon the subject. It was the dowager."

"Then, Val, she must have said it with an object in view. I am sure Maude did love him. I know she did."

He shook his head. "You are wrong, Anne, depend upon it. She did not like him, and she and her mother were at variance upon the point. However, it is of no moment to discuss it now: and it might never have come to an issue had Edward lived, for he did not care for her; and I dare say never would have cared for her."

Anne said no more. It was of no moment as he observed; but she retained her own opinion. They strolled to the end of the short walk in silence, and Anne said she must go in.

"Am I quite forgiven?" whispered Lord Hartledon, bending his head down to her.

"I never thought I had very much to forgive," she rejoined, after a pause.

"My darling! I mean by your father."

"Ah, I don't know. You must talk to him. He knows we have been writing to each other. I think he means to trust you."

"The best plan will be for you to come soon to Hartledon, Anne. I shall never go wrong when once you are my wife."

"Do you go so very wrong now?" she asked.

"On my honour, no! You need not doubt me, Anne; now or ever. I have paid up what I owed, and will take very good care to keep out of trouble for the future. I incurred debts for others, more than for myself, and have bought experience dearly. My darling, surely you can trust me now?"

"I always did trust you," she murmured.

He took a long, fervent kiss from her lips, and then led her to the open lawn and across to the house.

"Ought you to come in, Percival?"

"Certainly. One word, Anne; because I may be speaking to the Rector—I don't mean to-night. You will make no objection to coming soon to Hartledon?"

"I can't come, you know, as long as Lady Kirton is its mistress," she said, half seriously, half jestingly.

He laughed at the notion. Lady Kirton must be going soon of her own accord; if not, he should have to pluck up courage and give her a hint, was his answer. At any rate, she'd surely take herself off before Christmas. The old dowager at Hartledon after he had Anne there! Not if he knew it, he added, as he went on with her into the presence of Dr. and Mrs. Ashton. The Rector started from his seat, at once telling him that he ought not to have come in. Which Val did not see at all, and decidedly refused to go out again.

Meanwhile the countess-dowager and Maude were wondering what had become of him. They supposed he was still sitting in the dining-room. The old dowager fidgeted about, her fingers ominously near the bell. She was burning to send to him, but hardly knew how he might take the message: it might be that he would object to leading strings, and her attempt to put them on would ruin all. But the time went on; grew late; and she was dying for her tea, which she had chosen should wait also. Maude sat before the fire in a large chair; her eyes, her hands, her whole air supremely listless.

"Don't you want tea, Maude?" suddenly cried her mother, who had cast innumerable glances at her from time to time.

"I have wanted it for hours—as it seems to me."

"It's a horrid custom for young men, this sitting long after dinner. If he gets into it—But you must see to that, and stop it, if ever you reign at Hartledon. I dare say he's smoking."

"If ever I reign at Hartledon—which I am not likely to do—I'll take care not to wait tea for any one, as you have made me wait for it this evening," was Maude's rejoinder, spoken with apathy.

"I'll send a message to him," decided Lady Kirton, ringing rather fiercely.

A servant appeared.

"Tell Lord Hartledon we are waiting tea for him."

"His lordship's not in, my lady."

"Not in!"

"He went out directly after dinner, as soon as he had taken coffee."

"Oh," said the countess-dowager. And she began to make the tea with vehemence—for it did not please her to have it brought in made—and knocked down and broke one of the delicate china cups.

# XIV

## ANOTHER PATIENT

It was eleven o'clock when Lord Hartledon entered. Lady Kirton was fanning herself vehemently. Maude had gone upstairs for the night.

"Where have you been?" she asked, laying down her fan. "We waited tea for you until poor Maude got quite exhausted."

"Did you? I am sorry for that. Never wait for me, pray, Lady Kirton. I took tea at the Rectory."

"Took—tea—where?"

"At the Rectory."

With a shriek the countess-dowager darted to the far end of the room, turning up her gown as she went, and muffling it over her head and face, so that only the little eyes, round now with horror, were seen. Lord Hartledon gazed in amazement.

"You have been at the Rectory, when I warned you not to go! You have been inside that house of infection, and come home—here—to me—to my darling Maude! May heaven forgive you, Hartledon!"

"Why, what have I done? What harm will it do?" exclaimed the astonished man. He would have approached her, but she warned him from her piteously with her hands. She was at the upper end of the room, and he near the door, so that she could not leave it without passing him. Hedges came in, and stood staring in the same wondering astonishment as his master.

"For mercy's sake, take off every shred of your clothes!" she cried. "You may have brought home death in them. They shall be thrown into the burning tar. Do you want to kill us? What has Maude done to you that you behave in this way?"

"I do think you must be going mad!" cried Lord Hartledon, in bewilderment; "and I hope you'll forgive me for saying so. I—"

"Go and change your clothes!" was all she could reiterate. "Every minute you stand in them is fraught with danger. If you choose to die yourself, it's downright wicked to bring death to us. Oh, go, that I may get out of here."

Lord Hartledon, to pacify her, left the room, and the countess-dowager rushed forth and bolted herself into her own apartments.

Was she mad, or making a display of affectation, or genuinely afraid? wondered Lord Hartledon aloud, as he went up to his chamber. Hedges gave it as his opinion that she was really afraid, because she had been as bad as this when she first heard of the illness, before his lordship arrived. Val retired to rest laughing: it was a good joke to him.

But it was no joke to the countess-dowager, as he found to his cost when the morning came. She got him out of his chamber betimes, and commenced a "fumigating" process. The clothes he had worn she insisted should be burnt; pleading so piteously that he yielded in his good nature.

But there was to be a battle on another score. She forbade him, in the most positive terms, to go again to the Rectory—to approach within half-a-mile of it. Lord Hartledon civilly told her he could not comply; he hinted that if her alarms were so great, she had better leave the place until all danger was over, and thereby nearly entailed on himself another war-dance.

News that came up that morning from the Rectory did not tend to assuage her fears. The poor dairymaid had died in the night, and another servant, one of the men, was sickening. Even Lord Hartledon looked grave: and the countess-dowager wormed a half promise from him, in the softened feelings of the moment, that he would not visit the infected house.

Before an hour was over he came to her to retract it. "I cannot be so unfeeling, so unneighbourly, as not to call," he said. "Even were my relations not what they are with Miss Ashton, I could not do it. It's of no use talking, ma'am; I am too restless to stay away."

A little skirmish of words ensued. Lady Kirton accused him of wishing to sacrifice them to his own selfish gratification. Lord Hartledon felt uncomfortable at the accusation. One of the best-hearted men living, he did nothing in his vacillation. He would go in the evening, he said to himself, when they could not watch him from the house.

But she was clever at carrying out her own will, that countess-dowager; more than a match for the single-minded young man. She wrote an urgent letter to Dr. Ashton, setting forth her own and her daughter's danger if her nephew, as she styled him, was received at the Rectory; and she despatched it privately.

It brought forth a letter from Dr. Ashton to Lord Hartledon; a kind but peremptory mandate, forbidding him to show himself at the Rectory until the illness was over. Dr. Ashton reminded his future son-in-law that it was not particularly on his own account he interposed this veto, but for the sake of the neighbourhood generally. If they were to prevent the fever from spreading, it was absolutely necessary that no chance visitors should be running into the Rectory and out of it again, to carry possible infection to the parish.

Lord Hartledon could only acquiesce. The note was written in terms so positive as rather to surprise him; but he never suspected the undercurrent that had been at work. In his straightforwardness he showed the letter to the dowager, who nodded her head approvingly, but told no tales.

And so his days went on in the society of the two women at Hartledon; and if he found himself oppressed with *ennui* at first, he subsided into a flirtation with Maude, and forgot care. Elster's folly! He was not hearing from Anne, for it was thought better that even notes should not pass out of the Rectory.

Curiously to relate, the first person beyond the Rectory to take the illness was the man Pike. How he could have caught it was a marvel to Calne. And yet, if Lady Kirton's theory were correct, that infection was conveyed by clothes, it might be accounted for, and Clerk Gum be deemed the culprit. One evening after the clerk had been for some little time at the Rectory with Dr. Ashton, he met Pike in going out; had brushed close to him in passing, as he well remembered. However it might have been, in a few days after that Pike was found to be suffering from the fever.

Whether he would have died, lying alone in that shed, Calne did not decide; and some thought he would, making no sign; some thought not, but would have called in assistance. Mr. Hillary, an observant man, as perhaps it was requisite he should be in time of public danger, halted one morning to speak to Clerk Gum, who was standing at his own gate.

"Have you seen anything lately of that neighbour of yours, Gum?"

"Which neighbour?" asked the clerk, in tones that seemed to resent the question.

Mr. Hillary pointed his umbrella in the direction of the shed. "Pike."

"No, I've seen nothing of him, that I remember."

"Neither have I. What's more, I've seen no smoke coming out of the chimney these two days. It strikes me he's ill. It may be the fever."

"Gone away, possibly," remarked the clerk, after a moment's pause; "in the same unceremonious manner that he came."

"I think somebody ought to see. He may be lying there helpless."

"Little matter if he is," growled the clerk, who seemed put out about something or other.

"It's not like you to say so, Gum. You might step over the stile and see; you're nearest to him. Nobody knows what the man is, or what he may have been; but humanity does not let even the worst die unaided."

"What makes you think he has the fever?" asked the clerk.

"I only say he may have it; having seen neither him nor his smoke these two days. Never mind; if it annoys you to do this, I'll look in myself some time to-day."

"You wouldn't get admitted; he keeps his door fastened," returned Gum. "The only way to get at him is to shout out to him through that glazed aperture he calls his window."

"Will you do it—or shall I?"

"I'll do it," said the clerk; "and tell you if your services are wanted."

Mr. Hillary walked off at a quick pace. There was a good deal of illness in Calne at that season, though the fever had not spread.

Whether Clerk Gum kept his word, or whether he did not, certain it was that Mr. Hillary heard nothing from him that day. In the evening the clerk was sitting in his office in a thoughtful mood, busy over some accounts connected with an insurance company for which he was agent, when he heard a quick sharp knock at the front-door.

"I wonder if it's Hillary?" he muttered, as he took the candle and rose to open it.

Instead of the surgeon, there entered a lady, with much energy. It was the *bête noire* of Clerk Gum's life, Mrs. Jones.

"What's the house shut up for at this early hour?" she began. "The door locked, the shutters up, and the blinds down, just as if everybody was dead or asleep. Where's Nance?"

"She's out," said the clerk. "I suppose she shut up before she went, and I've been in my office all the afternoon. Do you want anything?"

"Do I want anything!" retorted Mrs. Jones. "I've come in to shelter from the rain. It's been threatening all the evening, and it's coming down now like cats and dogs."

The clerk was leading the way to the little parlour; but she ignored the movement, and went on to the kitchen. He could only follow her. "It's a pity you came out when it threatened rain," said he.

"Business took me out," replied Mrs. Jones. "I've been up to the mill. I heard young Rip was ill, and going to leave; so I went up to ask if they'd try our Jim. But young Rip isn't going to leave, and isn't ill, mother Floyd says, though it's certain he's not well. She can't think what's the matter with the boy; he's always fancying he sees ghosts in the river. I've had my trapes for nothing."

She had given her gown a good shake from the rain-drops in the middle of the kitchen, and was now seated before the fire. The clerk stood by the table, occasionally snuffing the candle, and wishing she'd take herself off again.

"Where's Nancy gone?" asked she.

"I didn't hear her say."

"And she'll be gone a month of Sundays, I suppose. I shan't wait for her, if the rain gives over."

"You'd be more comfortable in the small parlour," said the clerk, who seemed rather fidgety; "there's a nice bit of fire there."

"I'm more comfortable here," contradicted Mrs. Jones. "Where's the good of a bit of fire for a gown as wet as mine?"

Jabez Gum made no response. There was the lady, a fixture; and he could only resign himself to the situation.

"How's your friend at the next house—Pike?" she began again sarcastically.

"He's no friend of mine," said the clerk.

"It looks like it, at all events; or you'd have given him into custody long ago. *I* wouldn't let a man harbour himself so close to me. He's taken to a new dodge now: going about with a pistol to shoot people."

"Who says so?" asked the clerk.

"I say so. He frighted that boy Ripper pretty near to death. The boy tore home one night in a state of terror, and all they could get out of him was that he'd met Pike with a pistol. It's weeks ago, and he hasn't got over it yet."

"Did Pike level it at him?"

"I tell you that's all they could get out of the boy. He's a nice jail-bird too, that young Rip, unless I'm mistaken. They might as well send him away, and make room for our Jim."

"I think you are about the most fanciful, unjust, selfish woman in Calne!" exclaimed the clerk, unable to keep down his anger any longer. "You'd take young Ripper's character away without scruple, just because his place might suit your Jim!"

"I'm what?" shrieked Mrs. Jones. "I'm unjust, am I—"

An interruption occurred, and Mrs. Jones subsided into silence. The back-door suddenly opened, not a couple of yards from that lady's head, and in came Mrs. Gum in her ordinary indoor dress, two basins in her hand. The sight of her visitor appeared to occasion her surprise; she uttered a faint scream, and nearly dropped the basins.

"Lawk a mercy! Is it Lydia Jones?"

Mrs. Jones had been drawing a quiet deduction—the clerk had said his wife was out only to deceive her. She rose from her chair, and faced him.

"I thought you told me she was gone out?"

The clerk coughed. He looked at his wife, as if asking an explanation. The meeker of the two women hastily put her basins down, and stood looking from one to the other, apparently recovering breath.

"Didn't you go out?" asked the clerk.

"I was going, Gum, but stepped out first to collect my basins, and then the rain came down. I had to shelter under the wood-shed, it was peppering so."

"Collect your basins!" interjected Mrs. Jones. "Where from?"

"I put them out with scraps for the cats."

"The cats must be well off in your quarter; better than some children in others," was the rejoinder, delivered with an unnecessary amount of spite. "What makes you so out of breath?" she tartly asked.

"I had a bit of a fright," said the woman, simply. "My breath seems to get affected at nothing of late, Lydia."

"A pity but you'd your hands full of work, as mine are: that's the best remedy for fright," said Mrs. Jones sarcastically. "What might your fright have been, pray?"

"I was standing, waiting to dart over here, when I saw a man come across the waste land and make for Pike's shed," said Mrs. Gum, looking at her husband. "It gave me a turn. We've never seen a soul go near the place of an evening since Pike has been there."

"Why should it give you a turn?" asked Mrs. Jones, who was in a mood to contradict everything. "You've seen Pike often enough not to be frightened at him when he keeps his distance."

"It wasn't Pike, Lydia. The man had an umbrella over him, and he looked like a gentleman. Fancy Pike with an umbrella!"

"Was it Mr. Hillary?" interposed the clerk.

She shook her head. "I don't think so; but it was getting too dark to see. Any way, it gave me a turn; and he's gone right up to Pike's shed."

"Gave you a turn, indeed!" scornfully repeated Mrs. Jones. "I think you're getting more of an idiot every day, Nance. It's to be hoped somebody's gone to take him up; that's what is to be hoped."

But Mr. Hillary it was. Hearing nothing from Jabez Gum all day, he had come to the conclusion that that respectable man had ignored his promise, and, unable to divest himself of the idea that Pike was ill, in the evening, having a minute to spare, he went forth to see for himself.

The shed-door was closed, but not fastened, and Mr. Hillary went in at once without ceremony. A lighted candle shed its rays around the rude dwelling-room: and the first thing he saw was a young man, who did not look in the least like Pike, stretched upon a mattress; the second was a bushy black wig and appurtenances lying on a chair; and the third was a formidable-looking pistol, conveniently close to the prostrate invalid.

Quick as thought, the surgeon laid his hand upon the pistol and removed it to a safe distance. He then bent over the sick man, examining him with his penetrating eyes; and what he saw struck him with consternation so great, that he sat down on a chair to recover himself, albeit not liable to be overcome by emotion.

When he left the shed—which was not for nearly half-an-hour after he had entered it—he heard voices at Clerk Gum's front-door. The storm was over, and their visitor was departing. Mr. Hillary took a moment's counsel with himself, then crossed the stile and appeared amongst them. Nodding to the three collectively, he gravely addressed the clerk and his wife.

"I have come here to ask, in the name of our common humanity, whether you will put aside your prejudices, and be Christians in a case of need," he began. "I don't forget that once, when an epidemic was raging in Calne, you"—turning to the wife—"were active and fearless, going about and nursing the sick when almost all others held aloof. Will you do the same now by a helpless man?"

The woman trembled all over. Clerk Gum looked questioningly at the doctor. Mrs. Jones was taking in everything with eyes and ears.

"This neighbour of yours has caught the fever. Some one must attend to him, or he will lie there and die. I thought perhaps you'd do it, Mrs. Gum, for our Saviour's sake—if from no other motive."

She trembled excessively. "I always was terribly afraid of that man, sir, since he came," said she, with marked hesitation.

"But he cannot harm you now. I don't ask you to go in to him one day after he is well again—if he recovers. Neither need you be with him as a regular nurse: only step in now and then to give him his physic, or change the wet cloths on his burning head."

Mrs. Jones found her voice. The enormous impudence of the surgeon's request had caused its temporary extinction.

"I'd see Pike in his coffin before I'd go a-nigh him as a nurse! What on earth will you be asking next, Mr. Hillary?"

"I didn't ask you, Mrs. Jones: you have your children to attend to; full employment for one pair of arms. Mrs. Gum has nothing to do with her time; and is near at hand besides. Gum, you stand in your place by Dr. Ashton every Sunday, and read out to us of the loving mercy of God: will you urge your wife to this little work of charity for His sake?"

Jabez Gum evidently did not know what to answer. On the one hand, he could hardly go against the precepts he had to respond to as clerk; on the other, there was his scorn and hatred of the disreputable Arab.

"He's such a loose character, sir," he debated at length.

"Possibly: when he is well. But he is ill now, and could not be loose if he tried. Some one *must* go in now and then to see after him: it struck me that perhaps your wife would do it, for humanity's sake; and I thought I'd ask her before going further."

"She can do as she likes," said Jabez.

Mrs. Gum—as unresisting in her nature as ever was Percival Elster— yielded to the prayer of the surgeon, and said she would do what she could. But she had never shown more nervousness over anything than she was showing as she gave her answer.

"Then I will step indoors and give you a few plain directions," said the surgeon. "Mrs. Jones has taken her departure, I perceive."

Mrs. Gum was as good as her word, and went in with dire trepidation. Calne's sentiments, on the whole, resembled Mrs. Jones's, and the woman was blamed for her yielding nature. But she contrived, with the help of Mr. Hillary's skill, to bring the man through the fever; and it was very singular that no other person out of the Rectory took it.

The last one to take it at the Rectory was Mrs. Ashton. Of the three servants who had it, one had died; the other two recovered. Mrs. Ashton did not take it until the rest were well, and she had it lightly. Anne nursed her and would do so; and it was an additional reason for prolonging the veto against Lord Hartledon.

One morning in December, Val, in passing down the road, saw the Rectory turned, as he called it, inside out. Every window was thrown open; curtains were taken down; altogether there seemed to be a comprehensive cleaning going on. At that moment Mr. Hillary passed, and Val arrested him, pointing to the Rectory.

"Yes, they are having a cleansing and purification. The family went away this morning."

"Went where?" exclaimed Hartledon, in amazement.

"Dr. Ashton has taken a cottage near Ventnor."

"Had Mrs. Ashton quite recovered?"

"Quite: or they would not have gone. The Rectory has had a clean bill of health for some time past."

"Then why did they not let me know it?" exclaimed Val, in his astonishment and anger.

"Perhaps you didn't ask," said the surgeon. "But no visitors were sought. Time enough for that when the house shall have been fumigated."

"They might have sent to me," he cried, in resentment. "To go away and never let me know it!"

"They may have thought you were too agreeably engaged to care to be disturbed," remarked the surgeon.

"What do you mean?" demanded Val, hotly.

Mr. Hillary laughed. "People will talk, you know; and rumour has it that Lord Hartledon has found attractions in his own home, whilst the Rectory was debarred to him."

Val wheeled round on his heel, and walked away in displeasure. Home truths are never palatable. But the kindly disposition of the man resumed its sway immediately: he turned back, and pointed to the shed.

"Is that interesting patient of yours on his legs again?"

"He is getting better. The disease attacked him fiercely and was unusually prolonged. It's strange he should have been the only one to take it."

"Gum's wife has been nursing him, I hear?"

"She has gone in and out to do such necessary offices as the sick require. I put it to her from a Christian point of view, you see, and on the score of humanity. She was at hand; and that's a great thing where the nurse is only a visiting one."

"Look here, Hillary; don't let the man want for anything; see that he has all he needs. He is a black sheep, no doubt; but illness levels us all to one standard. Good day."

"Good day, Lord Hartledon."

And when the surgeon had got to a distance with his quick step, Lord Hartledon turned back to the Rectory.

# XV

## VAL'S DILEMMA

It was a mild day in spring. The air was balmy, but the skies were grey and lowering; and as a gentleman strolled across a field adjoining Hartledon Park he looked up at them more than once, as if asking whether they threatened rain.

Not that he had any great personal interest in the question. Whether the skies gave forth sunshine or rain is of little moment to a mind not at rest. He had only looked up in listlessness. A stranger might have taken him at a distance for a gamekeeper: his coat was of velveteen; his boots were muddy: but a nearer inspection would have removed the impression.

It was Lord Hartledon; but changed since you last saw him. For some time past there had been a worn, weary look upon his face, bespeaking a mind ill at ease; the truth is, his conscience was not at rest, and in time that tells on the countenance.

He had been by the fish-pond for an hour. But the fish had not shown themselves inclined to bite, and he grew too impatient to remain. Not altogether impatient at the wary fish, but in his own mental restlessness. The fishing-rod was carried in his hand in pieces; and he splashed along, in a brown study, on the wet ground, flinging himself over the ha-ha with an ungracious movement. Some one was approaching across the park from the house, and Lord Hartledon walked on to a gate, and waited there for him to come up. He began beating the bars with the thin end of the rod, and—broke it!

"That's the way you use your fishing-rods," cried the free, pleasant voice of the new-comer. "I shouldn't mind being appointed purveyor of tackle to your lordship."

The stranger was an active little man, older than Hartledon; his features were thin, his eyes dark and luminous. I think you have heard his name—Thomas Carr. Lord Hartledon once called him the greatest friend he possessed on earth. He had been wont to fly to him in his past dilemmas, and the habit was strong upon him still. A mandate that would have been peremptory, but for the beseeching terms in which it was couched, had reached Mr. Carr on circuit; and he had hastened across country to obey it, reaching Hartledon the previous evening. That something was wrong, Mr. Carr of course was aware; but what, he did not yet know. Lord Hartledon, with his natural vacillation, his usual shrinking from the discussion of unpleasant topics relating to himself, had not entered upon it at all on the previous night; and when breakfast was over that morning, Mr. Carr had craved an hour alone for letter-writing. It was the first time Mr. Carr had visited his friend at his new inheritance; indeed the first time he had been at all at Hartledon. Lord Hartledon seated himself on the gate; the barrister leaned his arms on the top bar whilst he talked to him.

"What is the matter?" asked the latter.

"Not much."

"I have finished my letters, so I came out to look for you. You are not changed, Elster."

"What should change me in so short a time?—it's only six months since you last saw me," retorted Hartledon, curtly.

"I alluded to your nature. I had to worm the troubles out of you in the old days, each one as it arose. I see I shall have to do the same now. Don't say there's not much the matter, for I am sure there is."

Lord Hartledon jerked his handkerchief out of his pocket, passed it over his face, and put it back again.

"What fresh folly have you got into?—as I used to ask you at Oxford. You are in some mess."

"I suppose it's of no use denying that I am in one. An awful mess, too."

"Well, I have pulled you out of many a one in my time. Let me hear it."

"There are some things one does not like to talk about, Carr. I sent for you in my perplexity; but I believe you can be of no use to me."

"So you have said before now. But it generally turned out that I was of use to you, and cleared you from your nightmare."

"All those were minor difficulties; this is different."

"I cannot understand your 'not liking' to speak of things to me. Why don't you begin?"

"Because I shall prove myself worse than a fool. You'll despise me to your heart's core. Carr, I think I shall go mad!"

"Tell me the cause first, and go mad afterwards. Come, Val; I am your true friend."

"I have made an offer of marriage to two women," said Hartledon, desperately plunging into the revelation. "Never was such a born idiot in the world as I have been. I can't marry both."

"I imagine not," quietly replied Mr. Carr.

"You knew I was engaged to Miss Ashton?"

"Yes."

"And I'm sure I loved her with all my"—he seemed to hesitate for a strong term—"might and main; and do still. But I have managed to get into mischief elsewhere."

"Elster's folly, as usual. What sort of mischief?"

"The worst sort, for there can be no slipping out of it. When that fever broke out at Doctor Ashton's—you heard us talking of it last night, Carr—I went to the Rectory just as usual. What did I care for fever?—it was not likely to attack me. But the countess-dowager found it out—"

"Why do they stay here so long?" interrupted Thomas Carr. "They have been here ever since your brother died."

"And before it. The old woman likes her quarters, and has no settled home. She makes a merit of stopping, and says I ought to feel under eternal obligation to her and Maude for sacrificing themselves to a solitary man and his household. But you should have heard the uproar she made upon discovering I had been to the Rectory. She had my room fumigated and my clothes burnt."

"Foolish old creature!"

"The best of it was, I pointed out by mistake the wrong coat, and the offending one is upstairs now. I shall show it her some day. She reproached me with holding her life and her daughter's dirt-cheap, and wormed a promise out of me not to visit the Rectory as long as fever was in it."

"Which you gave?"

"She wormed it out of me, I tell you. I don't know that I should have kept it, but Dr. Ashton put in his veto also; and between the two I was kept away. For many weeks afterwards I never saw or spoke to Anne. She did not come out at all, even to church; they were so anxious the fever should not spread."

"Well? Go on, Val."

"Well: how does that proverb run, about idleness being the root of all evil? During those weeks I was an idle man, wretchedly bored; and I fell into a flirtation with Maude. She began it, Carr, on my solemn word of honour—though it's a shame to tell these tales of a woman; and I joined in from sheer weariness, to kill time. But you know how one gets led on in such things—or I do, if you, you cautious fellow, don't—and we both went in pretty deep."

"Elster's folly again! How deep?"

"As deep as I well could, short of committing myself to a proposal. You see the ill-luck of it was, those two and I being alone in the house. I may as well say Maude and I alone; for the old woman kept her room very much; she had a cold, she said, and was afraid of the fever."

"Tush!" cried Thomas Carr angrily. "And you made love to the young lady?"

"As fast as I could make it. What a fool I was! But I protest I only did it in amusement; I never thought of her supplanting Anne Ashton. Now, Carr, you are looking as you used to look at Oxford; get your brow smooth again. You just shut up yourself for weeks with a fascinating girl, and see if you wouldn't find yourself in some horrible entanglement, proof against such as you think you are."

"As I am obliged to be. I should take care not to lay myself open to the temptation. Neither need you have done it."

"I don't see how I was to help myself. Often and often I wished to have visitors in the house, but the old woman met me with reproaches that I was forgetting the recent death of my brother. She won't have any one now if she knows it, and I had to send for you quietly. Did you see how she stared last night when you came in?"

Mr. Carr drew down his lips. "You might have gone away yourself, Elster."

"Of course I might," was the testy reply. "But I was a fool, and didn't. Carr, I swear to you I fell into the trap unconsciously; I did not foresee danger. Maude is a charming girl, there's no denying it; but as to love, I never glanced at it."

"Was it not suspected in town last year that Lady Maude had a liking for your brother?"

"It was suspected there and here; I thought it myself. We were mistaken. One day lately Maude offended me, and I hinted at something of the sort: she turned red and white with indignation, saying she wished he could rise from his grave to refute it. I only wish he could!" added the unhappy man.

"Have you told me all?"

"All! I wish I had. In December I was passing the Rectory, and saw it dismantled. Hillary, whom I met, said the family had gone to Ventnor. I went in, but could not learn any particulars, or get the address. I chanced a letter, written I confess in anger, directing it Ventnor only, and it found them. Anne's answer was cool: mischief-making tongues had been talking about me and Maude; I learned so much from Hillary; and Anne no doubt resented it. I resented that—can you follow me, Carr?—and I said to myself I wouldn't write again for some time to come. Before that time came the climax had occurred."

"And while you were waiting for your temper to come round in regard to Miss Ashton, you continued to make love to the Lady Maude?" remarked Mr. Carr. "On the face of things, I should say your love had been transferred to her."

"Indeed it hadn't. Next to Anne, she's the most charming girl I know; that's all. Between the two it will be awful work for me."

"So I should think," returned Mr. Carr. "The ass between two bundles of hay was nothing to it."

"He was not an ass at all, compared with what I am," assented Val, gloomily.

"Well, if a man behaves like an ass—"

"Don't moralize," interrupted Hartledon; "but rather advise me how to get out of my dilemma. The morning's drawing on, and I have promised to ride with Maude."

"You had better ride alone. All the advice I can give you is to draw back by degrees, and so let the flirtation subside. If there is no actual entanglement—"

"Stop a bit, Carr; I had not come to it," interrupted Lord Hartledon, who in point of fact had been holding back what he called the climax, in his usual vacillating manner. "One ill-starred day, when it was pouring cats and dogs, and I could not get out, I challenged Maude to a game at billiards. Maude lost. I said she should pay me, and put my arm round her waist and snatched a kiss. Just at that moment in came the dowager, who I believe must have been listening—"

"Not improbably," interrupted Mr. Carr, significantly.

"'Oh, you two dear turtle-doves,' cried she, 'Hartledon, you have made me so happy! I have seen for some weeks what you were thinking of. There's nobody living I'd confide that dear child to but yourself: you shall have her, and my blessing shall be upon you both.'

"Carr," continued poor Val, "I was struck dumb. All the absurdity of the thing rose up before me. In my confusion I could not utter a word. A man with more moral courage might have spoken out; acknowledged the shame and folly of his conduct and apologized. I could not."

"Elster's folly! Elster's folly!" thought the barrister. "You never had the slightest spark of moral courage," he observed aloud, in pained tones. "What did you say?"

"Nothing. There's the worst of it. I neither denied the dowager's assumption, nor confirmed it. Of course I cannot now."

"When was this?"

"In December."

"And how have things gone on since? How do you stand with them?"

"Things have gone on as they went on before; and I stand engaged to Maude, in her mother's opinion; perhaps in hers: never having said myself one word to support the engagement."

"Only continued to 'make love,' and 'snatch a kiss,'" sarcastically rejoined Mr. Carr.

"Once in a way. What is a man to do, exposed to the witchery of a pretty girl?"

"Oh, Percival! You are worse than I thought for. Where is Miss Ashton?"

"Coming home next Friday," groaned Val. "And the dowager asked me yesterday whether Maude and I had arranged the time for our marriage. What on earth I shall do, I don't know. I might sail for some remote land and convert myself into a savage, where I should never be found or recognized; there's no other escape for me."

"How much does Miss Ashton know of this?"

"Nothing. I had a letter from her this morning, more kindly than her letters have been of late."

"Lord Hartledon!" exclaimed Mr. Carr, in startled tones. "Is it possible that you are carrying on a correspondence with Miss Ashton, and your love-making with Lady Maude?"

Val nodded assent, looking really ashamed of himself.

"And you call yourself a man of honour! Why, you are the greatest humbug—"

"That's enough; no need to sum it up. I see all I've been."

"I understood you to imply that your correspondence with Miss Ashton had ceased."

"It was renewed. Dr. Ashton came up to preach one Sunday, just before Christmas, and he and I got friendly again; you know I never can be unfriendly with any one long. The next day I wrote to Anne, and we have corresponded since; more coolly though than we used to do. Circumstances have been really against me. Had they continued at Ventnor, I should have gone down and spent my Christmas with them, and nothing of this would have happened; but they must needs go to Dr. Ashton's sister's in Yorkshire for Christmas; and there they are still. It was in that miserable Christmas week that the mischief occurred. And now you have the whole, Carr. I know I've been a fool; but what is to be done?"

"Lord Hartledon," was the grave rejoinder, "I am unable to give you advice in this. Your conduct is indefensible."

"Don't 'Lord Hartledon' me: I won't stand it. Carr?"

"Well?"

"If you bring up against me a string of reproaches lasting until night will that mend matters? I am conscious of possessing but one true friend in the world, and that's yourself. You must stand by me."

"I was your friend; never a truer. But I believed you to be a man of honour."

Hartledon lifted his hat from his brow; as though the brow alone were heavy enough just then. At least the thought struck Mr. Carr.

"I have been drawn unwittingly into this, as I have into other things. I never meant to do wrong. As to dishonour, Heaven knows my nature shrinks from it."

"If your nature does, you don't," came the severe answer. "I should feel ashamed to put forth the same plea always of 'falling unwittingly' into disgrace. You have done it ever since you were a schoolboy. Talk of the Elster folly! this has gone beyond it. This is dishonour. Engaged to one girl, and corresponding with her; making hourly love for weeks to another! May I inquire which of the two you really care for?"

"Anne—I suppose."

"You suppose!"

"You make me wild, talking like this. Of course it's Anne. Maude has managed to creep into my regard, though, in no common degree. She is very lovely, very fascinating and amiable."

"May I ask which of the two you intend to marry!" continued the barrister, neither suppressing nor attempting to soften his indignant tones. "As this country's laws are against a plurality of wives, you will be unable, I imagine, to espouse them both."

Hartledon looked at him, beseechingly, and a sudden compassion came over Mr. Carr. He asked himself whether it was quite the way to treat a perplexed man who was very dear to him.

"If I am severe, it is for your sake. I assure you I scarcely know what advice to give. It is Miss Ashton, of course, whom you intend to make Lady Hartledon?"

"Of course it is. The difficulty in the matter is getting clear of Maude."

"And the formidable countess-dowager. You must tell Maude the truth."

"Impossible, Carr. I might have done it once; but the thing has gone on so long. The dowager would devour me."

"Let her try to. I should speak to Maude alone, and put her upon her generosity to release you. Tell her you presumed upon your cousinship; and confess that you have long been engaged to marry Miss Ashton."

"She knows that: they have both known it all along. My brother was the first to tell them, before he died."

"They knew it?" inquired Mr. Carr, believing he had not heard correctly.

"Certainly. There has been no secret made of my engagement to Anne. All the world knows of that."

"Then—though I do not in the least defend or excuse you—your breaking with Lady Maude may be more pardonable. They are poor, are they not, this Dowager Kirton and Lady Maude?"

"Poor as Job. Hard up, I think."

"Then they are angling for the broad lands of Hartledon. I see it all. You have been a victim to fortune-hunting."

"There you are wrong, Carr. I can't answer for the dowager one way or the other; but Maude is the most disinterested—"

"Of course: girls on the look-out for establishments always are. Have it as you like."

He spoke in tones of ridicule; and Hartledon jumped off the stile and led the way home.

That Lord Hartledon had got himself into a very serious predicament, Mr. Carr plainly saw. His good nature, his sensitive regard for the feelings of others, rendering it so impossible for him to say no, and above all his vacillating disposition, were his paramount characteristics still: in a degree they ever would be. Easily led as ever, he was as a very reed in the hands of the crafty old woman of the world, located with him. She had determined that he should become the husband of her daughter; and was as certain of accomplishing her end as if she had foreseen the future. Lord Hartledon himself afterwards, in his bitter repentance, said, over and over again, that circumstances were against him; and they certainly were so, as you will find.

Lord Hartledon thought he was making headway against it now, in sending for his old friend, and resolving to be guided by his advice.

"I will take an opportunity of speaking to Maude, Carr," he resumed. "I would rather not do it, of course; but I see there's no help for it."

"Make the opportunity," said Mr. Carr, with emphasis. "Don't delay a day; I shall expect you to write me a letter to-morrow saying you've done it."

"But you won't leave to-day," said Hartledon, entreatingly, feeling an instant prevision that with the departure of Thomas Carr all his courage would ignominiously desert him.

"I must go. You know I told you last night that my stay could only be four-and-twenty hours. You can accomplish it whilst I am here, if you like, and get it over; the longer a nauseous medicine is held to the lips the more difficult it is to swallow it. You say you are going to ride with Lady Maude presently; let that be your opportunity."

And get it over! Words that sounded as emancipation in Val's ear. But somehow he did not accomplish it in that ride. Excuses were on his lips five hundred times, but his hesitating lips never formed them. He really was on the point of speaking; at least he said so to himself; when Mr. Hillary overtook them on horseback, and rode with them some distance. After that, Maude put her horse to a canter, and so they reached home.

"Well?" said Mr. Carr.

"Not yet," answered Hartledon; "there was no opportunity."

"My suggestion was to make your opportunity."

"And so I will. I'll speak to her either to-night or to-morrow. She chose to ride fast to-day; and Hillary joined us part of the way. Don't look as if you doubted me, Carr: I shall be sure to speak."

"Will he?" thought Thomas Carr, as he took his departure by the evening train, having promised to run down the following Saturday for a few hours. "It is an even bet, I think. Poor Val!"

Poor Val indeed! Vacillating, attractive, handsome Val! shrinking, sensitive Val! The nauseous medicine was never taken. And when the Ashtons returned to the Rectory on the Friday night he had not spoken.

And the very day of their return a rumour reached his ear that Mrs. Ashton's health was seriously if not fatally shattered, and she was departing immediately for the South of France.

# XVI

## BETWEEN THE TWO

Not in the Rectory drawing-room, but in a pretty little sitting-room attached to her bed-chamber, where the temperature was regulated, and no draughts could penetrate, reclined Mrs. Ashton. Her invalid gown sat loosely upon her shrunken form, her delicate, lace cap shaded a fading face. Anne sat by her side in all her loveliness, ostensibly working; but her fingers trembled, and her face looked flushed and pained.

It was the morning after their return, and Mrs. Graves had called in to see Mrs. Ashton—gossiping Mrs. Graves, who knew all that took place in the parish, and a great deal of what never did take place. She had just been telling it all unreservedly in her hard way; things that might be said, and things that might as well have been left unsaid. She went out leaving a whirr and a buzz behind her and an awful sickness of desolation upon one heart.

"Give me my little writing-case, Anne," said Mrs. Ashton, waking up from a reverie and sitting forward on her sofa.

Anne took the pretty toy from the side-table, opened it, and laid it on the table before her mother.

"Is it nothing I can write for you, mamma?"

"No, child."

Anne bent her hot face over her work again. It had not occurred to her that it could concern herself; and Mrs. Ashton wrote a few rapid lines:

> My Dear Percival,
>     "Can you spare me a five-minutes' visit? I wish to speak with you. We go away again on Monday.
> > Ever sincerely yours,
> > Catherine Ashton

She folded it, enclosed it in an envelope, and addressed it to the Earl of Hartledon. Pushing away the writing-table, she held out the note to her daughter.

"Seal it for me, Anne. I am tired. Let it go at once."

"Mamma!" exclaimed Anne, as her eye caught the address. "Surely you are not writing to him! You are not asking him to come here?"

"You see that I am writing to him, Anne. And it is to ask him to come here. My dear, you may safely leave me to act according to my own judgment. But as to what Mrs. Graves has said, I don't believe a word of it."

"I scarcely think I do," murmured Anne; a smile hovering on her troubled countenance, like sunshine after rain.

Anne had the taper alight, and the wax held to it, the note ready in her hand, when the room-door was thrown open by Mrs. Ashton's maid.

"Lord Hartledon."

He came in in a hurried manner, talking fast, making too much fuss; it was unlike his usual quiet movements, and Mrs. Ashton noticed it. As he shook hands with her, she held the note before him.

"See, Percival! I was writing to ask you to call upon me."

Anne had put out the light, and her hand was in Lord Hartledon's before she well knew anything, save that her heart was beating tumultuously. Mrs. Ashton made a place for him on the sofa, and Anne quietly left the room.

"I should have been here earlier," he began, "but I had the steward with me on business; it is little enough I have attended to since my brother's death. Dear Mrs. Ashton! I grieve to hear this poor account of you. You are indeed looking ill."

"I am so ill, Percival, that I doubt whether I shall ever be better in this world. It is my last chance, this going away to a warmer place until winter has passed."

He was bending towards her in earnest sympathy, all himself again; his dark blue eyes very tender, his pleasant features full of concern as he gazed on her face. And somehow, looking at that attractive countenance, Mrs. Ashton's doubts went from her.

"But what I have said is to you alone," she resumed. "My husband and children do not see the worst, and I refrain from telling them. A little word of confidence between us, Val."

"I hope and trust you may come back cured!" he said, very fervently. "Is it the fever that has so shattered you?"

"It is the result of it. I have never since been able to recover strength, but have become weaker and more weak. And you know I was in ill health before. We leave on Monday morning for Cannes."

"For Cannes?" he exclaimed.

"Yes. A place not so warm as some I might have gone to; but the doctors say that will be all the better. It is not heat I need; only shelter from our cold northern winds until I can get a little strength into me. There's nothing the matter with my lungs; indeed, I don't know that anything is the matter with me except this terrible weakness."

"I suppose Anne goes with you?"

"Oh yes. I could not go without Anne. The doctor will see us settled there, and then he returns."

A thought crossed Lord Hartledon: how pleasant if he and Anne could have been married, and have made this their wedding tour. He did not speak it: Mrs. Ashton would have laughed at his haste.

"How long shall you remain away?" he asked.

"Ah, I cannot tell you. I may not live to return. If all goes well—that is, if there should be a speedy change for the better, as the medical men who have been attending me think there may be—I shall be back perhaps in April or May. Val—I cannot forget the old familiar name, you see—"

"I hope you never will forget it," he warmly interposed.

"I wanted very particularly to see you. A strange report was brought here this morning and I determined to mention it to you. You know what an old-fashioned, direct way I have of doing things; never choosing a roundabout road if I can take a straight one. This note was a line asking you to call upon me," she added, taking it from her lap, where it had been lying, and tossing it on to the table, whilst her hearer, his conscience rising up, began to feel a very little uncomfortable. "We heard you had proposed marriage to Lady Maude Kirton."

Lord Hartledon's face became crimson. "Who on earth could have invented that?" cried he, having no better answer at hand.

"Mrs. Graves mentioned it to me. She was dining at Hartledon last week, and the countess-dowager spoke about it openly."

Mrs. Ashton looked at him; and he, confused and taken aback, looked down on the carpet, devoutly wishing himself in the remote regions he had spoken of to Mr. Carr. Anywhere, so that he should never be seen or recognized again.

"What am I to do?" thought he. "I wish Mother Graves was hanged!"

"You do not speak, Percival!"

"Well, I—I was wondering what could have given rise to this," he stammered. "I believe the old dowager would like to see her daughter mistress of Hartledon: and suppose she gave utterance to her thoughts."

"Very strange that she should!" observed Mrs. Ashton.

"I think she's a little cracked sometimes," coughed Val; and, in truth, he now and then did think so. "I hope you have not told Anne?"

"I have told no one. And had I not felt sure it had no foundation, I should have told the doctor, not you. But Anne was in the room when Mrs. Graves mentioned it."

"What a blessing it would be if Mrs. Graves were out of the parish!" exclaimed Val, hotly. "I wonder Dr. Ashton keeps Graves on, with such a mother! No one ever had such a mischief-making tongue as hers."

"Percival, may I say something to you?" asked Mrs. Ashton, who was devouring him with her eyes. "Your manner would almost lead me to believe that there *is* something in it. Tell me the truth; I can never be anything but your friend."

"Believe one thing, dear Mrs. Ashton—that I have no intention of marrying anyone but Anne; and I wish with all my heart and soul you'd give her to me to-day. Shut up with those two women, the one pretty, the other watching any chance word to turn it to her own use, I dare say the Mrs. Graveses of the place have talked, forgetting that Maude is my cousin. I believe I paid some attention to Maude because I was angry at being kept out of the Rectory; but my attentions meant nothing, upon my honour."

"Elster's folly, Val! Lady Maude may have thought they did."

"At any rate she knew of my engagement to Anne."

"Then there is nothing in it?"

"There shall be nothing in it," was the emphatic answer. "Anne was my first love, and she will be my last. You must promise to give her to me as soon as you return from Cannes."

"About that you must ask her father. I dare say he will do so."

Lord Hartledon rose from his seat; held Mrs. Ashton's hand between his whilst he said his adieu, and stooped to kiss her with a son's affection. She was a little surprised to find it was his final farewell. They were not going to start until Monday. But Hartledon could not have risked that cross-questioning again; rather would he have sailed away for the savage territories at once. He went downstairs searching for Anne, and found her in the room where you first saw her—her own. She looked up with quite an affectation of surprise when he entered, although she had probably gone there to await him. The best of girls are human.

"You ran away, Anne, whilst mamma and I held our conference?"

"I hope it has been satisfactory," she answered demurely, not looking up, and wondering whether he suspected how violently her heart was beating.

"Partly so. The end was all right. Shall I tell it you?"

"The end! Yes, if you will," she replied unsuspectingly.

"The decision come to is, that a certain young friend of ours is to be converted, with as little delay as circumstances may permit, into Lady Hartledon."

Of course there came no answer except a succession of blushes. Anne's work, which she had carried with her, took all her attention just then.

"Can you guess her name, Anne?"

"I don't know. Is it Maude Kirton?"

He winced. "If you have been told that abominable rubbish, Anne, it is not necessary to repeat it. It's not so pleasant a theme that you need make a joke of it."

"Is it rubbish?" asked Anne, lifting her eyes.

"I think you ought to know that if any one does. But had anything happened, Anne, recollect it would have been your fault. You have been very cool to me of late. You forbid me the house for weeks and weeks; you went away for an indefinite period without letting me know, or giving me the chance of seeing you; and when the correspondence was at length renewed, your letters were cold and formal—quite different from what they used to be. It almost looks as if you wished to part from me."

Repentance was stealing over her: why had she ever doubted him?

"And now you are going away again! And although this interview may be our last for months, you scarcely deign to give me a word or a look of farewell."

Anne had already been terribly tried by Mrs. Graves: this was the climax: she lost her self-control and burst into tears. Lord Hartledon was softened at once. He took her two hands in his; he clasped her to his heart, half devouring her face with passionate kisses. Ah, Lady Maude! this impassioned love was never felt for you.

"You don't love her?" whispered Anne.

"Love her! I never loved but you, my best and dearest. I never shall, or can, love another."

He spoke in all good faith; fully believing what he said; and it was indeed true. And Anne? As though a prevision had been upon her of the future, she remained passively in his arms sobbing hysterically, and suffering his kisses; not drawing away from him in maiden modesty, as was her wont. She had never clung to him like this.

"You will write to me often?" he whispered.

"Yes. Won't you come to Cannes?"

"I don't know that it will be possible, unless you remain beyond the spring. And should that be the case, Anne, I shall pray your father and mother that the marriage may take place there. I am going up to town next month to take my seat in the House. It will be a busy session; and I want to see if I can't become a useful public man. I think it would please the doctor to find I've some stuff in me; and a man must have a laudable object in life."

"I would rather die," murmured Anne, passionately in her turn, "than hear again what Mrs. Graves said."

"My darling, we cannot stop people's gossip. Believe in me; I will not fail you. Oh, Anne, I wish you were already my wife!" he aspirated fervently, his perplexities again presenting themselves to his mind.

"The time will come," she whispered.

Lord Hartledon walked home full of loyal thought, saying to himself what an utter idiot he had been in regard to Maude, and determined to lose no time in getting clear of the entanglement. He sought an opportunity of speaking to her that afternoon; he really did; but could not find it. The dowager had taken her out to pay a visit.

Mr. Carr was as good as his word, and got down in time for dinner. One glance at Lord Hartledon's face told him what he half expected to see—that the word of emancipation had not yet been spoken.

"Don't blame me, Carr. I shall speak to-night before I sleep, on my word of honour. Things have come to a crisis now; and if I wished to hold back I could not. I would say what a fool I have been not to speak before; only you know I'm one already."

Thomas Carr laughed.

"Mrs. Ashton has heard some tattle about Maude, and spoke to me this afternoon. Of course I could only deny it, my face feeling on fire with its sense of dishonour, for I don't think I ever told a deliberate lie in my life; and—and, in short, I should like my marriage with Anne to take place as soon as possible."

"Well, there's only one course to pursue, as I told you when I was down before. Tell Lady Maude the candid truth, and take shame and blame to yourself, as you deserve. Her having known of the engagement to Miss Ashton renders your task the easier."

Very restless was Lord Hartledon until the moment came. He knew the best time to speak to Maude would be immediately after dinner, whilst the countess-dowager took her usual nap. There was no hesitation now; and he speedily followed them upstairs, leaving his friend at the dinner-table.

He went up, feeling a desperate man. To those of his temperament having to make a disagreeable communication such as this is almost as cruel as parting with life.

No one was in the drawing-room but Lady Kirton—stretched upon a sofa and apparently fast asleep. Val crossed the carpet with softened tread to the adjoining rooms: small, comfortable rooms, used by the dowager in preference to the more stately rooms below. Maude had drawn aside the curtain and was peering out into the frosty night.

"Why, how soon you are up!" she cried, turning at his entrance.

"I came on purpose, Maude. I want to speak to you."

"Are you well?" she asked, coming forward to the fire, and taking her seat on a sofa. In truth, he did not look very well just then. "What is it?"

"Maude," he answered, his fair face flushing a dark red as he plunged into it blindfold: "I am a rogue and a fool!"

Lady Maude laughed. "Elster's folly!"

"Yes. You know all this time that we—that I—" (Val thought he should never flounder through this first moment, and did not remain an instant in one place as he talked)—"have been going on so foolishly, I was—almost as good as a married man."

"Were you?" said she, quietly. "Married to whom?"

"I said as good as married, Maude. You know I have been engaged for years to Miss Ashton; otherwise I would have *knelt* to ask you to become my wife, so earnestly should I desire it."

Her calm imperturbability presented a curious contrast to his agitation. She was regarding him with an amused smile.

"And, Maude, I have come now to ask you to release me. Indeed, I—"

"What's all this about?" broke in the countess-dowager, darting upon the conference, her face flushed and her head-dress awry. "Are you two quarrelling?"

"Val was attempting to explain something about Miss Ashton," answered Maude, rising from the sofa, and drawing herself up to her stately height. "He had better do it to you instead, mamma; I don't understand it."

She stood up by the mantelpiece, in the ray of the lustres. They fell across her dark, smooth hair, her flushed cheeks, her exquisite features. Her dress was of flowing white crêpe, with jet ornaments; and Lord Hartledon, even in the midst of his perplexity, thought how beautiful she was, and what a sad thing it was to lose her. The truth was, his senses had been caught by the girl's beauty although his heart was elsewhere. It is a very common case.

"The fact is, ma'am," he stammered, turning to the dowager in his desperation, "I have been behaving very foolishly of late, and am asking your daughter's pardon. I should have remembered my engagement to Miss Ashton."

"Remembered your engagement to Miss Ashton!" echoed the dowager, her voice becoming a little shrill. "What engagement?"

Lord Hartledon began to recover himself, though he looked foolish still. With these nervous men it is the first plunge that tells; get that over and they are brave as their fellows.

"I cannot marry two women, Lady Kirton, and I am bound to Anne."

The old dowager's voice toned down, and she pulled her black feathers straight upon her head.

"My dear Hartledon, I don't think you know what you are talking about. You engaged yourself to Maude some weeks ago."

"Well—but—whatever may have passed, engagement or no engagement, I could not legally do it," returned the unhappy young man, too considerate to say the engagement was hers, not his. "You knew I was bound to Anne, Lady Kirton."

"Bound to a fiddlestick!" said the dowager. "Excuse my plainness, Hartledon. When you engaged yourself to the young woman you were poor and a nobody, and the step was perhaps excusable. Lord Hartledon is not bound by the promises of Val Elster. All the young women in the kingdom, who have parsons for fathers, could not oblige him to be so."

"I am bound to her in honour; and"—in love he was going to say, but let the words die away unspoken.

"Hartledon, you are bound in honour to my daughter; you have sought her affections, and gained them. Ah, Percival, don't you know that it is you she has loved all along? In the days when I was worrying her about your brother, she cared only for you. You cannot be so infamous as to desert her."

"I wish to Heaven she had never seen me!" cried the unfortunate man, beginning to wonder whether he could break through these trammels. "I'd sacrifice myself willingly, if that would put things straight."

"You cannot sacrifice Maude. Look at her!" and the crafty old dowager flourished her hand towards the fireplace, where Maude stood in all her beauty. "A daughter of the house of Kirton cannot be taken up and cast aside at will. What would the world say of her?"

"The world need never know."

"Not know!" shrieked the dowager; "not know! Why, her trousseau is ordered, and some of the things have arrived. Good Heavens, Hartledon, you dare not trifle with Maude in this way. You could never show your face amongst men again."

"But neither dare I trifle with Anne Ashton," said Lord Hartledon, completely broken down by the gratuitous information. He saw that the situation was worse than even he had bargained for, and all his irresolution began to return upon him. "If I knew what was right to be done, I'm sure I'd do it."

"Right, did you say? Right? There cannot be a question about that. Which is the more fitting to grace your coronet: Maude, or a country parson's daughter?"

"I'm sure if this goes on I shall shoot myself," cried Val. "Taken to task at the Rectory, taken to task here—shooting would be bliss to it."

"No doubt," returned the dowager. "It can't be a very pleasant position for you. Any one but you would get out of it, and set the matter at rest."

"I should like to know how."

"So long as you are a single man they naturally remain on the high ropes at the Rectory, with their fine visions for Anne—"

"I wish you would understand once for all, Lady Kirton, that the Ashtons are our equals in every way," he interrupted: "and," he added, "in worth and goodness infinitely our superiors."

The dowager gave a sniff. "You think so, I know, Hart. Well, the only plan to bring you peace is this: make Maude your wife. At once; without delay."

The proposition took away Val's breath. "I could not do it, Lady Kirton. To begin with, they'd bring an action against me for breach of promise."

"Breach of nonsense!" wrathfully returned the dowager. "Was ever such a thing heard of yet, as a doctor of divinity bringing an action of that nature? He'd lose his gown."

"I wish I was at the bottom of a deep well, never to come up again!" mentally aspirated the unfortunate man.

"Will—you—marry—Maude?" demanded the dowager, with a fixed denunciation in every word, which was as so much slow torture to her victim.

"I wish I could. You must see for yourself, Lady Kirton, that I cannot. Maude must see it."

"I see nothing of the sort. You are bound to her in honour."

"All I can do is to remain single to the end of my days," said Val, after a pause. "I have been a great villain to both, and I cannot repair it to either. The one stands in the way of the other."

"But—"

"I beg your pardon, ma'am," he interrupted, so peremptorily that the old woman trembled for her power. "This is my final decision, and I will not hear another word. I feel ready to hang myself, as it is. You tell me I cannot marry any other than Maude without being a scoundrel; the same thing precisely applies to Anne. I shall remain single."

"You will give me one promise—for Maude's sake. Not, after this, to marry Anne Ashton."

"Why, how can I do it?" asked he, in tones of exasperation. "Don't you see that it is impossible? I shall not see the Ashtons again, ma'am; I would rather go a hundred miles the other way than face them."

The countess-dowager probably deemed she had said sufficient for safety; for she went out and shut the door after her. Lord Hartledon dashed his hair from his brow with a hasty hand, and was about to leave the room by the other door, when Maude came up to him.

"Is this to be the end of it, Percival?"

She spoke in tones of pain, of tremulous tenderness; all her pride gone out of her. Lord Hartledon laid his hand upon her shoulder, meeting the dark eyes that were raised to his through tears.

"Do you indeed love me like this, Maude? Somehow I never thought it."

"I love you better than the whole world. I love you enough to give up everything for you."

The emphasis conveyed a reproach—that he did not "give up everything" for her. But Lord Hartledon kept his head for once.

"Heaven knows my bitter repentance. If I could repair this folly of mine by any sacrifice on my own part, I would gladly do it. Let me go, Maude! I have been here long enough, unless I were more worthy. I would ask you to forgive me if I knew how to frame the petition."

　　　　　　　　　　　　　　　　　MRS. HENRY WOOD

She released the hand of which she had made a prisoner—released it with a movement of petulance; and Lord Hartledon quitted the room, the words she had just spoken beating their refrain on his brain. It did not occur to him in his gratified vanity to remember that Anne Ashton, about whose love there could be no doubt, never avowed it in those pretty speeches.

"Well?" said Mr. Carr, when he got back to the dining-room.

"It is not well, Carr; it is ill. There can be no release. The old dowager won't have it."

"But surely you will not resign Miss Ashton for Lady Maude!" cried the barrister, after a pause of amazement.

"I resign both; I see that I cannot do anything else in honour. Excuse me, Carr, but I'd rather not say any more about it just now; I feel half maddened."

"Elster's folly," mentally spoke Thomas Carr.

# XVII

## AN AGREEABLE WEDDING

That circumstances, combined with the countess-dowager, worked terribly against Lord Hartledon, events proved. Had the Ashtons remained at the Rectory all might have been well; but they went away, and he was left to any influence that might be brought to bear upon him.

How the climax was accomplished the world never knew. Lord Hartledon himself did not know the whole of it for a long while. As if unwilling to trust himself longer in dangerous companionship, he went up to town with Thomas Carr. Whilst there he received a letter from Cannes, written by Dr. Ashton; a letter that angered him.

It was a cool letter, a vein of contemptuous anger running through it; meant to be hidden, but nevertheless perceptible to Lord Hartledon. Its purport was to forbid all correspondence between him and Miss Ashton: things had better "remain in abeyance" until they met, ran the words, "if indeed any relations were ever renewed between them again."

It might have angered Lord Hartledon more than it did, but for the hopelessness which had taken up its abode within him. Nevertheless he resented it. He did not suppose it possible that the Ashtons could have heard of the dilemma he was in, or that he should be unable to fulfil his engagement with Anne, having with his usual vacillation put off any explanation with them; which of course must come sometime. He had taken an idea into his head long before, that Dr. Ashton wished to part them, and he looked upon the letter as resulting from that. Hartledon was feeling weary of the world.

How little did he divine that the letter of the doctor was called forth by a communication from the countess-dowager. An artful communication, with a charming candour lying on its surface. She asked—she actually asked that Dr. Ashton would allow "fair play;" she said the "deepest affection" had grown up between Lord Hartledon and Lady Maude; and she only craved that the young man might not be coerced either way, but might be allowed to choose between them. The field after Miss Ashton's return would be open to the two, and ought to be left so.

You may imagine the effect this missive produced upon the proud, high-minded doctor of divinity. He took a sheet of paper and wrote a stinging letter to Lord Hartledon, forbidding him to think again of Anne. But when he was in the act of sealing it a sudden doubt like an instinct rushed over him, whether it might not be a ruse, and nothing else, of the crafty old dowager's. The doubt was sufficiently strong to cause him to tear up the letter. But he was not satisfied with Lord Hartledon's own behaviour; had not been for some few months; and he then wrote a second letter, suspending matters until they should meet again. It was in effect what was asked for by the countess-dowager; and he wrote a cold proud letter to that lady, stating what he had done. Of course any honourable woman— any woman with a spark of justice in her heart—would have also forbidden all intercourse with Lady Maude. The countess-dowager's policy lay in the opposite direction.

But Lord Hartledon remained in London, utterly oblivious to the hints and baits held out for his return to Calne. He chiefly divided his time between the House of Lords and sitting at home, lamenting over his own ill-starred existence. He was living quite en garçon, with only one man, his house having been let for the season. We always want what we cannot obtain, and because marriage was denied him, he fell into the habit of dwelling upon it as the only boon in life. Thomas Carr was on circuit, so that Hartledon was alone.

Easter was early that year, the latter end of March. On the Monday in Passion-week there arrived a telegram for Lord Hartledon sent apparently by the butler, Hedges. It was vaguely worded; spoke of a railway accident and somebody dying. Who he could not make out, except that it was a Kirton: and it prayed him to hasten down immediately. All his goodness of heart aroused, Val lost not a moment. He had been engaged to spend Easter with some people in Essex, but dispatched a line of apology, and hastened down to Calne, wondering whether it was the dowager or Maude, and whether death would have taken place before his arrival.

"What accident has there been?" he demanded, leaping out of the carriage at Calne Station; and the man he addressed happened to be the porter, Jones.

"Accident?" returned Jones, touching his cap.

"An accident on the line; somewhere about here, I conclude. People wounded; dying."

"There has been no accident here," said Jones, in his sulky way. "Maybe your lordship's thinking of the one on the branch line, the bridge that fell in?"

"Nonsense," said Lord Hartledon, "that took place a fortnight ago. I received a telegram this morning from my butler, saying some one was dying at Hartledon from a railway accident," he impatiently added. "I took it to be either Lady Kirton or her daughter."

Mr. Jones swung round a large iron key he held in his hand, and light dawned upon him.

"I know now," he said. "There was a private accident at the station here last night; your lordship must mean that. A gentleman got out of a carriage before it stopped, and fell between the rail and the platform. His name was Kirton. I saw it on his portmanteau."

"Lord Kirton?"

"No, my lord. Captain Kirton."

"Was he seriously hurt?"

"Well, it was thought so. Mr. Hillary feared the leg would have to come off. He was carried to Hartledon."

Very much relieved, Lord Hartledon jumped into a fly and was driven home. The countess-dowager embraced him and fell into hysterics.

The crafty old dowager, whose displayed emotion was as genuine as she was! She had sent for this son of hers, hoping he might be a decoy-duck to draw Hartledon home again, for she was losing heart; and the accident, which she had not bargained for, was a very godsend to her.

"Why don't you word your telegrams more clearly, Hedges?" asked Lord Hartledon of his butler.

"It wasn't me worded it at all, my lord. Lady Kirton went to the station herself. She informed me she had sent it in my name."

"Has Hillary told you privately what the surgeons think of the case?"

"Better of it than they did at first, my lord. They are trying to save the leg."

This Captain Kirton was really the best of the Kirton bunch: a quiet, unassuming young man, somewhat delicate in health. Lord Hartledon was grieved for his accident, and helped to nurse him with the best heart in the world.

And now what devilry (there were people in Calne who called it nothing less) the old countess-dowager set afloat to secure her ends I am unable to tell you. She was a perfectly unscrupulous woman—

poverty had rendered her wits keen; and her captured lion was only feebly struggling to escape from the net. He was to blame also. Thrown again into the society of Maude and her beauty, Val basked in its sunshine, and went drifting down the stream, never heeding where the current led him. One day the countess-dowager put it upon his honour—he must marry Maude. He might have held out longer but for a letter that came from some friend of the dowager's opportunely located at Cannes; a letter that spoke of the approaching marriage of Miss Ashton to Colonel Barnaby, eldest son of a wealthy old baronet, who was sojourning there with his mother. No doubt was implied or expressed; the marriage was set forth as an assured fact.

"And I believe you meant to wait for her?" said the countess-dowager, as she put the letter into his hand, with a little laugh. "You are free now for my darling Maude."

"This may not be true," observed Lord Hartledon, with compressed lips. "Every one knows what this sort of gossip is worth."

"I happen to know that it is true," spoke Lady Kirton, in a whisper. "I have known of it for some time past, but would not vex you with it."

Well, she convinced him; and from that moment had it all her own way, and carried out her plots and plans according to her own crafty fancy. Lord Hartledon yielded; for the ascendency of Maude was strong upon him. And yet—and yet—whilst he gave all sorts of hard names to Anne Ashton's perfidy, lying down deep in his heart was a suspicion that the news was not true. How he hated himself for his wicked assumption of belief in after-years!

"You will be free as air," said the dowager, joyously. "You and Maude shall get ahead of Miss Ashton and her colonel, and have the laugh at them. The marriage shall be on Saturday, and you can go away together for months if you like, and get up your spirits again; I'm sure you have both been dull enough."

Lord Hartledon was certainly caught by the words "free as air;" as he had been once before. But he stared at the early day mentioned.

"Marriages can't be got up as soon as that."

"They can be got up in a day if people choose, with a special license; which, of course, you will have," said the dowager. "I'll arrange things, my dear Val; leave it all to me. I intend Maude to be married in the little chapel."

"What little chapel?"

"Your own private chapel."

Lord Hartledon stared with all his eyes. The private chapel, built out from the house on the side next Calne, had not been used for years and years.

"Why, it's all dust and rust inside; its cushions moth-eaten and fallen to pieces."

"Is it all dust and rust!" returned the dowager. "That shows how observant you are. I had it put in order whilst you were in London; it was a shame to let a sacred place remain in such a state. I should like it to be used for Maude; and mind, I'll see to everything; you need not give yourself any trouble at all. There's only one thing I must enjoin on you."

"What's that?"

"*Secrecy.* Don't let a hint of your intentions get abroad. Whatever you do, don't write a word to that Carr friend of yours; he's as sharp as a two-edged sword. As well let things be done privately; it is Maude's wish."

"I shall not write to him," cried Hartledon, feeling a sudden heat upon his face, "or to any one else."

"Here's Maude. Step this way, Maude. Hartledon wants the ceremony to take place on Saturday, and I have promised for you."

Lady Maude advanced; she had really come in by accident; her head was bent, her eyelashes rested on her flushed cheeks. A fair prize; very, very fair! The old dowager put her hand into Lord Hartledon's.

"You will love her and cherish her, Percival?"

What was the young man to do? He murmured some unintelligible assent, and bent forward to kiss her. But not until that moment had he positively realized the fact that there would be any marriage.

Time went on swimmingly until the Saturday, and everything was in progress. The old dowager deserved to be made commander of a garrison for her comprehensive strategy, the readiness and skill she displayed in carrying out her arrangements. For what reason, perhaps she could not have explained to herself; but an instinct was upon her that secrecy in all ways was necessary; at any rate, she felt surer of success whilst it was maintained. Hence her decision in regard to the unused little chapel; and that this one particular portion of the project had been long floating in her mind was proved by the fact that she had previously caused the chapel to be renovated. But that it was to serve her own turn, she would have let it remain choked up with dust for ever.

The special license had arrived; the young clergyman who was to perform the service was located at Hartledon. Seven o'clock was the hour fixed for the marriage: it would be twilight then, and dinner over. Immediately afterwards the bride and bridegroom were to depart. So far, so good. But Lady Kirton was not to have it quite her own way on this same Saturday, although she had enjoyed it hitherto.

A rumour reached her ears in the afternoon that Dr. Ashton was at the Rectory. The doctor had been spending Easter at Cannes, and the dowager had devoutly prayed that he might not yet return. The news turned her cheeks blue and yellow; a prevision rushing over her that if he and Lord Hartledon met there might be no wedding after all. She did her best to keep Lord Hartledon indoors, and the fact of the Rector's return from him.

Now who is going to defend Lord Hartledon? Not you or I. More foolish, more culpable weakness was never shown than in thus yielding to these schemes. Though ensnared by Maude's beauty, that was no excuse for him.

An accident—or what may be called one—delayed dinner. Two county friends of Hartledon's, jolly fox-hunters in the season, had come riding a long way across country, and looked in to beg some refreshment. The dowager fumed, and was not decently civil; but she did not see her way to turning them out.

They talked and laughed and ate; and dinner was indefinitely prolonged. When the dowager and Lady Maude rose from table the former cast a meaning look at Lord Hartledon. "Get rid of them as soon as you can," it plainly said.

But the fox-hunters liked good drinking as well as good eating, and sat on, enjoying their wine; their host, one of the most courteous of living men, giving no sign, by word or look, that he wished for their departure. He was rather silent, they observed; but the young clergyman, who made the fourth at the table, was voluble by nature. Captain Kirton had not yet left his sick bed.

Lady Maude sat alone in her room; the white robes upon her, the orthodox veil, meant to shade her fair face thrown back from it. She had sent away her attendants, bolted the door against her mother, and sat waiting her summons. Waiting and thinking. Her cheek rested on her hand, and her eyes were dreamy.

Is it true that whenever we are about to do an ill or unjust deed a shadow of the fruits it will bring comes over us as a warning? Some people will tell you so. A vision of the future seemed to rest on Maude Kirton as she sat there; and for the first time all the injustice of the approaching act rose in her mind as a solemn omen. The true facts were terribly distinct. Her own dislike (it was indeed no less than dislike) of the living lord, her lasting love for the dead one. All the miserable stratagems they had been guilty of to win him; the dishonest plotting and planning. What was she about to do? For her own advancement, to secure herself a position in the great world, and not for love, she was about to separate two hearts, which but for her would have been united in this world and the next. She was thrusting herself upon Lord Hartledon, knowing that in his true heart it was another that he loved, not her. Yes, she knew that full well. He admired her beauty, and was marrying her; marrying partly in pique against Anne Ashton; partly in blindfold submission to the deep schemes of her mother, brought to bear on his yielding nature. All the injustice done to Anne Ashton was in that moment beating its refrain upon her heart; and a thought crossed her—would God not avenge it? Another time she might have smiled at the thought as fanciful: it seemed awfully real now. "I might give Val up yet," she murmured; "there's just time."

She did not act upon the suggestion. Whether it was her warning, or whether it was not, she allowed it to slip from her. Hartledon's broad lands and coronet resumed their fascination over her soul; and when her door was tried, Lady Maude had lost herself in that famous Spanish château we have all occupied on occasion, touching the alterations she had mentally planned in their town-house.

"Goodness, Maude, what do you lock yourself in for?"

Maude opened the door, and the countess-dowager floundered in. She was resplendent in one of her old yellow satin gowns, a white turban with a silver feather, and a pink scarf thrown on for ornament. The colours would no doubt blend well by candlelight.

"Come, Maude. There's no time to be lost."

"Are the men gone?"

"Yes, they are gone; no thanks to Hartledon, though. He sat mooning on, never giving them the least hint to depart. Priddon told me so. I'll tell you what it is, Maude, you'll have to shake your husband out of no end of ridiculous habits."

"It is growing dark," exclaimed Maude, as she stepped into the corridor.

"Dark! of course it's dark," was the irascible answer; "and they have had to light up the chapel, or Priddon couldn't have seen to read his book. And all through those confounded fox-hunters!"

Lord Hartledon was not in the drawing-room, where Lady Kirton had left him only a minute before; and she looked round sharply.

"Has he gone on to the chapel?" she asked of the young clergyman.

"No, I think not," replied Mr. Priddon, who was already in his canonicals. "Hedges came in and said something to him, and they went out together."

A minute or two of impatience—she was in no mood to wait long—and then she rang the bell. It should be remarked that the old lady, either from excitement or some apprehension of failure, was shaking and jumping as if she had St. Vitus's dance. Hedges came in.

"Where's your master?" she tartly asked.

"With Mr. Carr, my lady."

"With Mr.—What did you say?"

"My lord is with Mr. Carr. He has just arrived."

A moment given to startled consternation and then the fury broke forth. The young parson had never had the pleasure of seeing one of these war-dances before, and backed against the wall in his starched surplice.

"What brings him here? How dare he come uninvited?"

"I heard him say, my lady, that finding he had a Sunday to spare, he thought he would come and pass it at Hartledon," said the well-trained Hedges.

Ere the words had left his lips Lord Hartledon and Mr. Carr were present; the latter in a state of utter amazement and in his travelling dress, having only removed his overcoat.

"You'll be my groomsman, Carr," said Hartledon. "We have no adherents; this is a strictly private affair."

"Did you send for Mr. Carr?" whispered the countess-dowager, looking white through her rouge.

"No; his coming has taken me by surprise," replied Hartledon, with a nervousness he could not wholly conceal.

They passed rapidly through the passages, marshalled by Hedges. Lord Hartledon led his bride, the countess-dowager walked with the clergyman, and Mr. Carr brought up the rear. The latter gentleman was wondering whether he had fallen into a dream that he should wake up from in the morning. The mode of procession was a little out of the common order of such affairs; but so was the marriage.

Now it happened, not very long before this, that Dr. Ashton was on his way home from a visit to a sick parishioner—a poor man, who said he believed life had been prolonged in him that his many years' minister should be at his deathbed. Dr. Ashton's road lay beyond Hartledon, and in returning he crossed the road, which brought him out near the river, between Hartledon and the Rectory. Happening to cast his eyes that way, he saw a light where he had never seen one before—in the little unused chapel. Peering through the trees at the two low diamond-paned windows, to make sure he was not mistaken, Dr. Ashton quickened his pace: his thoughts glancing at fire.

He was well acquainted with Hartledon; and making his way in by the nearest entrance, he dashed along the passages to the chapel, meeting at length one of the servants.

"John," he panted, quite out of breath with hurrying, "there's a light in the chapel. I fear it is on fire."

"Not at all, sir," replied the man. "We have been lighting it up for my lord's marriage. They have just gone in."

"Lighting it up for what?" exclaimed Dr. Ashton.

"For my lord's marriage, sir. He's marrying Lady Maude. It's the old dowager, sir, who has got it up in this queer way," continued the man, venturing on a little confidential gossip with his Rector.

Dr. Ashton paused to collect his wits ere he walked into the chapel. The few wax-candles the servants had been able to put about only served to make the gloom visible. The party were taking their places, the young clergyman directing them where to stand. He opened his book and was commencing, when a hand was laid upon Hartledon's shoulder.

"Lord Hartledon, what is the meaning of this?"

Lord Hartledon recognised the voice, and broke into a cold perspiration. He gave no answer; but the countess-dowager made up for his silence. Her temper, none of the mildest, had been considerably exasperated by the visit of the fox-hunters; it was made worse by the arrival of Mr. Carr. When she turned and saw what *this* formidable interruption was, she lost it altogether, as few, calling themselves gentlewomen, can lose it. As she peered into the face of Dr. Ashton, her own was scarlet and yellow, and her voice rose to a shriek.

"You prying parson, where did you spring from? Are you not ashamed to dodge Lord Hartledon in his own house? You might be taken up and imprisoned for it."

"Lord Hartledon," said Dr. Ashton, "I—"

"How dare you persist, I ask you?" shrieked the old woman, whilst the young clergyman stood aghast, and Mr. Carr folded his arms, and resolutely fixed his eyes on the floor. "Because Hartledon once had a flirtation with your daughter, does that give you leave to haunt him as if you were his double?"

"Madam," said Dr. Ashton, contriving still to subdue his anger, "I must, I will speak to Lord Hartledon. Allow me to do so without disturbance. Lord Hartledon, I wait for an answer: Are you about to marry this young lady?"

"Yes, he is," foamed the dowager; "I tell you so. Now then?"

"Then, madam," proceeded the doctor, "this marriage owes its rise to you. You will do well to consider whether you are doing them a kindness or an injury in permitting it. You have deliberately set yourself to frustrate the hopes of Lord Hartledon and my daughter: will a marriage, thus treacherously entered into, bring happiness with it?"

"Oh, you wicked man!" cried the dowager. "You would like to call a curse upon them."

"No," shuddered Dr. Ashton; "if a curse ever attends them, it will not be through any wish of mine. Lord Hartledon, I knew you as a boy; I have loved you as a son; and if I speak now, it is as your pastor, and for your own sake. This marriage looks very like a clandestine one, as though you were ashamed of the step you are taking, and dared not enter on it in the clear face of day. I would have you consider that this sort of proceeding does not usually bring a blessing with it."

If ever Val felt convicted of utter cowardice, he felt so then. All the wretched sophistry by which he had been beguiled into the step, by which he had beguiled himself; all the iniquity of his past conduct to Miss Ashton, rose up before his mind in its naked truth. He dared not reply to the doctor for very shame. A sorry figure he cut, standing there, Lady Maude beside him.

"The last time you entered my house, Lord Hartledon, it was to speak of your coming marriage with Anne—"

"And you would like him to go there again and arrange it," interrupted the incensed dowager, whose head had begun to nod so vehemently that she could not stop it. "Oh yes, I dare say!"

"By what right have you thus trifled with her?" continued the Rector, ignoring the nodding woman and her words, and confronting Lord Hartledon. "Is it a light matter, think you, to gain a maiden's best love, and then to desert her for a fresh face? You have been playing fast-and-loose for some little time: and I gave you more than one opportunity of retiring, if you so willed it—of openly retiring, you understand; not of doing so in this secret, disreputable manner. Your conscience will prick you in after-life, unless I am mistaken."

Val opened his lips, but the Rector put up his hand.

"A moment yet. That I am not endeavouring to recall Anne's claims on you in saying this, I am sure you are perfectly aware, knowing me as you do. I never deemed you worthy of her—you know that, Lord Hartledon; and you never were so. Were you a free man at this moment, and went down on your knees to implore me to give you Anne, I would not do it. You have forfeited her; you have forfeited the esteem of all good men. But that I am a Christian minister, I should visit your dishonour upon you as you deserve."

"Will you cease?" raved the dowager; and Dr. Ashton wheeled round upon her.

"There is less excuse for your past conduct, madam, than for his. You have played on Lord Hartledon's known irresolution to mould him to your will. I see now the aim of the letter you favoured me with at Cannes, when you requested, with so much candour, that he might be left for a time unfettered by any correspondence with Miss Ashton. Well, you have obtained your ends. Your covetous wish that you and your daughter should reign at Hartledon is on the point of being gratified. The honour of marrying Lady Maude was intended both by you and her for the late Lord Hartledon. Failing him, you transferred your hopes to the present one, regardless of who suffered, or what hearts or honour might be broken in the process."

"Will nobody put this disreputable parson outside?" raved the dowager.

"I do not seek to bring reproach home to you; let that, ladies, lie between yourselves and conscience. I only draw your attention to the facts; which have been sufficiently patent to the world, whatever Lord Hartledon may think. And now I have said my say, and leave you; but I declare that were I performing this burlesque of a marriage, as that young clergyman is about to do, I should feel my prayers for the divine blessing to attend it were but a vain mockery."

He turned to leave the chapel with quick steps, when Lord Hartledon, shaking off Maude, darted forward and caught his arm.

"You will tell me one thing at least: Is Anne *not* going to marry Colonel Barnaby?"

"Sir!" thundered the doctor. "Going to marry *whom*?"

"I heard it," he faltered. "I believed it to be the truth."

"You may have heard it, but you did not believe it, Lord Hartledon. You knew Anne better. Do not add this false excuse to the rest."

Pleasant! Infinitely so for the bridegroom's tingling ears. Dr. Ashton walked out of the chapel, and Val stood for a few moments where he was, looking up and down in the dim light. It might be that in his mental confusion he was deliberating what his course should be; but thought and common sense came to him, and he knew he could not desert Lady Maude, having brought matters so far to an end.

"Proceed," he said to the young clergyman, stalking back to the altar. "Get—it—over quickly."

Mr. Carr unfolded his arms and approached Lord Hartledon. He was the only one who had caught the expression of the bride's face when Hartledon dropped her arm. It spoke of bitter malice; it spoke, now that he had returned to her, of an evil triumph; and it occurred to Thomas Carr to think that he should not like a wife of his to be seen with that expression on her bridal face.

"Lord Hartledon, you must excuse me if I do not remain to countenance this wedding," he said in low but distinct tones. "Before hearing what I have heard from that good man, I had hesitated about it; but I was lost in surprise. Fare you well. I shall have left by the time you quit the chapel."

He held out his hand, and Val mechanically shook it. The retreating steps of Mr. Carr, following in the wake of Dr. Ashton, were heard, as Lord Hartledon spoke again to the clergyman with irritable sharpness:

"Why don't you begin?"

And the countess-dowager fanned herself complacently, and neither she nor Maude cared for the absence of a groomsman. But Maude was not quite hardened yet; and the shame of her situation was tingeing her eyelids.

# XVIII

## THE STRANGER

Lord Hartledon was leading his bride through the chapel at the conclusion of the ceremony, when his attention was caught by something outside one of the windows. At first he thought it was a black cat curled up in some impossible fashion, but soon saw it was a dark human face. And that face he discovered to be Mr. Pike's, peering earnestly in.

"Hedges, send that man away. How dare he intrude himself in this manner? How has he got up to the window?"

For these windows were high beyond the ordinary height of man. Hedges went out, a sharp reprimand on his tongue, and found that Mr. Pike had been at the trouble of carrying a heap of stones from a distance and piling them up to stand upon.

"Well, you must have a curiosity!" he exclaimed, in his surprise. "Just put those stones back in their places, and take yourself away."

"You are right," said the man. "I have a curiosity in all that concerns the new lord. But I am going away now."

He leaped down as he spoke, and began to replace the stones. Hedges went in again.

The carriage, waiting to convey them away, was already at the door, the impatient horses pawing the ground. Maude changed her dress with all speed; and in driving down the road by starlight they overtook Thomas Carr, carrying his own portmanteau. Lord Hartledon let down the window impulsively, as if he would have spoken, but seemed to recollect himself, and drew it up again.

"What is it?" asked Maude.

"Mr. Carr."

It was the first word he had spoken to her since the ceremony. His silence had frightened her: what if he should resent on *her* the cruel words spoken by Dr. Ashton? Sick, trembling, her beautiful face humble and tearful enough now, she bent it on his shoulder in a shower of bitter tears.

"Oh, Percival, Percival! surely you are not going to punish me for what has passed?"

A moment's struggle with himself, and he turned and took both her hands in his.

"It may be that neither of us is free from blame, Maude, in regard to the past. All we can now do, as it seems to me, is to forget it together, and make the best of the future."

"And you will forget Anne Ashton?" she whispered.

"Of course I shall forget her. I ask nothing better than to forget her from this moment. I have made *you* my wife; and I will try to make your happiness."

He bent and kissed her face. Maude, in some restlessness, as it seemed, withdrew to her own corner of the carriage and cried softly; and Lord Hartledon let down the glass again to look back after Thomas Carr and his portmanteau in the starlight.

The only perfectly satisfied person was the countess-dowager. All the little annoying hindrances went for nothing now that the desired end was accomplished, and she was in high feather when she bade adieu to the amiable young clergyman, who had to depart that night for his curacy, ten miles away, to be in readiness for the morrow's services.

"If you please, my lady, Captain Kirton has been asking for you once or twice," said Hedges, entering the dowager's private sitting-room.

"Then Captain Kirton must ask," retorted the dowager, who was sitting down to her letters, which she had left unopened since their arrival in the morning, in her anxiety for other interests. "Hedges, I should like some supper: I had only a scrambling sort of dinner. You can bring it up here. Something nice; and a bottle of champagne."

Hedges withdrew with the order, and Lady Kirton applied herself to her letters. The first she opened was from the daughter who had married the French count. It told a pitiful tale of distress, and humbly craved to be permitted to come over on a fortnight's visit, she and her two sickly children, "for a little change."

"I dare say!" emphatically cried the dowager. "What next? No, thank you, my lady; now that I have at least a firm footing in this house—as that blessed parson said—I am not going to risk it by filling it with every bothering child I possess. Bob departs as soon as his leg's well. Why what's this?"

She had come upon a concluding line as she was returning the letter to the envelope. "P.S. If I don't hear from you *very* decisively to the contrary, I shall come, and trust to your good nature to forgive it. I want to see Bob."

"Oh, that's it, is it!" said the dowager. "She means to come, whether I will or no. That girl always had enough impudence for a dozen."

Drawing a sheet of paper out of her desk, she wrote a few rapid lines.

> Dear Jane,
>
> "For *mercy's* sake keep those *poor* children and yourself *away*! We have had an *aweful infectious fever* rageing in the place, which it was thought to be *cured*, but it's on the break *out* again-several *deaths*, Hartledon and Maude (*married* of course) have gone out of its reach and I'm thinking of it if *Bob's* leg which is *better* permits. You'd not like I dare say to see the children in a *coffin apiece* and yourself in a *third*, as might be the end. *Small-pox* is raging at *Garchester* a neighbouring town, that *will* be awful if it gets to *us* and I *hear* it's on the *road* and with kind love *believe* me your *affectionate*
>
> MOTHER
>
> "P.S. I am sorry for *what* you tell me about *Ugo* and the *state* of affairs chey vous. But you know you *would marry* him so there's *nobody* to blame. Ah! *Maude* has gone by *my* advice and done as *I* said and the consequence is *she's* a peeress for life and got a handsome young husband *without* a *will* of his own."

The countess-dowager was not very adroit at spelling and composition, whether French or English, as you observe. She made an end of her correspondence, and sat down to a delicious little supper alone; as she best liked to enjoy these treats. The champagne was excellent, and she poured out a full tumbler of it at once, by way of wishing good luck to Maude's triumphant wedding.

"And it *is* a triumph!" she said, as she put down the empty glass. "I hope it will bring Jane and the rest to a sense of *their* folly."

A triumph? If you could only have looked into the future, Lady Kirton! A triumph!

The above was not the only letter written that evening. At the hotel where Lord and Lady Hartledon halted for the night, when she had retired under convoy of her maid, then Val's restrained remorse broke out. He paced the room in a sort of mad restlessness; in the midst of which he suddenly sat down to a table on which lay pens, ink, and paper, and poured forth hasty sentences in his mind's wretched tumult.

My Dear Mrs. Ashton,

"I cannot address you in any more formal words, although you will have reason to fling down the letter at my presuming to use these now—for dear, most dear, you will ever be to me.

"What can I say? Why do I write to you? Indeed to the latter question I can only answer I do not know, save that some instinct of good feeling, not utterly dead within me, is urging me to it.

"Will you let me for a moment throw conventionality aside; will you for that brief space of time let me speak truly and freely to you, as one might speak who has passed the confines of this world?

"When a man behaves to a woman as I, to my eternal shame, have this day behaved to Anne, it is, I think, a common custom to regard the false man as having achieved a sort of triumph; to attribute somewhat of humiliation to the other.

"Dear Mrs. Ashton, I cannot sleep until I have said to you that in my case the very contrary is the fact. A more abject, humiliated man than I stand at this hour in my own eyes never yet took his sins upon his soul. Even you might be appeased if you could look into mine and see its sense of degradation.

"That my punishment has already come home to me is only just; that I shall have to conceal it from all the world, including my wife, will not lessen its sting.

"I have this evening married Maude Kirton. I might tell you of unfair play brought to bear upon me, of a positive assurance, apparently well grounded, that Anne had entered into an engagement to wed another, could I admit that these facts were any excuse for me. They are no excuse; not the slightest palliation. My own yielding folly alone is to blame, and I shall take shame to myself for ever.

"I write this to you as I might have written it to my own mother, were she living; not as an expiation; only to tell of my pain; that I am not utterly hardened; that I would sue on my knees for pardon, were it not shut out from me by my own act. There is no pardon for such as I. When you have torn it in pieces, you will, I trust, forget the writer.

"God bless you, dear Mrs. Ashton! God bless and comfort another who is dear to you!—and believe me with true undying remorse your once attached friend,

Hartledon

It was a curious letter to write; but men of Lord Hartledon's sensitive temperament in regard to others' feelings often do strange things; things the world at large would stare at in their inability to understand them. The remorse might not have come home to him quite so soon as this, his wedding-day, but for the inopportune appearance of Dr. Ashton in the chapel, speaking those words that told home so forcibly. Such reproach on these vacillating men inflicts a torture that burns into the heart like living fire.

He sealed the letter, addressing it to Cannes; called a waiter, late as it was, and desired him to post it. And then he walked about the room, reflecting on the curse of his life—his besetting sin—irresolution. It seemed almost an anomaly for *him* to make resolves; but he did make one then; that he would, with the help of Heaven, be a MAN from henceforth, however it might crucify his sensitive feelings. And for the future, the obligation he had that day taken upon himself he determined to fulfil to his uttermost in all honour and love; to cherish his wife as he would have cherished Anne Ashton. For the past—but Lord Hartledon rose up now with a start. There was one item of that past he dared not glance at, which did not, however, relate to Miss Ashton: and it appeared inclined to thrust itself prominently forward to-night.

Could Lord Hartledon have borrowed somewhat of the easy indifference of the countess-dowager, he had been a happier man. That lady would have made a female Nero, enjoying herself while Rome was burning. She remained on in her snug quarters at Hartledon, and lived in clover.

One evening, rather more than a week after the marriage, Hedges had been on an errand to Calne, and was hastening home. In the lonely part of the road near Hartledon, upon turning a sharp corner, he came upon Mirrable, who was standing talking to Pike, very much to the butler's surprise. Pike walked away at once; and the butler spoke.

"He is not an acquaintance of yours, that man, Mrs. Mirrable?"

"Indeed no," she answered, tossing her head. "It was like his impudence to stop me. Rather flurried me too," she continued: and indeed Hedges noticed that she seemed flurried.

"What did he stop you for? To beg?"

"Not that. I've never heard that he does beg. He accosted me with a cool question as to when his lordship was coming back to Hartledon. I answered that it could not be any business of his. And then you came up."

"He is uncommon curious as to my lord. I can't make it out. I've seen him prowling about the grounds: and the night of the marriage he was mounted up at the chapel window. Lord Hartledon saw him, too. I should like to know what he wants."

"By a half-word he let drop, I fancy he has a crotchet in his head that his lordship will find him some work when he comes home. But I must go on my way," added Mirrable. "Mrs. Gum's not well, and I sent word I'd look in for half-an-hour this evening."

Hedges had to go on his way also, for it was close upon the countess-dowager's dinner-hour, at which ceremony he must attend. Putting his best foot forward, he walked at more than an ordinary pace, and overtook a gentleman almost at the very door of Hartledon. The stranger was approaching the front entrance, Hedges was wheeling off to the back; but the former turned and spoke. A tall, broad-shouldered, grey-haired man, with high cheek-bones. Hedges took him for a clergyman from his attire; black, with a white neckcloth.

"This is Hartledon House, I believe," he said, speaking with a Scotch accent.

"Yes, sir."

"Do you belong to it?"

"I am Lord Hartledon's butler."

"Is Lord Hartledon at home?"

"No, sir. He is in France."

"I read a notice of his marriage in the public papers," continued the stranger, whose eyes were fixed on Hedges. "It was, I suppose, a correct one?"

"My lord was married the week before last: about ten or eleven days ago."

"Ay; April the fourteenth, the paper said. She is one of the Kirton family. When do you expect him home?"

"I don't know at all, sir. I've not heard anything about it."

"He is in France, you say, Paris, I suppose. Can you furnish me with his address?"

Up to this point the colloquy had proceeded smoothly on both sides: but it suddenly flashed into the mind of Hedges that the stranger's manner was somewhat mysterious, though in what the mystery lay he could not have defined. The communicative man, true to the interests of his master, became cautious at once: he supposed some of Lord Hartledon's worries, contracted when he was Mr. Elster, were returning upon him.

"I cannot give his address, sir. And for the matter of that, it might not be of use if I could. Lord and Lady Hartledon did not intend remaining any length of time in one place."

The stranger had dug the point of his umbrella into the level greensward that bounded the gravel, and swayed the handle about with his hand, pausing in thought.

"I have come a long way to see Lord Hartledon," he observed. "It might be less trouble and cost for me to go on to Paris and see him there, than to start back for home, and come here again when he returns to England. Are you sure you can't give me his address?"

"I'm very sorry I can't, sir. There was a talk of their going on to Switzerland," continued Hedges, improvising the journey, "and so coming back through Germany; and there *was* a talk of their making Italy before the heat came on, and stopping there. Any way, sir, I dare say they are already away from Paris."

The stranger regarded Hedges attentively, rather to the discomfiture of that functionary, who thought he was doubted. He then asked a great many questions, some about Lord Hartledon's personal habits, some about Lady Maude: the butler answered them freely or cautiously, as he thought he might, feeling inclined all the while to chase the intruder off the premises. Presently he turned his attention on the house.

"A fine old place, this, Mr. Butler."

"Yes, sir."

"I suppose I could look over it, if I wished?"

Hedges hesitated. He was privately asking himself whether the law would allow the stranger, if he had come after any debt of Lord Hartledon's, to refuse to leave the house, once he got into it.

"I could ask Lady Kirton, sir, if you particularly wished it."

"Lady Kirton? You have some one in the house, then!"

"The Dowager Lady Kirton's here, sir. One of her sons also—Captain Kirton; but he is confined to his room."

"Then I would rather not go in," said the stranger quickly. "I'm very disappointed to have come all this way and not find Lord Hartledon."

"Can I forward any letter for you, sir? If you'd like to intrust one to me, I'll send it as soon as we know of any certain address."

"No—no, I think not," said the stranger, musingly. "There might be danger," he muttered to himself, but Hedges caught the words.

He stood swaying the umbrella-handle about, looking down at it, as if that would assist his decision. Then he looked at Hedges.

"My business with Lord Hartledon is quite private, and I would rather not write. I'll wait until he is back in England: and see him then."

"What name, sir?" asked Hedges, as the stranger turned away.

"I would prefer not to leave my name," was the candid answer. "Good evening."

He walked briskly down the avenue, and Hedges stood looking after him, slightly puzzled in his mind.

"I don't believe it's a creditor; that I don't. He looks like a parson to me. But it's some trouble though, if it's not debt. 'Danger' was the word: 'there might be danger.' Danger in writing, he meant. Any way, I'm glad he didn't go in to that ferreting old dowager. And whatever it may be, his lordship's able to pay it now."

# XIX

## A Chance Meeting

Some few weeks went by. On a fine June morning Lord and Lady Hartledon were breakfasting at their hotel in the Rue Rivoli. She was listlessly playing with her cup; he was glancing over *Galignani's*.

"Maude," he suddenly exclaimed, "the fountains are to play on Sunday at Versailles. Will you go to see them?"

"I am tired of sight-seeing, and tired of Paris too," was Lady Hartledon's answer, spoken with apathy.

"Are you?" he returned, with animation, as though not sorry to hear the avowal. "Then we won't stay in Paris any longer. When shall we leave?"

"Are the letters not late this morning?" she asked, allowing the question to pass.

Lord Hartledon glanced at the clock. "Very late: and we are late also. Are you expecting any in particular?"

"I don't know. This chocolate is cold."

"That is easily remedied," said he, rising to ring the bell. "They can bring in some fresh."

"And keep us waiting half-an-hour!" she grumbled.

"The hotel is crammed up to the mansarde," said good-natured Lord Hartledon, who was easily pleased, and rather tolerant of neglect in French hotels. "Is not that the right word, Maude? You took me to task yesterday for saying garret. The servants are run off their legs."

"Then the hotel should keep more servants. I am quite sick of having to ring twice. A week ago I wished I was out of the place."

"My dear Maude, why did you not say so? If you'd like to go on at once to Germany—"

"Lettres et journal pour monsieur," interrupted a waiter, entering with two letters and the *Times*.

"One for you, Maude," handing a letter to his wife. "Don't go," he continued to the waiter; "we want some more chocolate; this is cold. Tell him in French, Maude."

But Lady Hartledon did not hear; or if she heard, did not heed; she was already absorbed in the contents of her letter.

MRS. HENRY WOOD

"Ici," said Hartledon, pushing the chocolate-pot towards the man, and rallying the best French he could command, "encore du chocolat. Toute froide, *this*. Et puis dépêchez vous; il est tarde, et nous avons besoin de sortir."

The man was accustomed to the French of Englishmen, and withdrew without moving a muscle of his face. But Lady Hartledon's ears had been set on edge.

"*Don't* attempt French again, Val. They'll understand you if you speak in English."

"Did I make any mistake?" he asked good-humouredly. "I could speak French once; but am out of practice. It's the genders bother one."

"Fine French it must have been!" thought her ladyship. "Who is your letter from?"

"My bankers, I think. About Germany, Maude—would you like to go there?"

"Yes. Later. After we have been to London."

"To London!"

"We will go to London at once, Percival; stay there for the rest of the season, and then—"

"My dear," he interrupted, his face overcast, "the season is nearly over. It will be of no use going there now."

"Plenty of use. We shall have quite six weeks of it. Don't look cross, Val; I have set my heart upon it."

"But have you considered the difficulties? In the first place, we have no house in town; in the second—"

"Oh yes we have: a very good house."

Lord Hartledon paused, and looked at her; he thought she was joking. "Where is it?" he asked in merry tones; "at the top of the Monument?"

"It is in Piccadilly," she coolly replied. "Do you remember, some days ago, I read out an advertisement of a house that was to be let there for the remainder of the season, and remarked that it would suit us?"

"That it might suit us, had we wanted one," put in Val.

"I wrote off at once to mamma, and begged her to see after it and engage it for us," she continued, disregarding her husband's amendment. "She now tells me she has done so, and ordered servants up from Hartledon. By the time this letter reaches me she says it will be in readiness."

Lord Hartledon in his astonishment could scarcely find words to reply. "You wrote—yourself—and ordered the house to be taken?"

"Yes. You are difficult to convince, Val."

"Then I think it was your duty to have first consulted me, Lady Maude," he said, feeling deeply mortified.

"Thank you," she laughed. "I have not been Lady Maude this two months."

"I beg your pardon, Lady Hartledon."

"Now don't pretend to be offended, Val. I have only saved you trouble."

"Maude," he said, rallying his good humour, "it was not right. Let us—for Heaven's sake let us begin as we mean to go on: our interests must be *one*, not separate. Why did you not tell me you wished to return to London, and allow me to see after an abode for us? It would have been the proper way."

"Well, the truth is, I saw you did not want to go; you kept holding back from it; and if I *had* spoken you would have shillyshallied over it until the season was over. Every one I know is in London now."

The waiter entered with the fresh chocolate, and retired again. Lord Hartledon was standing at the window then. His wife went up to him, and stole her hand within his arm.

"I'm sorry if I have offended you, Val. It's no great matter to have done."

"I think it was, Maude. However—don't act for yourself in future; let me know your wishes. I do not think you have expressed a wish, or half a wish, since our marriage, but I have felt a pleasure in gratifying it."

"You good old fellow! But I am given to having a will of my own, and to act independently. I'm like mamma in that. Val, we will start to-morrow: have you any orders for the servants? I can transmit them through mamma."

"I have no orders. This is your expedition, Maude, not mine; and, I assure you, I feel like a man in utter darkness in regard to it. Allow me to see your mother's letter."

Lady Hartledon had put the letter safely into her pocket.

"I would rather not, Percival: it contains a few private words to myself, and mamma has always an objection to her letters being shown. I'll read you all necessary particulars. You must let me have some money to-day."

"How much?" asked he, from between his compressed lips.

"Oceans. I owe for millinery and things. And, Val, I'll go to Versailles this afternoon, if you like. I want to see some of the rooms again."

"Very well," he answered.

She poured out some chocolate, took it hurriedly, and quitted the room, leaving her husband in a disheartening reverie. That Lady

Hartledon and Maude Kirton were two very distinct persons he had discovered already; the one had been all gentleness and childlike suavity, the other was positive, extravagant, and self-willed; the one had made a pretence of loving him beyond all other things in life, the other was making very little show of loving him at all, or of concealing her indifference. Lord Hartledon was not the only husband who has been disagreeably astonished by a similar metamorphosis.

The following was the letter of the countess-dowager:

Darling Maude,

"I have *secured* the *house* you write about and send by this *post* for Hedges and a few of the rest from *Hartledon*. It won't accommodate a large *establishment* I can tell you and you'll be *disappointed* when you come over to take *possession* which you can do when you *choose*. Val was a *fool* for letting his town house in the spring but of course we know he is *one* and must put up with it. Whatever you *do*, don't *consult* him about *any earthly thing* take *your own way*, he never did have *much* of a will and you must let him *have none* for the future. You've got a splendid *chance* can spend *what you like* and rule in *society* and he'll subside into a *tame spaniel*.

"Maude if you are such an idiot I'll *shake* you. Find you've made a *dredful* mistake?—can't bear your husband?—keep thinking always of *Edward*? A child might write such utter *rubish* but not you, what does it matter whether one's husband is *liked* or *disliked*, provided he gives one *position* and *wealth*? Go to Amiens and stop with *Jane* for a *week* and see her *plight* and then grumble at your own, you *are* an idiot.

"I'm quite *glad* about your taking this town-*house*, and shall enter into *posession* myself as soon as the servants are up, and await you. *Bob's* quite *well* and joins to-day and of course *gives up* his lodgings, which have been *wretchedly confined* and uncomfortable and where I should have gone to but for this *move* of yours I don't know. Mind you bring me over a Parisian *bonnet* or two or some articles of that *sort*. I'm nearly in *rags*, Kirton's as undutiful as he *can* be but it's that *wife* of his.

Your affectionate mother,
C. Kirton

The letter will give you some guide to the policy of Maude Hartledon since her marriage. She did find she had made a mistake. She cared no more for her husband now than she had cared for him before; and it was a positive fact that she despised him for walking so tamely into the snare laid for him by herself and her mother. Nevertheless she triumphed; he had made her a peeress, and she did care for that; she cared also for the broad lands of Hartledon. That she was unwise in assuming her own will so promptly, with little regard to consulting his, she might yet discover.

At Versailles that day—to which place they went in accordance with Maude's wish—there occurred a rencontre which Lord Hartledon would willingly have gone to the very ends of the earth to avoid. It happened to be rather full for Versailles; many of the visitors in Paris apparently having taken it into their minds to go; indeed, Maude's wish was induced by the fact that some of her acquaintances in the gay capital were going also.

You may possibly remember a very small room in the galleries, exceedingly small as compared with the rest, chiefly hung with English portraits. They were in this room, amidst the little crowd that filled it, when Lord Hartledon became aware that his wife had encountered some long-lost friend. There was much greeting and shaking of hands. He caught the name—Kattle; and being a somewhat singular name, he recognised it for that of the lady who had been sojourning at Cannes, and had sent the news of Miss Ashton's supposed engagement to the countess-dowager. There was the usual babble on both sides—where each was staying, had been staying, would be staying; and then Lord Hartledon heard the following words from Mrs. Kattle.

"How strange I should have seen you! I have met you, the Fords, and the Ashtons here, and did not know that any of you were in Paris. It's true I only arrived yesterday. Such a long illness, my dear, I had at Turin!"

"The Ashtons!" involuntarily repeated Maude. "Are they here?—in the château?" And it instantly occurred to her how she should like to meet them, and parade her triumph. If ever a spark of feeling for her husband arose within Maude's heart, it was when she thought of Anne Ashton. She was bitterly jealous of her still.

"Yes, here; I saw them not three minutes ago. They are only now on their road home from Cannes. Fancy their making so long a stay!"

"You wrote mamma word that Miss Ashton was about to marry some Colonel Barnaby."

Mrs. Kattle laughed. It is possible that written news might have been *asked for* by the countess-dowager.

"Well, my dear, and so I did; but it turned out to be a mistake. He did admire her; there was no mistake about that; and I dare say she might have had him if she liked. How's your brother and his poor leg?"

"Oh, he is well," answered Maude. "Au revoir; I can't stand this crush any longer."

It was really a crush just then in the room; and though Maude escaped from it dexterously, Lord Hartledon did not. He was wedged in behind some stout women, and had the pleasure of hearing another word or two from Mrs. Kattle.

"Who was that?" asked a lady, who appeared to be her companion.

"Lady Hartledon. He was only the younger brother until a few months ago, but the elder one got drowned in some inexplicable manner on his own estate, and this one came into the title. The old dowager began at once to angle for him, and succeeded in hooking him. She used to write me word how it progressed."

"She is very beautiful."

"Very."

Lord Hartledon made his escape, and found his wife looking round for him. She was struck by the aspect of his face.

"Are you ill, Percival?"

"Ill? No. But I don't care how soon we get out of these rooms. I can't think what brings so many people in them to-day."

"He has heard that *she's* here, and would like to avoid her," thought Maude as she took the arm he held out. "The large rooms are empty enough, I'm sure," she remarked. "Shall we have time to go to the Trianon?"

"If you like. Yes."

He began to hurry through the rooms. Maude, however, was in no mood to be hurried, but stopped here and stopped there. All at once they met a large party of friends; those she had originally expected to meet. Quitting her husband's arm, she became lost amongst them.

There was no help for it; and Lord Hartledon, resigning himself to the detention, took up his standing before the pictures and stared at them, his back to the room. He saw a good deal to interest him, in spite of his rather tumultuous state of mind, and remained there until he found himself surrounded by other spectators. Turning hastily with a view to escaping, he trod upon a lady's dress. She looked up at his word of apology, and they stood face to face—himself and Miss Ashton!

That both utterly lost their presence of mind would have been conclusive to the spectators, had any regarded them; but none did so. They were strangers amidst the crowd. For the space of a moment each gazed on the other, spell-bound. Lord Hartledon's honest blue eyes were riveted on her face with a strangely yearning expression of repentance—her sweet face, which had turned as white as ashes. He wore mourning still for his brother, and was the most distinguished-looking man in the château that day. Anne was in a trailing lilac silk, with a white gossamer-bonnet. That the heart of each went out to the other, as it had perhaps never gone out before, it may be no sin to say. Sin or no sin, it was the truth. The real value of a thing, as you know, is never felt until it is lost. For two months each had been dutifully striving to forget the other, and believed they were succeeding; and this first accidental meeting roused up the past in all its fever of passion.

No more conscious of what he did than if he had been in a dream, Lord Hartledon held out his hand; and she, quite as unconscious, mechanically met it with hers. What confused words of greeting went forth from his lips he never knew; she as little; but this state of bewildered feeling lasted only a minute; recollection came to both, and she strove to withdraw her hand to retreat.

"God bless you, Anne!" was all he whispered, his fervent words marred by their tone of pain; and he wrung her hand as he released it.

Turning away he caught the eyes of his wife riveted on them; she had evidently seen the meeting, and her colour was high. Lord Hartledon walked straight into the next room, and Maude went up to Anne.

"How do you do, Miss Ashton? I am so glad to meet you. I have just heard you were here from Mrs. Kattle. You have been speaking to my husband."

Anne bowed; she did not lose her presence of mind at *this* encounter. A few civil words of reply given with courteous dignity, and she moved away with a bright flush on her cheek, towards Dr. and Mrs. Ashton, who were standing arm-in-arm enraptured before a remote picture, cognizant of nothing else.

"How thin she looks!" exclaimed Maude, as she rejoined her husband, and took his arm.

"Who looks thin?"

"Miss Ashton. I wonder she did not fling your hand away, instead of putting her own into it!"

"Do you wish to see the Trianon? We shall be late."

"Yes, I do wish to see it. But you need not speak in that tone: it was not my fault that we met her."

He answered never a syllable. His lips were compressed to pain, and his face was hectic; but he would not be drawn into reproaching his wife by so much as a word, for the sort of taste she was displaying. The manner in which he had treated Miss Ashton and her family was ever in his mind, more or less, in all its bitter, humiliating disgrace. The worst part of it to Val was, that there could be no reparation.

The following day Lord Hartledon and his wife took their departure from Paris; and if anything could have imparted especial gratification on his arriving in London at the hired house, it was to find that his wife's mother was not in it. Val had come home against his will; he had not wished to be in London that season; rather would he have buried himself and his haunting sense of shame on the tolerant Continent; and he certainly had not wished his wife to make her debut in a small hired house. When he let his own, nothing could have been further from his thoughts than marriage. As to this house—Lady Kirton had told her daughter she would be disappointed in it; but when Maude saw its dimensions, its shabby entrance, its want of style altogether, she was dismayed. "And after that glowing advertisement!" she breathed resentfully. It was one of the smallest houses facing the Green Park.

Hedges came forward with an apology from the countess-dowager. An apology for not invading their house and inflicting her presence upon them uninvited! A telegraphic despatch from Lord Kirton had summoned her to Ireland on the previous day; and Val's face grew bright as he heard it.

"What was the matter, Hedges?" inquired his mistress. "I'm sure my brother would not telegraph unless it was something."

"The message didn't say, my lady. It was just a few words, asking her ladyship to go off by the first train, but giving no reason."

"I wonder she went, then," observed Val to his wife, as they looked into the different rooms. But Maude did not wonder: she knew how anxious her mother was to be on good terms with her eldest son, from whom she received occasional supplies. Rather would she quarrel with the whole world than with him.

"I think it a good thing she has gone, Maude," said he. "There certainly would not have been room for her and for us in this house."

"And so do I," answered Maude, looking round her bed-chamber. "If mamma fancies she's going to inflict herself upon us for good she's mistaken. She and I might quarrel, perhaps; for I know she'd try to control me. Val, what are we to do in this small house?"

"The best we can. We have made the bargain, you know, and taken possession now."

"You are laughing. I declare I think you are glad it has turned out what it is!"

"I am not sorry," he avowed. "You'll let me cater for you another time, Maude."

She put up her face to be kissed. "Don't be angry with me. It is our home-coming."

"Angry!" he repeated. "I have never shown anger to you yet, Maude. Never a woman had a more indulgent husband than you shall have in me."

"You don't say a loving one, Val!"

"And a loving one also: if you will only let me be so."

"What do you mean?"

"Love requires love in return. We shall be happy, I am sure, if you so will it. Only let us pull together; one mind, one interest. Here's your maid. I wonder where my dressing room is?"

And thus they entered on what remained of the London season. The newspapers announced the arrival of Lord and Lady Hartledon, and Maude read it aloud to her husband. She might have retained peace longer, however, had that announcement not gone forth to the four corners of the land.

"Only let us pull together!" A very few days indeed sufficed to dissipate that illusion. Lady Hartledon plunged madly into all the gaieties of the dying season, as though to make up for lost time; Lord Hartledon never felt less inclined to plunge into anything, unless it was the waters of oblivion. He held back from some places, but she did not appear to care, going her way in a very positive, off-hand manner, according to her own will, and paying not the slightest deference to his.

# XX

## The Stranger Again

On a burning day at the end of June, Lord Hartledon was walking towards the Temple. He had not yet sought out his friend Thomas Carr; a sense of shame held him back; but he was on his way to do so now.

Turning down Essex Street and so to the left, he traversed the courts and windings, and mounted the stairs to the barrister's rooms. Many a merry hour had he passed in those three small rooms, dignified with the name of "Mr. Carr's chambers," but which were in fact also Mr. Carr's dwelling-place—and some sad ones.

Lord Hartledon knocked at the outer door with his stick—a somewhat faint, doubtful knock; not with the free hand of one at ease with himself and the world. For one thing, he was uncertain as to the reception he should meet with.

Mr. Carr came to the door himself; his clerk was out. When he saw who was his visitor he stood in comic surprise. Val stepped in, extending his hand; and it was heartily taken.

"You are not offended with me, then, Carr?"

"Nay," said Mr. Carr, "I have no reason to be offended. Your sin was not against me."

"That's a strong word, 'sin.'"

"It is spoken," was the answer; "but I need not speak it again. I don't intend to quarrel with you. I was not, I repeat, the injured party."

"Yet you took yourself off in dudgeon, as though you were, leaving me without a groomsman."

"I would not remain to witness a marriage that—that you ought not to have entered upon."

"Well, it's done and over, and need not be brought up again," returned Hartledon, a shade of annoyance in his tones.

"Certainly not. I have no wish or right to bring it up. How is Lady Hartledon?"

"She is very well. And now what has kept you away, Carr? We have been in London nearly a fortnight, and you've never been near me. I thought you *were* going to quarrel."

"I did not know you had returned."

"Not know it! Why all the newspapers had it in amongst the 'fashionable intelligence.'"

"I have more to do with my time than to look at the fashionable portion of the papers. Not being fashionable myself, it doesn't interest me."

"Yes, it's about a fortnight since we came back to this hateful place," returned Hartledon, his light tone subsiding into seriousness. "I am out of conceit with England just now; and would far rather have gone to the Antipodes."

"Then why did you come back to it?" inquired the barrister, in surprise.

"My wife gave me no choice. She possesses a will of her own. It is the ordinary thing, perhaps, for wives to do so."

"Some do, and some don't," observed Thomas Carr, who never flattered at the expense of truth. "Are you going down to Hartledon?"

"Hartledon!" with a perceptible shiver. "In the mind I am in, I shall never visit Hartledon again; there are some in its vicinity I would rather not insult by my presence. Why do you bring up disagreeable subjects?"

"You will have to get over that feeling," observed Mr. Carr, disregarding the hint, and taking out his probing-knife. "And the sooner it is got over the better for all parties. You cannot become an exile from your own place. Are they at Calne now?"

"Yes. They were in Paris just before we left it, and there was an encounter at Versailles. I wished myself dead; I declare I did. A day or two after we came to England they crossed over, and went straight down to Calne. There—don't say any more."

"The longer you keep away from Hartledon the greater effort it will cost you to go down to it; and—"

"I won't go to Hartledon," he interrupted, in a sort of fury; "neither perhaps would you, in my place."

"Sir," cried Mr. Carr's clerk, bustling in and addressing his master, "you are waited for at the chambers of Serjeant Gale. The consultation is on."

Lord Hartledon rose.

"I will not detain you, Carr; business must be attended to. Will you come and dine with us this evening? Only me and my wife. Here's where we are staying—Piccadilly. My own house is let, you know."

"I have no engagement, and will come with pleasure," said Mr. Carr, taking the card. "What hour?"

"Ah, that's just what I can't tell you. Lady Hartledon orders dinner to suit her engagements—any time between six and nine! I never know. We are a fashionable couple, don't you see?"

"Stay, though, Hartledon; I forget. I have a business appointment for half-past eight. Perhaps I can put it off."

"Come up at six. You'll be all right, then, in any case."

Lord Hartledon left the Temple, and sauntered towards home. He had no engagement on hand—nothing to kill time. He and his wife were falling naturally into the way of—as he had just cynically styled it—fashionable people. She went her way and he went his.

Many a cabman held up his hand or his whip; but in his present mood walking was agreeable to him: why should he hurry home, when he had nothing on earth to do there? So he stared here, and gazed there, and stopped to speak to this acquaintance, and walked a few steps with that, went into his club for ten minutes, and arrived home at last.

His wife's carriage was at the door waiting for her. She was bound on an expedition to Chiswick: Lord Hartledon had declined it. He met her hastening out as he entered, and she was looking very cross.

"How late you are going, Maude!"

"Yes, there has been a mistake," she said peevishly, turning in with him to a small room they used as a breakfast-room. "I have been waiting all this time for Lady Langton, and she, I find, has been waiting for me. I'm now going round to take her up. Oh, I have secured that opera-box, Val, but at an extravagant price, considering the little time that remains of the season."

"What opera-box?"

"Didn't I tell you? It's one I heard of yesterday. I was not going again to put up with the wretched little box they palmed you off with. I did tell you that."

"It was the only one I could get, Maude: there was no other choice."

"Yes, I know. Well, I have secured another for the rest of the season, and you must not talk about extravagance, please."

"Very well," said Val, with a smile. "For what hour have you ordered dinner?"

"Nine o'clock."

"Nine o'clock! That's awkward—and late."

"Why awkward? You may have to wait for me even then. It is impossible to say when we shall get home from Chiswick. All the world will be there."

"I have just asked Carr to dine with us, and told him to come at six. I don't fancy these hard-working men care to wait so long for their dinner. And he has an appointment for half-past eight."

The colour came flushing into Lady Hartledon's face, an angry light into her eyes.

"You have asked Carr to dinner! How dared you?"

Val looked up in quiet amazement.

"Dared!"

"Well—yes. Dared!"

"I do not understand you, Maude. I suppose I may exercise the right of inviting a friend to dinner."

"Not when it is objectionable to me. I dislike that man Carr, and will not receive him."

"You can have no grounds for disliking him," returned Lord Hartledon warmly. "He has been a good and true friend to me ever since I knew what friendship meant; and he is a good and true man."

"Too much of a friend," she sarcastically retorted. "You don't need him now, and can drop him."

"Maude," said Lord Hartledon, very quietly, "I have fancied several times lately that you are a little mistaking me. I am not to have a will of my own; I am to bend in all things to yours; you are to be mistress and master, I a nonentity: is it not so? This is a mistake. No woman ever had a better or more indulgent husband than you shall find in me: but in all necessary things, where it is needful and expedient that I should exercise my own judgment, and act as master, I shall do it."

She paused in very astonishment: the tone was so calmly decisive.

"My dear, let us have no more of this; something must have vexed you to-day."

"We will have no more of it," she passionately retorted; "and I'll have no more of your Thomas Carrs. It is not right that you should bring a man here who has deliberately insulted me. Be quiet, Lord Hartledon; he has. What else was it but an insult—his going out of the chapel in the manner he did, when we were before the altar? It was a direct intimation that he did not countenance the marriage. He would have preferred, I suppose, that you should marry your country sweetheart, Anne Ashton."

A hot flush rose to Lord Hartledon's brow, but his tone was strangely temperate. "I have already warned you, Maude, that we shall do well to discard that name from our discussions, and if possible from our thoughts; it may prove better for both of us."

"Better for you, perhaps; but you are *not* going to exercise any control over my will, or words, or action; and so I tell you at once. I'm quite old enough to be out of leading-strings, and I'll be mistress in my own house. You will do well to send a note to your amiable friend Carr; it may save him a useless journey; for at my table he shall not sit. Now you know, Val."

She spoke impatiently, haughtily, and swept out to her carriage. Val did not follow to place her in; he positively did not, but left her to the servants. Never in his whole life perhaps had he felt so nettled, never so resolute: the once vacillating, easily-persuaded man, when face to face with people, was speedily finding the will he had only exercised behind their backs. He rang the bell for Hedges.

"Her ladyship has ordered dinner for nine o'clock," he said, when the butler appeared.

"I believe so, my lord."

"It will be inconvenient to me to wait so long to-day. I shall dine at seven. You can serve it in this room, leaving the dining-room for Lady Hartledon. Mr. Carr dines with me."

So Hedges gave the necessary orders, and dinner was laid in the breakfast-room. Thomas Carr came in, bringing the news that he had succeeded in putting off his appointment. Lord Hartledon received him in the same room, fearing possibly the drawing-room might be invaded by his wife. She was just as likely to be home early from Chiswick as late.

"We have it to ourselves, Carr, and I am not sorry. There was no certainty about my wife's return, so I thought we'd dine alone."

They very much enjoyed their tête-à-tête dinner; as they had enjoyed many a one in Hartledon's bachelor days. Thomas Carr—one of the quiet, good men in a fast world—was an admirable companion, full of intelligence and conversation. Hedges left them alone after the cloth was removed, but in a very few minutes returned; his step rather more subdued than usual, as if he came upon some secret mission.

"Here's that stranger come again, sir," he began, in low tones; and it may as well be remarked that in moments of forgetfulness he often did address his master as he used to address him in the past. "He asked if—"

"What stranger?" rather testily interposed Lord Hartledon. "I am at dinner, and can't see any stranger now. What are you thinking about, Hedges?"

"It is what I said," returned Hedges; "but he would not take the answer. He said he had come a long way to see your lordship, and he would see you; his business was very important. My lady asked him—"

"Has Lady Hartledon returned?"

"She came in now, my lord, while I was denying you to him. Her ladyship heard him say he would see you, and she inquired what his business was; but he did not tell her. It was private business, he remarked, and could only be entered into with your lordship."

"Who is it, Hedges? Do you know him?"

Lord Hartledon had dropped his voice to confidential tones. Hedges was faithful, and had been privy to some of his embarrassments in the old days. The man looked at the barrister, and seemed to hesitate.

"Speak out. You can say anything before Mr. Carr."

"I don't know him," answered Hedges. "It is the gentleman who came to Hartledon the week after your lordship's marriage, asking five hundred questions, and wanting—"

"He, is it?" interrupted Val. "You told me about him when I came home, I remember. Go on, Hedges."

"That's all, my lord. Except that he is here now"—and Hedges nodded his head towards the room-door. "He seems very inquisitive. When my lady went upstairs, he asked whether that was the countess, and followed her to the foot of the stairs to look after her. I never saw any gentleman stare so."

Val played with his wine-glass, and pondered. "I don't believe I owe a shilling in the world," quoth he—betraying the bent of his thoughts, and speaking to no one in particular. "I have squared-up every debt, as far as I know."

"He does not look like a creditor," observed Hedges, with a fatherly air. "Quite superior to that: more like a parson. It's his manner that makes one doubt. There was a mystery about it at Hartledon that I didn't like; and he refused to give his name. His insisting on seeing your lordship now, at dinner or not at dinner, is odd too; his voice is quiet, just as if he possessed the right to do this. I didn't know what to do, and as I say, he's in the hall."

"Show him in somewhere, Hedges. Lady Hartledon is in the drawing-room, I suppose: let him go into the dining-room."

"Her ladyship's dinner is being laid there, my lord," dissented the cautious retainer. "She said it was to be served as soon as it was ready, having come home earlier than she expected."

"Deuce take it!" testily responded Val, "one can't swing a cat in these cramped hired houses. Show him into my smoking-den upstairs."

"Let me go there," said Mr. Carr, "and you can see him in this room."

"No; keep to your wine, Carr. Take him up there, Hedges."

The butler retired, and Lord Hartledon turned to his guest. "Carr, can you give a guess at the fellow's business?"

"It's nothing to trouble you. If you have overlooked any old debt, you are able to give a cheque for it. But I should rather suspect your persevering friend to be some clergyman or missionary, bent on drawing a good subscription from you."

Val did not raise his eyes. He was playing again with his empty wine-glass, his face grave and perplexed.

"Do they serve writs in these cases?" he suddenly asked.

Mr. Carr laughed. "Is the time so long gone by that you have forgotten yours? You have had some in your day."

"I am not thinking of debt, Carr: that is over for me. But there's no denying that I behaved disgracefully to—you know—and Dr. Ashton has good reason to be incensed. Can he be bringing an action against me, and is this visit in any way connected with it?"

"Nonsense," said Mr. Carr.

"Is it nonsense! I'm sure I've heard of their dressing-up these serving-officers as clergymen, to entrap the unwary. Well, call it nonsense, if you like. What of my suggestion in regard to Dr. Ashton?"

Thomas Carr paused to consider. That it was most improbable in all respects, he felt sure; next door to impossible.

"The doctor is too respectable a man to do anything of the sort," he answered. "He is high-minded, honourable, wealthy: there's no inducement whatever. *No.* "

"Yes, there may be one: that of punishing me by bringing my disgrace before the world."

"You forget that he would bring his daughter's name before it at the same time. It is quite out of the range of possibility. The Ashtons are not people to seek legal reparation for injury of this sort. But that your fears are blinding you, you would never suspect them of being capable of it."

"The stranger is upstairs, my lord," interrupted Hedges, coming back to the room. "I asked him what name, and he said your lordship would know him when you saw him, and there was no need to give it."

Lord Hartledon went upstairs, marshalled by the butler. Hedges was resenting the mystery; very much on his master's account, a little on his own, for it cannot be denied that he was given to curiosity. He threw open the door of the little smoking-den, and in his loftiest, loudest, most uncompromising voice, announced:

"The gentleman, my lord."

Then retired, and shut them in.

Thomas Carr remained alone. He was not fond of wine, and did not help himself during his host's absence. Five minutes, ten minutes, half-an-hour, an hour; and still he was alone. At the end of the first half-hour he began to think Val a long time; at the end of the hour he feared something must have happened. Could he be quarrelling with the mysterious stranger? Could he have forgotten him and gone out? Could he—

The door softly opened, and Lord Hartledon came in. Was it Lord Hartledon? Thomas Carr rose from his chair in amazement and dread. It was like him, but with some awful terror upon him. His face was of an ashy whiteness; the veins of his brow stood out; his dry lips were drawn.

"Good Heavens, Hartledon!" uttered Thomas Carr. "What is it? You look as if you had been accused of murder."

"I have been accused of it," gasped the unhappy man, "of worse than murder. Ay, and I have done it."

The words called up a strange confusion of ideas in the mind of Thomas Carr. Worse than murder!

"What is it?" cried he, aloud. "I am beginning to dream."

"Will you stand by me?" rejoined Hartledon, his voice seeming to have changed into something curiously hollow. "I have asked you before for trifles; I ask you now in the extremity of need. Will you stand by me, and aid me with your advice?"

"Y—es," answered Mr. Carr, his excessive astonishment causing a hesitation. "Where is your visitor?"

"Upstairs. He holds a fearful secret, and has me in his power. Do you come back with me, and combat with him against its betrayal."

"A fearful secret!" was Thomas Carr's exclamation. "What brings you with one?"

Lord Hartledon only groaned. "You will stand by me, Carr? Will you come upstairs and do what you can for me?"

"I am quite ready," replied Thomas Carr, quickly. "I will stand by you now, as ever. But—I seem to be in a maze. Is it a true charge?"

"Yes, in so far as that—But I had better tell you the story," he broke off, wiping his brow. "I must tell it you before you go upstairs."

He linked his arm within his friend's, and drew him to the window. It was broad daylight still, but gloomy there: the window had the pleasure of reposing under the leads, and was gloomy at noon. Lord Hartledon hesitated still. "Elster's folly!" were the words mechanically floating in the mind of Thomas Carr.

"It is an awful story, Carr; bad and wicked."

"Let me hear it at once," replied Thomas Carr.

"I am in danger of—of—in short, that person upstairs could have me apprehended to-night. I would not tell you but that I must do so. I must have advice, assistance; but you'll start from me when you hear it."

"I will stand by you, whatever it may be. If a man has ever need of a friend, it must be in his extremity."

Lord Hartledon stood, and whispered a strange tale. It was anything but coherent to the clear-minded barrister; nevertheless, as he gathered one or two of its points he did start back, as Hartledon had foretold, and an exclamation of dismay burst from his lips.

"And you could *marry*—with this hanging over your head!"

"Carr—"

The butler came in with an interruption.

"My lady wishes to know whether your lordship is going out with her to-night."

"Not to-night," answered Lord Hartledon, pointing to the door for the man to make his exit. "It is of her I think, not of myself," he murmured to Mr. Carr.

"And he"—the barrister pointed above to indicate the stranger— "threatens to have you apprehended on the charge?"

"I hardly know what he threatens. *You* must deal with him, Carr; I cannot. Let us go; we are wasting time."

As they left the room to go upstairs Lady Hartledon came out of the dining-room and crossed their path. She was deeply mortified at her husband's bringing Mr. Carr to the house after what she had said; and most probably came out at the moment to confront them with her haughty and disapproving face. However that might have been, all other emotions gave place to surprise, when she saw *their* faces, each bearing a livid look of fear.

"I hope you are well, Lady Hartledon," said Mr. Carr.

She would not see the offered hand, but swept onwards with a cold curtsey, stopping just a moment to speak to her husband.

"You are not going out with me, Lord Hartledon?"

"I cannot to-night, Maude. Business detains me."

She passed up the stairs, vouchsafing no other word. They lingered a minute to let her get into the drawing-room.

"Poor Maude! What will become of her if this is brought home to me?"

"And if it is not brought home to you—the fact remains the same," said Mr. Carr, in his merciless truth.

"And our children, our children!" groaned Hartledon, a hot flush of dread arising in his white face.

They shut themselves in with the stranger, and the conference was renewed. Presently lights were rung for; Hedges brought them himself, but gained nothing by the movement; for Mr. Carr heard him coming, rose unbidden, and took them from him at the door.

Lady Hartledon's curiosity was excited. It had been aroused a little by the stranger himself; secondly by their scared faces; thirdly by this close conference.

"Who is that strange gentleman, Hedges?" she asked, from the drawing-room, as the butler descended.

"I don't know, my lady."

"What is his name?"

"I have not heard it, my lady."

"He looks like a clergyman."

"He does, my lady."

Apparently Hedges was impenetrable, and she allowed him to go down. Her curiosity was very much excited; it may be said, uneasily excited; there is no accounting for these instincts that come over us, shadowing forth a vague sense of dread. Although engaged out that night to more than one place, Lady Hartledon lingered on in the drawing-room.

They came out of the room at last and passed the drawing-room door. She pushed it to, only peeping out when they had gone by. There was nothing to hear; they were talking of ordinary matters. The stranger, in his strong Scotch accent, remarked what a hot day it had been. In travelling, no doubt very, responded Mr. Carr. Lady Hartledon condescended to cautiously put her head over the balustrades. There was no bell rung; Lord Hartledon showed his visitor out himself.

"And now for these criminal law books, Carr, that bear upon the case," he said, returning from the front-door.

"I must go down to my chambers for them."

"I know they can't bring it home to me; I know they can't!" he exclaimed, in tones so painfully eager as to prove to Lady Hartledon's ears that he thought they could, whatever the matter might be. "I'll go with you, Carr; this uncertainty is killing me."

"There's little uncertainty about it, I fear," was the grave reply. "You had better look the worst in the face."

They went out, intending to hail the first cab. Very much to Lord Hartledon's surprise he saw his wife's carriage waiting at the door, the impatient horses chafing at their delay. What could have detained her? "Wait for me one moment, Carr," he said. "Stop a cab if you see one."

He dashed up to the drawing-room; his wife was coming forth then, her cloak and gloves on, her fan in her hand. "Maude, my darling," he exclaimed, "what has kept you? Surely you have not waited for me?—you did not misunderstand me?"

"I hardly know what has kept me," she evasively answered. "It is late, but I'm going now."

It never occurred to Lord Hartledon that she had been watching or listening. Incapable of any meanness of the sort, he could not suspect it in another. Lady Hartledon's fertile brain had been suggesting a solution of this mystery. It was rather curious, perhaps, that her suspicions should take the same bent that her husband's did at first—that of instituting law proceedings by Dr. Ashton.

She said nothing. Her husband led her out, placed her in the carriage, and saw it drive away. Then he and the barrister got into a cab and went to the Temple.

"We'll take the books home with us, Carr," he said, feverishly. "You often have fellows dropping in to your chambers at night; at my house we shall be secure from interruption."

It was midnight when Lady Hartledon returned home. She asked after her husband, and heard that he was in the breakfast-room with Mr. Carr.

She went towards it with a stealthy step, and opened the door very softly. Had Lord Hartledon not been talking, they might, however, have heard her. The table was strewed with thick musty folios; but they appeared to be done with, and Mr. Carr was leaning back in his chair with folded arms.

"I have had nothing but worry all my life," Val was saying; "but compared with this, whatever has gone before was as nothing. When I think of Maude, I feel as if I should go mad."

"You must quietly separate from her," said Mr. Carr.

A slight movement. Mr. Carr stopped, and Lord Hartledon looked round. Lady Hartledon was close behind him.

"Percival, what is the matter?" she asked, turning her back on Mr. Carr, as if ignoring his presence. "What bad news did that parson bring you?—a friend, I presume, of Dr. Ashton's."

They had both risen. Lord Hartledon glanced at Mr. Carr, the perspiration breaking out on his brow. "It—it was not a parson," he said, in his innate adherence to truth.

"I ask *you*, Lord Hartledon," she resumed, having noted the silent appeal to Mr. Carr. "It requires no third person to step between man and wife. Will you come upstairs with me?"

Words and manner were too pointed, and Mr. Carr hastily stacked the books, and carried them to a side-table.

"Allow these to remain here until to-morrow," he said to Lord Hartledon; "I'll send my clerk for them. I'm off now; it's later than I thought. Good-night, Lady Hartledon."

He went out unmolested; Lady Hartledon did not answer him; Val nodded his good-night.

"Are you not ashamed to face me, Lord Hartledon?" she then demanded. "I overheard what you were saying."

"Overheard what we were saying?" he repeated, gazing at her with a scared look.

"I heard that insidious man give you strange advice—'*you must quietly separate from her*,' he said; meaning from me. And you listened patiently, and did not knock him down!"

"Maude! Maude! was that all you heard?"

"*All!* I should think it was enough."

"Yes, but—" He broke off, so agitated as scarcely to know what he was saying. Rallying himself somewhat, he laid his hand upon the white cloak covering her shoulders.

"Do not judge him harshly, Maude. Indeed he is a true friend to you and to me. And I have need of one just now."

"A true friend!—to advise that! I never heard of anything so monstrous. You must be out of your mind."

"No, I am not, Maude. Should—disgrace"—he seemed to hesitate for a word—"fall upon me, it must touch you as connected with me. I *know*, Maude, that he was thinking of your best and truest interests."

"But to talk of separating husband and wife!"

"Yes—well—I suppose he spoke strongly in the heat of the moment."

There was a pause. Lord Hartledon had his hand still on his wife's shoulder, but his eyes were bent on the table near which they stood. She was waiting for him to speak.

"Won't you tell me what has happened?"

"I can't tell you, Maude, to-night," he answered, great drops coming out again on his brow at the question, and knowing all the time that he should never tell her. "I—I must learn more first."

"You spoke of disgrace," she observed gently, swaying her fan before her by its silken cord. "An ugly word."

"It is. Heaven help me!"

"Val, I do think you are the greatest simpleton under the skies!" she exclaimed out of all patience, and flinging his hand off. "It's time you got rid of this foolish sensitiveness. I know what is the matter quite well; and it's not so very much of a disgrace after all! Those Ashtons are going to make you pay publicly for your folly. Let them do it."

He had opened his lips to undeceive her, but stopped in time. As a drowning man catches at a straw, so did he catch at this suggestion in his hopeless despair; and he suffered her to remain in it. Anything to stave off the real, dreadful truth.

"Maude," he rejoined, "it is for your sake. If I am sensitive as to any—any disgrace being brought home to me, I declare that I think of you more than of myself."

"Then don't think of it. It will be fun for me, rather than anything else. I did not imagine the Ashtons would have done it, though. I wonder what damages they'll go in for. Oh, Val, I should like to see you in the witness-box!"

He did not answer.

"And it was not a parson?" she continued. "I'm sure he looked as much like one as old Ashton himself. A professional man, then, I suppose, Val?"

"Yes, a professional man." But even that little answer was given with some hesitation, as though it had evasion in it.

Maude broke into a laugh. "Your friend, Pleader Carr—or whatever he calls himself—must be as thin-skinned as you are, Val, to fancy that a rubbishing action of that sort, brought against a husband, can reflect disgrace on the wife! Separate, indeed! Has he lived in a wood all his life? Well, I am going upstairs."

"A moment yet, Maude! You will take a caution from me, won't you? Don't speak of this; don't allude to it, even to me. It may be arranged yet, you know."

"So it may," acquiesced Maude. "Let your friend Carr see the doctor, and offer to pay the damages down."

He might have resented this speech for Dr. Ashton's sake, in a happier moment, but resentment had been beaten out of him now. And Lady Hartledon decided that her husband was a simpleton, for instead of going to sleep like a reasonable man, he tossed and turned by her side until daybreak.

# XXI

## Secret Care

From that hour Lord Hartledon was a changed man. He went about as one who has some awful fear upon him, starting at shadows. That his manner was inexplicable, even allowing that he had some great crime on his conscience, a looker-on had not failed to observe. He was very tender with his wife; far more so than he had been at all; anxious, as it seemed, to indulge her every fancy, gratify her every whim. But when it came to going into society with her, then he hesitated; he would and he wouldn't, reminding Maude of his old vacillation, which indeed had seemed to have been laid aside for ever. It was as though he appeared not to know what to do; what he ought to do; his own wish or inclination having no part in it.

"Why *won't* you go with me?" she said to him angrily one day that he had retracted his assent at the last moment. "Is it that you care so much for Anne Ashton, that you don't care to be seen with me?"

"Oh, Maude! If you knew how little Anne Ashton is in my thoughts now! When by chance I do think of her, it is to be thankful I did not marry her," he added, in a tone of self-communing.

Maude laughed a light laugh. "This movement of theirs is putting you out of conceit of your old love, Val."

"What movement?" he rejoined; and he would not have asked the question had his thoughts not gone wool-gathering.

"You are dreaming, Val. The action."

"Ah, yes, to be sure."

"Have you heard yet what damages they claim?"

He shook his head. "You promised not to speak of this, Maude; even to me."

"Who is to help speaking of it, when you allow it to take your ease away? I never in my life saw any one so changed as you are. I wish the thing were over and done with, though it left you a few thousand pounds the poorer. *Will* you accompany me to this dinner to-day? I am sick of appearing alone and making excuses for you."

"I wish I knew what to do for the best—what my course ought to be!" thought Hartledon within his conscience. "I can't bear to be seen with her in public. When I face people with her on my arm, it seems as if they must know what sort of man she, in her unconsciousness, is leaning upon."

"I'll go with you to-day, Maude, as you press it. I was to have seen Mr. Carr, but can send down to him."

"Then don't be five minutes dressing: it is time we went."

She heard him despatch a footman to the Temple with a message that he should not be at Mr. Carr's chambers that evening; and she lay back in her chair, waiting for him in her dinner-dress of black and white. They were in mourning still for his brother. Lord Hartledon had not left it off, and Maude had loved him too well to grumble at the delay.

She had grown tolerant in regard to the intimacy with Mr. Carr. That her husband should escape as soon and as favourably as possible out of the dilemma in which he was plunged, she naturally wished; that he should require legal advice and assistance to accomplish it, was only reasonable, and therefore she tolerated the visits of Mr. Carr. She had even gone so far one evening as to send tea in to them when he and Val were closeted together.

But still Lady Hartledon was not quite prepared to find Mr. Carr at their house when they returned. She and Lord Hartledon went forth to the dinner; the latter behaving as though his wits were in some far-off hemisphere rather than in this one, so absent-minded was he. From the dinner they proceeded to another place or two; and on getting home, towards one in the morning, there was the barrister.

"Mr. Carr is waiting to see you, my lord," said Hedges, meeting them in the passage. "He is in the dining-room."

"Mr. Carr! Now!"

The hall-lamp shone full on his face as he spoke. He had been momentarily forgetting care; was speaking gaily to his wife as they entered. She saw the change that came over it; the look of fear, of apprehension, that replaced its smile. He went into the dining-room, and she followed him.

"Why, Carr!" he exclaimed. "Is it you?"

Mr. Carr, bowing to Lady Hartledon, made a joke of the matter. "Having waited so long, I thought I'd wait it out, Hartledon. As good be hung for a sheep as a lamb, you know, and I have no wife sitting up for me at home."

"You had my message?"

"Yes, and that brought me here. I wanted just to say a word to you, as I am going out of town to-morrow."

"What will you take?"

"Nothing at all. Hedges has been making me munificent offers, but I declined them. I never take anything after dinner, except a cup of tea or so, as you may remember, keeping a clear head for work in the morning."

There was a slight pause. Lady Hartledon saw of course that she was *de trop* in the conference; that Mr. Carr would not speak his "word" whilst she was present. She had never understood why the matter should be kept apart from her; and in her heart resented it.

"You won't say to my husband before me what you have come to say, Mr. Carr."

It was strictly the truth, but the abrupt manner of bringing it home to him momentarily took away Mr. Carr's power of repartee, although he was apt enough in general, as became a special pleader.

"You have had news from the Ashtons; that is, of their cause, and you have come to tell it. I don't see why you and Lord Hartledon should so cautiously keep everything from me."

There was an eager look on Lord Hartledon's face as he stood behind his wife. It was directed to Mr. Carr, and said as plainly as look could say, "Don't undeceive her; keep up the delusion." But Thomas Carr was not so apt at keeping up delusions at the expense of truth, and he only smiled in reply.

"What damages are they suing for?"

"Oh," said Mr. Carr, with a laugh, and ready enough now: "ten thousand pounds will cover it."

"Ten thousand pounds!" she echoed. "Of course they won't get half of it. In this sort of action—breach of promise—parties never get so much as they ask for, do they?"

"Not often."

She laughed a little as she quitted the room. It was difficult to remain longer, and it never occurred to her to suspect that any graver matter than this action was in question.

"Now, Carr?" began Lord Hartledon, seating himself near the table as he closed the door after her, and speaking in low tones.

"I received this letter by the afternoon mail," said Mr. Carr, taking one from the safe enclosure of his pocket-book. "It is satisfactory, so far as it goes."

"I call it very satisfactory," returned Hartledon, glancing through it. "I thought he'd listen to reason. What is done cannot be undone, and exposure will answer no end. I wrote him an urgent letter the other day, begging him to be silent for Maude's sake. Were I to expiate the past with my life, it could not undo it. If he brought me to the bar of my country to plead guilty or not guilty, the past would remain the same."

"And I put the matter to him in my letter somewhat in the same light, though in a more business-like point of view," returned Mr. Carr. "There was no entreaty in mine. I left compassion, whether for you or others, out of the argument; and said to him, what will you gain by exposure, and how will you reconcile it to your conscience to inflict on innocent persons the torture exposure must bring?"

"I shall breathe freely now," said Hartledon, with a sigh of relief." If that man gives his word not to stir in the matter, not to take proceedings against me; in short, to bury what he knows in secrecy and silence, as he has hitherto done; it will be all I can hope for."

Mr. Carr lifted his eyebrows.

"I perceive what you think: that the fact remains. Carr, I know it as well as you; I know that *nothing* can alter it. Don't you see that remorse is ever present with me? driving me mad? killing me by inches with its pain?"

"Do you know what I should be tempted to do, were the case mine?"

"Well?"

"Tell my wife."

"Carr!"

"I almost think I should; I am not quite sure. Should the truth ever come to her—"

"But I trust it never will come to her," interrupted Hartledon, his face growing hot.

"It's a delicate point to argue," acknowledged Mr. Carr, "and I cannot hope to bring you into my way of looking at it. Had you married Miss Ashton, it appears to me that you would have no resource but to tell her: the very fact of being bound to you would kill a religious, high-principled woman."

"Not if she remained in ignorance."

"There it is. Ought she to remain in ignorance?"

Lord Hartledon leaned his head on his hand as one faint and weary. "Carr, it is of no use to go over all this ground again. If I disclose the whole to Maude, how would it make it better for her? Would it not render it a hundred times worse? She could not inform against me; it would be contrary to human nature to suppose it; and all the result would be, that she must go through life with the awful secret upon her, rendering her days a hell upon earth, as it is rendering mine. It's true she might separate from me; I dare say she would; but what satisfaction would that bring her? No; the kinder course is to allow her to remain in ignorance. Good Heavens! tell my wife! I should never dare do it!"

Mr. Carr made no reply, and a pause ensued. In truth, the matter was encompassed with difficulties on all sides; and the barrister could but acknowledge that Val's argument had some sort of reason in it. Having bound her to himself by marriage, it might be right that he should study her happiness above all things.

"It has put new life into me," Val resumed, pointing to the letter. "Now that he has promised to keep the secret, there's little to fear; and I know that he will keep his word. I must bear the burden as I best can, and keep a smiling face to the world."

"Did you read the postscript?" asked Mr. Carr; a feeling coming over him that Val had not read it.

"The postscript?"

"There's a line or two over the leaf."

Lord Hartledon glanced at it, and found it ran thus:

"You must be aware that another person knows of this besides myself. He who was a witness at the time, and from whom *I* heard the particulars. Of course for him I cannot answer, and I think he is in England. I allude to G.G. Lord H. will know."

"Lord H." apparently did know. He gazed down at the words with a knitted brow, in which some surprise was mingled.

"I declare that I understood him that night to say the fellow had died. Did not you?"

"I did," acquiesced Mr. Carr. "I certainly assumed it as a fact, until this letter came to-day. Gordon was the name, I think?"

"George Gordon."

"Since reading the letter I have been endeavouring to recollect exactly what he did say; and the impression on my mind is, that he spoke of Gordon as being *probably* dead; not that he knew it for a certainty. How I could overlook the point so as not to have inquired into it more fully, I cannot imagine. But, you see, we were not discussing details that night, or questioning facts: we were trying to disarm him—get him not to proceed against you; and for myself, I confess I was so utterly stunned that half my wits had left me."

"What is to be done?"

"We must endeavour to ascertain where Gordon is," replied Mr. Carr, as he re-enclosed the letter in his pocket-book. "I'll write and inquire what *his* grounds are for thinking he is in England; and then trace him out—if he is to be traced. You give me carte-blanche to act?"

"You know I do, Carr."

"All right."

"And when you have traced him—what then?"

"That's an after-question, and I must be guided by circumstances. And now I'll wish you good-night," continued the barrister, rising. "It's a shame to have kept you up; but the letter contains some consolation, and I knew I could not bring it you to-morrow."

The drawing-room was lighted when Lord Hartledon went upstairs; and his wife sat there with a book, as if she meant to remain up all night. She put it down as he entered.

"Are you here still, Maude! I thought you were tired when you came home."

"I felt tired because I met no one I cared for," she answered, in rather fractious tones. "Every one we know is leaving town, or has left."

"Yes, that's true."

"I shall leave too. I don't mind if we go to-morrow."

"To-morrow!" he echoed. "Why, we have the house for three weeks longer."

"And if we have? We are not obliged to remain in it."

Lord Hartledon put back the curtain, and stood leaning out at the open window, seeking a breath of air that hot summer's night, though indeed there was none to be found; and if there had been, it could not have cooled the brow's inward fever. The Park lay before him, dark and misty; the lights of the few vehicles passing gleamed now and again; the hum of life was dying out in the streets, men's free steps, careless voices. He looked down, and wondered whether any one of those men knew what care meant as *he* knew it; whether the awful skeleton, that never quitted him night or day, could hold such place with another. He was Earl of Hartledon; wealthy, young, handsome; he had no bad habits to hamper him; and yet he would willingly have changed lots at hazard

MRS. HENRY WOOD

with any one of those passers-by, could his breast, by so doing, have been eased of its burden.

"What are you looking at, Val?"

His wife had come up and stolen her arm within his, as she asked the question, looking out too.

"Not at anything in particular," he replied, making a prisoner of her hand. "The night's hot, Maude."

"Oh, I am getting tired of London!" she exclaimed. "It is always hot now; and I believe I ought to be away from it."

"Yes."

"That letter I had this morning was from Ireland, from mamma. I told her, when I wrote last, how I felt; and you never read such a lecture as she gave me in return. She asked me whether I was mad, that I should be going galvanizing about when I ought rather to be resting three parts of my time."

"Galvanizing?" said Lord Hartledon.

"So she wrote: she never waits to choose her words—you know mamma! I suppose she meant to imply that I was always on the move."

"Do you feel ill, Maude?"

"Not exactly ill; but—I think I ought to be careful. Percival," she breathed, "mamma asked me whether I was trying to destroy the hope of an heir to Hartledon."

An ice-bolt shot through him at the reminder. Better an heir should never be born, if it must call him father!

"I fainted to-day, Val," she continued to whisper.

He passed his arm round his wife's waist, and drew her closer to him. Not upon her ought he to visit his sin: she might have enough to bear, without coldness from him; rather should he be doubly tender.

"You did not tell me about it, love. Why have you gone out this evening?" he asked reproachfully.

"It has not harmed me. Indeed I will take care, for your sake. I should never forgive myself."

"I have thought since we married, Maude, that you did not much care for me."

Maude made no immediate answer. She was looking out straight before her, her head on his shoulder, and Lord Hartledon saw that tears were glistening in her eyes.

"Yes, I do," she said at length; and as she spoke she felt very conscious that she *was* caring for him. His gentle kindness, his many attractions were beginning to tell upon her heart; and a vision of the possible future, when she should love him, crossed her then and there as she stood. Lord Hartledon bent his face, and let it rest on hers.

"We shall be happy yet, Val; and I will be as good as gold. To begin with, we will leave London at once. I ought not to remain, and I know you have not liked it all along. It would have been better to wait until next year, when we could have had our own house; only I was impatient. I felt proud of being married; of being your wife—I did indeed, Val—and I was in a fever to be amidst my world of friends. And there's a real confession!" she concluded, laughing.

"Any more?" he asked, laughing with her.

"I don't remember any more just now. Which day shall we go? You shall manage things for me now: I won't be wilful again. Shall the servants go on first to Hartledon, or with us?"

"To Hartledon!" exclaimed Val. "Is it to Hartledon you think of going?"

"Of course it is," she said, standing up and looking at him in surprise. "Where else should I go?"

"I thought you wished to go to Germany!"

"And so I did; but that would not do now."

"Then let us go to the seaside," he rather eagerly said. "Somewhere in England."

"No, I would rather go to Hartledon. In one's own home rest and comfort can be insured; and I believe I require them. Don't you wish to go there?" she added, watching his perplexed face.

"No, I don't. The truth is, I cannot go to Hartledon."

"Is it because you do not care to face the Ashtons? I see! You would like to have this business settled first."

Lord Hartledon hardly heard the words, as he stood leaning against the open casement, gazing into the dark and misty past. No man ever shrank from a prison as he shrank from Hartledon.

"I cannot leave London at all just yet. Thomas Carr is remaining here for me, when he ought to be on circuit, and I must stay with him. I wish you would go anywhere else, rather than to Hartledon."

The tone was so painfully earnest, that a momentary suspicion crossed her of his having some other motive. It passed away almost as it arose, and she accused him of being unreasonable.

Unreasonable it did appear to be. "If you have any real reason to urge against Hartledon, tell it me," she said. But he mentioned none—save that it was his "wish" not to go.

And Lady Hartledon, rather piqued, gave the necessary orders on the following day for the removal. No further confidential converse, or approach to it, took place between her and her husband; but up to the last moment she thought he would relent and accompany her. Nothing of the sort. He was anxious for her every comfort on the journey, and saw her off himself: nothing more.

"I never thought you would allow me to go alone," she resentfully whispered, as he held her hand after she was seated in the train.

He shook his head. "It is your fault, Maude. I told you I could not go to Hartledon."

And so she went down in rather an angry frame of mind. Many a time and oft had she pictured to herself the triumph of their first visit to Calne, the place where she had taken so much pains to win him: but the arrival was certainly shorn of its glory.

# XXII

## ASKING THE RECTOR

Perhaps Lady Hartledon had never in all her life been so much astonished as when she reached Hartledon, for the first person she saw there was her mother: her mother, whom she had believed to be in some remote district of Ireland. For the moment she almost wondered whether it was really herself or her ghost. The countess-dowager came flying down the steps—if that term may be applied to one of her age and size—with rather demonstrative affection; which, however, was not cordially received.

"What's the matter, Maude? How you stare!"

"*Is* it you, mamma? How *can* it be you?"

"How can it be me?" returned the dowager, giving Maude's bonnet a few kisses. "It *is* me, and that's enough. My goodness, Maude, how thin you look! I see what it is! you've been killing yourself in that racketing London. It's well I've come to take care of you."

Maude went in, feeling that she could have taken care of herself, and listening to the off-hand explanations of the countess-dowager. "Kirton offended me," she said. "He and his wife are like two bears; and so I packed up my things and came away at once, and got here straight from Liverpool. And now you know."

"And is Lady Kirton quite well again?" asked Maude, helplessly, knowing she could not turn her mother out.

"She'd be well enough but for temper. She *was* ill, though, when they telegraphed for me; her life for three days and nights hanging on a shred. I told that fool of a Kirton before he married her that she had no constitution. I suppose you and Hart were finely disappointed to find I was not in London when you got there."

"Agreeably disappointed, I think," said Maude, languidly.

"Indeed! It's civil of you to say so."

"On account of the smallness of the house," added Maude, endeavouring to be polite. "We hardly knew how to manage in it ourselves."

"You wrote me word to take it. As to me, I can accommodate myself to any space. Where there's plenty of room, I take plenty; where there's not, I can put up with a closet. I have made Mirrable give me my old rooms here: you of course take Hart's now."

"I am very tired," said Maude. "I think I will have some tea, and go to bed."

"Tea!" shrieked the dowager. "I have not yet had dinner. And it's waiting; that's more."

"You can dine without me, mamma," she said, walking upstairs to the new rooms. The dowager stared, and followed her. There was an indescribable something in Maude's manner that she did not like; it spoke of incipient rebellion, of an influence that had been, but was now thrown off. If she lost caste once, with Maude, she knew that she lost it for ever.

"You could surely take a little dinner, Maude. You must keep up your strength, you know."

"Not any dinner, thank you. I shall be all right to-morrow, when I've slept off my fatigue."

"Well, I know I should like mine," grumbled the countess-dowager, feeling her position in the house already altered from what it had been during her former sojourn, when she assumed full authority, and ordered things as she pleased, completely ignoring the new lord.

"You can have it," said Maude.

"They won't serve it until Hartledon arrives," was the aggrieved answer. "I suppose he's walking up from the station. He always had a queer habit of doing that."

Maude lifted her eyes in slight surprise. Her solitary arrival was a matter of fact so established to herself, that it sounded strange for any one else to be in ignorance of it.

"Lord Hartledon has not come down. He is remaining in London."

The old dowager peered at Maude through her little eyes. "What's that for?"

"Business, I believe."

"Don't tell me an untruth, Maude. You have quarrelled."

"We have not quarrelled. We are perfectly good friends."

"And do you mean to tell me that he sent you down alone?"

"He sent the servants with me."

"Don't be insolent, Maude. You know what I mean."

"Why, mamma, I do not wish to be insolent. I can't tell you more, or tell it differently. Lord Hartledon did not come down with me, and the servants did."

She spoke sharply. In her tired condition the petty conversation was wearying her; and underlying everything else in her heart, was the mortifying consciousness that he had *not* come down with her, chafing her temper almost beyond repression. Considering that Maude did not profess to love her husband very much, it was astonishing how keenly she felt this.

"Are you and Hartledon upon good terms?" asked the countess-dowager after a pause, during which she had never taken her eyes from her daughter's face.

"It would be early days to be on any other."

"Oh," said the dowager. "And you did not write me word from Paris that you found you had made a mistake, that you could not bear your husband! Eh, Maude?"

A tinge came into Maude's cheeks. "And you, mamma, told me that I was to rule my husband with an iron hand, never allowing him to have a will of his own, never consulting him! Both you and I were wrong," she continued quietly. "I wrote that letter in a moment of irritation; and you were assuming what has not proved to be a fact. I like my husband now quite well enough to keep friends with him; his kindness to me is excessive; but I find, with all my wish to rule him, if I had the wish, I could not do it. He has a will of his own, and he exerts it in spite of me; and I am quite sure he will continue to exert it, whenever he fancies he is in the right. You never saw any one so changed from what he used to be."

"How do you mean?"

"I mean in asserting his own will. But he is changed in other ways. It seems to me that he has never been quite the same man since that night in the chapel. He has been more thoughtful; and all the old vacillation is gone."

The countess-dowager could not understand at all; neither did she believe; and she only stared at Maude.

"His *not* coming down with me is a proof that he exercises his own will now. I wished him to come very much, and he knew it; but you see he has not done so."

"And what do you say is keeping him?" repeated the countess-dowager.

"Business—"

"Ah," interrupted the dowager, before Maude could finish, "that's the general excuse. Always suspect it, my dear."

"Suspect what?" asked Maude.

"When a man says that, and gets his wife out of the way with it, rely upon it he is pursuing some nice little interests of his own."

Lady Hartledon understood the implication; she felt nettled, and a flush rose to her face. In her husband's loyalty (always excepting his feeling towards Miss Ashton) she rested fully assured.

"You did not allow me to finish," was the cold rejoinder. "Business *is* keeping him in town, for one thing; for another, I think he cannot get over his dislike to face the Ashtons."

"Rubbish!" cried the wrathful dowager. "He does not tell you what the business is, does he?" she cynically added.

"I happen to know," answered Maude. "The Ashtons are bringing an action against him for breach of promise; and he and Mr. Carr the barrister are trying to arrange it without its coming to a trial."

The old lady opened her eyes and her mouth.

"It is true. They lay the damages at ten thousand pounds!"

With a shriek the countess-dowager began to dance. Ten thousand pounds! Ten thousand pounds would keep her for ever, invested at good interest. She called the parson some unworthy names.

"I cannot give you any of the details," said Maude, in answer to the questions pressed upon her. "Percival will never speak of it, or allow me to do so. I learnt it—I can hardly tell you how I learnt it—by implication, I think; for it was never expressly told me. We had a mysterious visit one night from some old parson—parson or lawyer; and Percival and Mr. Carr, who happened to be at our house, were closeted with him for an hour or two. I saw they were agitated, and guessed what it was; Dr. Ashton was bringing an action. They could not deny it."

"The vile old hypocrite!" cried the incensed dowager. "Ten thousand pounds! Are you sure it is as much as that, Maude?"

"Quite. Mr. Carr told me the amount."

"I wonder you encourage that man to your house."

"It was one of the things I stood out against—fruitlessly," was the quiet answer. "But I believe he means well to me; and I am sure he is doing what he can to serve my husband. They are often together about this business."

"*Of course* Hartledon resists the claim?"

"I don't know. I think they are trying to compromise it, so that it shall not come into court."

"What does Hartledon think of it?"

"It is worrying his life out. No, mamma, it is not too strong an expression. He says nothing; but I can see that it is half killing him. I don't believe he has slept properly since the news was brought to him."

"What a simpleton he must be! And that man will stand up in the pulpit to-morrow and preach of charity!" continued the dowager, turning her animadversions upon Dr. Ashton. "You are a hypocrite too, Maude, for trying to deceive me. You and Hartledon are *not* on good terms; don't tell me! He would never have let you come down alone."

Lady Hartledon would not reply. She felt vexed with her mother, vexed with her husband, vexed on all sides; and she took refuge in her fatigue and was silent.

The dowager went to church on the following day. Maude would not go. The hot anger flushed into her face at the thought of showing herself there for the first time, unaccompanied by her husband: to Maude's mind it seemed that she must look to others so very much like a deserted wife. She comes home alone; he stays in London! "Ah, why did he not come down only for this one Sunday, and go back again—if he must have gone?" she thought.

A month or two ago Maude had not cared enough for him to reason like this. The countess-dowager ensconced herself in a corner of the Hartledon state-pew, and from her blinking eyes looked out upon the Ashtons. Anne, with her once bright face looking rather wan, her modest demeanour; Mrs. Ashton, so essentially a gentlewoman; the doctor, sensible, clever, charitable, beyond all doubt a good man—a feeling came over the mind of the sometimes obtuse woman that of all the people before her they looked the least likely to enter on the sort of lawsuit spoken of by Maude. But never a doubt occurred to her that they *had* entered on it.

Lady Hartledon remained at home, her prayer-book in her hand. She was thinking she could steal out to the evening service; it might not be so much noticed then, her being alone. Listlessly enough she sat, toying with her prayer-book rather than reading it. She had never pretended to be religious, had not been trained to be so; and reading a prayer-book, when not in church, was quite unusual to her. But there are seasons in a woman's life, times when peril is looked forward to, that bring thought even to the most careless nature. Maude was trying to play at "being good," and was reading the psalms for the day in an absent fashion, her thoughts elsewhere; and the morning passed on. The quiet apathy of her present state, compared with the restless fever which had stirred her during her last sojourn at Hartledon, was remarkable.

Suddenly there burst in upon her the countess-dowager: that estimable lady's bonnet awry, her face scarlet, herself in a commotion.

"I didn't suppose you'd have done it, Maude! You might play tricks upon other people, I think, but not upon your own mother."

The interlude was rather welcome to Maude, rousing her from her apathy. Not for some few moments, however, could she understand the cause of complaint.

It appeared that the countess-dowager, with that absence of all sense of the fitness of things which so eminently characterized her, had joined the Ashtons after service, inquiring with quite motherly solicitude after Mrs. Ashton's health, complimenting Anne upon her charming looks; making herself, in short, as agreeable as she knew how, and completely ignoring the past in regard to her son-in-law. Gentlewomen in mind and manners, they did not repulse her, were even courteously civil; and she graciously accompanied them across the road to the Rectory-gate, and there took a cordial leave, saying she would look in on the morrow.

In returning she met Dr. Ashton. He was passing her with nothing but a bow; but he little knew the countess-dowager. She grasped his hand; said how grieved she was not to have had an opportunity of explaining away her part in the past; hoped he would let bygones be bygones; and finally, whilst the clergyman was scheming how to get away from her without absolute rudeness, she astonished him with a communication touching the action-at-law. There ensued a little mutual misapprehension, followed by a few emphatic words of denial from Dr. Ashton; and the countess-dowager walked away with a scarlet face, and an explosion of anger against her daughter.

Lady Hartledon was not yet callous to the proprieties of life; and the intrusion on the Ashtons, which her mother confessed to, half frightened, half shamed her. But the dowager's wrath at having been misled bore down everything. Dr. Ashton had entered no action whatever against Lord Hartledon; had never thought of doing it.

"And you, you wicked, ungrateful girl, to come home to me with such an invention, and cause me to start off on a fool's errand! Do you suppose I should have gone and humbled myself to those people, but for hoping to bring the parson to a sense of what he was doing in going-in for those enormous damages?"

"I have not come home to you with any invention, mamma. Dr. Ashton has entered the action."

"He has not," raved the dowager. "It is an infamous hoax you have played off upon me. You couldn't find any excuse for your husband's staying in London, and so invented this. What with you, and what with Kirton's ingratitude, I shall be driven out of house and home!"

"I won't say another word until you are calm and can talk common sense," said Maude, leaning back in her chair, and putting down her prayer-book.

"Common sense! What am I talking but common sense? When a child begins to mislead her own mother, the world ought to come to an end."

Maude took no notice.

There happened to be some water standing on a table, and the dowager poured out a tumblerful and drank it, though not accustomed to the beverage. Untying her bonnet-strings she sat down, a little calmer.

"Perhaps you'll explain this at your convenience, Maude."

"There is nothing to explain," was the answer. "What I told you was the truth. The action *has* been entered by the Ashtons."

"And I tell you that the action has not."

"I assure you that it has," returned Maude. "I told you of the evening we first had notice of it, and the damages claimed; do you think I invented that, or went to sleep and dreamt it? If Val has gone down once to that Temple about it, he has gone fifty times. He would not go for pleasure."

The countess-dowager sat fanning herself quietly: for her daughter's words were gaining ground.

"There's a mistake somewhere, Maude, and it is on your side and not mine. I'll lay my life that no action has been entered by Dr. Ashton. The man spoke the truth; I can read the truth when I see it as well as anyone: his face flushed with pain and anger at such a thing being said of him. It may not be difficult to explain this contradiction."

"Do you think not?" returned Maude, her indifference exciting the listener to anger.

"*I* should say Hartledon is deceiving you. If any action is entered against him at all, it isn't that sort of action; or perhaps the young lady is not Miss Ashton, but some other; he's just the kind of man to be drawn into promising marriage to a dozen or two. Very clever of him to palm you off with this tale: a man may get into five hundred troubles not convenient to disclose to his wife."

Except that Lady Hartledon's cheek flushed a little, she made no answer; she held firmly—at least she thought she held firmly—to her own side of the case. Her mother, on the contrary, adopted the new view, and dismissed it from her thoughts accordingly.

Maude went to church in the evening, sitting alone in the great pew, pale and quiet. Anne Ashton was also alone; and the two whilom rivals, the triumphant and the rejected, could survey each other to their heart's content.

Not very triumphant was Maude's feeling. Strange perhaps to say, the suggestion of the old dowager, like instilled poison, was making its way into her very veins. Her thoughts had been busy with the matter ever since. One positive conviction lay in her heart—that Dr. Ashton, now reading the first lesson before her, for he was taking the whole of the service that evening, could not, under any circumstance, be guilty of a false assertion or subterfuge. One solution of the difficulty presented itself to her—that her mother, in her irascibility, had misunderstood the Rector; and yet that was improbable. As Maude half sat, half lay back in the pew, for the faint feeling was especially upon her that evening, she thought she would give a great deal to set the matter at rest.

When the service was over she took the more secluded way home; those of the servants who had attended returning as usual by the road. On reaching the turning where the three paths diverged, the faintness which had been hovering over her all the evening suddenly grew worse; and but for a friendly tree, she might have fallen. It grew better in a few moments, but she did not yet quit her support.

Very surprised was the Rector of Calne to come up and see Lady Hartledon in this position. Every Sunday evening, after service, he went to visit a man in one of the cottages, who was dying of consumption, and he was on his way there now. He would have preferred to pass without speaking: but Lady Hartledon looked in need of assistance; and in common Christian kindness he could not pass her by.

"I beg your pardon, Lady Hartledon. Are you ill?"

She took his offered arm with her disengaged hand, as an additional support; and her white face turned a shade whiter.

"A sudden faintness overtook me. I am better now," she said, when able to speak.

"Will you allow me to walk on with you?"

"Thank you; just a little way. If you will not mind it."

That he must have understood the feeling which prompted the concluding words was undoubted: and perhaps had Lady Hartledon been in possession of her keenest senses, she might never have spoken them. Pride and health go out of us together. Dr. Ashton took her on his arm, and they walked slowly in the direction of the little bridge. Colour was returning to her face, strength to her frame.

"The heat of the day has affected you, possibly?"

"Yes, perhaps; I have felt faint at times lately. The church was very hot to-night."

Nothing more was said until the bridge was gained, and then Maude released his arm.

"Dr. Ashton, I thank you very much. You have been a friend in need."

"But are you sure you are strong enough to go on alone? I will escort you to the house if you are not."

"Quite strong enough now. Thank you once again."

As he was bowing his farewell, a sudden impulse to speak, and set the matter that was troubling her at rest, came over her. Without a moment's deliberation, without weighing her words, she rushed upon it; the ostensible plea an apology for her mother's having spoken to him.

"Yes, I told Lady Kirton she was labouring under some misapprehension," he quietly answered.

"Will you forgive *me* also for speaking of it?" she murmured. "Since my mother came home with the news of what you said, I have been lost in a sea of conjecture: I could not attend to the service for dwelling upon it, and might as well not have been in church—a curious confession to make to you, Dr. Ashton. Is it indeed true that you know nothing of the matter?"

"Lady Kirton told me in so many words that I had entered an action against Lord Hartledon for breach of promise, and laid the damages at ten thousand pounds," returned Dr. Ashton, with a plainness of speech and a cynical manner that made her blush. And she saw at once that he had done nothing of the sort; saw it without any more decisive denial.

"But the action has been entered," said Lady Hartledon.

"I beg your pardon, madam. Lord Hartledon is, I should imagine, the only man living who could suppose me capable of such a thing."

"And you have *not* entered on it!" she reiterated, half bewildered by the denial.

"Most certainly not. When I parted with Lord Hartledon on a certain evening, which probably your ladyship remembers, I washed my hands of him for good, desiring never to approach him in any way whatever, never hear of him, never see him again. Your husband, madam, is safe for me: I desire nothing better than to forget that such a man is in existence."

Lifting his hat, he walked away. And Lady Hartledon stood and gazed after him as one in a dream.

# XXIII

## Mr. Carr at Work

Thomas Carr was threading his way through the mazy precincts of Gray's Inn, with that quick step and absorbed manner known only, I think, to the busy man of our busy metropolis. He was on his way to make some inquiries of a firm of solicitors, Messrs. Kedge and Reck, strangers to him in all but name.

Up some dark and dingy stairs, he knocked at a dark and dingy door: which, after a minute, opened of itself by some ingenious contrivance, and let him into a passage, whence he turned into a room, where two clerks were writing at a desk.

"Can I see Mr. Kedge?"

"Not in," said one of the clerks, without looking up.

"Mr. Reck, then?"

"Not in."

"When will either of them be in?" continued the barrister; thinking that if he were Messrs. Kedge and Reck the clerk would get his discharge for incivility.

"Can't say. What's your business?"

"My business is with them: not with you."

"You can see the managing clerk."

"I wish to see one of the partners."

"Could you give your name?" continued the gentleman, equably.

Mr. Carr handed in his card. The clerk glanced at it, and surreptitiously showed it to his companion; and both of them looked up at him. Mr. Carr of the Temple was known by reputation, and they condescended to become civil.

"Take a seat for a moment, sir," said the one. "I'll inquire how long Mr. Kedge will be; but Mr. Reek's not in town to-day."

A few minutes, and Thomas Carr found himself in a small square room with the head of the firm, a youngish man and somewhat of a dandy, especially genial in manner, as though in contrast to his clerk. He welcomed the rising barrister.

"There's as much difficulty in getting to see you as if you were Pope of Rome," cried Mr. Carr, good humouredly.

The lawyer laughed. "Hopkins did not know you: and strangers are generally introduced to Mr. Reck, or to our managing clerk. What can I do for you, Mr. Carr?"

"I don't know that you can do anything for me," said Mr. Carr, seating himself; "but I hope you can. At the present moment I am engaged in sifting a piece of complicated business for a friend; a private matter entirely, which it is necessary to keep private. I am greatly interested in it myself, as you may readily believe, when it is keeping me from circuit. Indeed it may almost be called my own affair," he added, observing the eyes of the lawyer fixed upon him, and not caring they should see into his business too clearly. "I fancy you have a clerk, or had a clerk, who is cognizant of one or two points in regard to it: can you put me in the way of finding out where he is? His name is Gordon."

"Gordon! We have no clerk of that name. Never had one, that I remember. How came you to fancy it?"

"I heard it from my own clerk, Taylor. One day last week I happened to say before him that I'd give a five-pound note out of my pocket to get at the present whereabouts of this man Gordon. Taylor is a shrewd fellow; full of useful bits of information, and knows, I really believe, three-fourths of London by name. He immediately said a young man of that name was with Messrs. Kedge and Reck, of Gray's Inn, either as clerk, or in some other capacity; and when he described this clerk of yours, I felt nearly sure that it was the man I am looking for. I got Taylor to make inquiries, and he did, I believe, of one of your clerks; but he could learn nothing, except that no one of that name was connected with you now. Taylor persists that he is or was connected with you; and so I thought the shortest plan to settle the matter was to ask yourselves."

"We have no clerk of that name," repeated Mr. Kedge, pushing back some papers on the table. "Never had one."

"Understand," said Mr. Carr, thinking it just possible the lawyer might be mistaking his motives, "I have nothing to allege against the man, and do not seek to injure him. The real fact is, that I do not want to see him or to be brought into personal contact with him; I only want to know whether he is in London, and, if so, where?"

"I assure you he is not connected with us," repeated Mr. Kedge. "I would tell you so in a moment if he were."

"Then I can only apologise for having troubled you," said the barrister, rising. "Taylor must have been mistaken. And yet I would have backed his word, when he positively asserts a thing, against the world. I hardly ever knew him wrong."

Mr. Kedge was playing with the locket on his watch-chain, his head bent in thought.

"Wait a moment, Mr. Carr. I remember now that we took a clerk temporarily into the office in the latter part of last year. His writing did not suit, and we kept him only a week or two. I don't know what his name was, but it might have been Gordon."

"Do you remember what sort of a man he was?" asked Mr. Carr, somewhat eagerly.

"I really do not. You see, I don't come much into contact with our clerks. Reck does; but he's not here to-day. I fancy he had red hair."

"Gordon had reddish hair."

"You had better see Kimberly," said the solicitor, ringing a bell. "He is our managing clerk, and knows everything."

A grey-haired, silent-looking man came in with stooping shoulders. Mr. Kedge, without any circumlocution, asked whether he remembered any clerk of the name of Gordon having been in the house. Mr. Kimberly responded by saying that they never had one in the house of the name.

"Well, I thought not," observed the principal. "There was one had in for a short time, you know, while Hopkins was ill. I forget his name."

"His name was Druitt, sir. We employed a man of the name of Gorton to do some outdoor business for us at times," continued the managing clerk, turning his eyes on the barrister; "but not lately."

"What sort of business?"

"Serving writs."

"Gorton is not Gordon," remarked Mr. Kedge, with legal acumen. "By the way, Kimberly, I have heard nothing of Gorton lately. What has become of him?"

"I have not the least idea, sir. We parted in a huff, so he wouldn't perhaps be likely to come in my way again. Some business that he mismanaged, if you remember, sir, down at Calne."

"When he arrested one man for another," laughed the lawyer, "and got entangled in a coroner's inquest, and I don't know what all."

Mr. Carr had pricked up his ears, scarcely daring to breathe. But his manner was careless to a degree.

"The man he arrested being Lord Hartledon; the man he ought to have arrested being the Honourable Percival Elster," he interposed, laughing.

"What! do you know about it?" cried the lawyer.

"I remember hearing of it; I was intimate with Mr. Elster at the time."

"He has since become Lord Hartledon."

"Yes. But about this Gorton! I should not be in the least surprised if he is the man I am inquiring for. Can you describe him to me, Mr. Kimberly?"

"He is a short, slight man, under thirty, with red hair and whiskers."

Mr. Carr nodded.

"Light hair with a reddish tinge it has been described to me. Do you happen to be at all acquainted with his antecedents?"

"Not I; I know nothing about, the man," said Mr. Kedge. "Kimberly does, perhaps."

"No, sir," dissented Kimberly. "He had been to Australia, I believe; and that's all I know about him."

"It is the same man," said Mr. Carr, quietly. "And if you can tell me anything about him," he continued, turning to the older man, "I shall be exceedingly obliged to you. To begin with—when did you first know him?"

But at this juncture an interruption occurred. Hopkins the discourteous came in with a card, which he presented to his principal. The gentleman was waiting to see Mr. Kedge. Two more clients were also waiting, he added, Thomas Carr rose, and the end of it was that he went with Mr. Kimberly to his own room.

"It's Carr of the Inner Temple," whispered Mr. Kedge in his clerk's ear.

"Oh, I know him, sir."

"All right. If you can help him, do so."

"I first knew Gorton about fifteen months ago," observed the clerk, when they were shut in together. "A friend of mine, now dead, spoke of him to me as a respectable young fellow who had fallen in the world, and asked if I could help him to some employment. I think he told me somewhat of his history; but I quite forget it. I know he was very low down then, with scarcely bread to eat."

"Did this friend of yours call him Gorton or Gordon?" interrupted Mr. Carr.

"Gorton. I never heard him called Gordon at all. I remember seeing a book of his that he seemed to set some store by. It was printed in old English, and had his name on the title-page: 'George Gorton. From his affectionate father, W. Gorton.' I employed him in some outdoor work. He knew London perfectly well, and seemed to know people too."

"And he had been to Australia?"

"He had been to Australia, I feel sure. One day he accidentally let slip some words about Melbourne, which he could not well have done unless he had seen the place. I taxed him with it, and he shuffled out of it with some excuse; but in such a manner as to convince me he had been there."

"And now, Mr. Kimberly, I am going to ask you another question. You spoke of his having been at Calne; I infer that you sent him to the place on the errand to Mr. Elster. Try to recollect whether his going there was your own spontaneous act, or whether he was the original mover in the journey?"

The grey-haired clerk looked up as though not understanding.

"You don't quite take me, I see."

"Yes I do, sir; but I was thinking. So far as I can recollect, it was our own spontaneous act. I am sure I had no reason to think otherwise at the time. We had had a deal of trouble with the Honourable Mr. Elster; and when it was found that he had left town for the family seat, we came to the resolution to arrest him."

Thomas Carr paused. "Do you know anything of Gordon's—or Gorton's doings in Calne? Did you ever hear him speak of them afterwards?"

"I don't know that I did particularly. The excuse he made to us for arresting Lord Hartledon was, that the brothers were so much alike he mistook the one for the other."

"Which would infer that he knew Mr. Elster by sight."

"It might; yes. It was not for the mistake that we discharged him; indeed, not for anything at all connected with Calne. He did seem to have gone about his business there in a very loose way, and to have paid less attention to our interests than to the gossip of the place; of which there was a tolerable amount just then, on account of Lord Hartledon's unfortunate death. Gorton was set upon another job or two when he returned; and one of those he contrived to mismanage so woefully, that I would give him no more to do. It struck me that he must drink, or else was accessible to a bribe."

Mr. Carr nodded his head, thinking the latter more than probable. His fingers were playing with a newspaper which happened to lie on the clerk's desk; and he put the next question with a very well-assumed air of carelessness, as if it were but the passing thought of the moment.

"Did he ever talk about Mr. Elster?"

"Never but once. He came to my house one evening to tell me he had discovered the hiding-place of a gentleman we were looking for. I was taking my solitary glass of gin and water after supper, the only stimulant I ever touch—and that by the doctor's orders—and I could not do less than ask him to help himself. You see, sir, we did not look upon him as a common sheriff's man: and he helped himself pretty freely. That made him talkative. I fancy his head cannot stand much; and he began rambling upon recent affairs at Calne; he had not been back above a week then—"

"And he spoke of Mr. Elster?"

"He spoke a good deal of him as the new Lord Hartledon, all in a rambling sort of way. He hinted that it might be in his power to bring home to him some great crime."

"The man must have been drunk indeed!" remarked Mr. Carr, with the most perfect assumption of indifference; a very contrast to the fear that shot through his heart. "What crime, pray? I hope he particularized it."

"What he seemed to hint at was some unfair play in connection with his brother's death," said the old clerk, lowering his voice. "'A man at his wits' end for money would do many queer things,' he remarked."

Mr. Carr's eyes flashed. "What a dangerous fool he must be! You surely did not listen to him!"

"I, sir! I stopped him pretty quickly, and bade him sew up his mouth until he came to his sober senses again. Oh, they make great simpletons of themselves, some of these young fellows, when they get a little drink into them."

"They do," said the barrister. "Did he ever allude to the matter again?"

"Never; and when I saw him the next day, he seemed ashamed of himself, and asked if he had not been talking a lot of nonsense. About a fortnight after that we parted, and I have never seen him since."

"And you really do not know what has become of him?"

"Not at all. I should think he has left London."

"Why?"

"Because had he remained in it he'd be sure to have come bothering me to employ him again; unless, indeed, he has found some one else to do it."

"Well," said Mr. Carr, rising, "will you do me this favour? If you come across the man again, or learn tidings of him in any way, let me know it at once. I do not want him to hear of me, or that I have made inquiries about him. I only wish to ascertain *where* he is, if that be possible. Any one bringing me this information privately will find it well worth his while."

He went forth into the busy streets again, sick at heart; and upon reaching his chambers wrote a note for a detective officer, and put some business into his hands.

Meanwhile Lord Hartledon remained in London. When the term for which they had engaged the furnished house was expired he took lodgings in Grafton Street; and there he stayed, his frame of mind restless and unsatisfactory. Lady Hartledon wrote to him sometimes, and he answered her. She said not a word about the discovery she had made in regard to the alleged action-at-law; but she never failed in every letter to ask what he was doing, and when he was coming home— meaning to Hartledon. He put her off in the best way he could: he and Carr were very busy together, he said: as to home, he could not mention any particular time. And Lady Hartledon bottled up her curiosity and her wrath, and waited with what patience she possessed.

The truth was—and, perhaps, the reader may have divined it—that graver motives than the sensitive feeling of not liking to face the Ashtons were keeping Lord Hartledon from his wife and home. He had once, in his bachelor days, wished himself a savage in some remote desert, where his civilized acquaintance could not come near him; he had a thousand times more reason to wish himself one now.

One dusty day, when the excessive heat of summer was on the wane, he went down to Mr. Carr's chambers, and found that gentleman out. Not out for long, the clerk thought; and sat down and waited. The room he was in looked out on the cool garden, the quiet river; in the one there was not a soul except Mr. Broom himself, who had gone in to watch the progress of his chrysanthemums, and was stooping lovingly over the beds; on the other a steamer, freighted with a straggling few, was paddling up the river against the tide, and a barge with its brown sail was coming down in all its picturesque charm. The contrast between this quiet scene and the bustling, dusty, jostling world he had come in from, was grateful even to his disturbed heart; and he felt half inclined to go round to the garden and fling himself on the lawn as a man might do who was free from care.

Mr. Carr indulged in the costly luxury of three rooms in the Temple; his sitting-room, which was his work-room, a bedroom, and a little outer room, the sanctum of his clerk. Lord Hartledon was in the sitting-room, but he could hear the clerk moving about in the ante-room, as if he had no writing on hand that morning. When tired of waiting, he called him in.

"Mr. Taylor, how long do you think he will be? I've been dozing, I think."

"Well, I thought he'd have been here before now, my lord. He generally tells me if he is going out for any length of time; but he said nothing to-day."

"A newspaper would be something to while away one's time, or a book," grumbled Hartledon. "Not those," glancing at a book-case full of ponderous law-volumes.

"Your lordship has taken the cream out of them already," remarked the clerk, with a laugh; and Hartledon's brow knitted at the words. He had "taken the cream" out of those old law-books, if studying them could do it, for he had been at them pretty often of late.

But Mr. Taylor's remarks had no ulterior meaning. Being a shrewd man, he could not fail to suspect that Lord Hartledon was in a scrape of some sort; but from a word dropped by his master he supposed it to involve nothing more than a question of debt; and he never suspected that the word had been dropped purposely. "Scamps would claim money twice over when they could," said Mr. Carr; and Elster was a careless man, always losing his receipts. He was a short, slight man, this clerk—in build something like his master—with an intelligent, silent face, a small, sharp nose, and fair hair. He had been born a gentleman, he was wont to say; and indeed he looked one; but he had not received an education commensurate with that fact, and had to make his own way in the world. He might do it yet, perhaps, he remarked one day to Lord Hartledon; and certainly, if steady perseverance could effect it, he would: all his spare time was spent in study.

"He has not gone to one of those blessed consultations in somebody's chambers, has he?" cried Val. "I have known them last three hours."

"I have known them last longer than that," said the clerk equably. "But there are none on just now."

"I can't think what has become of him. He made an appointment with me for this morning. And where's his *Times*?"

Mr. Taylor could not tell where; he had been looking for the newspaper on his own account. It was not to be found; and they could only come to the conclusion that the barrister had taken it out with him.

"I wish you'd go out and buy me one," said Val.

"I'll go with pleasure, my lord. But suppose any one comes to the door?"

"Oh, I'll answer it. They'll think Carr has taken on a new clerk."

Mr. Taylor laughed, and went out. Hartledon, tired of sitting, began to pace the room and the ante-room. Most men would have taken their departure; but he had nothing to do; he had latterly shunned that portion of the world called society; and was as well in Mr. Carr's chambers as in his own lodgings, or in strolling about with his troubled heart. While thus occupied, there came a soft tap to the outer door—as was sure to be the case, the clerk being absent—and Val opened it. A middle-aged, quiet-looking man stood there, who had nothing specially noticeable in his appearance, except a pair of deep-set dark eyes, under bushy eyebrows that were turning grey.

"Mr. Carr within?"

"Mr. Carr's not in," replied the temporary clerk. "I dare say you can wait."

"Likely to be long?"

"I should think not. I have been waiting for him these two hours."

The applicant entered, and sat down in the clerk's room. Lord Hartledon went into the other, and stood drumming on the window-pane, as he gazed out upon the Temple garden.

"I'd go, but for that note of Carr's," he said to himself. "If—Halloa! that's his voice at last."

Mr. Carr and his clerk had returned together. The former, after a few moments, came in to Lord Hartledon.

"A nice fellow you are, Carr! Sending me word to be here at eleven o'clock, and then walking off for two mortal hours!"

"I sent you word to wait for me at your own home!"

"Well, that's good!" returned Val. "It said, 'Be here at eleven,' as plainly as writing could say it."

"And there was a postscript over the leaf telling you, on second thought, *not* to be here, but to wait at home for me," said Mr. Carr. "I remembered a matter of business that would take me up your way this morning, and thought I'd go on to you. It's just your careless fashion, Hartledon, reading only half your letters! You should have turned it over."

"Who was to think there was anything on the other side? Folk don't turn their letters over from curiosity when they are concluded on the first page."

"I never had a letter in my life but I turned it over to make sure," observed the more careful barrister. "I have had my walk for nothing."

"And I have been cooling my heels here! And you took the newspaper with you!"

"No, I did not. Churton sent in from his rooms to borrow it."

"Well, let the misunderstanding go, and forgive me for being cross. Do you know, Carr, I think I am growing ill-tempered from trouble. What news have you for me?"

"I'll tell you by-and-by. Do you know who that is in the other room?"

"Not I. He seemed to stare me inside-out in a quiet way as I let him in."

"Ay. It's Green, the detective. At times a question occurs to me whether that's his real name, or one assumed in his profession. He has come to report at last. Had you better remain?"

"Why not?"

Mr. Carr looked dubious.

"You can make some excuse for my presence."

"It's not that. I'm thinking if you let slip a word—"

"Is it likely?"

"Inadvertently, I mean."

"There's no fear. You have not mentioned my name to him?"

"I retort in your own words—Is it likely? He does not know why he is being employed or what I want with the man I wish traced. At present he is working, as far as that goes, in the dark. I might have put him on a false scent, just as cleverly and unsuspiciously as I dare say he could put me; but I've not done it. What's the matter with you to-day, Hartledon? You look ill."

"I only look what I am, then," was the answer. "But I'm no worse than usual. I'd rather be transported—I'd rather be hanged, for that matter—than lead the life of misery I am leading. At times I feel inclined to give in, but then comes the thought of Maude."

# XXIV

## Somebody Else at Work

They were shut in together: the detective officer, Mr. Carr, and Lord Hartledon. "You may speak freely before this gentleman," observed Mr. Carr, as if in apology for a third being present. "He knows the parties, and is almost as much interested in the affair as I am."

The detective glanced at Lord Hartledon with his deep eyes, but he did not know him, and took out a note-book, on which some words and figures were dotted down, hieroglyphics to any one's eyes but his own. Squaring his elbows on the table, he begun abruptly; and appeared to have a habit of cutting short his words and sentences.

"Haven't succeeded yet as could wish, Mr. Carr; at least not altogether: have had to be longer over it, too, than thought for. George Gordon: Scotch birth, so far as can learn; left an orphan; lived mostly in London. Served time to medical practitioner, locality Paddington. Idle, visionary, loose in conduct, good-natured, fond of roving. Surgeon wouldn't keep him as assistant; might have done it, he says, had G.G. been of settled disposition: saw him in drink three times. Next turns up in Scotland, assistant to a doctor there; name Mair, locality Kirkcudbrightshire. Remained less than a year; left, saying was going to Australia. So far," broke off the speaker, raising his eyes to Mr. Carr's, "particulars tally with the information supplied by you."

"Just so."

"Then my further work began," continued Mr. Green. "Afraid what I've got together won't be satisfactory; differ from you in opinion, at any rate. G.G. went to Australia; no doubt of that; friend of his got a letter or two from him while there: last one enclosed two ten-pound notes, borrowed by G.G. before he went out. Last letter said been up to the diggings; very successful; coming home with his money, mentioned ship he meant to sail in. Hadn't been in Australia twelve months."

"Who was the friend?" asked Mr. Carr.

"Respectable man; gentleman; former fellow-pupil with Gordon in London; in good practice for himself now; locality Kensington. After last letter, friend perpetually looking out for G.G. G.G. did not make his appearance; conclusion friend draws is he did not come back. Feels sure Gordon, whether rich or poor, in ill-report or good-report, would have come direct to him."

"I happen to know that he did come back," said Mr. Carr.

"Don't think it," was the unceremonious rejoinder.

"I know it positively. And that he was in London."

The detective looked over his notes, as if completely ignoring Mr. Carr's words.

"You heard, gentlemen, of that mutiny on board the ship *Morning Star*, some three years ago? Made a noise at the time."

"Well?"

"Ringleader was this same man, George Gordon."

"No!" exclaimed Mr. Carr.

"No reasonable doubt about it. Friend of his feels none: can't understand how G.G. could have turned suddenly cruel; never was that. Pooh! when men have been leading lawless lives in the bush, perhaps taken regularly to drinking—which G.G. was inclined to before—they're ready for any crime under the sun."

"But how do you connect Gordon with the ringleader of that diabolical mutiny?"

"Easy enough. Same name, George Gordon: wrote to a friend the ship he was coming home in—*Morning Star*. It *was* the same; price on G.G.'s head to this day: shouldn't mind getting it. Needn't pother over it, sir; 'twas Gordon: but he'd never put his foot in London."

"If true, it would account for his not showing himself to his friend—assuming that he did come back," observed Mr. Carr.

"Friend says not. Sure that G.G., whatever he might have been guilty of, would go to him direct; knew he might depend on him in any trouble. A proof, he argues, that G.G. never came back."

"But I tell you he did come back," repeated the barrister. "Strange the similarity of name never struck me," he added, turning to Lord Hartledon. "I took some interest in that mutiny at the time; but it never occurred to me to connect this man or his name with it. A noted name, at any rate, if not a very common one."

Lord Hartledon nodded. He had sat silent throughout, a little apart, his face somewhat turned from them, as though the business did not concern him.

"And now I will relate to you what more I know of Gordon," resumed Mr. Carr, moving his chair nearer the detective, and so partially screening Lord Hartledon. "He was in London last year, employed by

Kedge and Reck, of Gray's Inn, to serve writs. What he had done with himself from the time of the mutiny—allowing that he was identical with the Gordon of that business—I dare say no one living could tell, himself excepted. He was calling himself Gorton last autumn. Not much of a change from his own name."

"George Gorton," assented the detective.

"Yes, George Gorton. I knew this much when I first applied to you. I did not mention it because I preferred to let you go to work without it. Understand me; that it is the same man, I *know*; but there are nevertheless discrepancies in the case that I cannot reconcile; and I thought you might possibly arrive at some knowledge of the man without this clue better than with it."

"Sorry to differ from you, Mr. Carr; must hold to the belief that George Gorton, employed at Kedge and Reck's, was not the same man at all," came the cool and obstinate rejoinder. "Have sifted the apparent similarity between the two, and drawn conclusions accordingly."

The remark implied that the detective was wiser on the subject of George Gorton than Mr. Carr had bargained for, and a shadow of apprehension stole over him. It was by no means his wish that the sharp detective and the man should come into contact with each other; all he wanted was to find out where he was at present, *not* that he should be meddled with. This he had fully explained in the first instance, and the other had acquiesced in his curt way.

"You are thinking me uncommon clever, getting on the track of George Gorton, when nothing on the surface connects him with the man wanted," remarked the detective, with professional vanity. "Came upon it accidentally; as well confess it; don't want to assume more credit than's due. It was in this way. Evening following your instructions, had to see managing clerk of Kedge and Reck; was engaged on a little matter for them. Business over, he asked me if I knew anything of a man named George Gorton, or Gordon— as I seemed to know something of pretty well everybody. Having just been asked here about George Gordon, I naturally connected the two questions together. Inquired of Kimberly *why* he suspected his clerk Gorton should be Gordon; Kimberly replied he did not suspect him, but a gentleman did, who had been there that day. This put me on Gorton's track."

"And you followed it up?"

"Of course; keeping my own counsel. Took it up in haste, though; no deliberation; went off to Calne, without first comparing notes with Gordon's friend the surgeon."

"To Calne!" explained Mr. Carr, while Lord Hartledon turned his head and took a sharp look at the speaker.

A nod was the only answer. "Got down; thought at first as you do, Mr. Carr, that man was the same, and was on right track. Went to work in my own way; was a countryman just come into a snug bit of inheritance, looking out for a corner of land. Wormed out a bit here and a bit there; heard this from one, that from another; nearly got an interview with my Lord Hartledon himself, as candidate for one of his farms."

"Lord Hartledon was not at Calne, I think," interrupted Mr. Carr, speaking impulsively.

"Know it now; didn't then; and wanted, for own purposes, to get a sight of him and a word with him. Went to his place: saw a queer old creature in yellow gauze; saw my lord's wife, too, at a distance; fine woman; got intimate with butler, named Hedges; got intimate with two or three more; altogether turned the recent doings of Mr. Gorton inside out."

"Well?" said Mr. Carr, in his surprise.

"Care to hear 'em?" continued the detective, after a moment's pause; and a feeling crossed Mr. Carr, that if ever he had a deep man to deal with it was this one, in spite of his apparent simplicity. "Gorton went down on his errand for Kedge and Reck, writ in pocket for Mr. Elster; had boasted he knew him. Can't quite make out whether he did or not; any rate, served writ on Lord Hartledon by mistake. Lordship made a joke of it; took up the matter as a brother ought; wrote himself to Kedge and Reck to get it settled. Brothers quarrelled; day or two, and elder was drowned, nobody seems to know how. Gorton stopped on, against orders from Kimberly; said afterwards, by way of excuse, had been served with summons to attend inquest. Couldn't say much at inquest, or *didn't*; was asked if he witnessed accident; said 'No,' but some still think he did. Showed himself at Hartledon afterwards trying to get interview with new lord; new lord wouldn't see him, and butler turned him out. Gorton in a rage, went back to inn, got some drink, said he might be able to *make* his lordship see him yet; hinted at some secret, but too far gone to know what he said; began boasting of adventures in Australia. Loose man there, one Pike, took him in charge, and saw him off by rail for London."

"Yes?" said Mr. Carr, for the speaker had stopped.

"That's pretty near all as far as Gorton goes. Got a clue to an address in London, where he might be heard of: got it oddly, too; but that's no matter. Came up again and went to address; could learn nothing; tracked here, tracked there, both for Gordon and Gorton; found Gorton disappeared close upon time he was cast adrift by Kimberly. Not in London as far as can be traced; where gone, can't tell yet. So much done, summed up my experiences and came here to-day to state them."

"Proceed," said Mr. Carr.

The detective put his note-book in his pocket, and with his elbows still on the table, pressed his fingers together alternately as he stated his points, speaking less abruptly than before.

"My conclusion is—the Gordon you spoke to me about was the Gordon who led the mutiny on board the *Morning Star*; that he never, after that, came back to England; has never been heard of, in short, by any living soul in it. That the Gorton employed by Kedge and Reck was another man altogether. Neither is to be traced; the one may have found his grave in the sea years ago; the other has disappeared out of London life since last October, and I can't trace how or where."

Mr. Carr listened in silence. To reiterate that the two men were identical, would have been waste of time, since he could not avow how he knew it, or give the faintest clue. The detective himself had unconsciously furnished a proof.

"Will you tell me your grounds for believing them to be different men?" he asked.

"Nay," said the keen detective, "the shortest way would be for you to give me your grounds for thinking them to be the same."

"I cannot do it," said Mr. Carr. "It might involve—no, I cannot do it."

"Well, I suspected so. I don't mind mentioning one or two on my side. The description of Gorton, as I had it from Kimberly, does not accord with that of Gordon as given me by his friend the surgeon. I wrote out the description of Gorton, and took it to him. 'Is this Gordon?' I asked. 'No, it is not,' said he; and I'm sure he spoke the truth."

"Gordon, on his return from Australia, might be a different-looking man from the Gordon who went to it."

"And would be, no doubt. But see here: Gorton was not disguised; Gordon would not dare to be in London without being so; his head's not worth a day's purchase. Fancy his walking about with only one letter in his name altered! Rely upon it, Mr. Carr, you are mistaken; Gordon would no more dare come back and put his head into the lion's mouth than you'd jump into a fiery furnace. He couldn't land without being dropped upon: the man was no common offender, and we've kept our eyes open. And that's all," added the detective, after a pause. "Not very satisfactory, is it, Mr. Carr? But, such as it is, I think you may rely upon it, in spite of your own opinion. Meanwhile, I'll keep on the look-out for Gorton, and tell you if he turns up."

The conference was over, and Mr. Green took his departure. Thomas Carr saw him out himself, returned and sat down in a reverie.

"It's a curious tale," said Lord Hartledon.

"I'm thinking how the fact, now disclosed, of Gordon's being Gordon of the mutiny, affects you," remarked Mr. Carr.

"You believe him to be the same?"

"I see no reason to doubt it. It's not probable that two George Gordons should take their passage home in the *Morning Star*. Besides, it explains points that seemed incomprehensible. I could not understand why you were not troubled by this man, but rely upon it he has found it expedient to go into effectual hiding, and dare not yet come out of it. This fact is a very great hold upon him; and if he turns round on you, you may keep him in check with it. Only let me alight on him; I'll so frighten him as to cause him to ship himself off for life."

"I don't like that detective's having gone down to Calne," remarked Lord Hartledon.

Neither did Mr. Carr, especially if Gordon, or Gorton, should have become talkative, as there was reason to believe he had.

"Gordon is in England, and in hiding; probably in London, for there's no place where you may hide so effectually. One thing I am astonished at: that he should show himself openly as George Gorton."

"Look here, Carr," said Lord Hartledon, leaning forward; "I don't believe, in spite of you and the detective, that Gordon, our Gordon, was the one connected with the mutiny. I might possibly get a description of that man from Gum of Calne; for his son was coming home in the same ship—was one of those killed."

"Who's Gum of Calne?"

"The parish clerk, and a very respectable man. Mirrable, our housekeeper whom you have seen, is related to them. Gum went to Liverpool at the time, I know, and saw the remnant of the passengers those pirates had spared; he was sure to hear a full description of Gordon. If ever I visit Hartledon again I'll ask him."

"If ever you visit Hartledon again!" echoed Mr. Carr. "Unless you leave the country—as I advise you to do—you cannot help visiting Hartledon."

"Well, I would almost as soon be hanged!" cried Val. "And now, what do you want me for, and why have you kept me here?"

Mr. Carr drew his chair nearer to Lord Hartledon. They alone knew their own troubles, and sat talking long after the afternoon was over. Mr. Taylor came to the room; it was past his usual hour of departure.

"I suppose I can go, sir?"

"Not just yet," replied Mr. Carr.

Hartledon took out his watch, and wondered whether it had been galloping, when he saw how late it was. "You'll come home and dine with me, Carr?"

"I'll follow you, if you like," was the reply. "I have a matter or two to attend to first."

A few minutes more, and Lord Hartledon and his care went out. Mr. Carr called in his clerk.

"I want to know how you came to learn that the man I asked you about, Gordon, was employed by Kedge and Reck?"

"I heard it through a man named Druitt," was the ready answer. "Happening to ask him—as I did several people—whether he knew any George Gordon, he at once said that a man of that name was at Kedge and Reck's, where Druitt himself had been temporarily employed."

"Ah," said Mr. Carr, remembering this same Druitt had been mentioned to him. "But the man was called Gorton, not Gordon. You must have caught up the wrong name, Taylor. Or perhaps he misunderstood you. That's all; you may go now."

The clerk departed. Mr. Carr took his hat and followed him down; but before joining Lord Hartledon he turned into the Temple Gardens, and strolled towards the river; a few moments of fresh air—fresh to those hard-worked denizens of close and crowded London—seemed absolutely necessary to the barrister's heated brain.

He sat down on a bench facing the water, and bared his brow to the breeze. A cool head, his; never a cooler brought thought to bear upon perplexity; nevertheless it was not feeling very collected now. He could not reconcile sundry discrepancies in the trouble he was engaged in fathoming, and he saw no release whatever for Lord Hartledon.

"It has only complicated the affair," he said, as he watched the steamers up and down, "this calling in Green the detective, and the news he brings. Gordon the Gordon of the mutiny! I don't like it: the other Gordon, simple enough and not bad-hearted, was easy to deal with in comparison; this man, pirate, robber, murderer, will stand at nothing.

We should have a hold on him, it's true, in his own crime; but what's to prevent his keeping himself out of the way, and selling Hartledon to another? Why he has not sold him yet, I can't think. Unless for some reason he is waiting his time."

He put on his hat and began to count the barges on the other side, to banish thought. But it would not be banished, and he fell into the train again.

"Mair's behaving well; with Christian kindness; but it's bad enough to be even in *his* power. There's something in Lord Hartledon he 'can't help loving,' he writes. Who can? Here am I, giving up circuit—such a thing as never was heard of—calling him friend still, and losing my rest at night for him! Poor Val! better he had been the one to die!"

"Please, sir, could you tell us the time?"

The spell was broken, and Mr. Carr took out his watch as he turned his eyes on a ragged urchin who had called to him from below.

The tide was down; and sundry Arabs were regaling their naked feet in the mud, sporting and shouting. The evening drew in earlier than they did, and the sun had already set.

Quitting the garden, Mr. Carr stepped into a hansom, and was conveyed to Grafton Street. He found Lord Hartledon knitting his brow over a letter.

"Maude is growing vexed in earnest," he began, looking up at Mr. Carr. "She insists upon knowing the reason that I do not go home to her."

"I don't wonder at it. You ought to do one of two things: go, or—"

"Or what, Carr?"

"You know. Never go home again."

"I wish I was out of the world!" cried the unhappy man.

# XXV

## At Hartledon

Hartledon,

"I wonder what you *think* of yourself, Galloping about *Rotten Row* with women when your wife's *dying*. Of *course* it's not your fault that reports of your goings-on *reach* her here oh dear no. You are a moddel husband you are, sending her down here *out of the way* that you may take your pleasure. Why did you *marry her*, nobody wanted you to she sits and *mopes* and *weeps* and she's going into the same way that her father *went*, you'll be glad no doubt to hear it it's what you're *aiming* at, once she is in *Calne churchyard* the *field* will be open for your Anne Ashton. I can tell you that if you've a spark of *proper feeling* you'll come *down* for its killing her,

Your wicked mother,<br>C. Kirton

Lord Hartledon turned this letter about in his hand. He scarcely noticed the mistake at the conclusion: the dowager had doubtless intended to imply that *he* was wicked, and the slip of the pen in her temper went for nothing.

Galloping about Rotten Row with women!

Hartledon sent his thoughts back, endeavouring to recollect what could have given rise to this charge. One morning, after a sleepless night, when he had tossed and turned on his uneasy bed, and risen unrefreshed, he hired a horse, for he had none in town, and went for a long ride. Coming back he turned into Rotten Row. He could not tell why he did so, for such places, affected by the gay, empty-headed votaries of fashion, were little consonant to his present state. He was barely in it when a lady's horse took fright: she was riding alone, with a groom following; Lord Hartledon gave her his assistance, led her horse until the animal was calm, and rode side by side with her to the end of the Row. He knew not who she was; scarcely noticed whether she was young or old; and had not given a remembrance to it since.

When your wife's dying! Accustomed to the strong expressions of the countess-dowager, he passed that over. But, "going the same way that her father went;" he paused there, and tried to remember how her father did "go." All he could recollect now, indeed all he knew at the time, was, that Lord Kirton's last illness was reported to have been a lingering one.

Such missives as these—and the countess-dowager favoured him with more than one—coupled with his own consciousness that he was not behaving to his wife as he ought, took him at length down to Hartledon. That his presence at the place so soon after his marriage was little short of an insult to Dr. Ashton's family, his sensitive feelings told him; but his duty to his wife was paramount, and he could not visit his sin upon her.

She was looking very ill; was low-spirited and hysterical; and when she caught sight of him she forgot her anger, and fell sobbing into his arms. The countess-dowager had gone over to Garchester, and they had a few hours' peace together.

"You are not looking well, Maude!"

"I know I am not. Why do you stay away from me?"

"I could not help myself. Business has kept me in London."

"Have *you* been ill also? You look thin and worn."

"One does grow to look thin in heated London," he replied evasively, as he walked to the window, and stood there. "How is your brother, Maude—Bob?"

"I don't want to talk about Bob yet; I have to talk to you," she said. "Percival, why did you practise that deceit upon me?"

"What deceit?"

"It was a downright falsehood; and made me look awfully foolish when I came here and spoke of it as a fact. That action."

Lord Hartledon made no reply. Here was one cause of his disinclination to meet his wife—having to keep up the farce of Dr. Ashton's action. It seemed, however, that there would no longer be any farce to keep up. Had it exploded? He said nothing. Maude gazing at him from the sofa on which she sat, her dark eyes looking larger than of yore, with hollow circles round them, waited for his answer.

"I do not know what you mean, Maude."

"You *do* know. You sent me down here with a tale that the Ashtons had entered an action against you for breach of promise—damages, ten thousand pounds—"

"Stay an instant, Maude. I did not 'send you down' with the tale. I particularly requested you to keep it private."

"Well, mamma drew it out of me unawares. She vexed me with her comments about your staying on in London, and it made me tell her why you had stayed. She ascertained from Dr. Ashton that there was not a word of truth in the story. Val, I betrayed it in your defence."

He stood at the window in silence, his lips compressed.

"I looked so foolish in the eyes of Dr. Ashton! The Sunday evening after I came down here I had a sort of half-fainting-fit, coming home from church. He overtook me, and was very kind, and gave me his arm. I said a word to him; I could not help it; mamma had worried me on so; and I learned that no such action had ever been thought of. You had no right to subject me to the chance of such mortification. Why did you do so?"

Lord Hartledon came from the window and sat down near his wife, his elbow on the table. All he could do now was to make the best of it, and explain as near to the truth as he could.

"Maude, you must not expect full confidence on this subject, for I cannot give it you. When I found I had reason to believe that some— some legal proceedings were about to be instituted against me, just at the first intimation of the trouble, I thought it must emanate from Dr. Ashton. You took up the same idea yourself, and I did not contradict it, simply because I could not tell you the real truth—"

"Yes," she interrupted. "It was the night that stranger called at our house, when you and Mr. Carr were closeted with him so long."

He could not deny it; but he had been thankful that she should forget the stranger and his visit. Maude waited.

"Then it was an action, but not brought by the Ashtons?" she resumed, finding he did not speak. "Mamma remarked that you were just the one to propose to half-a-dozen girls."

"It was not an action at all of that description; and I never proposed to any girl except Miss Ashton," he returned, nettled at the remark.

"Is it over?"

"Not quite;" and there was some hesitation in his tone. "Carr is settling it for me. I trust, Maude, you will never hear of it again—that it will never trouble you."

She sat looking at him with her wistful eyes.

"Won't you tell me its nature?"

"I cannot tell you, Maude, believe me. I am as candid with you as it is possible to be; but there are some things best—best not spoken of.

Maude," he repeated, rising impulsively and taking both her hands in his, "do you wish to earn my love—my everlasting gratitude? Then you may do it by nevermore alluding to this."

It was a mistaken request; an altogether unwise emotion. Better that he had remained at the window, and drawled out a nonchalant denial. But he was apt to be as earnestly genuine on the surface as he was in reality. It set Lady Hartledon wondering; and she resolved to "bide her time."

"As you please, of course, Val. But why should it agitate you?"

"Many a little thing seems to agitate me now," he answered. "I have not felt well of late; perhaps that's the reason."

"I think you might have satisfied me a little better. I expect it is some enormous debt risen up against you."

Better she should think so! "I shall tide it over," he said aloud. "But indeed, Maude, I cannot bear for you delicate women to be brought into contact with these things; they are fit for us only. Think no more about it, and rely on me to keep trouble from you if it can be kept. Where's Bob? He is here, I suppose?"

"Bob's in his room. He is going into a way, I think. When he wrote and asked me if I would allow him to come here for a little change, the medical men saying he must have it, mamma sent a refusal by return of post; she had had enough of Bob, she said, when he was here before. But I quietly wrote a note myself, and Bob came. He looked ill, and gets worse instead of better."

"What do you mean by saying he is going into a way?" asked Lord Hartledon.

"Consumption, or something of that sort. Papa died of it. You are not angry with me for having Bob?"

"Angry! My dear Maude, the house is yours; and if poor Bob stayed with us for ever, I should welcome him as a brother. Every one likes Bob."

"Except mamma. She does not like invalids in the house, and has been saying you don't like it; that it was helping to keep you away. Poor Bob had out his portmanteau and began to pack; but I told him not to mind her; he was my guest, not hers."

"And mine also, you might have added."

He left the room, and went to the chamber Captain Kirton had occupied when he was at Hartledon in the spring. It was empty, evidently not being used; and Hartledon sent for Mirrable. She came, looking just as usual, wearing a dark-green silk gown; for the twelve-month had expired, and their mourning was over.

"Captain Kirton is in the small blue rooms facing south, my lord. They were warmer for him than these."

"Is he very ill, Mirrable?"

"Very, I think," was the answer. "Of course he may get better; but it does not look like it."

He was a tall, thin, handsome man, this young officer—a year or two older than Maude, whom he greatly resembled. Seated before a table, he was playing at that delectable game "solitaire;" and his eyes looked large and wild with surprise, and his cheeks became hectic, when Lord Hartledon entered.

"Bob, my dear fellow, I am glad to see you."

He took his hands and sat down, his face full of the concern he did not care to speak. Lady Hartledon had said he was going into a way; it was evidently the way of the grave.

He pushed the balls and the board from him, half ashamed of his employment. "To think you should catch me at this!" he exclaimed. "Maude brought it to me yesterday, thinking I was dull up here."

"As good that as anything else. I often think what a miserably restless invalid *I* should make. But now, what's wrong with you?"

"Well, I suppose it's the heart."

"The heart?"

"The doctors say so. No doubt they are right; those complaints are hereditary, and my father had it. I got quite unfit for duty, and they told me I must go away for change; so I wrote to Maude, and she took me in."

"Yes, yes; we are glad to have you, and must try and get you well, Bob."

"Ah, I can't tell about that. He died of it, you know."

"Who?"

"My father. He was ill for some time, and it wore him to a skeleton, so that people thought he was in a decline. If I could only get sufficiently well to go back to duty, I should not mind; it is so sad to give trouble in a strange house."

"In a strange house it might be, but it would be ungrateful to call this one strange," returned Lord Hartledon, smiling on him from his pleasant blue eyes. "We must get you to town and have good advice for you. I suppose Hillary comes up?"

"Every-day."

"Does *he* say it's heart-disease?"

"I believe he thinks it. It might be as much as his reputation is worth to say it in this house."

"How do you mean?"

"My mother won't have it said. She ignores the disease altogether, and will not allow it to be mentioned, or hinted at. It's bronchitis, she tells everyone; and of course bronchitis it must be. I did have a cough when I came here: my chest is not strong."

"But why should she ignore heart-disease?"

"There was a fear that Maude would be subject to it when she was a child. Should it be disclosed to her that it is my complaint, and were I to die of it, she might grow so alarmed for herself as to bring it on; and agitation, as we know, is often fatal in such cases."

Lord Hartledon sat in a sort of horror. Maude subject to heart-disease! when at any moment a certain fearful tale, of which he was the guilty centre, might be disclosed to her! Day by day, hour by hour, he lived in dread of this story's being brought to light. This little unexpected communication increased that dread fourfold.

"Have I shocked you?" asked Captain Kirton. "I may yet get the better of it."

"I believe I was thinking of Maude," answered Hartledon, slowly recovering from his stupor. "I never heard—I had no idea that Maude's heart was not perfectly sound."

"And I don't know but that it is sound; it was only a fancy when she was a child, and there might have been no real grounds for it. My mother is full of crotchets on the subject of illness; and says she won't have anything about heart-disease put into Maude's head. She is right, of course, so far, in using precaution; so please remember that I am suffering from any disorder but that," concluded the young officer with a smile.

"How did yours first show itself?"

"I hardly know. I used to be subject to sudden attacks of faintness; but I am not sure that they had anything to do with the disease itself."

Just what Maude was becoming subject to! She had told him of a fainting-fit in London; had told him of another now.

"I suppose the doctors warn you against sudden shocks, Bob?"

"More than against anything. I am not to agitate myself in the least; am not to run or jump, or fly into a temper. They would put me in a glass case, if they could."

d, we'll see what skill can do for you," said Hartledon, rousing
elf. "I wonder if a warmer climate would be of service? You might
ve that without exertion, travelling slowly."

"Couldn't afford it," was the ingenuous answer. "I have forestalled
my pay as it is."

Lord Hartledon smiled. Never a more generous disposition than his;
and if money could save this poor Bob Kirton, he should not want it.

Walking forth, he strolled down the road towards Calne, intending
to ask a question or two of the surgeon. Mr. Hillary was at home. His
house was at this end of Calne, just past the Rectory and opposite the
church, with a side view of Clerk Gum's. The door was open, and Lord
Hartledon strolled into the surgery unannounced, to the surprise of
Mr. Hillary, who did not know he was at Calne.

The surgeon's opinion was not favourable. Captain Kirton had
heart-disease beyond any doubt. His chest was weak also, the lungs
not over-sound; altogether, the Honourable Robert Kirton's might be
called a bad life.

"Would a warmer climate do anything for him?" asked Lord
Hartledon.

The surgeon shrugged his shoulders. "He would be better there for
some things than here. On the whole it might temporarily benefit him."

"Then he shall go. And now, Hillary, I want to ask you something
else—and you must answer me, mind. Captain Kirton tells me the fact
of his having heart-disease is not mentioned in the house lest it should
alarm Lady Hartledon, and develop the same in her. Is there any fear
of this?"

"It is true that it's not spoken of; but I don't think there's any
foundation for the fear."

"The old dowager's very fanciful!" cried Lord Hartledon, resentfully.

"A queer old—girl," remarked the surgeon. "Can't help saying it,
though she is your mother-in-law."

"I wish she was any one else's! She's as likely as not to let out
something of this to Maude in her tantrums. But I don't believe a word
of it; I never saw the least symptom of heart-disease in my wife."

"Nor I," said the doctor. "Of course I have not examined her; neither
have I had much opportunity for ordinary observation."

"I wish you would contrive to get the latter. Come up and call often;
make some excuse for seeing Lady Hartledon professionally, and watch
her symptoms."

"I am seeing her professionally now; once or twice a week. She had one or two fainting-fits after she came down, and called me in."

"Kirton says he used to have those fainting-fits. Are they a symptom of heart-disease?"

"In Lady Hartledon I attribute them entirely to her present state of health. I assure you, I don't see the slightest cause for fear as regards your wife's heart. She is of a calm temperament too; as far as I can observe."

They stood talking for a minute at the door, when Lord Hartledon went out. Pike happened to pass on the other side of the road.

"He is here still, I see," remarked Hartledon.

"Oh dear, yes; and likely to be."

"I wonder how the fellow picks up a living?"

The surgeon did not answer. "Are you going to make a long stay with us?" he asked.

"A very short one. I suppose you have had no return of the fever?"

"Not any. Calne never was more healthy than it is now. As I said to Dr. Ashton yesterday, but for his own house I might put up my shutters and take a lengthened holiday."

"Who is ill at the Rectory? Mrs. Ashton?"

"Mrs. Ashton is not strong, but she's better than she was last year. I have been more concerned for Anne than for her."

"Is *she* ill?" cried Lord Hartledon, a spasm seizing his throat.

"Ailing. But it's an ailing I do not like."

"What's the cause?" he rejoined, feeling as if some other crime were about to be brought home to him.

"That's a question I never inquire into. I put it upon the air of the Rectory," added the surgeon in jesting tones, "and tell them they ought to go away for a time, but they have been away too much of late, they say. She's getting over it somewhat, and I take care that she goes out and takes exercise. What has it been? Well, a sort of inward fever, with flushed cheeks and unequal spirits. It takes time for these things to be got over, you know. The Rector has been anything but well, too; he is not the strong, healthy man he was."

"And all *my* work; my work!" cried Hartledon to himself, almost gnashing his teeth as he went back down the street. "What *right* had I to upset the happiness of that family? I wish it had pleased God to take me first! My father used to say that some men seem born into the world only to be a blight to it; it's what I have been, Heaven knows."

He knew only too well that Anne Ashton was suffering from the shock caused by his conduct. The love of these quiet, sensitive, refined natures, once awakened, is not given for a day, but for all time; it becomes a part of existence; and cannot be riven except by an effort that brings destruction to even future hope of happiness. Not even Mr. Hillary, not even Dr. and Mrs. Ashton, could discern the utter misery that was Anne's daily portion. She strove to conceal it all. She went about the house cheerfully, wore a smiling face when people were present, dressed well, laughed with their guests, went about the parish to rich and poor, and was altogether gay. Ah, do you know what it is, this assumption of gaiety when the heart is breaking?—this dread fear lest those about you should detect the truth? Have *you* ever lived with this mask upon your face?—which can only be thrown off at night in the privacy of your own chamber, when you may abandon yourself to your desolation, and pray heaven to take you or give you increased strength to *live* and *bear*? It may seem a light thing, this state of heart that I am telling you about; but it has killed both men and women, for all that; and killed them in silence.

Anne Ashton had never complained. She did everything she had been used to doing, was particular about all her duties; but a nervous cough attacked her, and her frame wasted, and her cheek grew hectic. Try as she would she could not eat: all she confessed to, when questioned by Mrs. Ashton, was "a pain in her throat;" and Mr. Hillary was called in. Anne laughed: there was nothing the matter with her, she said, and her throat was better; she had strained it perhaps. The doctor was a wise doctor; his professional visits were spent in gossip; and as to medicine, he sent her a tonic, and told her to take it or not as she pleased. Only time, he said to Mrs. Ashton—she would be all right in time; the summer heat was making her languid.

The summer heat had nearly passed now, and perhaps some of the battle was passing with it. None knew—let me repeat it—what that battle had been; none ever can know, unless they go through it themselves. In Miss Ashton's case there was a feature some are spared— her love had been known—and it increased the anguish tenfold. She would overcome it if she could only forget him; but it would take time; and she would come out of it an altogether different woman, her best hope in life gone, her heart dead.

"What brought him down here?" mentally questioned Mr. Hillary, in an explosion of wrath, as he watched his visitor down the street. "It will undo all I have been doing. He, and his wife too, might have had the grace to keep away for this year at least. I loved him once, with all his faults; but I should like to see him in the pillory now. It has told on him also, if I'm any reader of looks. And now, Miss Anne, you go off from Calne to-morrow an I can prevail. I only hope you won't come across him in the meantime."

# XXVI

## Under the Trees

It was the same noble-looking man Calne had ever known, as he went down the road, throwing a greeting to one and another. Lord Hartledon was not a whit less attractive than Val Elster, who had won golden opinions from all. None would have believed that the cowardly monster Fear was for ever feasting upon his heart.

He came to a standstill opposite the clerk's house, looked at it for a moment, as if deliberating whether he should enter, and crossed the road. The shades of evening had begun to fall whilst he talked with the surgeon. As he advanced up the clerk's garden, some one came out of the house with a rush and ran against him.

"Take care," he lazily said.

The girl—it was no other than Miss Rebecca Jones—shrank away when she recognized her antagonist. Flying through the gate she rapidly disappeared up the street. Lord Hartledon reached the house, and made his way in without ceremony. At a table in the little parlour sat the clerk's wife, presiding at a solitary tea-table by the light of a candle.

"How are you, Mrs. Gum?"

She had not heard him enter, and started at the salutation. Lord Hartledon laughed.

"Don't take me for a housebreaker. Your front-door was open, and I came in without knocking. Is your husband at home?"

What with shaking and curtseying, Mrs. Gum could scarcely answer. It was surprising how a little shock of this sort, or indeed of any sort, would upset her. Gum was away on some business or other, she replied—which caused their tea-hour to be delayed—but she expected him in every moment. Would his lordship please to wait in the best parlour, she asked, taking the candle to marshal him into the state sitting-room.

No; his lordship would not go into the best parlour; he would wait two or three minutes where he was, provided she did not disturb herself, and went on with her tea.

Mrs. Gum dusted a large old-fashioned oak chair with her apron; but he perched himself on one of its elbows.

"And now go on with your tea, Mrs. Gum, and I'll look on with all the envy of a thirsty man."

Mrs. Gum glanced up tremblingly. Might she dare offer his lordship a cup? She wouldn't make so bold but tea *was* refreshing to a parched throat.

"And mine's always parched," he returned. "I'll drink some with you, and thank you for it. It won't be the first time, will it?"

"Always parched!" remarked Mrs. Gum. "Maybe you've a touch of fever, my lord. Many folk get it at the close of summer."

Lord Hartledon sat on, and drank his tea. He said well that he was always thirsty, though Mrs. Gum's expression was the better one. That timid matron, overcome by the honour accorded her, sat on the edge of her chair, cup in hand.

"I want to ask your husband if he can give me a description of the man who was concerned in that wretched mutiny on board the *Morning Star*," said Lord Hartledon, somewhat abruptly. "I mean the ringleader, Gordon. Why—What's the matter?"

Mrs. Gum had jumped up from her chair and began looking about the room. The cat, or something else, had "rubbed against her legs."

No cat could be found, and she sat down again, her teeth chattering. Lord Hartledon came to the conclusion that she was only fit for a lunatic asylum. Why did she keep a cat, if its fancied caresses were to terrify her like that?

"It was said, you know—at least it has been always assumed—that Gordon did not come back to England," he continued, speaking openly of his business, where a more prudent man would have kept his lips closed. "But I have reason to believe that he did come back, Mrs. Gum; and I want to find him."

Mrs. Gum wiped her face, covered with drops of emotion.

"Gordon never did come back, I am sure, sir," she said, forgetting all about titles in her trepidation.

"You don't know that he did not. You may think it; the public may think it; what's of more moment to Gordon, the police may think it: but you can't *know* it. I know he did."

"My lord, he did not; I could—I almost think I could be upon my oath he did not," she answered, gazing at Lord Hartledon with frightened eyes and white lips, which, to say the truth, rather puzzled him as he gazed back from his perch.

"Will you tell me why you assert so confidently that Gordon did not come back?"

She could not tell, and she knew she could not.

"I can't bear to hear him spoken of, my lord," she said. "He—we look upon him as my poor boy's murderer," she broke off, with a sob; "and it is not likely that I could."

Not very logical; but Lord Hartledon allowed for confusion of ideas following on distress of mind.

"I don't like to speak about him any more than you can like to hear," he said kindly. "Indeed I am sorry to have grieved you; but if the man is in London, and can be traced—"

"In London!" she interrupted.

"He was in London last autumn, as I believe—living there."

An expression of relief passed over her features that was quite perceptible to Lord Hartledon.

"I should not like to hear of his coming near us," she sighed, dropping her voice to a whisper. "London: that's pretty far off."

"I suppose you are anxious to bring him to justice, Mrs. Gum?"

"No, sir, not now; neither me nor Gum," shaking her head. "Time was, sir—my lord—that I'd have walked barefoot to see him hanged; but the years have gone by; and if sorrow's not dead, it's less keen, and we'd be thankful to let the past rest in peace. Oh, my lord, *don't* rake him up again!"

The wild, imploring accents quite startled Lord Hartledon.

"You need not fear," he said, after a pause. "I do not care to see Gordon hanged either; and though I want to trace his present abode— if it can be traced—it is not with a view to injuring him."

"But we don't know his abode, my lord," she rejoined in faint remonstrance.

"I did not suppose you knew it. All I want to ask your husband is, to give me a description of Gordon. I wish to see if it tallies with— with some one I once knew," he cautiously concluded. "Perhaps you remember what the man was said to be like?"

She put her fingers up to her brow, leaning her elbow on the table. He could not help observing how the hand shook.

"I think it was said that he had red hair," she began, after a long pause; "and was—tall, was it?—either tall or short; one of the two. And his eyes—his eyes were dark eyes, either brown or blue."

Lord Hartledon could not avoid a smile. "That's no description at all."

"My memory is not over-good, my lord: I read his description in the handbills offering the reward; and that's some time ago now."

"The handbills!—to be sure!" interrupted Lord Hartledon, springing from his perch. "I never thought of them; they'll give me the best description possible. Do you know where—"

The conference was interrupted by the clerk. He came in with a large book in his hand; and a large dog, which belonged to a friend, and had followed him home. For a minute or two there was only commotion, for the dog was leaping and making friends with every one. Lord Hartledon then said a few words of explanation, and the quiet demeanour of the clerk, as he calmly listened, was in marked contrast to his wife's nervous agitation.

"Might I inquire your lordship's reasons for thinking that Gordon came back?" he quietly asked, when Lord Hartledon had ceased.

"I cannot give them in detail, Gum. That he did come back, there is no doubt about whatever, though how he succeeded in eluding the vigilance of the police, who were watching for him, is curious. His coming back, however, is not the question: I thought you might be able to give me a close description of him. You went to Liverpool when the unfortunate passengers arrived there."

But Clerk Gum was unable to give any satisfactory response. No doubt he had heard enough of what Gordon was like at the time, he observed, but it had passed out of his memory. A fair man, he thought he was described, with light hair. He had heard nothing of Gordon since; didn't want to, if his lordship would excuse his saying it; firmly believed he was at the bottom of the sea.

Patient, respectful, apparently candid, he spoke, attending his guest, hat in hand, to the outer gate, when it pleased him to depart. But, take it for all in all, there remained a certain doubtful feeling in Lord Hartledon's mind regarding the interview; for some subtle discernment had whispered to him that both Gum and his wife could have given him the description of Gordon, and would not do so.

He turned slowly towards home, thinking of this. As he passed the waste ground and Pike's shed, he cast his eyes towards it; a curl of smoke was ascending from the extemporized chimney, still discernible in the twilight. It occurred to Lord Hartledon that this man, who had the character of being so lawless, had been rather suspiciously intimate with the man Gorton. Not that the intimacy in itself was suspicious; birds of a feather flocked together; but the most simple and natural thing connected with Gorton would have borne suspicion to Hartledon's mind now.

He had barely passed the gate when some shouting arose in the road behind him. A man, driving a cart recklessly, had almost come in contact with another cart, and some hard language ensued. Lord Hartledon turned his head quickly, and just caught Mr. Pike's head, thrust a little over the top of the gate, watching him. Pike must have crouched down when Lord Hartledon passed. He went back at once; and Pike put a bold face on the matter, and stood up.

"So you occupy your palace still, Pike?"

"Such as it is. Yes."

"I half-expected to find that Mr. Marris had turned you from it," continued Lord Hartledon, alluding to his steward.

"He wouldn't do it, I expect, without your lordship's orders; and I don't fancy you'll give 'em," was the free answer.

"I think my brother would have given them, had he lived."

"But he didn't live," rejoined Pike. "He wasn't let live."

"What do you mean?" asked Lord Hartledon, mystified by the words.

Pike ignored the question. "'Twas nearly a smash," he said, looking at the two carts now proceeding on their different ways. "That cart of Floyd's is always in hot water; the man drinks; Floyd turned him off once."

The miller's cart was jogging up the road towards home, under convoy of the offending driver; the boy, David Ripper, sitting inside on some empty sacks, and looking over the board behind: looking very hard indeed, as it seemed, in their direction. Mr. Pike appropriated the gaze.

"Yes, you may stare, young Rip!" he apostrophized, as if the boy could hear him; "but you won't stare yourself out of my hands. You're the biggest liar in Calne, but you don't mislead me."

"Pike, when you made acquaintance with that man Gorton—you remember him?" broke off Lord Hartledon.

"Yes, I do," said Pike emphatically.

"Did he make you acquainted with any of his private affairs?—his past history?"

"Not a word," answered Pike, looking still after the cart and the boy.

"Were those fine whiskers of his false? that red hair?"

Pike turned his head quickly. The question had aroused him.

"False hair and whiskers! I never knew it was the fashion to wear them."

"It may be convenient sometimes, even if not the fashion," observed Lord Hartledon, his tone full of cynical meaning; and Mr. Pike surreptitiously peered at him with his small light eyes.

"If Gorton's hair was false, I never noticed it, that's all; I never saw him without a hat, that I remember, except in that inquest-room."

"Had he been to Australia?"

Pike paused to take another surreptitious gaze.

"Can't say, my lord. Never heard."

"Was his name Gorton, or Gordon? Come, Pike," continued Lord Hartledon, good-humouredly, "there's a sort of mutual alliance between you and me; you did me a service once unasked, and I allow you to live free and undisturbed on my ground. I think you *do* know something of this man; it is a fancy I have taken up."

"I never knew his name was anything but Gorton," said Pike carelessly; "never heard it nor thought it."

"Did you happen to hear him ever speak of that mutiny on board the Australian ship *Morning Star*? You have heard of it, I daresay: a George Gordon was the ringleader."

If ever the cool impudence was suddenly taken out of a man, this question seemed to take it out of Pike. He did not reply for some time; and when he did, it was in low and humble tones.

"My lord, I hope you'll pardon my rough thoughts and ways, which haven't been used to such as you—and the sight of that boy put me up, for reasons of my own. As to Gorton—I never did hear him speak of the thing you mention. His name's Gorton, and nothing else, as far as I know; and his hair's his own, for all I ever saw."

"He did not give you his confidence, then?"

"No, never. Not about himself nor anything else, past or present."

"And did not let a word slip? As to—for instance, as to his having been a passenger on board the *Morning Star* at the time of the mutiny?"

Pike had moved away a step, and stood with his arms on the hurdles, his head bent on them, his face turned from Lord Hartledon.

"Gorton said nothing to me. As to that mutiny—I think I read something about it in the newspapers, but I forget what. I was just getting up from some weeks of rheumatic fever at the time; I'd caught it working in the fields; and news don't leave much impression in illness. Gorton never spoke of it to me. I never heard him say who or what he was; and I couldn't speak more truly if your lordship offered to give me the shed as a bribe."

"Do you know where Gorton might be found at present?"

"I swear before Heaven that I know nothing of the man, and have never heard of him since he went away," cried Pike, with a burst of either fear or passion. "He was a stranger to me when he came, and he was a stranger when he left. I found out the little game he had come about, and saved your lordship from his clutches, which he doesn't know to this day. I know nothing else about him at all."

"Well, good evening, Pike. You need not put yourself out for nothing."

He walked away, taking leave of the man as civilly as though he had been a respectable member of society. It was not in Val's nature to show discourtesy to any living being. Why Pike should have shrunk from the questions he could not tell; but that he did shrink was evident; perhaps from a surly dislike to being questioned at all; but on the whole Lord Hartledon thought he had spoken the truth as to knowing nothing about Gorton.

Crossing the road, he turned into the field-path near the Rectory; it was a little nearer than the road-way, and he was in a hurry, for he had not thought to ask at what hour his wife dined, and might be keeping her waiting.

Who was this Pike, he wondered as he went along; as he had wondered before now. When the man was off his guard, the roughness of his speech and demeanour was not so conspicuous; and the tone assumed a certain refinement that seemed to say he had some time been in civilized society. Again, how did he live? A tale was told in Calne of Pike's having been disturbed at supper one night by a parcel of rude boys, who had seen him seated at a luxurious table; hot steak and pudding before him. They were not believed, certainly; but still Pike must live; and how did he find the means to do so? Why did he live there at all? what had caused him to come to Calne? Who—

These reflections might have lasted all the way home but for an interruption that drove every thought out of Lord Hartledon's mind, and sent the heart's blood coursing swiftly through his veins. Turning a corner of the dark winding path, he came suddenly upon a lady seated on a bench, so close to the narrow path that he almost touched her in passing. She seemed to have sat down for a moment to do something to her hat, which was lying in her lap, her hands busied with it.

A faint cry escaped her, and she rose up. It was caused partly by emotion, partly by surprise at seeing him, for she did not know he was within a hundred miles of the place. And very probably she would have liked to box her own ears for showing any. The hat fell from her knees as she rose, and both stooped for it.

"Forgive me," he said. "I fear I have startled you."

"I am waiting for papa," she answered, in hasty apology for being found there. And Lord Hartledon, casting his eyes some considerable distance ahead, discerned the indistinct forms of two persons talking together. He understood the situation at once. Dr. Ashton and his daughter had been to the cottages; and the doctor had halted on their return to speak to a day-labourer going home from his work, Anne walking slowly on.

And there they stood face to face, Anne Ashton and her deceitful lover! How their hearts beat to pain, how utterly oblivious they were of everything in life save each other's presence, how tumultuously confused were mind and manner, both might remember afterwards, but certainly were not conscious of then. It was a little glimpse of Eden. A corner of the dark curtain thrown between them had been raised, and so unexpectedly that for the moment nothing else was discernible in the dazzling light.

Forget! Not in that instant of sweet confusion, during which nothing seemed more real than a dream. He was the husband of another; she was parted from him for ever; and neither was capable of deliberate thought or act that could intrench on the position, or tend to return, even momentarily, to the past. And yet there they stood with beating hearts, and eyes that betrayed their own tale—that the marriage and the parting were in one sense but a hollow mockery, and their love was indelible as of old.

Each had been "forgetting" to the utmost of the poor power within, in accordance with the high principles enshrined in either heart. Yet what a mockery that forgetting seemed, now that it was laid before them naked and bare! The heart turning sick to faintness at the mere sight of each other, the hands trembling at the mutual touch, the wistful eyes shining with a glance that too surely spoke of undying love!

But not a word of this was spoken. However true their hearts might be, there was no fear of the tongue following up the error. Lord Hartledon would no more have allowed himself to speak than she to listen. Neither had the hands met in ordinary salutation; it was only when he resigned the hat to her that the fingers touched: a touch light, transient, almost imperceptible; nevertheless it sent a thrill through the whole frame. Not exactly knowing what to do in her confusion, Miss Ashton sat down on the bench again and put her hat on.

"I must say a word to you before I go on my way," said Lord Hartledon. "I have been wishing for such a meeting as this ever since I saw you at Versailles; and indeed I think I wished for nothing else before it. When you think of me as one utterly heartless—"

"Stay, Lord Hartledon," she interrupted, with white lips. "I cannot listen to you. You must be aware that I cannot, and ought not. What are you thinking about?"

"I know that I have forfeited all right to ask you; that it is an unpardonable intrusion my presuming even to address you. Well, perhaps, you are right," he added, after a moment's pause; "it may be better that I should not say what I was hoping to say. It cannot mend existing things; it cannot undo the past. I dare not ask your forgiveness: it would seem too much like an insult; nevertheless, I would rather have it than any earthly gift. Fare you well, Anne! I shall sometimes hear of your happiness."

"Have you been ill?" she asked in a kindly impulse, noticing his altered looks in that first calm moment.

"No—not as the world counts illness. If remorse and shame and repentance can be called illness, I have my share. Ill deeds of more kinds than one are coming home to me. Anne," he added in a hoarse whisper; his face telling of emotion, "if there is one illumined corner in my heart, where all else is very dark, it is caused by thankfulness to Heaven that you were spared."

"Spared!" she echoed, in wonder, so completely awed by his strange manner as to forget her reserve.

"Spared the linking of your name with mine. I thank God for it, for your sake, night and day. Had trouble fallen on you through me, I don't think I could have survived it. May you be shielded from all such for ever!"

He turned abruptly away, and she looked after him, her heart beating a great deal faster than it ought to have done.

That she was his best and dearest love, in spite of his marriage, it was impossible not to see; and she strove to think him very wicked for it, and her cheek was red with a feeling that seemed akin to shame. But— trouble?—thankful for her sake, night and day, that her name was not linked with his? He must allude to debt, she supposed: some of those old embarrassments had augmented themselves into burdens too heavy to be safely borne.

The Rector was coming on now at a swift pace. He looked keenly at Lord Hartledon; looked twice, as if in surprise. A flush rose to Val's sensitive face as he passed, and lifted his hat. The Rector, dark and proud, condescended to return the courtesy: and the meeting was over.

Toiling across Lord Hartledon's path was the labourer to whom the Rector had been speaking. He had an empty bottle slung over his shoulder, and carried a sickle. The man's day's work was over, and had left fatigue behind it.

"Good-night to your lordship!"

"Is it you, Ripper?"

He was the father of the young gentleman in the cart, whom Mr. Pike had not long before treated to his opinion: young David Ripper, the miller's boy. Old Ripper, a talkative, discontented man, stopped and ventured to enter on his grievances. His wife had been pledging things to pay for a fine gown she had bought; his two girls were down with measles; his son, young Rip, plagued his life out.

"How does he plague your life out?" asked Lord Hartledon, when he had listened patiently.

"Saying he'll go off and enlist for a soldier, my lord; he's saying it always: and means it too, only he's over-young for't."

"Over-young for it; I should think so. Why, he's not much more than a child. Our sergeants don't enlist little boys."

"Sometimes he says he'll drown himself by way of a change," returned old Ripper.

"Oh, does he? Folk who say it never do it. I should whip it out of him."

"He's never been the same since the lord's death that time. He's always frightened: gets fancying things, and saying sometimes he sees his shadder."

"Whose shadow?"

"His'n: the late lord's."

"Why does he fancy that?" came the question, after a perceptible pause.

Old Ripper shook his head. It was beyond his ken, he said. "There be only two things he's afeared of in life," continued the man, who, though generally called old Ripper, was not above five-and-thirty. "The one's that wild man Pike; t'other's the shadder. He'd run ten mile sooner than see either."

"Does Pike annoy the boy?"

"Never spoke to him, as I knows on, my lord. Afore that drowning of his lordship last year, Davy was the boldest rip going," added the man, who had long since fallen into the epithet popularly applied to his son. "Since then he don't dare say his soul's his own. We had him laid up before the winter, and I know 'twas nothing but fear."

Lord Hartledon could not make much of the story, and had no time to linger. Administering a word of general encouragement, he continued his way, his thoughts going back to the interview with Anne Ashton, a line or two of Longfellow's "Fire of Driftwood" rising up in his mind—

> *"Of what had been and might have been,*
> *And who was changed, and who was dead."*

# XXVII

## A Tête-à-Tête Breakfast

The Dowager-Countess of Kirton stood in the sunny breakfast-room at Hartledon, surveying the well-spread table with complacency; for it appeared to be rather more elaborately set out than usual, and no one loved good cheer better than she. When she saw two cups and saucers on the cloth instead of one, it occurred to her that Maude must, by caprice, be coming down, which she had not done of late. The dowager had arrived at midnight from Garchester, in consequence of having missed the earlier train, and found nearly all the house in retirement. She was in a furious humour, and no one had told her of the arrival of her son-in-law; no one ever did tell her any more than they were obliged to do; for she was not held in estimation at Hartledon.

"Potted tongue," she exclaimed, dodging round the table, and lifting various covers. "Raised pie; I wonder what's in it? And what's that stuff in jelly? It looks delicious. This is the result of the blowing-up I gave Hedges the other day; nothing like finding fault. Hot dishes too. I suppose Maude gave out that she should be down this morning. All rubbish, fancying herself ill: she's as well as I am, but gives way like a sim—A-a-a-ah!"

The exclamation was caused by the unexpected vision of Lord Hartledon.

"How are you, Lady Kirton?"

"Where on earth did you spring from?"

"From my room."

"What's the good of your appearing before people like a ghost, Hartledon? When did you arrive?"

"Yesterday afternoon."

"And time you did, I think, with your poor wife fretting herself to death about you. How is she this morning?"

"Very well."

"Ugh!" You must imagine this sound as something between a grunt and a groan, that the estimable lady gave vent to whenever put out. It is not capable of being written. "You might have sent word you were coming. I should think you frightened your wife to death."

"Not quite."

He walked across the room and rang the bell. Hedges appeared. It had been the dowager's pleasure that no one else should serve her at that meal—perhaps on account of her peculiarities of costume.

"Will you be good enough to pour out the coffee in Maude's place to-day, Lady Kirton? She has promised to be down another morning."

It was making her so entirely and intentionally a guest, as she thought, that Lady Kirton did not like it. Not only did she fully intend Hartledon House to be her home, but she meant to be its one ruling power. Keep Maude just now to her invalid fancies, and later to her gay life, and there would be little fear of her asserting very much authority.

"Are you in the habit of serving this sort of breakfast, Hedges?" asked Lord Hartledon; for the board looked almost like an elaborate dinner.

"We have made some difference, my lord, this morning."

"For me, I suppose. You need not do so in future. I have got out of the habit of taking breakfast; and in any case I don't want this unnecessary display. Captain Kirton gets up later, I presume."

"He's hardly ever up before eleven," said Hedges. "But he makes a good breakfast, my lord."

"That's right. Tempt him with any delicacy you can devise. He wants strength."

The dowager was fuming. "Don't you think I'm capable of regulating these things, Hartledon, I'd beg leave to ask?"

"No doubt. I beg you will make yourself at home whilst you stay with us. Some tea, Hedges."

She could have thrown the coffee-pot at him. There was incipient defiance in his every movement; latent war in his tones. He was no longer the puppet he had been; that day had gone by for ever.

Perhaps Val could not himself have explained the feeling that was this morning at work within him. It was the first time he and the dowager had met since the marriage, and she brought before him all too prominently the ill-omened past: her unjustifiable scheming—his own miserable weakness. If ever Lord Hartledon felt shame and repentance for his weak yielding, he felt it now—felt it in all its bitterness; and something very like rage against the dowager was bubbling up in his spirit, which he had some trouble to suppress.

He did suppress it, however, though it rendered him less courteous than usual; and the meal proceeded partly in silence; an interchanged word, civil on the surface, passing now and then. The dowager thoroughly entered into her breakfast, and had little leisure for anything else.

"What makes you take nothing?" she asked, perceiving at length that he had only a piece of toast on his plate, and was playing with that.

"I have no appetite."

"Have you left off taking breakfast?"

"To a great extent."

"What's the matter with you?"

Lord Hartledon slightly raised his eyebrows. "One can't eat much in the heat of summer."

"Heat of summer! it's nothing more than autumn now. And you are as thin as a weasel. Try some of that excellent raised pie."

"Pray let my appetite alone, Lady Kirton. If I wanted anything I should take it."

"Let you alone! yes, of course! You don't want it noticed that you are out of sorts," snapped the dowager. "Oh, *I* know the signs. You've been raking about London—that's what you've been at."

The "raking about London" presented so complete a contrast to the lonely life he had really passed, that Hartledon smiled in very bitterness. And the smile incensed the dowager, for she misunderstood it.

"It's early days to begin! I don't think you ought to have married Maude."

"I don't think I ought."

She did not expect the rejoinder, and dropped her knife and fork. "Why *did* you marry her?"

"Perhaps you can tell that better than I."

The countess-dowager pushed up her hair.

"Are you going to throw off the mask outright, and become a bad husband as well as a neglectful one?"

Val rose from his seat and went to the window, which opened to the ground. He did not wish to quarrel with her if he could help it. Lady Kirton raised her voice.

"Staying away, as you have, in London, and leaving Maude here to pine alone."

"Business kept me in London."

"I dare say it did!" cried the wrathful dowager. "If Maude died of ennui, you wouldn't care. She can't go about much herself just now, poor thing! I do wish Edward had lived."

"I wish he had, with all my heart!" came the answer; and the tone struck surprise on the dowager's ear—it was so full of pain. "Maude's coming to Hartledon without me was her own doing," he remarked. "I wished her not to come."

"I dare say you did, as her heart was set upon it. The fact of her wishing to do a thing would be the signal for your opposing it; I've gathered that much. My advice to Maude is, to assert her own will, irrespective of yours."

"Don't you think, Lady Kirton, that it may be as well if you let me and my wife alone? We shall get along, no doubt, without interference; *with* interference we might not do so."

What with one thing and another, the dowager's temper was inflammable that morning; and when it reached that undesirable state she was apt to say pretty free things, even for her.

"Edward would have made her the better husband."

"But she didn't like him, you know!" he returned, his eyes flashing with the remembrance of an old thought; and the countess-dowager took the sentence literally, and not ironically.

"Not like him. If you had had any eyes as Val Elster, you'd have seen whether she liked him or not. She was dying for him—not for you."

He made no reply. It was only what he had suspected, in a half-doubting sort of way, at the time. A little spaniel, belonging to one of the gardeners, ran up and licked his hand.

"The time that I had of it!" continued the dowager. "But for me, Maude never would have been forced into having you. And she *shouldn't* have had you if I'd thought you were going to turn out like this."

He wheeled round and faced her; his pale face working with emotion, but his voice subdued to calmness. Lady Kirton's last words halted, for his look startled even her in its resolute sternness.

"To what end are you saying this, madam? You know perfectly well that you almost moved heaven and earth to get me: *you*, I say; I prefer to leave my wife's name out of this: and I fell into the snare. I have not complained of my bargain; so far as I know, Maude has not done so: but if it be otherwise—if she and you repent of the union, I am willing to dissolve it, as far as it can be dissolved, and to institute measures for living apart."

Never, never had she suspected it would come to this. She sat staring at him, her eyes round, her mouth open: scarcely believing the calm resolute man before her could be the once vacillating Val Elster.

"Listen whilst I speak a word of truth," he said, his eyes bent on her with a strange fire that, if it told of undisguised earnestness, told also of inward fever. "I married your daughter, and I am ready and willing to do my duty by her in all honour, as I have done it since the day of the marriage. Whatever my follies may have been as a young man, I am at least incapable of wronging my wife as a married one. *She* has had no cause to complain of want of affection, but—"

"Oh, what a hypocrite!" interrupted the dowager, with a shriek. "And all the time you've left her here neglected, while you were taking your amusement in London! You've been dinner-giving and Richmond-going, and theatre-frequenting, and card-playing, and race-horsing—and I shouldn't wonder but you've been cock-fighting, and a hundred other things as disreputable, and have come down here worn to a skeleton!"

"But if she is discontented, if she does not care for me, as you would seem to intimate," he resumed, passing over the attack without notice; "in short, if Maude would be happier without me, I am quite willing, as I have just said, to relieve her of her distasteful husband."

"Of all the wicked plotters, you must be the worst! My darling unoffending Maude! A divorce for her!"

"We are neither of us eligible for a divorce," he coolly rejoined. "A separation alone is open to us, and that an amicable one. Should it come to it, every possible provision can be made for your daughter's comfort; she shall retain this home; she shall have, if she wishes, a town-house; I will deny her nothing."

Lady Kirton rubbed her face carefully with her handkerchief. Not until this moment had she believed him to be in earnest, and the conviction frightened her.

"Why do you wish to separate from her?" she asked, in a subdued tone.

"I do not wish it. I said I was willing to do so if she wished it. You have been taking pains to convince me that Maude's love was not mine, that she was only forced into the marriage with me. Should this have been the case, I must be distasteful to her still; an encumbrance she may wish to get rid of."

The countess-dowager had overshot her mark, and saw it.

"Oh well! Perhaps I was mistaken about the past," she said, staring at him very hard, and in a sort of defiance. "Maude was always very close. If you said anything about separation now, I dare say it would kill her. My belief is, she does care for you, and a great deal more than you deserve."

"It may be better to ascertain the truth from Maude——"

"You won't say a syllable to her!" cried the dowager, starting up in terror. "She'd never forgive me; she'd turn me out of the house. Hartledon, *promise* you won't say a word to her."

He stood back against the window, never speaking.

"She does love you; but I thought I'd frighten you, for you had no right to send Maude home alone; and it made me very cross, because I saw how she felt it. Separation indeed! What can you be thinking of?"

He was thinking of a great deal, no doubt; and his thoughts were as bitter as they could well be. He did not wish to separate; come what might, he felt his place should be by his wife's side as long as circumstances permitted it.

"Let me give you a word of warning, Lady Kirton. I and my wife will be happy enough together, I daresay, if we are allowed to be; but the style of conversation you have just adopted to me will not conduce to it; it might retaliate on Maude, you see. Do not again attempt it."

"How you have changed!" was her involuntary remark.

"Yes; I am not the yielding boy I was. And now I wish to speak of your son. He seems very ill."

"A troublesome intruding fellow, why can't he keep his ailments to his own barracks?" was the wrathful rejoinder. "I told Maude I wouldn't have him here, and what does she do but write off and tell him to come! I don't like sick folk about me, and never did. What do *you* want?"

The last question was addressed to Hedges, who had come in unsummoned. It was only a letter for his master. Lord Hartledon took it as a welcome interruption, went outside, and sat down on a garden-seat at a distance. How he hated the style of attack just made on him; the style of the dowager altogether! He asked himself in what manner he could avoid this for the future. It was a debasing, lowering occurrence, and he felt sure that it could hardly have taken place in his servants' hall. But he was glad he had said what he did about the separation. It might grieve him to part from his wife, but Mr. Carr had warned him that he ought to do it. Certainly, if she disliked him so very much—if she forced it upon him—why, then, it would be an easier task; but he felt sure she did not dislike him. If she had done so before marriage, she had learnt to like him now; and he believed that the bare mention of parting would shock her; and so—his duty seemed to lie in remaining by her side.

He held the letter in his hand for some minutes before he opened it. The handwriting warned him that it was from Mr. Carr, and he knew that no pleasant news could be in it. In fact, he had placed himself in so unsatisfactory a position as to render anything but bad news next door to an impossibility.

It contained only a few lines—a word of caution Mr. Carr had forgotten to speak when he took leave of Lord Hartledon the previous morning. "Let me advise you not to say anything to those people—Gum, I think the name is—about G.G. It might not be altogether prudent for you to do so. Should you remain any time at Hartledon, I will come down for a few days and question for myself."

"I've done it already," thought Val, as he folded the letter and returned it to his pocket. "As to my staying any time at Hartledon—not if I know it."

Looking up at the sound of footsteps, he saw Hedges approaching. Never free from a certain apprehension when any unexpected interruption occurred—an apprehension that turned his heart sick, and set his pulses beating—he waited, outwardly very calm.

"Floyd has called, my lord, and is asking to see you. He seems rather—rather concerned and put out. I think it's something about—about the death last summer."

Hedges hardly knew how to frame his words, and Lord Hartledon stared at him.

"Floyd can come to me here," he said.

The miller soon made his appearance, carrying a small case half purse, half pocket-book, in his hand, made of Russian leather, with rims of gold. Val knew it in a moment, in spite of its marks of defacement.

"Do you recognize it, my lord?" asked the miller.

"Yes, I do," replied Lord Hartledon. "It belonged to my brother."

"I thought so," returned the miller. "On the very day before that unfortunate race last year, his lordship was talking to me, and had this in his hand. I felt sure it was the same the moment I saw it."

"He had it with him the day of the race," observed Lord Hartledon. "Mr. Carteret said he saw it lying in the boat when they started. We always thought it had been lost in the river. Where did you find it?"

"Well, it's very odd, my lord, but I found it buried."

"Buried!"

"Buried in the ground, not far from the river, alongside the path that leads from where his lordship was found to Hartledon. I was getting up some dandelion roots for my wife this morning early, and dug up this close to one. There's where the knife touched it. My lord," added the miller, "I beg to say that I have not opened it. I wiped it, wrapped it in paper, and said nothing to anybody, but came here with it as soon as I thought you'd be up. That lad of mine, Ripper, said last night you were at Hartledon."

The miller was quite honest; and Lord Hartledon knew that when he said he had not opened it, he had not done so. It still contained some small memoranda in his brother's writing, but no money; and this was noticeable, since it was quite certain to have had money in it on that day.

"Those who buried it might have taken it out," he observed, following the bent of his thoughts.

"But who did bury it; and where did they find it, to allow of their burying it?" questioned the miller. "How did they come by it?—that's the odd thing. I am certain it was not in the skiff, for I searched that over myself."

Lord Hartledon said little. He could not understand it; and the incident, with the slips of paper, was bringing his brother all too palpably before him. One of them had concerned himself, though in what manner he would never know now. It ran as follows: "Not to forget Val." Poor fellow! Poor Lord Hartledon!

"Would your lordship like to come and see the spot where I found it?" asked the miller.

Lord Hartledon said he should, and would go in the course of the day; and Floyd took his departure. Val sat on for a time where he was, and then went in, locked up the damp case with its tarnished rims, and went on to the presence of his wife.

She was dressed now, but had not left her bedroom. It was evident that she meant to be kind and pleasant with him; different from what she had been, for she smiled, and began a little apology for her tardiness, saying she would get up to breakfast in future.

He motioned her back to her seat on the sofa before the open window, and sat down near her. His face was grave; she thought she had never seen it so much so—grave and firm, and his voice was grave too, but had a kindly tone in it. He took both her hands between his as he spoke; not so much, it seemed in affection, as to impress solemnity upon her.

"Maude, I'm going to ask you a question, and I beg you to answer me as truthfully as you could answer Heaven. Have you any wish that we should live apart from each other?"

"I do not understand you," she answered, after a pause, during which a flush of surprise or emotion spread itself gradually over her face.

"Nay, the question is plain. Have you any wish to separate from me?"

"I never thought of such a thing. Separate from you! What can you mean?"

"Your mother has dropped a hint that you have not been happy with me. I could almost understand her to imply that you have a positive dislike to me. She sought to explain her words away, but certainly spoke them. Is it so, Maude? I fancied something of the sort myself in the earlier days of our marriage."

He turned his head sharply at a sudden sound, but it was only the French clock on the mantelpiece striking eleven.

"Because," he resumed, having waited in vain for an answer, "if such should really be your wish, I will accede to it. I desire your comfort, your happiness beyond any earthly thing; and if living apart from me would promote it, I will sacrifice my own feelings, and you shall not hear a murmur. I would sacrifice my life for you."

She burst into tears. "Are you speaking at all for yourself? Do you wish this?" she murmured.

"No."

"Then how can you be so cruel?"

"I should have thought it unjustifiably cruel, but that it has been suggested to me. Tell me the truth, Maude."

Maude was turning sick with apprehension. She had begun to like her husband during the latter part of their sojourn in London; had missed him terribly during this long period of lonely ennui at Hartledon; and his tender kindness to her for the past few fleeting hours of this their meeting had seemed like heaven as compared with the solitary past. Her whole heart was in her words as she answered:

"When we first married I did not care for you; I almost think I did not like you. Everything was new to me, and I felt as one in an unknown sea. But it wore off; and if you only knew how I have thought of you, and wished for you here, you would never have said anything so cruel. You are my husband, and you cannot put me from you. Percival, promise me that you will never hint at this again!"

He bent and kissed her. His course lay plain before him; and if an ugly mountain rose up before his mind's eye, shadowing forth not voluntary but forced separation, he would not look at it in that moment.

"What could mamma mean?" she asked. "I shall ask her."

"Maude, oblige me by saying nothing about it. I have already warned Lady Kirton that it must not be repeated; and I am sure it will not be. I wish you would also oblige me in another matter."

"In anything," she eagerly said, raising her tearful eyes to his. "Ask me anything."

"I intend to take your brother to the warmest seaside place England can boast of, at once; to-day or to-morrow. The sea-air may do me good also. I want that, or something else," he added; his tone assuming a sad weariness as he remembered how futile any "sea-air" would be for a mind diseased. "Won't you go with us, Maude?"

"Oh yes, gladly! I will go with you anywhere."

He left her to proceed to Captain Kirton's room, thinking that he and his wife might have been happy together yet, but for that one awful shadow of the past, which she did not know anything about; and he prayed she never might know.

But after all, it would have been a very moonlight sort of happiness.

# XXVIII

## Once More

The months rolled on, and Lord and Lady Hartledon did not separate. They remained together, and were, so far, happy enough—the moonlight happiness hinted at; and it is as I believe, the best and calmest sort of happiness for married life. Maude's temper was unequal, and he was subject to prolonged hours of sadness. But the time went lightly enough over their heads, for all the world saw, as it goes over the heads of most people.

And Lord Hartledon was a free man still, and stood well with the world. Whatever the mysterious accusation brought against him had been, it produced no noisy effects as yet; in popular phrase, it had come to nothing. As yet; always as yet. Whether he had shot a man, or robbed a bank, or fired a church, the incipient accusation died away. But the fear, let it be of what nature it would, never died away in his mind; and he lived as a man with a sword suspended over his head. Moreover, the sword, in his own imagination, was slipping gradually from its fastenings; his days were restless, his nights sleepless, an inward fever for ever consumed him.

As none knew better than Thomas Carr. There were two witnesses who could bring the facts home to Lord Hartledon; and, so far as was known, only two: the stranger, who had paid him a visit, and the man Gordon, or Gorton. The latter was the more dangerous; and they had not yet been able to trace him. Mr. Carr's friend, Detective Green, had furnished that gentleman with a descriptive bill of Gordon of the mutiny: "a young, slight man, with light eyes and fair hair." This did not answer exactly to the Gorton who had played his part at Calne; but then, in regard to the latter, there remained the suspicion that the red hair was false. Whether it was the same man or whether it was two men—if the phrase may be allowed—neither of them, to use Detective Green's expressive words, turned up. And thus the months had passed on, with nothing special to mark them. Captain Kirton had been conveyed abroad for the winter, and they had good news of him; and the countess-dowager was inflicting a visit upon one of her married daughters in Germany, the baroness with the unpronounceable name.

And the matter had nearly faded from the mind of Lady Hartledon. It would quite have faded, but for certain interviews with Thomas Carr at his chambers, when Hartledon's look of care precluded the idea that they could be visits of mere idleness or pleasure; and for the secret trouble that unmistakably sat on her husband like an incubus. At times he would moan in his sleep as one in pain; but if told of this, had always some laughing answer ready for her—he had dreamed he was fighting a lion or being tossed by a bull.

This was the pleasantest phase of Lady Hartledon's married life. Her health did not allow of her entering into gaiety; and she and her husband passed their time happily together. All her worst qualities seemed to have left her, or to be dormant; she was yielding and gentle; her beauty had never been so great as now that it was subdued; her languor was an attraction, her care to please being genuine; and they were sufficiently happy. They were in their town-house now, not having gone back to Hartledon. A large, handsome house, very different from the hired one they had first occupied.

In January the baby was born; and Maude's eyes glistened with tears of delight because it was a boy: a little heir to the broad lands of Hartledon. She was very well, and it seemed that she could never tire of fondling her child.

But in the first few days succeeding that of the birth a strange fancy took possession of her: she observed, or thought she observed, that her husband did not seem to care for the child. He did not caress it; she once heard him sighing over it; and he never announced it in the newspapers. Other infants, heirs especially, could be made known to the world, but not hers. The omission might never have come to her knowledge, since at first she was not allowed to see newspapers, but for a letter from the countess-dowager. The lady wrote in a high state of wrath from Germany; she had looked every day for ten days in the *Times*, and saw no chronicle of the happy event; and she demanded the reason. It afforded a valve for her temper, which had been in an explosive state for some time against Lord Hartledon, that ungracious son-in-law having actually forbidden her his house until Maude's illness should be over; telling her plainly that he would not have his wife worried. Lady Hartledon said nothing for a day or two; she was watching her husband; watching for signs of the fancy which had taken possession of her.

He was in her room one dark afternoon, standing with his elbow on the mantelpiece whilst he talked to her: a room of luxury and comfort it must have been almost a pleasure to be ill in. Lady Hartledon had been allowed to get up, and sit in an easy-chair: she seemed to be growing strong rapidly; and the little red gentleman in the cradle, sleeping quietly, was fifteen days old.

"About his name, Percival; what is it to be?" she asked. "Your own?"

"No, no, not mine," said he, quickly; "I never liked mine. Choose some other, Maude."

"What do you wish it to be?"

"Anything."

The short answer did not please the young mother; neither did the dreamy tone in which it was spoken. "Don't you care what it is?" she asked rather plaintively.

"Not much, for myself. I wish it to be anything you shall choose."

"I thought perhaps you would have liked it named after your brother," she said, very much offended on the baby's account.

"George?"

"George, no. I never knew George; I should not be likely to think of him. Edward."

Lord Hartledon looked at the fire, absently pushing back his hair. "Yes, let it be Edward. It will do as well as anything else."

"Good gracious, Percival, one would think you had been having babies all your life!" she exclaimed resentfully. "'Do as well as anything else!' If he were our tenth son, instead of our first, you could not treat it with more indifference. I have done nothing but deliberate on the name since he was born; and I don't believe you have once given it a thought."

Lord Hartledon turned his face upon her; and when illumined with a smile, as now, it could be as bright as before care came to it. "I don't think we men attach the importance to names in a general way that you do, Maude. I shall like to have it Edward."

"Edward William Algernon—"

"No, no, no," as if the number alarmed him. "Pray don't have a string of names: one's quite enough."

"Oh, very well," she returned, biting her lips. "William was your father's name. Algernon is my eldest brother's: I supposed you might like them. I thought," she added, after a pause, "we might ask Lord Kirton to be its godfather."

"I have decided on the godfathers already. Thomas Carr will be one, and I intend to be the other."

"Thomas Carr! A poor hard-working barrister, that not a soul knows, and of no family or influence whatever, godfather to the future Lord Hartledon!" uttered the offended mother.

"I wish it, Maude. Carr is the most valued friend I have in the world, or ever can have. Oblige me in this."

"Then my brother can be the other."

"No; I myself; and I wish you would be its godmother."

"Well, it's quite reversing the order of things!" she said, tacitly conceding the point.

A silence ensued. The firelight played on the lace curtains of the baby's bed, as it did on Lady Hartledon's face; a thoughtful face just now. Twilight was drawing on, and the fire lighted the room.

"Percival, do you care for the child?"

The tone had a sound of passion in it, breaking upon the silence. Lord Hartledon lifted his bent face and glanced at his wife.

"Do I care for the child, Maude? What a question! I do care for him: more than I allow to appear."

And if her voice had passion in it, his had pain. He crossed the room, and stood looking down on the sleeping baby, touching at length its cheek with his finger. He could have knelt, there and then, and wept over the child, and prayed, oh, how earnestly, that God would take it to Himself, not suffer it to live. Many and many a prayer had ascended from his heart in their earlier married days, that his wife might not bear him children; for he could only entail upon them an inheritance of shame.

"I don't think you have once taken him in your arms, Percival; you never kiss him. It's quite unnatural."

"I give my kisses in the dark," he laughed, as he returned to where she was sitting. And this was in a sense true; for once when he happened to be alone for an instant with the baby, he had clasped it and kissed it in a sort of delirious agony.

"You never had it in the *Times*, you know!"

"Never what?"

"Never announced its birth in the *Times*. Did you forget it?"

"It must have been very stupid of me," he remarked. "Never mind, Maude; he won't grow the less for the omission. When are you coming downstairs?"

"Mamma is in a rage about it; she says such neglect ought to be punished; and she knows you have done it on purpose."

"She is always in a rage with me, no matter what I do," returned Val, good-humouredly. "She hoped to be here at this time, and sway us all—you and me and the baby; and I stopped it. Ho, ho! young sir!"

The baby had wakened with a cry, and a watchful attendant came gliding in at the sound. Lord Hartledon left the room and went straight down to the Temple to Mr. Carr's chambers. He found him in all the bustle of departure from town. A cab stood at the foot of the stairs, and Mr. Carr's laundress, a queer old body with an inverted black bonnet, was handing the cabman a parcel of books.

"A minute more and you'd have been too late," observed Mr. Carr, as Lord Hartledon met him on the stairs, a coat on his arm.

"I thought you did not start till to-morrow."

"But I found I must go to-day. I can give you three minutes. Is it anything particular?"

Lord Hartledon drew him into his room. "I have come to crave a favour, Carr. It has been on my lips to ask you before, but they would not frame the words. This child of mine: will you be its godfather with myself?"

One moment's hesitation, quite perceptible to the sensitive mind of Lord Hartledon, and then Mr. Carr spoke out bravely and cheerily.

"Of course I will."

"I see you hesitate: but I do not like to ask any one else."

"If I hesitated, it was at the thought of the grave responsibility attaching to the office. I believe I look upon it in a more serious light than most people do, and have never accepted the charge yet. I will be sponsor to this one with all my heart."

Lord Hartledon clasped his hand in reply, and they began to descend the stairs. "Poor Maude was dreaming of making a grand thing of the christening," he said; "she wanted to ask Lord Kirton to come to it. It will take place in about a fortnight."

"Very well; I must run up for it, unless you let me stand by proxy. I wish, Hartledon, you would hear me on another point," added the barrister, halting on the stairs, and dropping his voice to a whisper.

"Well?"

"If you are to go away at all, now's the time. Can't you be seized with an exploring fit, and sail to Africa, or some other place, where your travels would occupy years?"

Lord Hartledon shook his head. "How can I leave Maude to battle alone with the exposure, should it come?"

"It is a great deal less likely to come if you are a few thousand miles away."

"I question it. Should Gorton turn up he is just the one to frighten a defenceless woman, and purchase his own silence. No; my place is beside Maude."

"As you please. I have spoken for the last time. By the way, any letters bearing a certain postmark, that come addressed to me during my absence, Taylor has orders to send to you. Fare you well, Hartledon; I wish I could help you to peace."

Hartledon watched the cab rattle away, and then turned homewards. Peace! There was no peace for him.

Lady Hartledon was not to be thwarted on all points, and she insisted on a ceremonious christening. The countess-dowager would come over for it, and did so; Lord Hartledon could not be discourteous enough to deny this; Lord and Lady Kirton came from Ireland; and for the first time since their marriage they found themselves entertaining guests. Lord Hartledon had made a faint opposition, but Maude had her own way. The countess-dowager was furiously indignant when she heard of the intended sponsors—its father and mother, and that cynical wretch, Thomas Carr! Val played the hospitable host; but there was a shadow on his face that his wife did not fail to see.

It was the evening before the christening, and a very snowy evening too. Val was dressing for dinner, and Maude, herself ready, sat by him, her baby on her knee. The child was attired for the first time in a splendidly-worked robe with looped-up sleeves; and she had brought it in to challenge admiration for its pretty arms, with all the pardonable pride of a young mother.

"Won't you kiss it for once, Val?"

He took the child in his arms; it had its mother's fine dark eyes, and looked straight up from them into his. Lord Hartledon suddenly bent his own face down upon that little one with what seemed like a gesture of agony; and when he raised it his own eyes were wet with tears. Maude felt startled with a sort of terror: love was love; but she did not understand love so painful as this.

She sat down with the baby on her knee, saying nothing; he did not intend her to see the signs of emotion. And this brings us to where we were. Lord Hartledon went on with his toilette, and presently someone knocked at the door.

Two letters: they had come by the afternoon post, very much delayed on account of the snow. He came back to the gaslight, opening one. A full letter, written closely; but he had barely glanced at it when he hastily folded it again, and crammed it into his pocket. If ever a movement expressed something to be concealed, that did. And Lady Hartledon was gazing at him with her questioning eyes.

"Wasn't that letter from Thomas Carr?"

"Yes."

"Is he coming up? Or is Kirton to be proxy?"

"He is—coming, I think," said Val, evidently knowing nothing one way or the other. "He'll be here, I daresay, to-morrow morning."

Opening the other letter as he spoke—a foreign-looking letter this one—he put it up in the same hasty manner, with barely a glance; and then went on slowly with his dressing.

"Why don't you read your letters, Percival?"

"I haven't time. Dinner will be waiting."

She knew that he had plenty of time, and that dinner would not be waiting; she knew quite certainly that there was something in both letters she must not see. Rising from her seat in silence, she went out of the room with her baby; resentment and an unhealthy curiosity doing battle in her heart.

Lord Hartledon slipped the bolt of the door and read the letters at once; the foreign one first, over which he seemed to take an instant's counsel with himself. Before going down he locked them up in a small ebony cabinet which stood against the wall. The room was his own exclusively; his wife had nothing to do with it.

Had they been alone he might have observed her coolness to him; but, with guests to entertain, he neither saw nor suspected it. She sat opposite him at dinner richly dressed, her jewels and smiles alike dazzling: but the smiles were not turned on him.

"Is that chosen sponsor of yours coming up for the christening; lawyer Carr?" tartly inquired the dowager from her seat, bringing her face and her turban, all scarlet together, to bear on Hartledon.

"He comes up by this evening's train; will be in London late to-night, if the snow allows him, and stay with us until Sunday night," replied Val.

"Oh! *That's* no doubt the reason why you settled the christening for Saturday: that your friend might have the benefit of Sunday?"

"Just so, madam."

And Lady Hartledon knew, by this, that her husband must have read the letters. "I wonder what he has done with them?" came the mental thought, shadowing forth a dim wish that she could read them too.

In the drawing-room, after dinner, someone proposed a carpet quadrille, but Lord Hartledon seemed averse to it. In his wife's present mood, his opposition was, of course, the signal for her approval, and she began pushing the chairs aside with her own hands. He approached her quietly.

"Maude, do not let them dance to-night."

"Why not?"

"I have a reason. My dear, won't you oblige me in this?"

"Tell me the reason, and perhaps I will; not otherwise."

"I will tell it you another time. Trust me, I have a good one. What is it, Hedges?"

The butler had come up to his master in the unobtrusive manner of a well-trained servant, and was waiting an opportunity to speak. He said a word in Lord Hartledon's ear, and Lady Hartledon saw a shiver of surprise run through her husband. He looked here, looked there, as one perplexed with fear, and finally went out of the room with a calm face, but one that was turning livid.

Lady Hartledon followed in an impulse of curiosity. She looked after him over the balustrades, and saw him turn into the library below. Hedges was standing near the drawing-room door.

"Does any one want Lord Hartledon?"

"Yes, my lady."

"Who is it?"

"I don't know, my lady. Some gentleman."

She ran lightly down the stairs, pausing at the foot, as if ashamed of her persistent curiosity. The well-lighted hall was before her; the dining-room on one side; the library and a small room communicating on the other. Throwing back her head, as in defiance, she boldly crossed the hall and opened the library door.

Now what Lady Hartledon had really thought was that the visitor was Mr. Carr; her husband was going to steal a quiet half-hour with him; and Hedges was in the plot. She had not lived with Hartledon the best part of a year without learning that Hedges was devoted heart and soul to his master.

She opened the library-door. Her husband's back was towards her; and facing him, his arms raised as if in anger or remonstrance, was the same stranger who had caused some commotion in the other house. She knew him in a moment: there he was, with his staid face, his black clothes, and his white neckcloth, looking so like a clergyman. Lord Hartledon turned his head.

"I am engaged, Maude; you can't come in," he peremptorily said; and closed the door upon her.

She went slowly up the stairs again, not choosing to meet the butler's eyes, past the drawing-rooms, and up to her own. The sight of the stranger, coupled with her husband's signs of emotion, had renewed all her old suspicions, she knew not, she never had known, of what. Jumping to the conclusion that those letters must be in some way connected with the mystery, perhaps an advent of the visit, it set her thinking, and rebellion arose in her heart.

"I wonder if he put them in the ebony cabinet?" she exclaimed. "I have a key that will fit that."

Yes, she had a key to fit it. A few weeks before, Lord Hartledon mislaid his keys; he wanted something out of this cabinet, in which he did not, as a rule, keep anything of consequence, and tried hers. One was found to unlock it, and he jokingly told her she had a key to his treasures. But himself strictly honourable, he could not suspect dishonour in another; and Lord Hartledon supposed it simply impossible that she should attempt to open it of her own accord.

They were of different natures; and they had been reared in different schools. Poor Maude Kirton had learnt to be anything but scrupulous, and really thought it a very slight thing she was about to do, almost justifiable under the circumstances. Almost, if not quite. Nevertheless she would not have liked to be caught at it.

She took her bunch of keys and went into her husband's dressing-room, which opened from their bedroom: but she went on tip-toe, as one who knows she is doing wrong. It took some little time to try the keys, for there were several on the ring, and she did not know the right one: but the lid flew open at last, and disclosed the two letters lying there.

She snatched at one, either that came first, and opened it. It happened to be the one from Mr. Carr, and she began to read it, her heart beating.

Dear Hartledon,
    "I think I have at last found some trace of Gorton. There's a man of that name in the criminal calendar here, down

for trial to-morrow; I shall see then whether it is the same, but the description tallies. Should it be our Gorton, I think the better plan will be to leave him entirely alone: a man undergoing a criminal sentence—and this man is sure of a long period of it—has neither the means nor the motive to be dangerous. He cannot molest you whilst he is working on Portland Island; and, so far, you may live a little eased from fear. I wish—"

Mr. Carr's was a close handwriting, and this concluded the first page. She was turning it over, when Lord Hartledon's voice on the stairs caught her ear. He seemed to be coming up.

Ay, and he would have caught her at her work but for the accidental circumstance of the old dowager's happening to look out of the drawing-room and detaining him, as he was hastening onwards up the stairs. She did her daughter good service that moment, if she had never done it before. Maude had time to fold the letter, put it back, lock the cabinet, and escape. Had she been a nervous woman, given to being flurried and to losing her presence of mind, she might not have succeeded; but she was cool and quick in emergency, her brain and fingers steady.

Nevertheless her heart beat a little as she stood within the other room, the door not latched behind her. She did not stir, lest he should hear her; and she hoped to remain unseen until he went down again. A ready excuse was on her lips, if he happened to look in, which was not probable: that she fancied she heard baby cry, and was listening.

Lord Hartledon was walking about his dressing-room, pacing it restlessly, and she very distinctly heard suppressed groans of mortal anguish breaking from his lips. How he had got rid of his visitor, and what the visitor came for, she knew not. He seemed to halt before the washhand-stand, pour out some water, and dash his face into it.

"God help me! God help Maude!" he exclaimed, as he went down again to the drawing-room.

And Lady Hartledon went down also, for the interruption had frightened her, and she did not attempt to open the cabinet again. She never knew more of the contents of Mr. Carr's letter; and only the substance of the other, as communicated to her by her husband.

# XXIX

## CROSS-QUESTIONING MR. CARR

Not until the Sunday morning did Lady Hartledon speak to her husband of the stranger's visit. There seemed to have been no previous opportunity. Mr. Carr had arrived late on the Friday night; indeed it was Saturday morning, for the trains were all detained; and he and Hartledon sat up together to an unconscionable hour. For this short visit he was Lord Hartledon's guest. Saturday seemed to have been given to preparation, to gaiety, and to nothing else. Perhaps also Lady Hartledon did not wish to mar that day by an unpleasant word. The little child was christened; the names given him being Edward Kirton: the countess-dowager, who was in a chronic state of dissatisfaction with everything and every one, angrily exclaimed at the last moment, that she thought at least her family name might have been given to the child; and Lord Hartledon interposed, and said, give it. Lord and Lady Hartledon, and Mr. Carr, were the sponsors: and it would afford food for weeks of grumbling to the old dowager. Hilarity reigned, and toasts were given to the new heir of Hartledon; and the only one who seemed not to enter into the spirit of the thing, but on the contrary to be subdued, absent, nervous, was the heir's father.

And so it went on to the Sunday morning. A cold, bleak, bitter morning, the wind howling, the snow flying in drifts. Mr. Carr went to church, and he was the only one of the party in the house who did go. The countess-dowager the previous night had proclaimed the fact that *she* meant to go—as a sort of reproach to any who meant to keep away. However, when the church-bells began, she was turning round in her warm bed for another nap.

Maude did not go down early; had not yet taken to doing so. She breakfasted in her room, remained toying with her baby for some time, and then went into her own sitting-room; a small cosy apartment on the drawing-room floor, into which visitors did not intrude. It looked on to Hyde Park, and a very white and dreary park it was on that particular day.

Drawing a chair to the window, she sat looking out. That is, her eyes were given to the outer world, but she was so deep in thought as to see nothing of it. For two nights and a day, burning with curiosity, she had been putting this and that together in her own mind, and drawing conclusions according to her own light. First, there was the advent of the visitor; secondly, there was the letter she had dipped into. She connected the two with each other and wondered WHAT the secret care could be that had such telling effect upon her husband.

Gorton. The name had struck upon her memory, even whilst she read it, as one associated with that terrible time—the late Lord Hartledon's death. Gradually the floodgates of recollection opened, and she knew him for the witness at the inquest about whom some speculation had arisen as to who he was, and what his business at Calne might have been with Lord Hartledon and his brother, Val Elster.

Why should her husband be afraid of this man?—as it seemed he *was* afraid, by Mr. Carr's letter. What power had he of injuring Lord Hartledon?—what secret did he possess of his, that might be used against him? Turning it about in her mind, and turning it again, searching her imagination for a solution, Lady Hartledon at length arrived at one, in default of others. She thought this man must know some untoward fact by which the present Lord Hartledon's succession was imperilled. Possibly the late Lord Hartledon had made some covert and degrading marriage; leaving an obscure child who possessed legal rights, and might yet claim them. A romantic, far-fetched idea, you will say; but she could think of no other that was in the least feasible. And she remembered some faint idea having arisen in her mind at the time, that the visit of the man Gorton was in some way connected with trouble, though she did not know with which brother.

Val came in and shut the door. He stirred the fire into a blaze, making some remark about the snow, and wondering how Carr would get down to the country again. Maude gave a slight answer, and then there was silence. Each was considering how best to say something to the other. She was the quicker.

"Lord Hartledon, what did that man want on Friday?"

"What man?" he rejoined, rather wincing—for he knew well enough to what she alluded.

"The man—gentleman, or whatever he is—who had you called down to him in the library."

"By the way, Maude—yes—you should not dart in when I am engaged with visitors on business."

"Well, I thought it was Mr. Carr," she replied, glancing at his heightened colour. "What did he want?"

"Only to say a word to me on a matter of business."

"It was the same person who upset you so when he called last autumn. You have never been the same man since."

"Don't take fancies into your head, Maude."

"Fancies! you know quite well there is no fancy about it. That man holds some unpleasant secret of yours, I am certain."

"Maude!"

"Will you tell it me?"

"I have nothing to tell."

"Ah, well; I expected you wouldn't speak," she answered, with subdued bitterness; as much as to say, that she made a merit of resigning herself to an injustice she could not help. "You have been keeping things from me a long time."

"I have kept nothing from you it would give you pleasure to know. It is not—Maude, pray hear me—it is not always expedient for a man to make known to his wife the jars and rubs he has himself to encounter. A hundred trifles may arise that are best spared to her. That gentleman's business concerned others as well as myself, and I am not at liberty to speak of it."

"You refuse, then, to admit me to your confidence?"

"In this I do. I am the best judge—and you must allow me to be so—of what ought, and what ought not, to be spoken of to you. You may always rely upon my acting for your best happiness, as far as lies in my power."

He had been pacing the room whilst he spoke. Lady Hartledon was in too resentful a mood to answer. Glancing at her, he stood by the mantelpiece and leaned his elbow upon it.

"I want to make known to you another matter, Maude. If I have kept it from you—"

"Does it concern this secret business of yours?" she interrupted.

"No."

"Then let us have done with this first, if you please. Who is Gorton?"

"Who is—Gorton?" he repeated, after a dumbfounded pause. "What Gorton?"

"Well, I don't know; unless it's that man who gave evidence at the inquest on your brother."

Lord Hartledon stared at her, as well he might; and gulped down his breath, which seemed choking him. "But what about Gorton? Why do you ask me the question?"

"Because I fancy he is connected with this trouble. I—I thought I heard you and Mr. Carr mention the name yesterday when you were whispering together. I'm sure I did—there!"

As far as Lord Hartledon remembered, he and Mr. Carr had not been whispering together yesterday; had not mentioned the name of Gorton. They had done with the subject at that late sitting, the night of the barrister's arrival; who had brought news that the Gorton, that morning tried for a great crime, was *not* the Gorton of whom they were in search. Lord Hartledon gazed at his wife with questioning eyes, but she persisted in her assertion. It was sinfully untrue; but how else could she account for knowing the name?

"Do you suppose I dreamed it, Lord Hartledon?"

"I don't know whether you dreamed it or not, Maude. Mr. Carr has certainly spoken to me since he came of a man of that name; but as certainly not in your hearing. One Gorton was tried for his life on Friday—or almost for his life—and he mentioned to me the circumstances of the case: housebreaking, accompanied by violence, which ended in death. I cannot understand you, Maude, or the fancies you seem to be taking up."

She saw how it was—he would admit nothing: and she looked straight out across the dreary park, a certain obstinate defiance veiled in her eyes. By the help of Heaven or earth, she would find out this secret that he refused to disclose to her.

"Almost every action of your life bespeaks concealment," she resumed. "Look at those letters you received in your dressing-room on Friday night: you just opened them and thrust them unread into your pocket, because I happened to be there. And yet you talk of caring for me! I know those letters contained some secret or other you dare not tell me."

She rose in some temper, and gave the fire a fierce stir.

Lord Hartledon kept her by him.

"One of those letters was from Mr. Carr; and I presume you can make no objection to my hearing from him. The other—Maude, I have waited until now to disclose its contents to you; I would not mar your happiness yesterday."

She looked up at him. Something in his voice, a sad pitying tenderness, caused her heart to beat a shade quicker. "It was a foreign letter, Maude. I think you observed that. It bore the French postmark."

A light broke upon her. "Oh, Percival, it is about Robert! Surely he is not worse!"

He drew her closer to him: not speaking.

"He is not dead?" she said, with a rush of tears. "Ah, you need not tell me; I see it. Robert! Robert!"

"It has been a happy death, Maude, and he is better off. He was quite ready to go. I wish we were as ready!"

Lord Hartledon took out the letter and read the chief portion of it to her. One little part he dexterously omitted, describing the cause of death—disease of the heart.

"But I thought he was getting so much better. What has killed him in this sudden manner?"

"Well, there was no great hope from the first. I confess I have entertained none. Mr. Hillary, you know, warned us it might end either way."

"Was it decline?" she asked, her tears falling.

"He has been declining gradually, no doubt."

"Oh, Percival! Why did you not tell me at once? It seems so cruel to have had all that entertainment yesterday! This is why you did not wish us to dance!"

"And if I had told you, and stopped the entertainment, allowing the poor little fellow to be christened in gloom and sorrow, you would have been the first to reproach me; you might have said it augured ill-luck for the child."

"Well, perhaps I should; yes, I am sure I should. You have acted rightly, after all, Val." And it was a candid admission, considering what she had been previously saying. He bent towards her with a smile, his voice quite unsteady with its earnestness.

"You see now with what motive I kept the letter from you. Maude! cannot this be an earnest that you should trust me for the rest? In all I do, as Heaven is my witness, I place your comfort first and foremost."

"Don't be angry with me," she cried, softening at the words.

He laid his hand on his wife's bent head, thinking how far he was from anger. Anger? He would have died for her then, at that moment, if it might have saved her from the sin and shame that she must share with him.

"Have you told mamma, Percival?"

"Not yet. It would not have been kept from you long had she known it. She is not up yet, I think."

"Who has written?"

"The doctor who attended him."

"You'll let me read the letter?"

"I have written to desire that full particulars may be sent to you: you shall read that one."

The tacit refusal did not strike her. She only supposed the future letter would be more explanatory. He was always anxious for her; and he had written off on the Friday night to ask for a letter giving fuller particulars, whilst avoiding mention of the cause of death.

Thus harmony for the hour was restored between them; and Lord Hartledon stood the dowager's loud reproaches with equanimity. In possession of the news of that darling angel's death ever since Friday night, and to have bottled it up within him till Sunday! She wondered what he thought of himself!

After all, Val had not quite "bottled it up." He had made it known to his brother-in-law, Lord Kirton, and also to Mr. Carr. Both had agreed that nothing had better be said until the christening-day was over.

But there came a reaction. When Lady Hartledon had got over her first grief, the other annoyance returned to her, and she fell again to brooding over it in a very disturbing fashion. She merited blame for this in a degree; but not so much as appears on the surface. If that idea, which she was taking up very seriously, were correct—that her husband's succession was imperilled—it would be the greatest misfortune that could happen to her in life. What had she married for but position?— rank, wealth, her title? any earthly misfortune would be less keen than this. Any earthly misfortune! Poor Maude!

It was a sombre dinner that evening; the news of Captain Kirton's death making it so. Besides relatives, very few guests were staying in the house; and the large and elaborate dinner-party of the previous day was reduced to a small one on this. The first to come into the drawing-room afterwards, following pretty closely on the ladies, was Mr. Carr. The dowager, who rarely paid attention to appearances, or to anything else, except her own comfort, had her feet up on a sofa, and was fast asleep; two ladies were standing in front of the fire, talking in undertones; Lady Hartledon sat on a sofa a little apart, her baby on her knee; and her sister-in-law, Lady Kirton, a fragile and rather cross-looking young woman, who looked as if a breath would blow her away, was standing over her, studying the infant's face. The latter lady moved away and joined the group at the fire as Mr. Carr approached Lady Hartledon.

"You have your little charge here, I see!"

"Please excuse it; I meant to have sent him away before any of you came up," she said, quite pleadingly. "Sarah took upon herself to proclaim aloud that his eyes were not straight, and I could not help having him brought down to refute her words. Not straight, indeed! She's only envious of him."

Sarah was Lady Kirton. Mr. Carr smiled.

"She has no children herself. I think you might be proud of your godson, Mr. Carr. But he ought not to have been here to receive you, for all that."

"I have come up soon to say good-bye, Lady Hartledon. In ten minutes I must be gone."

"In all this snow! What a night to travel in!"

"Necessity has no law. So, sir, you'd imprison my finger, would you!"

He had touched the child's hand, and in a moment it was clasped round his finger. Lady Hartledon laughed.

"Lady Kirton—the most superstitious woman in the world—would say that was an omen: you are destined to be his friend through life."

"As I will be," said the barrister, his tone more earnest than the occasion seemed to call for.

Lady Hartledon, with a graciousness she was little in the habit of showing to Mr. Carr, made room for him beside her, and he sat down. The baby lay on his back, his wide-open eyes looking upwards, good as gold.

"How quiet he is! How he stares!" reiterated the barrister, who did not understand much about babies, except for a shadowy idea that they lived in a state of crying for the first six months.

"He is the best child in the world; every one says so," she returned. "He is not the least—Hey-day! what do you mean by contradicting mamma like that? Behave yourself, sir."

For the infant, as if to deny his goodness, set up a sudden cry. Mr. Carr laughed. He put down his finger again, and the little fingers clasped round it, and the cry ceased.

"He does not like to lose his friend, you see, Lady Hartledon."

"I wish you would be my friend as well as his," she rejoined; and the low meaning tones struck on Mr. Carr's ear.

"I trust I am your friend," he answered.

She was still for a few moments; her pale beautiful face inclining towards the child's; her large dark eyes bent upon him. She turned them on Mr. Carr.

"This has been a sad day."

"Yes, for you. It is grievous to lose a brother."

"And to lose him without the opportunity of a last look, a last farewell. Robert was my best and favourite brother. But the day has been marked as unhappy for other causes than that."

Was it an uncomfortable prevision of what was coming that caused Mr. Carr not to answer her? He talked to the unconscious baby, and played with its cheeks.

"What secret is this that you and my husband have between you, Mr. Carr?" she asked abruptly.

He ceased his laughing with the baby, said something about its soft face, was altogether easy and careless in his manner, and then answered in half-jesting tones:

"Which one, Lady Hartledon?"

"Which one! Have you more than one?" she continued, taking the words literally.

"We might count up half-a-dozen, I daresay. I cannot tell you how many things I have not confided to him. We are quite—"

"I mean the secret that affects *him*," she interrupted, in aggrieved tones, feeling that Mr. Carr was playing with her.

"There is some dread upon him that's wearing him to a shadow, poisoning his happiness, making his days and nights one long restlessness. Do you think it right to keep it from me, Mr. Carr? Is it what you and he are both doing—and are in league with each other to do?"

"*I* am not keeping any secret from you, Lady Hartledon."

"You know you are. Nonsense! Do you think I have forgotten that evening that was the beginning of it, when a tall strange man dressed as a clergyman, came here, and you both were shut up with him for I can't tell how long, and Lord Hartledon came out from it looking like a ghost? You and he both misled me, causing me to believe that the Ashtons were entering an action against him for breach of promise; laying the damages at ten thousand pounds. I mean *that* secret, Mr. Carr," she added with emphasis. "The same man was here on Friday night again; and when you came to the house afterwards, you and Lord Hartledon sat up until nearly daylight."

Mr. Carr, who had his eyes on the exacting baby, shook his head, and intimated that he was really unable to understand her.

"When you are in town he is always at your chambers; when you are away he receives long letters from you that I may not read."

"Yes, we have been on terms of close friendship for years. And Lord Hartledon is an idle man, you know, and looks me up."

"He said you were arranging some business for him last autumn."

"Last autumn? Let me see. Yes, I think I was."

"Mr. Carr, is it of any use playing with me? Do you think it right or kind to do so?"

His manner changed at once; he turned to her with eyes as earnest as her own.

"Lady Hartledon, I would tell you anything that I could and ought to tell you. That your husband has been engaged in some complicated business, which I have been—which I have taken upon myself to arrange for him, is very true. I know that he does not wish it mentioned, and therefore my lips are sealed: but it is as well you did not know it, for it would give you no satisfaction."

"Does it involve anything very frightful?"

"It might involve the—the loss of a large sum of money," he answered, making the best reply he could.

Lady Hartledon sank her voice to a whisper. "Does it involve the possible loss of his title?—of Hartledon?"

"No," said Mr. Carr, looking at her with surprise.

"You are sure?"

"Certain. I give you my word. What can have got into your head, Lady Hartledon?"

She gave a sigh of relief. "I thought it just possible—but I will not tell you why I thought it—that some claimant might be springing up to the title and property."

Mr. Carr laughed. "That would be a calamity. Hartledon is as surely your husband's as this watch"—taking it out to look at the time—"is mine. When his brother died, he succeeded to him of indisputable right. And now I must go, for my time is up; and when next I see you, young gentleman, I shall expect a good account of your behaviour. Why, sir, the finger's mine, not yours. Good-bye, Lady Hartledon."

She gave him her hand coolly, for she was not pleased. The baby began to cry, and was sent away with its nurse.

And then Lady Hartledon sat on alone, feeling that if she were ever to arrive at the solution of the mystery, it would not be by the help of Mr. Carr. Other questions had been upon her lips—who the stranger was—what he wanted—five hundred of them: but she saw that she might as well have put them to the moon.

And Lord Hartledon went out with Mr. Carr in the inclement night, and saw him off by a Great-Western train.

# XXX

## Maude's Disobedience

A gain the months went on, it may almost be said the years, and little took place worthy of record. Time obliterates as well as soothes; and Lady Hartledon had almost forgotten the circumstances which had perplexed and troubled her, for nothing more had come of them.

And Lord Hartledon? But for a certain restlessness, a hectic flush and a worn frame, betraying that the inward fever was not quenched, a startled movement if approached or spoken to unexpectedly, it might be thought that he also was at rest. There were no more anxious visits to Thomas Carr's chambers; he went about his ordinary duties, sat out his hours in the House of Lords, and did as other men. There was nothing very obvious to betray mental apprehension; and Maude had certainly dismissed the past, so far, from her mind.

Not again had Val gone down to Hartledon. With the exception of that short visit of a day or two, already recorded, he had not been there since his marriage. He would not go: his wife, though she had her way in most things, could not induce him to go. She went once or twice, in a spirit of defiance, it may be said, and meanwhile he remained in London, or took a short trip to the Continent, as the whim prompted him. Once they had gone abroad together, and remained for some months; taking servants and the children, for there were two children now; and the little fellow who had clasped the finger of Mr. Carr was a sturdy boy of three years old.

Lady Hartledon's health was beginning to fail. The doctors told her she must be more quiet; she went out a great deal, and seemed to live only in the world. Her husband remonstrated with her on the score of health; but she laughed, and said she was not going to give up pleasure just yet. Of course these gay habits are more easily acquired than relinquished. Lady Hartledon had fainting-fits; she felt occasional pain and palpitation in the region of the heart; and she grew thin without apparent cause. She said nothing about it, lest it should be made a plea for living more quietly; never dreaming of danger. Had she known what caused her brother's death her fears might possibly have been awakened. Lord Hartledon suspected mischief might be arising, and cautiously questioned her; she denied that anything was the matter, and he felt reassured. His chief care was to keep her free from excitement; and in this hope he gave way to her more than he would otherwise have done. But alas! the moment was approaching when all his care would be in vain; when the built-up security of years was destroyed by a single act of wilful disobedience to him. The sword so long suspended over his head, was to fall on hers at last.

One spring afternoon, in London, he was in his wife's sitting-room; the little room where you have seen her before, looking upon the Park. The children were playing on the carpet—two pretty little things; the girl eighteen months old.

"Take care!" suddenly called out Lady Hartledon.

Some one was opening the door, and the little Maude was too near to it. She ran and picked up the child, and Hedges came in with a card for his master, saying at the same time that the gentleman was waiting. Lord Hartledon held it to the fire to read the name.

"Who is it?" asked Lady Hartledon, putting the little girl down by the window, and approaching her husband. But there came no answer.

Whether the silence aroused her suspicions—whether any look in her husband's face recalled that evening of terror long ago—or whether some malicious instinct whispered the truth, can never be known. Certain it was that the past rose up as in a mirror before Lady Hartledon's imagination, and she connected this visitor with the former. She bent over his shoulder to peep at the card; and her husband, startled out of his presence of mind, tore it in two and threw the pieces into the fire.

"Oh, very well!" she exclaimed, mortally offended. "But you cannot blind me: it is your mysterious visitor again."

"I don't know what you mean, Maude. It is only someone on business."

"Then I will go and ask him his business," she said, moving to the door with angry resolve.

Val was too quick for her. He placed his back against the door, and lifted his hands in agitation. It was a great fault of his, or perhaps a misfortune—for he could not help it—this want of self-control in moments of emergency.

"Maude, I forbid you to interfere in this; you must not. For Heaven's sake, sit down and remain quiet."

"I'll see your visitor, and know, at last, what this strange trouble is. I will, Lord Hartledon."

"You must not: do you hear me?" he reiterated with deep emotion, for she was trying to force her way out of the room. "Maude—listen—I do not mean to be harsh, but for your own good I conjure you to be still. I forbid you, by the obedience you promised me before God, to inquire into or stir in this matter. It is a private affair of my own, and not yours. Stay here until I return."

Maude drew back, as if in compliance; and Lord Hartledon, supposing he had prevailed, quitted the room and closed the door. He was quite mistaken. Never had her solemn vows of obedience been so utterly despised; never had the temptation to evil been so rife in her heart.

She unlatched the door and listened. Lord Hartledon went downstairs and into the library, just as he had done the evening before the christening. And Lady Hartledon was certain the same man awaited him there. Ringing the nursery-bell, she took off her slippers, unseen, and hid them under a chair.

"Remain here with the children," was her order to the nurse who appeared, as she shut the woman into the room.

Creeping down softly she opened the door of the room behind the library, and glided in. It was a small room, used exclusively by Lord Hartledon, where he kept a heterogeneous collection of things—papers, books, cigars, pipes, guns, scientific models, anything—and which no one but himself ever attempted to enter. The intervening door between that and the library was not quite closed; and Lady Hartledon, cautiously pushed it a little further open. Wilful, unpardonable disobedience! when he had so strongly forbidden her! It was the same tall stranger. He was speaking in low tones, and Lord Hartledon leaned against the wall with a blank expression of face.

She saw; and heard. But how she controlled her feelings, how she remained and made no sign, she never knew. But that the instinct of self-esteem was one of her strongest passions, the dread of detection in proportion to it, she never had remained. There she was, and she could not get away again. The subtle dexterity which had served her in coming might desert her in returning. Had their senses been on the alert they might have heard her poor heart beating.

The interview did not last long—about twenty minutes; and whilst Lord Hartledon was attending his visitor to the door she escaped upstairs again, motioned away the nurse, and resumed her shoes. But what did she look like? Not like Maude Hartledon. Her face was as that of one upon whom some awful doom has fallen; her breath was coming painfully; and she kneeled down on the carpet and clasped her children to her beating heart with an action of wild despair.

"Oh, my boy! my boy! Oh, my little Maude!"

Suddenly she heard her husband's step approaching, and pushing them from her, rose and stood at the window, apparently looking out on the darkening world.

Lord Hartledon came in, gaily and cheerily, his manner lighter than it had been for years.

"Well, Maude, I have not been long, you see. Why don't you have lights?"

She did not answer: only stared straight out. Her husband approached her. "What are you looking at, Maude?"

"Nothing," she answered: "my head aches. I think I shall lie down until dinner-time. Eddie, open the door, and call Nurse, as loud as you can call."

The little boy obeyed, and the nurse returned, and was ordered to take the children. Lady Hartledon was following them to go to her own room, when she fell into a chair and went off in a dead faint.

"It's that excitement," said Val. "I do wish Maude would be reasonable!"

The illness, however, appeared to be more serious than an ordinary fainting-fit; and Lord Hartledon, remembering the suspicion of heart-disease, sent for the family doctor Sir Alexander Pepps, an oracle in the fashionable world.

A different result showed itself—equally caused by excitement—and the countess-dowager arrived in a day or two in hot haste. Lady Hartledon lay in bed, and did not attempt to get up or to get better. She lay almost as one without life, taking no notice of any one, turning her head from her husband when he entered, refusing to answer her mother, keeping the children away from the room.

"Why doesn't she get up, Pepps?" demanded the dowager, wrathfully, pouncing upon the physician one day, when he was leaving the house.

Sir Alexander, who might have been supposed to have received his baronetcy for his skill, but that titles, like kissing, go by favour, stopped short, took off his hat, and presumed that Lady Hartledon felt more comfortable in bed.

"Rubbish! We might all lie in bed if we studied comfort. Is there any earthly reason why she should stay there, Pepps?"

"Not any, except weakness."

"Except idleness, you mean. Why don't you order her to get up?"

"I have advised Lady Hartledon to do so, and she does not attend to me," replied Sir Alexander.

"Oh," said the dowager. "She was always wilful. What about her heart?"

"Her heart!" echoed Sir Alexander, looking up now as if a little aroused.

"Dear me, yes; her heart; I didn't say her liver. Is it sound, Pepps?"

"It's sound, for anything I know to the contrary. I never suspected anything the matter with her heart."

"Then you are a fool!" retorted the complimentary dowager.

Sir Alexander's temperament was remarkably calm. Nothing could rouse him out of his tame civility, which had been taken more than once for obsequiousness. The countess-dowager had patronized him in earlier years, when he was not a great man, or had begun to dream of becoming one.

"Don't you recollect I once consulted you on the subject—what's your memory good for? She was a girl then, of fourteen or so; and you were worth fifty of what you are now, in point of discernment."

The oracle carried his thoughts back, and really could not recollect it. "Ahem! yes; and the result was—was—"

"The result was that you said the heart had nothing the matter with it, and I said it had," broke in the impatient dowager.

"Ah, yes, madam, I remember. Pray, have you reason to suspect anything wrong now?"

"That's what you ought to have ascertained, Pepps, not me. What d'you mean by your neglect? What, I ask, does she lie in bed for? If her heart's right, there's nothing more the matter with her than there is with you."

"Perhaps your ladyship can persuade Lady Hartledon to exert herself," suggested the bland doctor. "I can't; and I confess I think that she only wants rousing."

With a flourish of his hat and his small gold-headed black cane the doctor bowed himself out from the formidable dowager. That lady turned her back upon him, and betook herself on the spur of the moment to Maude's room, determined to "have it out."

Curious sounds greeted her, as of some one in hysterical pain. On the bed, clasped to his mother in nervous agony, was the wondering child, little Lord Elster: words of distress, nay, of despair, breaking from her. It seemed, the little boy, who was rather self-willed and rebellious on occasion, had escaped from the nursery, and stolen to his mother's room. The dowager halted at the door, and looked out from her astonished eyes.

"Oh, Edward, if we were but dead! Oh, my darling, if it would only please Heaven to take us both! I couldn't send for you, child; I couldn't see you; the sight of you kills me. You don't know; my babies, you don't know!"

"What on earth does all this mean?" interrupted the dowager, stepping forward. And Lady Hartledon dropped the boy, and fell back on the bed, exhausted.

"What have you done to your mamma, sir?"

The child, conscious that he had not done anything, but frightened on the whole, repented of his disobedience, and escaped from the chamber more quickly than he had entered it. The dowager hated to be puzzled, and went wrathfully up to her daughter.

"Perhaps you'll tell me what's the matter, Maude."

Lady Hartledon grew calm. The countess-dowager pressed the question.

"There's nothing the matter," came the tardy and rather sullen reply.

"Why do you wish yourself dead, then?"

"Because I do."

"How dare you answer me so?"

"It's the truth. I should be spared suffering."

The countess-dowager paused. "Spared suffering!" she mentally repeated; and being a woman given to arriving at rapid conclusions without rhyme or reason, she bethought herself that Maude must have become acquainted with the suspicion regarding her heart.

"Who told you that?" shrieked the dowager. "It was that fool Hartledon."

"He has told me nothing," said Maude, in an access of resentment, all too visible. "Told me what?"

"Why, about your heart. That's what I suppose it is."

Maude raised herself upon her elbow, her wan face fixed on her mother's. "Is there anything the matter with my heart?" she calmly asked.

And then the old woman found that she had made a grievous mistake, and hastened to repair it.

"I thought there might be, and asked Pepps. I've just asked him now; and he's says there's nothing the matter with it."

"I wish there were!" said Maude.

"You wish there were! That's a pretty wish for a reasonable Christian," cried the tart dowager. "You want your husband to lecture you; saying such things."

"I wish he were hanged!" cried Maude, showing her glistening teeth.

"My gracious!" exclaimed the wondering old lady, after a pause. "What has he done?"

"Why did you urge me to marry him? Oh, mother, can't you see that I am dying—dying of horror—and shame—and grief? You had better have buried me instead."

For once in her selfish and vulgar mind the countess-dowager felt a feeling akin to fear. In her astonishment she thought Maude must be going mad.

"You'd do well to get some sleep, dear," she said in a subdued tone; "and to-morrow you must get up; Pepps says so; he thinks you want rousing."

"I have not slept since; it's not sleep, it's a dead stupor, in which I dream things as horrible as the reality," murmured Maude, unconscious perhaps that she spoke aloud. "I shall never sleep again."

"Not slept since when?"

"I don't know."

"Can't you say what you mean?" cried the puzzled dowager. "If you've any grievance, tell it out; if you've not, don't talk nonsense."

But Lady Hartledon, though thus sweetly allured to confession, held her tongue. Her half-scattered senses came back to her, and with them a reticence she would not break. The countess-dowager hardly knew whether she deserved pitying or shaking, and went off in a fit of exasperation, breaking in upon her son-in-law as he was busy looking over some accounts in the library.

"I want to know what is the matter with Maude."

He turned round in his chair, and met the dowager's flaxen wig and crimson face. Val did not know what was the matter with his wife any more than the questioner did. He supposed she would be all right when she grew stronger.

"She says it's *you*," said the gentle dowager, improving upon her information. "She has just been wishing you were hanged."

"Ah, you have been teasing her," he returned, with composure. "Maude says all sorts of things when she's put out."

"Perhaps she does," was the retort; "but she meant this, for she showed her teeth when she said it. You can't blind me; and I have seen ever since I came here that there was something wrong between you and Maude."

For that matter, Val had seen it too. Since the night of his wife's fainting-fit she had scarcely spoken a word to him; had appeared as if she could not tolerate his presence for an instant in her room. Lord Hartledon felt persuaded that it arose from resentment at his having refused to allow her to see the stranger. He rose from his seat.

"There's nothing wrong between me and Maude, Lady Kirton. If there were, you must pardon me for saying that I could not suffer any interference in it. But there is not."

"Something's wrong somewhere. I found her just now sobbing and moaning over Eddie, wishing they were both dead, and all the rest of it. If she goes on like this for nothing, she's losing her senses, that's all."

"She'll be all right when she's stronger. Pray don't worry her. She'll be well soon, I daresay. And now I shall be glad if you'll leave me, for I am very busy."

She did not leave him any the quicker for the request, but stayed to worry him, as it was in her nature to worry every one. Getting rid of her at last, he turned the key of the door, and wished her a hundred miles away.

The wish bore fruit. In a few days some news she heard regarding her eldest son—who was a widower now—took the dowager to Ireland, and Lord Hartledon wished he could as easily turn the key of the house upon her as he had turned that of the room.

# XXXI

## The Sword Slipped

S ummer dust was in the London streets, summer weather in the air, and the carriage of that fashionable practitioner, Sir Alexander Pepps, still waited before Lord Hartledon's house. It had waited there more frequently in these later weeks than of old.

The great world—*her* world—wondered what was the matter with her: Sir Alexander wondered also. Perhaps had he been a less courtly man he might have rapped out "obstinacy," if questioned upon the point; as it was, he murmured of "weakness." Weak she undoubtedly was; and she did not seem to try in the least to grow strong again. She did not go into society now; she dressed as usual, and sat in her drawing-room, and received visitors if the whim took her; but she was usually denied to all; and said she was not well enough to go out. From her husband she remained bitterly estranged. If he attempted to be friendly with her, to ask what was ailing her, she either sharply refused to say, or maintained a persistent silence. Lord Hartledon could not account for her behaviour, and was growing tired of it.

Poor Maude! That some grievous blow had fallen upon her was all too evident. Resentment, anguish, bitter despair alternated within her breast, and she seemed really not to care whether she lived or died. Was it for *this* that she had schemed, and so successfully, to wrest Lord Hartledon from his promised bride Anne Ashton? She would lie back in her chair and ask it. No labour of hers could by any possibility have brought forth a result by which Miss Ashton could be so well avenged. Heaven is true to itself, and Dr. Ashton had left vengeance with it. Lady Hartledon looked back on her fleeting triumph; a triumph at the time certainly, but a short one. It had not fulfilled its golden promises: that sort of triumph perhaps never does. It had been followed by ennui, repentance, dissatisfaction with her husband, and it had resulted in a very moonlight sort of happiness, which had at length centred only in the children. The children! Maude gave a cry of anguish as she thought of them. No; take it altogether, the play from the first had not been worth the candle. And now? She clasped her thin hands in a frenzy of impotent rage—with Anne Ashton had lain the real triumph, with herself the sacrifice. Too well Maude understood a remark her husband once made in answer to a reproach of hers in the first year of their marriage—that he was thankful not to have wedded Anne.

One morning Sir Alexander Pepps, on his way from the drawing-room to his chariot—a very old-fashioned chariot that all the world knew well—paused midway in the hall, with his cane to his nose, and condescended to address the man with the powdered wig who was escorting him.

"Is his lordship at home?"

"Yes, sir."

"I wish to see him."

So the wig changed its course, and Sir Alexander was bowed into the presence. His lordship rose with what the French would call *empressement*, to receive the great man.

"Thank you, I have not time to sit," said he, declining the offered chair and standing, cane in hand. "I have three consultations to-day, and some urgent cases. I grieve to have a painful duty to fulfil; but I must inform you that Lady Hartledon's health gives me uneasiness."

Lord Hartledon did not immediately reply; but it was not from want of genuine concern.

"What is really the matter with her?"

"Debility; nothing else," replied Sir Alexander. "But these cases of extreme debility cause so much perplexity. Where there is no particular disease to treat, and the patient does not rally, why—"

He understood the doctor's pause to mean something ominous. "What can be done?" he asked. "I have remarked, with pain, that she does not gain strength. Change of air? The seaside—"

"She says she won't go," interrupted the physician. "In fact, her ladyship objects to everything I can suggest or propose."

"It's very strange," said Lord Hartledon.

"At times it has occurred to me that she has something on her mind," continued Sir Alexander. "Upon my delicately hinting this opinion to Lady Hartledon, she denied it with a vehemence which caused me to suspect that I was correct. Does your lordship know of anything likely to—to torment her?"

"Not anything," replied Lord Hartledon, confidently. "I think I can assure you that there is nothing of the sort."

And he spoke according to his belief; for he knew of nothing. He would have supposed it simply impossible that Lady Hartledon had been made privy to the dreadful secret which had weighed on him; and he never gave that a thought.

Sir Alexander nodded, reassured on the point.

"I should wish for a consultation, if your lordship has no objection."

"Then pray call it without delay. Have anything, do anything, that may conduce to Lady Hartledon's recovery. You do not suspect heart-disease?"

"The symptoms are not those of any heart-disease known to me. Lady Kirton spoke to me of this; but I see nothing to apprehend at present on that score. If there's any latent affection, it has not yet shown itself. Then we'll arrange the consultation for to-morrow."

Sir Alexander Pepps was bowed out; and the consultation took place; which left the matter just where it was before. The wise doctors thought there was nothing radically wrong; but strongly recommended change of air. Sir Alexander confidently mentioned Torbay; he had great faith in Torbay; perhaps his lordship could induce Lady Hartledon to try it? She had flatly told the consultation that she would *not* try it.

Lady Hartledon was seated in the drawing-room when he went in, willing to do what he could; any urging of his had not gone far with her of late. A white silk shawl covered her dress of green check silk; she wore a shawl constantly now, having a perpetual tendency to shiver; her handsome features were white and attenuated, but her eyes were brilliant still, and her dark hair was dressed in elaborate braids.

"So you have had the doctors here, Maude," he remarked, cheerfully.

She nodded a reply, and began to fidget with the body of her gown. It seemed that she had to do something or other always to her attire whenever he spoke to her—which partially took away her attention.

"Sir Alexander tells me they have been recommending you Torbay."

"I am not going to Torbay."

"Oh yes, you are, Maude," he soothingly said. "It will be a change for us all. The children will benefit by it as much as you, and so shall I."

"I tell you I shall not go to Torbay."

"Would you prefer any other place?"

"I will not go anywhere; I have told them so."

"Then I declare that I'll carry you off by force!" he cried, rather sharply. "Why do you vex me like this? You know you must go?"

She made no reply. He drew a chair close to her and sat down.

"Maude," he said, speaking all the more gently for his recent outbreak, "you must be aware that you do not recover as quickly as we could wish—"

"I do not recover at all," she interrupted. "I don't want to recover."

"My dear, how can you talk so? There is nothing the matter with you but weakness, and that will soon be overcome if you exert yourself."

"No, it won't. I shall not leave home."

"Somewhere you must go, for the workmen are coming into the house; and for the next two months it will not be habitable."

"Who is bringing them in?" she asked, with flashing eyes.

"You know it was decided long ago that the house should be done up this summer. It wants it badly enough. Torbay—"

"I will not go to Torbay, Lord Hartledon. If I am to be turned out of this house, I'll go to the other."

"What other?"

"Hartledon."

"Not to Hartledon," said he, quickly, for his dislike to the place had grown with time, and the word grated on his ear.

"Then I remain where I am."

"Maude," he resumed in quiet tones, "I will not urge you to try sea-air for my sake, because you do what you can to show me I am of little moment to you; but I will say try it for the sake of the children. Surely, they are dear to you!"

A subdued sound of pain broke from her lips, as if she could not bear to hear them named.

"It's of no use prolonging this discussion," she said. "An invalid's fancies may generally be trusted, and mine point to Hartledon—if I am to be disturbed at all. I should not so much mind going there."

A pause ensued. Lord Hartledon had taken her hand, and was mechanically turning round her wedding-ring, his thoughts far away; it hung sufficiently loosely now on the wasted finger. She lay back in her chair, looking on with apathy, too indifferent to withdraw her hand.

"Why did you put it on?" she asked, abruptly.

"Why indeed?" returned his lordship, deep in his abstraction. "What did you say, Maude?" he added, awaking in a flurry. "Put what on?"

"My wedding-ring."

"My dear! But about Hartledon—if you fancy that, and nowhere else, I suppose we must go there."

"You also?"

"Of course."

"Ah! when your wife's chord of life is loosening what model husbands you men become!" she uttered. "You have never gone to Hartledon with me; you have suffered me to be there alone, through a ridiculous reminiscence; but now that you are about to lose me you will go!"

"Why do you encourage these gloomy thoughts about yourself, Maude?" he asked, passing over the Hartledon question. "One would think you wished to die."

"I do not know," she replied in tones of deliberation. "Of course, no one, at my age, can be tired of the world, and for some things I wish to live; but for others, I shall be glad to die."

"Maude! Maude! It is wrong to say this. You are not likely to die."

"I can't tell. All I say is, I shall be glad for some things, if I do."

"What is all this?" he exclaimed, after a bewildered pause. "Is there anything on your mind, Maude? Are you grieving after that little infant?"

"No," she answered, "not for him. I grieve for the two who remain."

Lord Hartledon looked at her. A dread, which he strove to throw from him, struggling to his conscience.

"I think you are deceived in my state of health. And if I object to going to the seaside, it is chiefly because I would not die in a strange place. If I am to die, I should like to die at Hartledon."

His hair seemed to rise up in horror at the words. "Maude! have you any disease you are concealing from me?"

"Not any. But the belief has been upon me for some time that I should not get over this. You must have seen how I appear to be sinking."

"And with no disease upon you! I don't understand it."

"No particular physical disease."

"You are weak, dispirited—I cannot pursue these questions," he broke off. "Tell me in a word: is there any cause for this?"

"Yes."

Percival gathered up his breath. "What is it?"

"What is it!" her eyes ablaze with sudden light. "What has weighed *you* down, not to the grave, for men are strong, but to terror, and shame, and sin? What secret is it, Lord Hartledon?"

His lips were whitening. "But it—even allowing that I have a secret—need not weigh you down."

"Not weigh me down!—to terror deeper than yours; to shame more abject? Suppose I know the secret?"

"You cannot know it," he gasped. "It would have killed you."

"And what *has* it done? Look at me."

"Oh, Maude!" he wailed, "what is it that you do, or do not know? How did you learn anything about it?"

"I learnt it through my own folly. I am sorry for it now. My knowing it can make the fact neither better nor worse; and perhaps I might have been spared the knowledge to the end."

"But what is it that you know?" he asked, rather wishing at the moment he was dead himself.

"*All.*"

"It is impossible."

"It is true."

And he felt that it was true; here was the solution to the conduct which had puzzled him, puzzled the doctors, puzzled the household and the countess-dowager.

"And how—and how?" he gasped.

"When that stranger was here last, I heard what he said to you," she replied, avowing the fact without shame in the moment's terrible anguish. "I made the third at the interview."

He looked at her in utter disbelief.

"You refused to let me go down. I followed you, and stood at the little door of the library. It was open, and I—heard—every word."

The last words were spoken with an hysterical sobbing. "Oh, Maude!" broke from the lips of Lord Hartledon.

"You will reproach me for disobedience, of course; for meanness, perhaps; but I *knew* there was some awful secret, and you would not tell me. I earned my punishment, if that will be any satisfaction to you; I have never since enjoyed an instant's peace, night or day."

He hid his face in his pain. This was the moment he had dreaded for years; anything, so that it might be kept from her, he had prayed in his never-ceasing fear.

"Forgive, forgive me! Oh, Maude, forgive me!"

She did not respond; she did not attempt to soothe him; if ever looks expressed reproach and aversion, hers did then.

"Have compassion upon me, Maude! I was more sinned against than sinning."

"What compassion had you for me? How dared you marry me? you, bound with crime?"

"The worst is over, Maude; the worst is over."

"It can never be over: you are guilty of wilful sophistry. The crime remains; and—Lord Hartledon—its fruits remain."

He interrupted her excited words by voice and gesture; he took her hands in his. She snatched them from him, and burst into a fit of hysterical crying, which ended in a faintness almost as of death. He did not dare to call assistance; an unguarded word might have slipped out unawares.

Shut them in; shut them in! they had need to be alone in a scene such as that.

Lord and Lady Hartledon went down to Calne, as she wished. But not immediately; some two or three weeks elapsed, and during that time Mr. Carr was a good deal with both of them. Their sole friend: the only man cognizant of the trouble they had yet to battle with; who alone might whisper a word of something like consolation.

Lady Hartledon seemed to improve. Whether it was the country, or the sort of patched-up peace that reigned between her and her husband, she grew stronger and better, and began to go out again and enjoy life as usual. But in saying life, it must not be thought that gaiety is implied; none could shun that as Lady Hartledon now seemed to shun it. And he, for the first time since his marriage, began to take some interest in his native place, and in his own home. The old sensitive feeling in regard to meeting the Ashtons lingered still; was almost as strong as ever; and he had the good sense to see that this must be overcome, if possible, if he made Hartledon his home for the future, as his wife now talked of doing.

As a preliminary step to it, he appeared at church; one, two, three Sundays. On the second Sunday his wife went with him. Anne was in her pew, with her younger brother, but not Mrs. Ashton: she, as Lord Hartledon knew by report, was too ill now to go out. Each day Dr. Ashton did the whole duty; his curate, Mr. Graves, was taking a holiday. Lord Hartledon heard another report, that the curate had been wanting to press his attentions on Miss Ashton. The truth was, as none had known better than Val Elster, Mr. Graves had wanted to press them years and years ago. He had at length made her an offer, and she had angrily refused him. A foolish girl! said indignant Mrs. Graves, reproachfully. Her son was a model son, and would make a model husband; and he would be a wealthy man, as Anne knew, for he must sooner or later come into the entailed property of his uncle. It was not at all pleasant to Lord Hartledon to stand there in his pew, with recollection upon him, and the gaze of the Ashtons studiously turned from him, and Jabez Gum looking out at him from the corners of his eyes as he made his sonorous responses. A wish for reconciliation took strong possession of Lord Hartledon, and he wondered whether he could not bring himself to sue for it. He wanted besides to stay for the after-service, which he had not done since he was a young man—never since his marriage. Maude had stayed occasionally, as was the fashion; but he never. I beg you not to quarrel with me for the word; some of the partakers in that after-service remain from no higher motive. Certainly poor Maude had not.

On the third Sunday, Lord Hartledon went to church in the evening—alone; and when service was over he waited until the church had emptied itself, and then made his way into the vestry. Jabez was passing out of it, and the Rector was coming out behind him. Lord Hartledon stopped the latter, and craved a minute's conversation. Dr. Ashton bowed rather stiffly, put his hat down, and Jabez shut them in.

"Is there any service you require of me?" inquired the Rector, coldly.

It was the impulsive Val Elster of old days who answered; his hand held out pleadingly, his ingenuous soul shining forth from his blue eyes.

"Yes, there is, Doctor Ashton; I have come to pray for it—your forgiveness."

"My Christian forgiveness you have had already," returned the clergyman, after a pause.

"But I want something else. I want your pardon as a man; I want you to look at me and speak to me as you used to do. I want to hear you call me 'Val' again; to take my hand in yours, and not coldly; in short, I want you to help me to forgive myself."

In that moment—and Dr. Ashton, minister of the gospel though he was, could not have explained it—all the old love for Val Elster rose bubbling in his heart. A stubborn heart withal, as all hearts are since Adam sinned; he did not respond to the offered hand, nor did his features relax their sternness in spite of the pleading look.

"You must be aware, Lord Hartledon, that your conduct does not merit pardon. As to friendship—which is what you ask for—it would be incompatible with the distance you and I must observe towards each other."

"Why need we observe it—if you accord me your true forgiveness?"

The question was one not easy to respond to candidly. The doctor could not say, Your intercourse with us might still be dangerous to the peace of one heart; and in his inner conviction he believed that it might be. He only looked at Val; the yearning face, the tearful eyes; and in that moment it occurred to the doctor that something more than the ordinary wear and tear of life had worn the once smooth brow, brought streaks of silver to the still luxuriant hair.

"Do you know that you nearly killed her?" he asked, his voice softening.

"I have known that it might be so. Had *any* atonement lain in my power; any means by which her grief might have been soothed; I would have gone to the ends of the earth to accomplish it. I would even have died if it could have done good. But, of all the world, I alone might attempt nothing. For myself I have spent the years in misery; not on that score," he hastened to add in his truth, and a thought crossed Dr. Ashton that he must allude to unhappiness with his wife—"on another. If it will be any consolation to know it—if you might accept it as even the faintest shadow of atonement—I can truly say that few have gone through the care that I have, and lived. Anne has been amply avenged."

The Rector laid his hand on the slender fingers, hot with fever, whiter than they ought to be, betraying life's inward care. He forgave him from that moment; and forgiveness with Dr. Ashton meant the full meaning of the word.

"You were always your own enemy, Val."

"Ay. Heaven alone knows the extent of my folly; and of my punishment."

From that hour Lord Hartledon and the Rectory were not total strangers to each other. He called there once in a way, rarely seeing any one but the doctor; now and then Mrs. Ashton; by chance, Anne. Times and again was it on Val's lips to confide to Dr. Ashton the nature of the sin upon his conscience; but his innate sensitiveness, the shame it would reflect upon him, stepped in and sealed the secret.

Meanwhile, perhaps he and his wife had never lived on terms of truer cordiality. *There were no secrets between them*: and let me tell you that is one of the keys to happiness in married life. Whatever the past had been, Lady Hartledon appeared to condone it; at least she no longer openly resented it to her husband. It is just possible that a shadow of the future, a prevision of the severing of the tie, very near now, might have been unconsciously upon her, guiding her spirit to meekness, if not yet quite to peace. Lord Hartledon thought she was growing strong; and, save that she would rather often go into a passion of hysterical tears as she clasped her children to her, particularly the boy, her days passed calmly enough. She indulged the children beyond all reason, and it was of no use for their father to interfere. Once when he stepped in to prevent it, she flew out almost like a tigress, asking what business it was of his, that he should dare to come between her and them. The lesson was an effectual one; and he never interfered again. But the indulgence was telling on the boy's naturally haughty disposition; and not for good.

# XXXII

## In the Park

As the days and weeks went on, and Lord and Lady Hartledon continued at Calne, there was one circumstance that began to impress itself on the mind of the former in a careless sort of way—that he was constantly meeting Pike. Go out when he would, he was sure to see Pike in some out-of-the-way spot; at a sudden turning, or peering forth from under a group of trees, or watching him from a roadside bank. One special day impressed itself on Lord Hartledon's memory. He was walking slowly along the road with Dr. Ashton, and found Pike keeping pace with them softly on the other side the hedge, listening no doubt to what he could hear. On one of these occasions Val stopped and confronted him.

"What is it you want, Mr. Pike?"

Perhaps Mr. Pike was about the last man in the world to be, as the saying runs, "taken aback," and he stood his ground, and boldly answered "Nothing."

"It seems as though you did," said Val. "Go where I will, you are sure to spring up before me, or to be peeping from some ambush as I walk along. It will not do: do you understand?"

"I was just thinking the same thing yesterday—that your lordship was always meeting *me*," said Pike. "No offence on either side, I dare say."

Val walked on, throwing the man a significant look of warning, but vouchsafing no other reply. After that Pike was a little more cautious, and kept aloof for a time; but Val knew that he was still watched on occasion.

One fine October day, when the grain had been gathered in and the fields were bare with stubble, Hartledon, alone in one of the front rooms, heard a contest going on outside. Throwing up the window, he saw his young son attempting to mount the groom's pony: the latter objecting. At the door stood a low basket carriage, harnessed with the fellow pony. They belonged to Lady Hartledon; sometimes she drove only one; and the groom, a young lad of fourteen, light and slim, rode the other: sometimes both ponies were in the carriage; and on those occasions the boy sat by her side, and drove.

"What's the matter, Edward?" called out Lord Hartledon to his son.

"Young lordship wants to ride the pony, my lord," said the groom. "My lady ordered me to ride it."

At this juncture Lady Hartledon appeared on the scene, ready for her drive. She had intended to take her little son with her—as she generally did—but the child boisterously demanded that he should ride the pony for once, and she weakly yielded. Lord Hartledon's private opinion, looking on, was that she was literally incapable of denying him any earthly thing he chose to demand. He went out.

"He had better go with you in the carriage, Maude."

"Not at all. He sits very well now, and the pony's perfectly quiet."

"But he is too young to ride by the side of any vehicle. It is not safe. Let him sit with you as usual."

"Nonsense! Edward, you shall ride the pony. Help him up, Ralph."

"No, Maude. He—"

"Be quiet!" said Lady Hartledon, bending towards her husband and speaking in low tones. "It is not for you to interfere. Would you deny him everything?"

A strangely bitter expression sat on Val's lips. Not of anger; not even mortification, but sad, cruel pain. He said no more.

And the cavalcade started. Lady Hartledon driving, the boy-groom sitting beside her, and Eddie's short legs striding the pony. They were keeping to the Park, she called to her husband, and she should drive slowly.

There was no real danger, as Val believed; only he did not like the child's wilful temper given way to. With a deep sigh he turned indoors for his hat, and went strolling down the avenue. Mrs. Capper dropped a curtsey as he passed the lodge.

"Have you heard from your son yet?" he asked.

"Yes, my lord, many thanks to you. The school suits him bravely."

Turning out of the gates, he saw Floyd, the miller, walking slowly along. The man had been confined to his bed for weeks in the summer, with an attack of acute rheumatism, and to the house afterwards. It was the first time they had met since that morning long ago, when the miller brought up the purse. Lord Hartledon did not know him at first, he was so altered; pale and reduced.

"Is it really you, Floyd?"

"What's left of me, my lord."

"And that's not much; but I am glad to see you so far well," said Hartledon, in his usual kindly tone. "I have heard reports of you from Mr. Hillary."

"Your lordship's altered too."

"Am I?"

"Well, it seems so to me. But it's some few years now since I saw you. Nothing has ever come to light about that pocket-book, my lord."

"I conclude not, or I should have heard of it."

"And your lordship never came down to see the place!"

"No. I left Hartledon the same day, I think, or the next. After all, Floyd, I don't see that it is of any use looking into these painful things: it cannot bring the dead to life again."

"That's, true," said the miller.

He was walking into Calne. Lord Hartledon kept by his side, talking to him. He promised to be as popular a man as his father had been; and that was saying a great deal. When they came opposite the Rectory, Lord Hartledon wished him good day and more strength, in his genial manner, and turned in at the Rectory gates.

About once a week he was in the habit of calling upon Mrs. Ashton. Peace was between them; and these visits to her sick chamber were strangely welcome to her heart. She had loved Val Elster all her life, and she loved him still, in spite of the past. For Val was curiously subdued; and his present mood, sad, quiet, thoughtful, was more endearing than his gayer one had been. Mrs. Ashton did not fail to read that he was a disappointed man, one with some constant care upon him.

Anne was in the hall when he entered, talking to a poor applicant who was waiting to see the Rector. Lord Hartledon lifted his hat to her, but did not offer to shake hands. He had never presumed to touch her hand since the reconciliation; in fact, he scarcely ever saw her.

"How is Mrs. Ashton to-day?"

"A little better, I think. She will be glad to see you."

He followed the servant upstairs, and Anne turned to the woman again. Mrs. Ashton was in an easy-chair near the window; he drew one close to her.

"You are looking wonderful to-day, do you know?" he began in tones almost as gay as those of the light-hearted Val Elster. "What is it? That very becoming cap?"

"The cap, of course. Don't you see its pink ribbons? Your favourite colour used to be pink, Val. Do you remember?"

"I remember everything. But indeed and in truth you look better, dear Mrs. Ashton."

"Yes, better to-day," she said, with a sigh. "I shall fluctuate to the end, I suppose; one day better, the next worse. Val, I think sometimes it is not far off now."

Very far off he knew it could not be. But he spoke of hope still: it was in his nature to do so. In the depths of his heart, so hidden from the world, there seemed to be hope for the whole living creation, himself excepted.

"How is your wife to-day?"

"Quite well. She and Edward are out with the ponies and carriage."

"She never comes to see me."

"She does not go to see anyone. Though well, she's not very strong yet."

"But she's young, and will grow strong. I shall only grow weaker. I am brave to-day; but you should have seen me last night. So prostrate! I almost doubted whether I should rise from my bed again. I do not think you will have to come here many more times."

"Oh, Mrs. Ashton!"

"A little sooner or a little later, what does it matter, I try to ask myself; but parting is parting, and my heart aches sometimes. One of my aches will be leaving you."

"A very minor one then," he said, with deprecation; but tears shone in his dark blue eyes.

"Not a minor one. I have loved you as a son. I never loved you more, Percival, than when that letter of yours came to me at Cannes."

It was the first time she had alluded to it: the letter written the evening of his marriage. Val's face turned red, for his perfidy rose up before him in its full extent of shame.

"I don't care to speak of that," he whispered. "If you only knew what my humiliation has been!"

"Not of that, no; I don't know why I mentioned it. But I want you to speak of something else, Val. Over and over again has it been on my lips to ask it. What secret trouble is weighing you down?"

A far greater change, than the one called up by recollection and its shame, came over his face now. He did not speak; and Mrs. Ashton continued. She held his hands as he bent towards her.

"I have seen it all along. At first—I don't mind confessing it—I took it for granted that you were on bad terms with yourself on account of the past. I feared there was something wrong between you and your wife, and that you were regretting Anne. But I soon put that idea from me, to replace it with a graver one."

"What graver one?" he asked.

"Nay, I know not. I want you to tell me. Will you do so?"

He shook his head with an unmistakable gesture, unconsciously pressing her hands to pain.

"Why not?"

"You have just said I am dear to you," he whispered; "I believe I am so."

"As dear, almost, as my own children."

"Then do not even wish to know it. It is an awful secret; and I must bear it without sympathy of any sort, alone and in silence. It has been upon me for some years now, taking the sweetness out of my daily bread; and it will, I suppose, go with me to my grave. Not scarcely to lift it off my shoulders, would I impart it to *you*."

She sighed deeply; and thought it must be connected with some of his youthful follies. But she loved him still; she had faith in him; she believed that he went wrong from misfortune more than from fault.

"Courage, Val," she whispered. "There is a better world than this, where sorrow and sighing cannot enter. Patience—and hope—and trust in God!—always bearing onwards. In time we shall attain to it."

Lord Hartledon gently drew his hands away, and turned to the window for a moment's respite. His eyes were greeted with the sight of one of his own servants, approaching the Rectory at full speed, some half-dozen idlers behind him.

With a prevision that something was wrong, he said a word of adieu to Mrs. Ashton, went down, and met the man outside. Dr. Ashton, who had seen the approach, also hurried out.

There had been some accident in the Park, the man said. The pony had swerved and thrown little Lord Elster: thrown him right under the other pony's feet, as it seemed. The servant made rather a bungle over his news, but this was its substance.

"And the result? Is he much hurt?" asked Lord Hartledon, constraining his voice to calmness.

"Well, no; not hurt at all, my lord. He was up again soon, saying he'd lash the pony for throwing him. He don't seem hurt a bit."

"Then why need you have alarmed us so?" interrupted Dr. Ashton, reprovingly.

"Well, sir, it's her ladyship seems hurt—or something," cried the man.

Lord Hartledon looked at him.

"What have you come to tell, Richard? Speak out."

Apparently Richard could not speak out. His lady had been frightened and fainted, and did not come to again. And Lord Hartledon waited to hear no more.

The people, standing about in the park here and there—for even this slight accident had gathered its idlers together—seemed to look at Lord Hartledon curiously as he passed them. Close to the house he met Ralph the groom. The boy was crying.

"'Twasn't no fault of anybody's, my lord; and there ain't any damage to the ponies," he began, hastening to excuse himself. "The little lord only slid off, and they stood as quiet as quiet. There wasn't no cause for my lady's fear."

"Is she fainting still?"

"They say she's—dead."

Lord Hartledon pressed onwards, and met Mr. Hillary at the hall-door. The surgeon took his arm and drew him into an empty room.

"Hillary! is it true?"

"I'm afraid it is."

Lord Hartledon felt his sight failing. For a moment he was a man groping in the dark. Steadying himself against the wall, he learned the details.

The child's pony had swerved. Ralph could not tell at what, and Lady Hartledon did not survive to tell. She was looking at him at the time, and saw him flung under the feet of the other pony, and she rose up in the carriage with a scream, and then fell back into the seat again. Ralph jumped out and picked up the child, who was not hurt at all; but when he hastened to tell her this, he saw that she seemed to have no life in her. One of the servants, Richard, happened to be going through the Park, within sight; others soon came up; and whilst Lady Hartledon was being driven home Richard ran for Mr. Hillary, and then sought his master, whom he found at the Rectory. The surgeon had found her dead.

"It must have been instantaneous," he observed in low tones as he concluded these particulars. "One great consolation is, that she was spared all suffering."

"And its cause?" breathed Lord Hartledon.

"The heart. I don't entertain the least doubt about it."

"You said she had no heart disease. Others said it."

"I said, if she had it, it was not developed. Sudden death from it is not at all uncommon where disease has never been suspected."

And this was all the conclusion come to in the case of Lady Hartledon. Examination proved the surgeon's surmise to be correct; and in answer to a certain question put by Lord Hartledon, he said the death was entirely irrespective of any trouble, or care, or annoyance she might have had in the past; irrespective even of any shock, except the shock at the moment of death, caused by seeing the child thrown. That, and that alone, had been the fatal cause. Lord Hartledon listened to this, and went away to his lonely chamber and fell on his knees in devout thankfulness to Heaven that he was so far innocent.

"If she had not given way to the child!" he bitterly aspirated in the first moments of sorrow.

That the countess-dowager should come down post-haste and invade Hartledon, was of course only natural; and Lord Hartledon strove not to rebel against it. But she made herself so intensely and disagreeably officious that his patience was sorely tried. Her first act was to insist on a stately funeral. He had given orders for one plain and quiet in every way; but she would have her wish carried out, and raved about the house, abusing him for his meanness and want of respect to his dead wife. For peace' sake, he was fain to give her her way; and the funeral was made as costly as she pleased. Thomas Carr came down to it; and the countess-dowager was barely civil to him.

Her next care was to assume the entire management of the two children, putting Lord Hartledon's authority over them at virtual, if not actual, defiance. The death of her daughter was in truth a severe blow to the dowager; not from love, for she really possessed no natural affection at all, but from fear that she should lose her footing in the house which was so desirable a refuge. As a preliminary step against this, she began to endeavour to make it more firm and secure. Altogether she was rendering Hartledon unbearable; and Val would often escape from it, his boy in his hand, and take refuge with Mrs. Ashton.

That Lord Hartledon's love for his children was intense there could be no question about; but it was nevertheless of a peculiarly reticent nature. He had rarely, if ever, been seen to caress them. The boy told tales of how papa would kiss him, even weep over him, in solitude; but he would not give him so much as an endearing name in the presence of others. Poor Maude had called him all the pet names in a fond mother's vocabulary; Lord Hartledon always called him Edward, and nothing more.

A few evenings after the funeral had taken place, Mirrable, who had been into Calne, was hurrying back in the twilight. As she passed Jabez Gum's gate, the clerk's wife was standing at it, talking to Mrs. Jones. The two were laughing: Mrs. Gum seemed in a less depressed state than usual, and the other less snappish.

"Is it you!" exclaimed Mrs. Jones, as Mirrable stopped. "I was just saying I'd not set eyes on you in your new mourning."

"And laughing over it," returned Mirrable.

"No!" was Mrs. Jones's retort. "I'd been telling of a trick I served Jones, and Nance was laughing at that. Silk and crêpe! It's fine to be you, Mrs. Mirrable!"

"How's Jabez, Nancy?" asked Mirrable, passing over Mrs. Jones's criticism.

"He's gone to Garchester," replied Mrs. Gum, who was given to indirect answers. "I thought I was never going to see you again, Mary."

"You could not expect to see me whilst the house was in its recent state," answered Mirrable. "We have been in a bustle, as you may suppose."

"You've not had many staying there."

"Only Mr. Carr; and he left to-day. We've got the old countess-dowager still."

"And likely to have her, if all's true that's said," put in Mrs. Jones.

Mirrable tacitly admitted the probability. Her private opinion was that nothing short of a miracle could ever remove the Dowager Kirton from the house again. Had any one told Mirrable, as she stood there, that her ladyship would be leaving of her own accord that night, she had simply said it was impossible.

"Mary," cried the weak voice of poor timid Mrs. Gum, "how was it none of the brothers came to the funeral? Jabez was wondering. She had a lot, I've heard."

"It was not convenient to them, I suppose," replied Mirrable. "The one in the Isle of Wight had gone cruising in somebody's yacht, or he'd have come with the dowager; and Lord Kirton telegraphed from Ireland that he was prevented coming. I know nothing about the rest."

"It was an awful death!" shivered Mrs. Gum. "And without cause too; for the child was not hurt after all. Isn't my lord dreadfully cut up, Mary?"

"I think so; he's very quiet and subdued. But he has seemed full of sorrow for a long while, as if he had some dreadful care upon him. I don't think he and his wife were very happy together," added Mirrable. "My lord's likely to make Hartledon his chief residence now, I fancy, for—My gracious! what's that?"

A crash as if a whole battery of crockery had come down inside the house. A moment of staring consternation ensued, and nervous Mrs. Gum looked ready to faint. The two women disappeared indoors, and Mirrable turned homewards at a brisk pace. But she was not to go on without an interruption. Pike's head suddenly appeared above the hurdles, and he began inquiring after her health. "Toothache gone?" asked he.

"Yes," she said, answering straightforwardly in her surprise. "How did you know I had toothache?" It was not the first time by several he had thus accosted her; and to give her her due, she was always civil to him. Perhaps she feared to be otherwise.

"I heard of it. And so my Lord Hartledon's like a man with some dreadful care upon him!" he went on. "What is the care?"

"You have been eavesdropping!" she angrily exclaimed.

"Not a bit of it. I was seated under the hedge with my pipe, and you three women began talking. I didn't tell you to. Well, what's his lordship's care?"

"Just mind your own business, and his lordship will mind his," she retorted. "You'll get interfered with in a way you won't like, Pike, one of these days, unless you mend your manners."

"A great care on him," nodded Pike to himself, looking after her, as she walked off in her anger. "A great care! I know. One of these fine days, my lord, I may be asking you questions about it on my own score. I might long before this, but for—"

The sentence broke off abruptly, and ended with a growl at things in general. Mr. Pike was evidently not in a genial mood.

Mirrable reached home to find the countess-dowager in a state more easily imagined than described. Some sprite, favourable to the peace of Hartledon, had been writing confidentially from Ireland regarding Kirton and his doings. That her eldest son was about to steal a march on her and marry again seemed almost indisputably clear; and the miserable dowager, dancing her war-dance and uttering reproaches, was repacking her boxes in haste. Those boxes, which she had fondly hoped would never again leave Hartledon, unless it might be for sojourns in Park Lane! She was going back to Ireland to mount guard, and prevent any such escapade. Only in September had she quitted him—and then had been as nearly ejected as a son could eject his mother with any decency—and had taken the Isle of Wight on her way to Hartledon. The son who lived in the Isle of Wight had espoused a widow twice his own age, with eleven hundred a year, and a house and carriage; so that he had a home: which the countess-dowager sometimes remembered.

Lord Hartledon was liberal. He gave her a handsome sum for her journey, and a cheque besides; most devoutly praying that she might keep guard over Kirton for ever. He escorted her to the station himself in a closed carriage, an omnibus having gone before them with a mountain of boxes, at which all Calne came out to stare.

And the same week, confiding his children to the joint care of Mirrable and their nurse—an efficient, kind, and judicious woman—Lord Hartledon departed from home and England for a sojourn on the Continent, long or short, as inclination might lead him, feeling as a bird released from its cage.

# XXXIII

## Coming Home

Some eighteen months after the event recorded in the last chapter, a travelling carriage dashed up to a house in Park Lane one wet evening in spring. It contained Lord Hartledon and his second wife. They were expected, and the servants were assembled in the hall.

Lord Hartledon led her into their midst, proudly, affectionately; as he had never in his life led any other. Ah, you need not ask who she was; he had contrived to win her, to win over Dr. Ashton; and his heart had at length found rest. Her fair countenance, her thoughtful eyes and sweet smile were turned on the servants, thanking them for their greeting.

"All well, Hedges?" asked Lord Hartledon.

"Quite well, my lord. But we are not alone."

"No!" said Val, stopping in his progress. "Who's here?"

"The Countess-Dowager of Kirton, my lord," replied Hedges, glancing at Lady Hartledon in momentary hesitation.

"Oh, indeed!" said Val, as if not enjoying the information. "Just see, Hedges, that the things inside the carriage are all taken out. Don't come up, Mrs. Ball; I will take Lady Hartledon to her rooms."

It was the light-hearted Val of the old, old days; his face free from care, his voice gay. He did not turn into any of the reception-rooms, but led his wife at once to her chamber. It was nearly dinner-time, and he knew she was tired.

"Welcome home, my darling!" he whispered tenderly ere releasing her. "A thousand welcomes to you, my dear, dear wife!"

Tears rose to his eyes with the fervour of the wish. Heaven alone knew what the past had been; the contrast between that time and this.

"I will dress at once, Percival," she said, after a few moments' pause. "I must see your children before dinner. Heaven helping me, I shall love them and always act by them as if they were my own."

"I am so sorry she is here, Anne—that terrible old woman. You heard Hedges say Lady Kirton had arrived. Her visit is ill-timed."

"I shall be glad to welcome her, Val."

"It is more than I shall be," replied Val, as his wife's maid came into the room, and he quitted it. "I'll bring the children to you, Anne."

They had been married nearly five weeks. Anne had not seen the children for several months. The little child, Edward, had shown symptoms of delicacy, and for nearly a year the children had sojourned at the seaside, having been brought to the town-house just before their father's marriage.

The nursery was empty, and Lord Hartledon went down. In the passage outside the drawing-room was Hedges, evidently waiting for his master, and with a budget to unfold.

"When did she come, Hedges?"

"My lord, it was only a few days after your marriage," replied Hedges. "She arrived in the most outrageous tantrum—if I shall not offend your lordship by saying so—and has been here ever since, completely upsetting everything."

"What was her tantrum about?"

"On account of your having married again, my lord. She stood in the hall for five minutes when she got here, saying the most audacious things against your lordship and Miss Ashton—I mean my lady," corrected Hedges.

"The old hag!" muttered Lord Hartledon.

"I think she's insane at times, my lord; I really do. The fits of passion she flies into are quite bad enough for insanity. The housekeeper told me this morning she feared she would be capable of striking my lady, when she first saw her. I'm afraid, too, she has been schooling the children."

Lord Hartledon strode into the drawing-room. There, as large as life—and a great deal larger than most lives—was the dowager-countess. Fortunately she had not heard the arrival: in fact, she had dropped into a doze whilst waiting for it; and she started up when Val entered.

"How are you, ma'am?" asked he. "You have taken me by surprise."

"Not half as much as your wicked letter took me," screamed the old dowager. "Oh, you vile man! to marry again in this haste! You—you—I can't find words that I should not be ashamed of; but Hamlet's mother, in the play, was nothing to it."

"It is some time since I read the play," returned Hartledon, controlling his temper under an assumption of indifference. "If my memory serves me, the 'funeral baked meats did coldly furnish forth the marriage table.' *My* late wife has been dead eighteen months, Lady Kirton."

"Eighteen months! for such a wife as Maude was to you!" raved the dowager. "You ought to have mourned her eighteen years. Anybody else would. I wish I had never let you have her."

Lord Hartledon wished it likewise, with all his heart and soul; had wished it in his wife's lifetime.

"Lady Kirton, listen to me! Let us understand each other. Your visit here is ill-timed; you ought to feel it so; nevertheless, if you stay it out, you must observe good manners. I shall be compelled to request you to terminate it if you fail one iota in the respect due to this house's mistress, my beloved and honoured wife."

"Your *beloved* wife! Do you dare to say it to me?"

"Ay; beloved, honoured and respected as no woman has ever been by me yet, or ever will be again," he replied, speaking too plainly in his warmth.

"What a false-hearted monster!" cried the dowager, shrilly, apostrophizing the walls and the mirrors. "What then was Maude?"

"Maude is gone, and I counsel you not to bring up her name to me," said Val, sternly. "Your treachery forced Maude upon me; and let me tell you now, Lady Kirton, if I have never told you before, that it wrought upon her the most bitter wrong possible to be inflicted; which she lived to learn. I was a vacillating simpleton, and you held me in your trammels. The less we rake up old matters the better. Things have altered. I am altered. The moral courage I once lacked does not fail me now; and I have at least sufficient to hold my own against the world, and protect from insult the lady I have made my wife. I beg your pardon if my words seem harsh; they are true; and I am sorry you have forced them from me."

She was standing still for a moment, staring at him, not altogether certain of her ground.

"Where are the children?" he asked.

"Where you can't get at them," she rejoined hotly. "You have your beloved wife; you don't want them."

He rang the bell, more loudly than he need have done; but his usually sweet temper was provoked. A footman came in.

"Tell the nurse to bring down the children."

"They are not at home, my lord."

"Not at home! Surely they are not out in this rain!—and so late!"

"They went out this afternoon, my lord: and have not come in, I believe."

"There, that will do," tartly interposed the dowager. "You don't know anything about it, and you may go."

"Lady Kirton, where are the children?"

"Where you can't get at them, I say," was Lady Kirton's response. "You don't think I am going to suffer Maude's children to be domineered over by a wretch of a step-mother—perhaps poisoned."

He confronted her in his wrath, his eyes flashing.

"Madam!"

"Oh, you need not 'Madam' me. Maude's gone, and I shall act for her."

"I ask you where my children are?"

"I have sent them away; you may make the most of the information. And when I have remained here as long as I choose, I shall take them with me, and keep them, and bring them up. You can at once decide what sum you will allow me for their education and maintenance: two maids, a tutor, a governess, clothes, toys, and pocket-money. It must be a handsome sum, paid quarterly in advance. And I mean to take a house in London for their accommodation, and shall expect you to pay the rent."

The coolness with which this was delivered turned Val's angry feelings into amusement. He could not help laughing as he looked at her.

"You cannot have my children, Lady Kirton."

"They are Maude's children," snapped the dowager.

"But I presume you admit that they are likewise mine. And I shall certainly not part with them."

"If you oppose me in this, I'll put them into Chancery," cried the dowager. "I am their nearest relative, and have a right to them."

"Nearest relative!" he repeated. "You must have lost your senses. I am their father."

"And have you lived to see thirty, and never learnt that men don't count for anything in the bringing up of infants?" shrilly asked the dowager. "If they had ten fathers, what's that to the Lord Chancellor? No more than ten blocks of wood. What they want is a mother."

"And I have now given them one."

Without another word, with the red flush of emotion on his cheek, he went up to his wife's room. She was alone then, dressed, and just coming out of it. He put his arm round her to draw her in again, as he shortly explained the annoyance their visitor was causing him.

"You must stay here, my dearest, until I can go down with you," he added. "She is in a vile humour, and I do not choose that you should encounter her, unprotected by me."

"But where are you going, Val?"

"Well, I really think I shall get a policeman in, and frighten her into saying what she has done with the children. She'll never tell unless forced into it."

Anne laughed, and Hartledon went down. He had in good truth a great mind to see what the effect would be. The old woman was not a reasonable being, and he felt disposed to show her very little consideration. As he stood at the hall-door gazing forth, who should arrive but Thomas Carr. Not altogether by accident; he had come up exploring, to see if there were any signs of Val's return.

"Ah! home at last, Hartledon!"

"Carr, what happy wind blew you hither?" cried Val, as he grasped the hands of his trusty friend. "You can terrify this woman with the thunders of the law if she persists in kidnapping children that don't belong to her." And he forthwith explained the state of affairs.

Mr. Carr laughed.

"She will not keep them away long. She is no fool, that countess-dowager. It is a ruse, no doubt, to induce you to give them up to her."

"Give them up to her, indeed!" Val was beginning, when Hedges advanced to him.

"Mrs. Ball says the children have only gone to Madame Tussaud's, my lord," quoth he. "The nurse told her so when she went out."

"I wish she was herself one of Madame Tussaud's figure-heads!" cried Val. "Mr. Carr dines here, Hedges. Nonsense, Carr; you can't refuse. Never mind your coat; Anne won't mind. I want you to make acquaintance with her."

"How did you contrive to win over Dr. Ashton?" asked Thomas Carr, as he went in.

"I put the matter before him in its true light," answered Val, "asking him whether, if Anne forgave me, he would condemn us to live out our lives apart from each other: or whether he would not act the part of a good Christian, and give her to me, that I might strive to atone for the past."

"And he did so?"

"After a great deal of trouble. There's no time to give you details. I had a powerful advocate in Anne's heart. She had never forgotten me, for all my misconduct."

"You have been a lucky man at last, taking one thing with another."

"You may well say so," was the answer, in tones of deep feeling. "Moments come over me when I fear I am about to awake and find the present a dream. I am only now beginning to *live*. The past few years have been—you know what, Carr."

He sent the barrister into the drawing room, went upstairs for Anne, and brought her in on his arm. The dowager was in her chamber, attiring herself in haste.

"My wife, Carr," said Hartledon, with a loving emphasis on the word. She was in an evening dress of white and black, not having yet put off mourning for Mrs. Ashton, and looked very lovely; far more lovely in Thomas Carr's eyes than Lady Maude, with her dark beauty, had ever looked. She held out her hand to him with a frank smile.

"I have heard so much of you, Mr. Carr, that we seem like old friends. I am glad you have come to see me so soon."

"My being here this evening is an accident, Lady Hartledon, as you may see by my dress," he returned. "I ought rather to apologize for intruding on you in the hour of your arrival."

"Don't talk about intrusion," said Val. "You will never be an intruder in my house—and Anne's smile is telling you the same—"

"Who's that, pray?"

The interruption came from the countess-dowager. There she stood, near the door, in a yellow gown and green turban. Val drew himself up and approached her, his wife still on his arm. "Madam," said he, in reply to her question, "this is my wife, Lady Hartledon."

The dowager's gauzes made acquaintance with the carpet in so elaborate a curtsey as to savour of mockery, but her eyes were turned up to the ceiling; not a word or look gave she to the young lady.

"The other one, I meant," cried she, nodding towards Thomas Carr.

"It is my friend Mr. Carr. You appear to have forgotten him."

"I hope you are well, ma'am," said he, advancing towards her.

Another curtsey, and the countess-dowager fanned herself, and sailed towards the fireplace.

Meanwhile the children came home in a cab from Madame Tussaud's, and dinner was announced. Lord Hartledon was obliged to take down the countess-dowager, resigning his wife to Mr. Carr. Dinner passed off pretty well, the dowager being too fully occupied to be annoying; also the good cheer caused her temper to thaw a little. Afterwards, the children came in; Edward, a bold, free boy of five, who walked straight up to his grandmother, saluting no one; and Maude, a timid, delicate little child, who stood still in the middle of the carpet where the maid placed her.

The dowager was just then too busy to pay attention to the children, but Anne held out her hand with a smile. Upon which the child drew up to her father, and hid her face in his coat.

He took her up, and carried her to his wife, placing her upon her knee. "Maude," he whispered, "this is your mamma, and you must love her very much, for she loves you."

Anne's arms fondly encircled the child; but she began to struggle to get down.

"Bad manners, Maude," said her father.

"She's afraid of her," spoke up the boy, who had the dark eyes and beautiful features of his late mother. "We are afraid of bad people."

The observation passed momentarily unnoticed, for Maude, whom Lady Hartledon had been obliged to release, would not be pacified. But when calmness ensued, Lord Hartledon turned to the boy, just then assisting himself to some pineapple.

"What did I hear you say about bad people, Edward?"

"She," answered the boy, pointing towards Lady Hartledon. "She shan't touch Maude. She's come here to beat us, and I'll kick if she touches me."

Lord Hartledon, with an unmistakable look at the countess-dowager, rose from his seat in silence and rang the bell. There could be no correction in the presence of the dowager; he and Anne must undo her work alone. Carrying the little girl in one arm, he took the boy's hand, and met the servant at the door.

"Take these children back to the nursery."

"I want some strawberries," the boy called out rebelliously.

"Not to-day," said his father. "You know quite well that you have behaved badly."

His wife's face was painfully flushed. Mr. Carr was critically examining the painted landscape on his plate; and the turban was enjoying some fruit with perfect unconcern. Lord Hartledon stood an instant ere he resumed his seat.

"Anne," he said in a voice that trembled in spite of its displeased tones, "allow me to beg your pardon, and I do it with shame that this gratuitous insult should have been offered you in your own house. A day or two will, I hope, put matters on their right footing; the poor children, as you see, have been tutored."

"Are you going to keep the port by you all night, Hartledon?"

Need you ask from whom came the interruption? Mr. Carr passed it across to her, leaving her to help herself; and Lord Hartledon sat down, biting his delicate lips.

When the dowager seemed to have finished, Anne rose. Mr. Carr rose too as soon as they had retired.

"I have an engagement, Hartledon, and am obliged to run away. Make my adieu to your wife."

"Carr, is it not a crying shame?—enough to incense any man?"

"It is. The sooner you get rid of her the better."

"That's easier said than done."

When Lord Hartledon reached the drawing-room, the dowager was sleeping comfortably. Looking about for his wife, he found her in the small room Maude used to make exclusively her own, which was not lighted up. She was standing at the window, and her tears were quietly falling. He drew her face to his own.

"My darling, don't let it grieve you! We shall soon right it all."

"Oh, Percival, if the mischief should have gone too far!—if they should never look upon me except as a step-mother! You don't know how sick and troubled this has made me feel! I wanted to go to them in the nursery when I came up, and did not dare! Perhaps the nurse has also been prejudiced against me!"

"Come up with me now, love," he whispered.

They went silently upstairs, and found the children were then in bed and asleep. They were tired with sight-seeing, the nurse said apologetically, curtseying to her new mistress.

The nurse withdrew, and they stood over the nursery fire, talking. Anne could scarcely account for the extreme depression the event seemed to have thrown upon her. Lord Hartledon quickly recovered his spirits, vowing he should like to "serve out" the dowager.

"I was thankful for one thing, Val; that you did not betray anger to them, poor little things. It would have made it worse."

"I was on the point of betraying something more than anger to Edward; but the thought that I should be punishing him for another's fault checked me. I wonder how we can get rid of her?"

"We must strive to please her while she stays."

"Please her!" he echoed. "Anne, my dear, that is stretching Christian charity rather too far."

Anne smiled. "I am a clergyman's daughter, you know, Val."

"If she is wise, she'll abstain from offending you in my presence. I'm not sure but I should lose command of myself, and send her off there and then."

"I don't fear that. She was quite civil when we came up from dinner, and—"

"As she generally is then. She takes her share of wine."

"And asked me if I would excuse her falling into a doze, for she never felt well without it."

Anne was right. The cunning old woman changed her tactics, finding those she had started would not answer. It has been remarked before, if you remember, that she knew particularly well on which side her bread was buttered. Nothing could exceed her graciousness from that evening. The past scene might have been a dream, for all traces that remained of it. Out of the house she was determined not to go in anger; it was too desirable a refuge for that. And on the following day, upon hearing Edward attempt some impudent speech to his new mother, she put him across her knee, pulled off an old slipper she was wearing, and gave him a whipping. Anne interposed, the boy roared; but the good woman had her way.

"Don't put yourself out, dear Lady Hartledon. There's nothing so good for them as a wholesome whipping. I used to try it on my own children at times."

# XXXIV

## Mr. Pike on the Wing

The time went on. It may have been some twelve or thirteen months later that Mr. Carr, sitting alone in his chambers, one evening, was surprised by the entrance of his clerk—who possessed a latch-key as well as himself.

"Why, Taylor! what brings you here?"

"I thought you would most likely be in, sir," replied the clerk. "Do you remember some few years ago making inquiries about a man named Gorton—and you could not find him?"

"And never have found him," was Mr. Carr's comment. "Well?"

"I have seen him this evening. He is back in London."

Thomas Carr was not a man to be startlingly affected by any communication; nevertheless he felt the importance of this, for Lord Hartledon's sake.

"I met him by chance, in a place where I sometimes go of an evening to smoke a cigar, and learned his name by accident," continued Mr. Taylor. "It's the same man that was at Kedge and Reck's, George Gorton; he acknowledged it at once, quite readily."

"And where has he been hiding himself?"

"He has been in Australia for several years, he says; went there directly after he left Kedge and Reck's that autumn."

"Could you get him here, Taylor? I must see him. Tell me: what coloured hair has he?"

"Red, sir; and plenty of it. He says he's doing very well over there, and has only come home for a short change. He does not seem to be in concealment, and gave me his address when I asked him for it."

According to Mr. Carr's wish, the man Gorton was brought to his chambers the following morning by Taylor. To the barrister's surprise, a well-dressed and really rather gentlemanly man entered. He had been accustomed to picturing this Gorton as an Arab of London life. Casting a keen glance at the red hair, he saw it was indisputably his own.

A few rapid questions, which Gorton answered without the slightest demur, and Mr. Carr leaned back in his chair, knowing that all the trouble he had been at to find this man might have been spared: for he was not the George Gordon they had suspected. But Mr. Carr was cautious, and betrayed nothing.

"I am sorry to have troubled you," he said. "When I inquired for you of Kedge and Reck some years ago, it was under the impression that you were some one else. You had left; and they did not know where to find you."

"Yes, I had displeased them through arresting a wrong man, and other things. I was down in the world then, and glad to do anything for a living, even to serving writs."

"You arrested the late Lord Hartledon for his brother," observed Mr. Carr, with a careless smile. "I heard of it. I suppose you did not know them apart."

"I had never set eyes on either of them before," returned Gorton; unconsciously confirming a point in the barrister's mind; which, however, was already sufficiently obvious.

"The man I wanted to find was named Gordon. I thought it just possible that you might have changed your name temporarily: some of us finding it convenient to do so on occasion."

"I never changed mine in my life."

"And if you had, I don't suppose you'd have changed it to one so notorious as George Gordon."

"Notorious?"

"It was a George Gordon who was the hero of that piratical affair; that mutiny on board the *Morning Star*."

"Ah, to be sure. And an awful villain too! A man I met in Australia knew Gordon well. But he tells a curious tale, though. He was a doctor, that Gordon; had come last from somewhere in Kirkcudbrightshire."

"He did," said Thomas Carr, quietly. "What curious tale does your friend tell?"

"Well, sir, he says—or rather said, for I've not seen him since my first visit there—that George Gordon did not sail in the *Morning Star*. He was killed in a drunken brawl the night before he ought to have sailed: this man was present and saw him buried."

"But there's pretty good proof that Gordon did sail. He was the ringleader of the mutiny."

"Well, yes. I don't know how it could have been. The man was positive. I never knew Gordon; so that the affair did not interest me much."

"You are doing well over there?"

"Very well. I might retire now, if I chose to live in a small way, but I mean to take a few more years of it, and go on to riches. Ah! and it was just the turn of a pin whether I went over there that second time, or whether I stopped in London to serve writs and starve."

"Val was right," thought the barrister.

On the following Saturday Mr. Carr took a return-ticket, and went down to Hartledon: as he had done once or twice before in the old days. The Hartledons had not come to town this season; did not intend to come: Anne was too happy in the birth of her baby-boy to care for London; and Val liked Hartledon better than any other place now.

In one single respect the past year had failed to bring Anne happiness—there was not entire confidence between herself and her husband. He had something on his mind, and she could not fail to see that he had. It was not that awful dread that seemed to possess him in his first wife's time; nevertheless it was a weight which told more or less on his spirits at all times. To Anne it appeared like remorse; yet she might never have thought this, but for a word or two he let slip occasionally. Was it connected with his children? She could almost have fancied so: and yet in what manner could it be? His behaviour was peculiar. He rather avoided them than not; but when with them was almost passionately demonstrative, exactingly jealous that due attention should be paid to them: and he seemed half afraid of caressing Anne's baby, lest it should be thought he cared for it more than for the others. Altogether Lady Hartledon puzzled her brains in vain: she could not make him out. When she questioned him he would deny that there was anything the matter, and said it was her fancy.

They were at Hartledon alone: that is, without the countess-dowager. That respected lady, though not actually domiciled with them during the past twelve-month, had paid them three long visits. She was determined to retain her right in the household—if right it could be called. The dowager was by far too wary to do otherwise; and her behaviour to Anne was exceedingly mild. But somehow she contrived to retain, or continually renew, her evil influence over the children; though so insidiously, that Lady Hartledon could never detect how or when it was done, or openly meet it. Neither could she effectually counteract it. So surely as the dowager came, so surely did the young boy and his sister become unruly with their step-mother; ill-natured and rude. Lady Hartledon was kind, judicious, and good; and things would so far be remedied during the crafty dowager's absences, as to promise a complete cure; but whenever she returned the evil broke out again. Anne was sorely perplexed. She did not like to deny the children to their grandmother, who was more nearly related to them than she herself; and she could only pray that time would bring about some remedy. The dowager passed her time pretty equally between their house and her son's. Lord Kirton had not married again, owing, perhaps, to the watch and ward kept over him. But as soon as he started off to the Continent, or elsewhere, where she could not follow him, then off she came, without notice, to England and Lord Hartledon's. And Val, in his good-nature, bore the infliction passively so long as she kept civil and peaceable.

In this also her husband's behaviour puzzled Anne. Disliking the dowager beyond every other created being, he yet suffered her to indulge his children; and if any little passage-at-arms supervened, took her part rather than his wife's.

"I cannot understand you, Val," Anne said to him one day, in tones of pain. "You are not as you used to be." And his only answer was to strain his wife to his bosom with an impassioned gesture of love.

But these were only episodes in their generally happy life. Never more happy, more free from any external influence, than when Thomas Carr arrived there on this identical Saturday. He went in unexpectedly: and Val's violet eyes, beautiful as ever, shone out their welcome; and Anne, who happened to have her baby on her lap, blushed and smiled, as she held it out for the barrister's inspection.

"I dare not take it," said he. "You would be up in arms if it were dropped. What is its name?"

"Reginald."

A little while, and she carried the child away, leaving them alone. Mr. Carr declined refreshment for the present; and he and Val strolled out arm-in-arm.

"I have brought you an item of news, Hartledon. Gorton has turned up."

"Not Gordon?"

"No. And what's more, Gorton never was Gordon. You were right, and I was wrong. I would have bet a ten-pound note—a great venture for a barrister—that the men were the same; never, in point of fact, had a doubt of it."

"You would not listen to me," said Val. "I told you I was sure I could not have failed to recognize Gordon, had he been the one who was down at Calne with the writ."

"But you acknowledged that it might have been he, nevertheless; that his red hair might have been false; that you never had a distinct view of the man's face; and that the only time you spoke to him was in the gloaming," reiterated Thomas Carr. "Well, as it turns out, we might have spared half our pains and anxiety, for Gorton was never any one but himself: an innocent sheriff's officer, as far as you are concerned, who had never, in his life set eyes on Val Elster until he went after him to Calne."

"Didn't I say so?" reiterated Val. "Gordon would have known me too well to arrest Edward for me."

"But you admitted the general likeness between you and your brother; and Gordon had not seen you for three years or more."

"Yes; I admitted all you say, and perhaps was a little doubtful myself. But I soon shook off the doubt, and of late years have been sure that Gordon was really dead. It has been more than a conviction. I always said there were no grounds for connecting the two together."

"I had my grounds for doing it," remarked the barrister. "Gorton, it seems, has been in Australia ever since. No wonder Green could not unearth him in London. He's back again on a visit, looking like a gentleman; and really I can't discover that there was ever anything against him, except that he was down in the world. Taylor met him the other day, and I had him brought to my chambers; and have told you the result."

"You do not now feel any doubt that Gordon's dead?"

"None at all. Your friend, Gordon of Kircudbright, was the one who embarked, or ought to have embarked, on the *Morning Star*, homeward bound," said Mr. Carr. And he forthwith told Lord Hartledon what the man had said.

A silence ensued. Lord Hartledon was in deep and evidently not pleasant thought; and the barrister stole a glance at him.

"Hartledon, take comfort. I am as cautious by nature as I believe it is possible for any one to be; and I am sure the man is dead, and can never rise up to trouble you."

"I have been sure of that for years," replied Hartledon quietly. "I have just said so."

"Then what is disturbing you?"

"Oh, Carr, how can you ask it?" came the rejoinder. "What is it lies on my mind day and night; is wearing me out before my time? Discovery may be avoided; but when I look at the children—at the boy especially—it would have turned some men mad," he more quietly added, passing his hand across his brow. "As long as he lives, I cannot have rest from pain. The sins of the fathers—"

"Yes, yes," interposed Mr. Carr, hastily. "Still the case is light, compared with what we once dreaded."

"Light for me, heavy for him."

Mr. Carr remained with them until the Monday: he then went back to London and work; and time glided on again. An event occurred the following winter which shall be related at once; more especially as nothing of moment took place in those intervening months needing special record.

The man Pike, who still occupied his shed undisturbed, had been ailing for some time. An attack of rheumatic fever in the summer had left him little better than a cripple. He crawled abroad still when he was able, and *would* do so, in spite of what Mr. Hillary said; would lie about the damp ground in a lawless, gipsying sort of manner; but by the time winter came all that was over, and Mr. Pike's career, as foretold by the surgeon, was drawing rapidly to a close. Mrs. Gum was his good Samaritan, as she had been in the fever some years before, going in and out and attending to him; and in a reasonable way Pike wanted for nothing.

"How long can I last?" he abruptly asked the doctor one morning. "Needn't fear to say. *She's* the only one that will take on; I shan't."

He alluded to Mrs. Gum, who had just gone out. The surgeon considered.

"Two or three days."

"As much as that?"

"I think so."

"Oh!" said Pike. "When it comes to the last day I should like to see Lord Hartledon."

"Why the last day?"

The man's pinched features broke into a smile; pleasant and fair features once, with a gentle look upon them. The black wig and whiskers lay near him; but the real hair, light and scanty, was pushed back from the damp brow.

"No use, then, to think of giving me up: no time left for it."

"I question if Lord Hartledon would give you up were you in rude health. I'm sure he would not," added Mr. Hillary, endorsing his opinion rather emphatically. "If ever there was a kindly nature in the world, it's his. What do you want with him?"

"I should like to say a word to him in private," responded Pike.

"Then you'd better not wait to say it. I'll tell him of your wish. It's all safe. Why, Pike, if the police themselves came they wouldn't trouble to touch you now."

"I shouldn't much care if they did," said the man. "*I* haven't cared for a long while; but there were the others, you know."

"Yes," said Mr. Hillary.

"Look here," said Pike; "no need to tell him particulars; leave them till I'm gone. I don't know that I'd like *him* to look me in the face, knowing them."

"As you will," said Mr. Hillary, falling in with the wish more readily than he might have done for anyone but a dying man.

He had patients out of Calne, beyond Hartledon, and called in returning. It was a snowy day; and as the surgeon was winding towards the house, past the lodge, with a quick step, he saw a white figure marching across the park. It was Lord Hartledon. He had been caught in the storm, and came up laughing.

"Umbrellas are at a premium," observed Mr. Hillary, with the freedom long intimacy had sanctioned.

"It didn't snow when I came out," said Hartledon, shaking himself, and making light of the matter. "Were you coming to honour me with a morning call?"

"I was and I wasn't," returned the surgeon. "I've no time for morning calls, unless they are professional ones; but I wanted to say a word to you. Have you a mind for a further walk in the snow?"

"As far as you like."

"There's a patient of mine drawing very near the time when doctors can do no more for him. He has expressed a wish to see you, and I undertook to convey the request."

"I'll go, of course," said Val, all his kindliness on the alert. "Who is it?"

"A black sheep," answered the surgeon. "I don't know whether that will make any difference?"

"It ought not," said Val rather warmly. "Black sheep have more need of help than white ones, when it comes to the last. I suppose it's a poacher wanting to clear his conscience."

"It's Pike," said Hillary.

"Pike! What can he want with me? Is he no better?"

"He'll never be better in this world; and to speak the truth, I think it's time he left it. He'll be happier, poor fellow, let's hope, in another than he has been in this. Has it ever struck you, Lord Hartledon, that there was something strange about Pike, and his manner of coming here?"

"Very strange indeed."

"Well, Pike is not Pike, but another man—which I suppose you will say is Irish. But that he is so ill, and it would not be worth while for the law to take him, he might be in mortal fear of your seeing him, lest you betrayed him. He wanted you not to be informed until the last hour. I told him there was no fear."

"I would not betray any living man, whatever his crime, for the whole world," returned Lord Hartledon; his voice so earnest as to amount to pain. And the surgeon looked at him; but there rose up in his remembrance how *he* had been avoiding betrayal for years. "Who is he?"

"Willy Gum."

Lord Hartledon turned his head sharply under cover of the surgeon's umbrella, for they were walking along together. A thought crossed him that the words might be a jest.

"Yes, Pike is Willy Gum," continued Mr. Hillary. "And there you have the explanation of the poor mother's nervous terrors. I do pity her. The clerk has taken it more philosophically, and seemed only to care lest the fact should become known. Ah, poor thing! what a life hers has been! Her fears of the wild neighbour, her basins for cats, are all explained now. She dreaded lest Calne should suspect that she occasionally stole into the shed under cover of the night with the basins containing food for its inmate. There the man has lived—if you can call such an existence living; Willy Gum, concealed by his borrowed black hair and whiskers. But that he was only a boy when he went away, Calne would have recognized him in spite of them."

"And he is not a poacher and a snarer, and I don't know what all, leading a lawless life, and thieving for his living?" exclaimed Lord Hartledon, the first question that rose to the surface, amidst the many that were struggling in his mind.

"I don't believe the man has touched the worth of a pin belonging to any one since he came here, even on your preserves. People took up the notion from his wild appearance, and because he had no ostensible means of living. It would not have done to let them know that he had his supplies—sometimes money, sometimes food—from respectable clerk Gum's."

"But why should he be in concealment at all? That bank affair was made all right at the time."

"There are other things he feared, it seems. I've not time to enter into details now; you'll know them later. There he is—Pike: and there he'll die—Pike always."

"How long have you known it?"

"Since that fever he caught from the Rectory some years ago. I recollect your telling me not to let him want for anything;" and Lord Hartledon winced at the remembrance brought before him, as he always did wince at the unhappy past. "I never shall forget it. I went in, thinking Pike was ill, and that he, wild and disreputable though he had the character of being, might want physic as well as his neighbours. Instead of the black-haired bear I expected to see, there lay a young, light, delicate fellow, with a white brow, and cheeks pink with fever. The features seemed familiar to me; little by little recognition came to me, and I saw it was Willy Gum, whom every one had been mourning as dead. He said a pleading word or two, that I would keep his secret, and not give him up to justice. I did not understand what there was to give him up for then. However, I promised. He was too ill to say much; and I went to the next door, and put it to Gum's wife that she should go and nurse Pike for humanity's sake. Of course it was what she wanted to do. Poor thing! she fell on her knees later, beseeching me not to betray him."

"And you have kept counsel all this time?"

"Yes," said the surgeon, laconically. "Would your lordship have done otherwise, even though it had been a question of hanging?"

"*I!* I wouldn't give a man a month at the treadmill if I could help it. One gets into offences so easily," he dreamily added.

They crossed over the waste land, and Mr. Hillary opened the door of the shed with a pass-key. A lock had been put on when Pike was lying in rheumatic fever, lest intruders might enter unawares, and see him without his disguise.

"Pike, I have brought you my lord. He won't betray you."

# XXXV

## THE SHED RAZED

C losing the door upon them, the surgeon went off on other business, and Lord Hartledon entered and bent over the bed; a more comfortable bed than it once had been. It was the Willy Gum of other days; the boy he had played with when they were boys together. White, wan, wasted, with the dying hectic on his cheek, the glitter already in his eye, he lay there; and Val's eyelashes shone as he took the worn hand.

"I am so sorry, Willy. I had no suspicion it was you. Why did you not confide in me?"

The invalid shook his head. "There might have been danger in it."

"Never from me," was the emphatic answer.

"Ah, my lord, you don't know. I haven't dared to make myself known to a soul. Mr. Hillary found it out, and I couldn't help myself."

Lord Hartledon glanced round at the strange place: the rafters, the rude walls. A fire was burning on the hearth, and the appliances brought to bear were more comfortable than might have been imagined; but still—

"Surely you will allow yourself to be removed to a better place, Willy?" he said.

"Call me Pike," came the feverish interruption. "Never that other name again, my lord; I've done with it for ever. As to a better place—I shall have that soon enough."

"You wanted to say something to me, Mr. Hillary said."

"I've wanted to say it some time now, and to beg your lordship's pardon. It's about the late earl's death."

"My brother's?"

"Yes. I was on the wrong scent a long time. And I can tell you what nobody else will."

Lord Hartledon lifted his head quickly; thoughts were crowding impulsively into his mind, and he spoke in the moment's haste.

"Surely you had not anything to do with that!"

"No; but I thought your lordship had."

"What do you mean?" asked Lord Hartledon, quietly.

"It's for my foolish and wicked and mistaken thought that I would crave pardon before I go. I thought your lordship had killed the late lord, either by accident or maliciously."

"You must be dreaming, Pike!"

"No; but I was no better than dreaming then. I had been living amidst lawless scenes, over the seas and on the seas, where a life's not of much account, and the fancy was easy enough. I happened to overhear a quarrel between you and the earl just before his death; I saw you going towards the spot at the time the accident happened, as you may remember—"

"I did not go so far," interrupted Hartledon, wondering still whether this might not be the wanderings of a dying man. "I turned back into the trees at once, and walked slowly home. Many a time have I wished I had gone on!"

"Yes, yes; I was on the wrong scent. And there was that blow on his temple to keep up the error, which I know now must have been done against the estrade. I did suspect at the time, and your lordship will perhaps not forgive me for it. I let drop a word that I suspected something before that man Gorton, and he asked me what I meant; and I explained it away, and said I was chaffing him. And I have been all this time, up to a few weeks ago, learning the true particulars of how his lordship died."

Lord Hartledon decided that the man's mind was undoubtedly wandering.

But Pike was not wandering. And he told the story of the boy Ripper having been locked up in the mill. Mr. Ripper was almost a match for Pike himself in deceit; and Pike had only learned the facts by dint of long patience and perseverance and many threats. The boy had seen the whole accident; had watched it from the window where he was enclosed, unable to get out, unless he had torn away the grating. Lord Hartledon had lost all command of the little skiff, his arm being utterly disabled; and it came drifting down towards the mill, and struck against the estrade. The skiff righted itself at once, but not its owner: there was a slight struggle, a few cries, and he lay motionless, drifting later to the place where he was found. Mr. Ripper's opinion was that he had lost his senses with the blow on the temple, and fell an easy prey to death. Had that gentleman only sacrificed the grating and his own reputation, he might have saved him easily; and that fact had since been upon his conscience, making him fear all sorts of things, not the least of which was that he might be hanged as a murderer.

This story he had told Pike at the time, with one reserve—he persisted that he had not *seen*, only heard. Pike saw that the boy was still not telling the whole truth, and suspected he was screening Lord Hartledon—he who now stood before him. Mr. Ripper's logic tended to the belief that he could not be punished if he stuck to the avowal of having seen nothing. He had only heard the cries; and when Pike asked if they were cries as if he were being assaulted, the boy evasively answered "happen they were." Another little item he suppressed: that he found the purse at the bottom of the skiff, after he got out of the mill, and appropriated it to himself; and when he had fairly done that, he grew more afraid of having done it than of all the rest. The money he secreted, using it when he dared, a sixpence at a time; the case, with its papers, he buried in the spot where his master afterwards found it. With all this upon the young man's conscience, no wonder he was a little confused and contradictory in his statements to Pike: no wonder he fancied the ghost of the man he could have saved and did not, might now and then be hovering about him. Pike learned the real truth at last; and a compunction had come over him, now that he was dying, for having doubted Lord Hartledon.

"My lord, I can only ask you to forgive me. I ought to have known you better. But things seemed to corroborate it so: I've heard people say the new lord was as a man who had some great care upon him. Oh, I was a fool!"

"At any rate it was not *that* care, Pike; I would have saved my brother's life with my own, had I been at hand to do it. As to Ripper—I shall never bear to look upon him again."

"He's gone away," said Pike.

"Where has he gone?"

"The miller turned him off for idleness, and he's gone away, nobody knows where, to get work: I don't suppose he'll ever come back again. This is the real truth of the matter as it occurred, my lord; and there's no more behind it. Ripper has now told all he knows, just as fully as if he had been put to torture."

Lord Hartledon remained with Pike some time longer, soothing the man as much as it was in his power and kindly nature to soothe. He whispered a word of the clergyman, Dr. Ashton.

"Father says he shall bring him to-night," was the answer. "It's all a farce."

"I am sorry to hear you say that," returned Lord Hartledon, gravely.

"If I had never said a worse thing than that, my lord, I shouldn't hurt. Unless the accounts are made up beforehand, parsons can't avail much at the twelfth hour. Mother's lessons to me when a child, and her reading the Bible as she sits here in the night, are worth more than Dr. Ashton could do. But for those old lessons' having come home to me now, I might not have cared to ask your forgiveness. Dr. Ashton! what is he? For an awful sinner—and it's what I've been—there's only Christ. At times I think I've been too bad even for Him. I've only my sins to take to Him: never were worse in this world."

Lord Hartledon went out rather bewildered with the occurrences of the morning. Thinking it might be only kind to step into the clerk's, he crossed the stile and went in without ceremony by the open back-door. Mrs. Gum was alone in the kitchen, crying bitterly. She dried her eyes in confusion, as she curtsied to her visitor.

"I know all," he interrupted, in low, considerate tones, to the poor suffering woman. "I have been to see him. Never mind explanations: let us think what we can best do to lighten his last hours."

Mrs. Gum burst into deeper tears. It was a relief, no doubt: but she wondered how much Lord Hartledon knew.

"I say that he ought to be got away from that place, Mrs. Gum. It's not fit for a man to die in. You might have him here. Calne! Surely my protection will sufficiently screen him against tattling Calne!"

She shook her head, saying it was of no use talking to Willy about removal; he wouldn't have it; and she thought herself it might be better not. Jabez, too; if this ever came out in Calne, it would just kill him; his lordship knew what he was, and how he had cared for appearances all his life. No; it would not be for many more hours now, and Willy must die in the shed where he had lived.

Lord Hartledon sat down on the ironing-board, the white table underneath the window, in the old familiar manner of former days; many and many a time had he perched himself there to talk to her when he was young Val Elster.

"Only fancy what my life has been, my lord," she said. "People have called me nervous and timid; but look at the cause I've had! I was just beginning to get over the grief for his death, when he came here; and to the last hour of my life I shan't get the night out of my mind! I and

Jabez were together in this very kitchen. I had come in to wash up the tea-things, and Jabez followed me. It was a cold, dark evening, and the parlour fire had got low. By token, my lord, we were talking of you; you had just gone away to be an ambassador, or something, and then we spoke of the wild, strange, black man who had crept into the shed; and Jabez, I remember, said he should acquaint Mr. Marris, if the fellow did not take himself off. I had seen him that very evening, at dusk, for the first time, when his great black face rose up against mine, nearly frightening me to death. Jabez was angry at such a man's being there, and said he should go up to Hartledon in the morning and see the steward. Just then there came a tap at the kitchen door, and Jabez went to it. It was the man; he had watched the servant out, and knew we were alone; and he came into the kitchen, and asked if we did not know him. Jabez did; he had seen Willy later than I had, and he recognized him; and the man took off his black hair and great black whiskers, and I saw it was Willy, and nearly fainted dead away."

There was a pause. Lord Hartledon did not speak, and she resumed, after a little indulgence in her grief.

"And since then all our aim has been to hide the truth, to screen him, and keep up the tale that we were afraid of the wild man. How it has been done I know not: but I do know that it has nearly killed me. What a night it was! When Jabez heard his story and forced him to answer all questions, I thought he would have given Willy up to the law there and then. My lord, we have just lived since with a sword over our heads!"

Lord Hartledon remembered the sword that had been over his own head, and sympathized with them from the depths of his heart.

"Tell me all," he said. "You are quite safe with me, Mrs. Gum."

"I don't know that there's much more to tell," she sighed. "We took the best precautions we could, in a quiet way, having the holes in the shutters filled up, and new locks put on the doors, lest people might look in or step in, while he sat here of a night, which he took to do. Jabez didn't like it, but I'm afraid I encouraged it. It was so lonely for him, that shed, and so unhealthy! We sent away the regular servant, and engaged one by day, so as to have the house to ourselves at night. If a knock came to the door, Willy would slip out to the wood-house before we opened it, lest it might be anybody coming in. He did not come in every night—two or three times a-week; and it never was pleasant; for Jabez would hardly open his mouth, unless it was to reproach him. Heaven alone knows what I've had to bear!"

"But, Mrs. Gum, I cannot understand. Why could not Willy have declared himself openly to the world?"

It was evidently a most painful question. Her eyes fell; the crimson of shame flushed into her cheeks; and he felt sorry to have asked it.

"Spare me, my lord, for I *cannot* tell you. Perhaps Jabez will: or Mr. Hillary; he knows. It doesn't much matter, now death's so near; but I think it would kill me to have to tell it."

"And no one except the doctor has ever known that it was Willy?"

"One more, my lord: Mirrable. We told her at once. I have had to hear all sorts of cruel things said of him," continued Mrs. Gum. "That he thieved and poached, and did I know not what; and we could only encourage the fancy, for it put people off the truth as to how he really lived."

"Amidst other things, they said, I believe, that he was out with the poachers the night my brother George was shot!"

"And that night, my lord, he sat over this kitchen fire, and never stirred from it. He was ill: it was rheumatism, caught in Australia, that took such a hold upon him; and I had him here by the fire till near daylight in the morning, so as to keep him out of the damp shed. What with fearing one thing and another, I grew into a state of perpetual terror."

"Then you will not have him in here now," said Lord Hartledon, rising.

"I cannot," she said, her tears falling silently.

"Well, Mrs. Gum, I came in just to say a word of true sympathy. You have it heartily, and my services also, if necessary. Tell Jabez so."

He quitted the house by the front-door, as if he had been honouring the clerk's wife with a morning-call, should any curious person happen to be passing, and went across through the snow to the surgeon's. Mr. Hillary, an old bachelor, was at his early dinner, and Lord Hartledon sat down and talked to him.

"It's only rump steak; but few cooks can beat mine, and it's very good. Won't your lordship take a mouthful by way of luncheon?"

"My curiosity is too strong for luncheon just now," said Val. "I have come over to know the rights and wrongs of this story. What has Willy Gum been doing in the past years that it cannot be told?"

"I am not sure that it would be safe to say while he's living."

"Not safe! with me! Was it safe with you?"

"But I don't consider myself obliged to give up to justice any poor criminal who comes in my way," said the surgeon; and Val felt a little vexed, although he saw that he was joking.

"Come, Hillary!"

"Well, then, Willy Gum was coming home in the *Morning Star*; and a mutiny broke out—mutiny and murder, and everything else that's bad; and one George Gordon was the ringleader."

"Yes. Well?"

"Willy Gum was George Gordon."

"What!" exclaimed Hartledon, not knowing how to accept the words. "How could he be George Gordon?"

"Because the real George Gordon never sailed at all; and this fellow Gum went on board in his name, calling himself Gordon."

Lord Hartledon leaned back in his chair and listened to the explanation. A very simple one, after all. Gum, one of the wildest and most careless characters possible when in Australia, gambled away, before sailing, the money he had acquired. Accident made him acquainted with George Gordon, also going home in the same ship and with money. Gordon was killed the night before sailing—(Mr. Carr had well described it as a drunken brawl)—killed accidentally. Gum was present; he saw his opportunity, went on board as Gordon, and claimed the luggage—some of it gold—already on board. How the mutiny broke out was less clear; but one of the other passengers knew Gum, and threatened to expose him; and perhaps this led to it. Gum, at any rate, was the ringleader, and this passenger was one of the first killed. Gum—Gordon as he was called—contrived to escape in the open boat, and found his way to land; thence, disguised, to England and to Calne; and at Calne he had since lived, with the price offered for George Gordon on his head.

It was a strange and awful story: and Lord Hartledon felt a shiver run through him as he listened. In truth, that shed was the safest and fittest place for him to die in!

As die he did ere the third day was over. And was buried as Pike, the wild man, without a mourner. Clerk Gum stood over the grave in his official capacity; and Dr. Ashton, who had visited the sick man, himself read the service, which caused some wonder in Calne.

And the following week Lord Hartledon caused the shed to be cleared away, and the waste land ploughed; saying he would have no more tramps encamping next door to Mr. and Mrs. Gum.

# XXXVI

## The Dowager's Alarm

Again the years went on, bringing not altogether comfort to the house of Hartledon. As Anne's children were born—there were three now—a sort of jealous rivalry seemed to arise between them and the two elder children; and this in spite of Anne's efforts to the contrary. The moving spring was the countess-dowager, who in secret excited the elder children against their little brothers and sister; but so craftily that Anne could produce nothing tangible to remonstrate against. Things would grow tolerably smooth during the old woman's absences; but she took good care not to make those absences lengthened, and then all the ill-nature and rebellion reigned triumphant.

Once only Anne spoke of this, and that was to her father. She hinted at the state of things, and asked his advice. Why did not Val interpose his authority, and forbid the dowager the house, if she could not keep herself from making mischief in it, sensibly asked the Rector. But Anne said neither she nor Val liked to do this. And then the Rector fancied there was some constraint in his daughter's voice, and she was not telling him the whole case unreservedly. He inquired no further, only gave her the best advice in his power: to be watchful, and counteract the dowager's influence, as far as she could; and trust to time; doing her own duty religiously by the children.

What Anne had not mentioned to Dr. Ashton was her husband's conduct in the matter. In that one respect she could read him no better than of old. Devoted to her as he was, as she knew him to be, in the children's petty disputes he invariably took the part of his first wife's—to the glowing satisfaction of the countess-dowager. No matter how glaringly wrong they might be, how tyrannical, Hartledon screened the elder, and—to use the expression of the nurses—snubbed the younger. Kind and good though Lady Hartledon was, she felt it acutely; and, to say the truth, was sorely puzzled and perplexed.

Lord Elster was an ailing child, and Mr. Brook, the apothecary, was always in attendance when they were in London. Lady Hartledon thought the boy's health might have been better left more to nature, but she would not have said so for the world. The dowager, on the contrary, would have preferred that half the metropolitan faculty should see him daily. She had a jealous dread of anything happening to the boy, and Anne's son becoming the heir.

Lord Hartledon was a busy man now, and had a place in the Government—though not as yet in the Cabinet. Whatever his secret care might have been, it was now passive; he was a general favourite, and courted in society. He was still young; the face as genial, the manners as free, the dark-blue eyes as kindly as of yore; eminently attractive in earlier days, he was so still; and his love for his wife amounted to a passion.

At the close of a sharp winter, when they had come up to town in January, that Lord Hartledon might be at his post, and the countess-dowager was inflicting upon them one of her long visits, it happened that Lord Elster seemed very poorly. Mr. Brook was called in, and said he would send a powder. He was called in so often to the boy as to take it quite as a matter of course; and, truth to say, thought the present indisposition nothing but a slight cold.

Late in the evening the two boys happened to be alone in the nursery, the nurse being temporarily absent from it. Edward was now a tall, slender, handsome boy in knickerbockers; Reginald a timid little fellow, several years younger—rendered timid by Edward's perpetual tyranny, which he might not resent. Edward was quiet enough this evening; he felt ill and shivery, and sat close to the fire. Casting his eyes upwards, he espied Mr. Brook's powder on the mantelpiece, with the stereotyped direction—"To be taken at bedtime." It was lying close to the jam-pot, which the head-nurse had put ready. Of course he had the greatest possible horror of medicine, and his busy thoughts began to run upon how he might avoid that detestable powder. The little fellow was sitting on the carpet playing with his bricks. Edward turned his eyes on his brother, and a bright thought occurred to him.

"Regy," said he, taking down the pot, "come here. Look at this jam: isn't it nice? It's raspberry and currant."

The child left his bricks to bend over the tempting compound.

"I'll give it you every bit to eat before nurse comes back," continued the boy, "if you'll eat this first."

Reginald cast a look upon the powder his brother exhibited. "What is it?" he lisped; "something good?"

"Delicious. It's just come in from the sweet-stuff shop. Open your mouth—wide."

Reginald did as he was bid: opened his mouth to its utmost width, and the boy shot in the powder.

It happened to be a preparation of that nauseous drug familiarly known as "Dover's powder." The child found it so, and set up a succession of shrieks, which aroused the house. The nurse rushed in; and Lord and Lady Hartledon, both of whom were dressing for dinner, appeared on the scene. There stood Reginald, coughing, choking, and roaring; and there sat the culprit, equably devouring the jam. With time and difficulty the facts were elicited from the younger child, and the elder scorned to deny them.

"What a wicked, greedy Turk you must be!" exclaimed the nurse, who was often in hot water with the elder boy.

"But Reginald need not have screamed so," testily interposed Lord Hartledon. "I thought one of them must be on fire. You naughty child, why did you scream?" he continued, giving Reginald a slight tap on the ear.

"Any child would scream at being so taken by surprise," said Lady Hartledon. "It is Edward who is in fault, not Reginald; and it is he who deserves punishment."

"And he should have it, if he were my son," boldly declared the nurse, as she picked up the unhappy Reginald. "A great greedy boy, to swallow down every bit of the jam, and never give his brother a taste, after poisoning him with that nasty powder!"

Edward rose, and gave the nurse a look of scorn. "The powder's good enough for him: he is nothing but a young brat, and I am Lord Elster."

Lady Hartledon felt provoked. "What is that you say, Edward?" she asked, laying her hand upon his shoulder in reproval.

"Let me alone, mamma. He'll never be anything but Regy Elster. *I* shall be Lord Hartledon, and jam's proper for me, and it's fair I should put upon him."

The nurse flounced off with Reginald, and Lady Hartledon turned to her husband. "Is this to be suffered? Will you allow it to pass without correction?"

"He means nothing," said Val. "Do you, Edward, my boy?"

"Yes, I do; I mean what I say. I shall stand up for myself and Maude."

Hartledon made no remonstrance: only drew the boy to him, with a hasty gesture, as though he would shield him from anger and the world.

Anne, hurt almost to tears, quitted the room. But she had scarcely reached her own when she remembered that she had left a diamond brooch in the nursery, which she had just been about to put into her dress when alarmed by the cries. She went back for it, and stood almost confounded by what she saw. Lord Hartledon, sitting down, had clasped his boy in his arms, and was sobbing over him; emotion such as man rarely betrays.

"Papa, Regy and the other two are not going to put me and Maude out of our places, are they? They can't, you know. We come first."

"Yes, yes, my boy; no one shall put you out," was the answer, as he pressed passionate kisses on the boy's face. "I will stand by you for ever."

Very judicious indeed! the once sensible man seemed to ignore the evident fact that the boy had been tutored. Lady Hartledon, a fear creeping over her, she knew not of what, left her brooch where it was, and stole back to her dressing-room.

Presently Val came in, all traces of emotion removed from his features. Lady Hartledon had dismissed her maid, and stood leaning against the arm of the sofa, indulging in bitter rumination.

"Silly children!" cried he; "it's hard work to manage them. And Edward has lost his pow—"

He broke off; stopped by the look of angry reproach from his wife, cast on him for the first time in their married life. He took her hand and bent down to her: fervent love, if ever she read it, in his eyes and tones.

"Forgive me, Anne; you are feeling this."

"Why do you throw these slights on my children? Why are you not more just?"

"I do not intend to slight our children, Anne, Heaven knows. But I—I cannot punish Edward."

"Why did you ever make me your wife?" sighed Lady Hartledon, drawing her hand away.

His poor assumption of unconcern was leaving him quickly; his face was changing to one of bitter sorrow.

"When I married you," she resumed, "I had reason to hope that should children be born to us, you would love them equally with your first; I had a right to hope it. What have I done that—"

"Stay, Anne! I can bear anything better than reproach from you."

"What have I and my children done to you, I was about to ask, that you take this aversion to them? lavishing all your love on the others and upon them only injustice?"

Val bent down, agitation in his face and voice.

"Hush, Anne! you don't know. The danger is that I should love your children better, far better than Maude's. It might be so if I did not guard against it."

"I cannot understand you," she exclaimed.

"Unfortunately, I understand myself only too well. I have a heavy burden to bear; do not you—my best and dearest—increase it."

She looked at him keenly; laid her hands upon him, tears gathering in her eyes. "Tell me what the burden is; tell me, Val! Let me share it."

But Val drew in again at once, alarmed at the request: and contradicted himself in the most absurd manner.

"There's nothing to share, Anne; nothing to tell."

Certainly this change was not propitiatory. Lady Hartledon, chilled and mortified, disdained to pursue the theme. Drawing herself up, she turned to go down to dinner, remarking that he might at least treat the children with more *apparent* justice.

"I am just; at least, I wish to be just," he broke forth in impassioned tones. "But I cannot be severe with Edward and Maude."

Another powder was procured, and, amidst much fighting and resistance, was administered. Lady Hartledon was in the boy's room the first thing in the morning. One grand quality in her was, that she never visited her vexation on the children; and Edward, in spite of his unamiable behaviour, did at heart love her, whilst he despised his grandmother; one of his sources of amusement being to take off that estimable old lady's peculiarities behind her back, and send the servants into convulsions.

"You look very hot, Edward," exclaimed Lady Hartledon, as she kissed him. "How do you feel?"

"My throat's sore, mamma, and my legs could not find a cold place all night. Feel my hand."

It was a child's answer, sufficiently expressive. An anxious look rose to her countenance.

"Are you sure your throat is sore?"

"It's very sore. I am so thirsty."

Lady Hartledon gave him some weak tea, and sent for Mr. Brook to come round as soon as possible. At breakfast she met the dowager, who had been out the previous evening during the powder episode. Lady Hartledon mentioned to her husband that she had sent a message to the doctor, not much liking Edward's symptoms.

"What's the matter with him?" asked the dowager, quickly. "What are his symptoms?"

"Nay, I may be wrong," said Lady Hartledon, with a smile. "I won't infect you with my fears, when there may be no reason for them."

The countess-dowager caught at the one word, and applied it in a manner never anticipated. She was the same foolish old woman she had ever been; indeed, her dread of catching any disorder had only grown with the years. And it happened, unfortunately for her peace, that the disorder which leaves its cruel traces on the most beautiful face was just then prevalent in London. Of all maladies the human frame is subject to, the vain old creature most dreaded that one. She rose up from her seat; her face turned pale, and her teeth began to chatter.

"It's small-pox! If I have a horror of one thing more than another, it's that dreadful, disfiguring malady. I wouldn't stay in a house where it was for a hundred thousand pounds. I might catch it and be marked for life!"

Lady Hartledon begged her to be composed, and Val smothered a laugh. The symptoms were not those of small-pox.

"How should you know?" retorted the dowager, drowning the reassuring words. "How should any one know? Get Pepps here directly. Have you sent for him?"

"No," said Anne. "I have more confidence in Mr. Brook where children are concerned."

"Confidence in Brook!" shrieked the dowager, pushing up her flaxen front. "A common, overworked apothecary! Confidence in him, Lady Hartledon! Elster's life may be in danger; he is my grandchild, and I insist on Pepps being fetched to him."

Anne sat down at once and wrote a brief note to Sir Alexander. It happened that the message sent to Mr. Brook had found that gentleman away from home, and the greater man arrived first. He looked at the child, asked a few bland questions, and wrote a prescription. He did not say what the illness might be: for he never hazarded a premature opinion. As he was leaving the chamber, a servant accosted him.

"Lady Kirton wishes to see you, sir."

"Well, Pepps," cried she, as he advanced, having loaded herself with camphor, "what is it?"

"I do not take upon myself to pronounce an opinion, Lady Kirton," rejoined the doctor, who had grown to feel irritated lately at the dowager's want of ceremony towards him. "In the early stage of a disorder it can rarely be done with certainty."

"Now don't let's have any of that professional humbug, Pepps," rejoined her ladyship. "You doctors know a common disorder as soon as you see it, only you think it looks wise not to say. Is it small-pox?"

"It's not impossible," said the doctor, in his wrath.

The dowager gasped.

"But I do not observe any symptoms of that malady developing themselves at present," added the doctor. "I think I may say it is not small-pox."

"Good patience, Pepps! you'll frighten me into it. It is and it isn't—what do you mean? What is it, if it's not that?"

"I may be able to tell after a second visit. Good morning, Lady Kirton," said he, backing out. "Take care you don't do yourself an injury with too much of that camphor. It is exciting."

In a short time Mr. Brook arrived. When he had seen the child and was alone with Lady Hartledon, she explained that the countess-dowager had wished Sir Alexander Pepps called in, and showed him the prescription just written. He read it and laid it down.

"Lady Hartledon," said he, "I must venture to disagree with that prescription. Lord Elster's symptoms are those of scarlet-fever, and it would be unwise to administer it. Sir Alexander stands of course much higher in the profession than I do, but my practice with children is larger than his."

"I feared it was scarlet-fever," answered Lady Hartledon. "What is to be done? I have every confidence in you, Mr. Brook; and were Edward my own child, I should know how to act. Do you think it would be dangerous to give him this prescription? You may speak confidentially."

"Not dangerous; it is a prescription that will do neither harm nor good. I suspect Sir Alexander could not detect the nature of the illness, and wrote this merely to gain time. It is not an infrequent custom to do so. In my opinion, not an hour should be lost in giving him a more efficacious medicine; early treatment is everything in scarlet-fever."

Lady Hartledon had been rapidly making up her mind. "Send in what you think right to be taken, immediately," she said, "and meet Sir Alexander in consultation later on."

Scarlet-fever it proved to be; not a mild form of it; and in a very few hours Lord Elster was in great danger, the throat being chiefly affected. The house was in commotion; the dowager worse than any one in it. A complication of fears beset her: first, terror for her own safety, and next, the less abject dread that death might remove *her* grandchild. In this latter fear she partly lost her personal fears, so far at any rate as to remain in the house; for it seemed to her that the child would inevitably die if she left it. Late in the afternoon she rushed into the presence of the doctors, who had just been holding a second consultation.

Sir Alexander Pepps recommended leeches to the throat: Mr. Brook disapproved of them. "It is the one chance for his life," said Sir Alexander.

"It is removing nearly all chance," said Mr. Brook.

Sir Alexander prevailed; and when they came forth it was understood that leeches were to be applied. But here Lady Hartledon stepped in.

"I dread leeches to the throat, Sir Alexander, if you will forgive me for saying so. I have twice seen them applied in scarlet-fever; and the patients—one a young lady, the other a child—in both cases died."

"Madam, I have given my opinion," curtly returned the physician. "They are necessary in Lord Elster's case."

"Do you approve of leeches?" cried Lady Hartledon, turning to Mr. Brook.

"Not altogether," was the cautious answer.

"Answer me one question, Mr. Brook," said Lady Hartledon, in her earnestness. "Would you apply these leeches were you treating the case alone?"

"No, madam, I would not."

Anne appealed to her husband. When the medical men differed, she thought the decision lay with him.

"I'm sure I don't know," returned Val, who felt perfectly helpless to advise. "Can't you decide, Anne? You know more about children and illness than I do."

"I would do so without hesitating a moment were it my own child," she replied. "I would not allow them to be put on."

"No, you would rather see him die," interrupted the dowager, who overheard the words, and most intemperately and unjustifiably answered them.

Anne coloured with shame for the old woman, but the words silenced her: how was it possible to press her own opinion after that? Sir Alexander had it all his own way, and the leeches were applied on either side the throat, Mr. Brook emphatically asserting in Lady Hartledon's private ear that he "washed his hands" of the measure. Before they came off the consequences were apparent; the throat was swollen outwardly, on both sides; within, it appeared to be closing.

The dowager, rather beside herself on the whole, had insisted on the leeches. Any one, seeing her conduct now, might have thought the invalid boy was really dear to her. Nothing of the sort. A hazy idea had been looming through her mind for years that Val was not strong; she had been mistaking mental disease for bodily illness; and a project to have full control of her grandchild, should he come into the succession prematurely, had coloured her dreams. This charming prospect would be ignominiously cut short if the boy went first.

Sir Alexander saw his error. There must be something peculiar in Lord Elster's constitution, he blandly said; it would not have happened in another. Of course, anything that turns out a mistake always is in the constitution—never in the treatment. Whether he lived or died now was just the turn of a straw: the chances were that he would die. All that could be done now was to endeavour to counteract the mischief by external applications.

"I wish you would let me try a remedy," said Lady Hartledon, wistfully. "A compress of cold water round the throat with oilsilk over it. I have seen it do so much good in cases of inward inflammation."

Mr. Brook smiled: if anything would do good that might, he said, speaking as if he had little faith in remedies now. Sir Alexander intimated that her ladyship might try it; graciously observing that it would do no harm.

The application was used, and the evening went on. The child had fallen into a sort of stupor, and Mr. Brook came in again before he had been away an hour, and leaned anxiously over the patient. He lay with his eyes half-closed, and breathed with difficulty.

"I think," he exclaimed softly, "there's the slightest shade of improvement."

"In the fever, or the throat?" whispered Lady Hartledon, who had not quitted the boy's bedside.

"In the throat. If so, it is due to your remedy, Lady Hartledon."

"Is he in danger?"

"In great danger. Still, I see a gleam of hope."

After the surgeon's departure, she went down to her husband, meeting Hedges on the stairs, who was coming to inquire after the patient for his master, for about the fiftieth time. Hartledon was in the library, pacing about incessantly in the darkness, for the room was only lighted by the fire. Anne closed the door and approached him.

"Percival, I do not bring you very good tidings," she said; "and yet they might be worse. Mr. Brook tells me he is in great danger, but thinks he sees a gleam of hope."

Lord Hartledon took her hand within his arm and resumed his pacing; his eyes were fixed on the carpet, and he said nothing.

"Don't grieve as those without hope," she continued, her eyes filling with tears. "He may yet recover. I have been praying that it may be so."

"Don't pray for it," he cried, his tone one of painful entreaty. "I have been daring to pray that it might please God to take him."

"Percival!" she exclaimed, starting away from him.

"I am not mad, Anne. Death would be a more merciful fate for my boy than life. Death now, whilst he is innocent, safe in Christ's love!—death, in Heaven's mercy!"

And Anne crept back to the upper chamber, sick with terror; for she did think that the trouble of his child's state was affecting her husband's brain.

# XXXVII

## A Painful Scene

Lord and Lady Hartledon were entertaining a family group. The everlasting dowager kept to them unpleasantly; making things unbearable, and wearing out her welcome in no slight degree, if she had only been wise enough to see it. She had escaped scarlet-fever and other dreaded ills; and was alive still. For that matter, the little Lord Elster had come out of it also: *not* unscathed; for the boy remained a sickly wreck, and there was very little hope that he would really recover. The final close might be delayed, but it was not to be averted. Before Easter they had left London for Hartledon, that he might have country air. Lord Hartledon's eldest sister, Lady Margaret Cooper, came there with her husband; and on this day the other sister, Lady Laura Level, had arrived from India. Lady Margaret was an invalid, and not an agreeable woman besides; but to Laura and Anne the meeting, after so many years' separation, was one of intense pleasure. They had been close friends from childhood.

They were all gathered together in the large drawing-room after luncheon. The day was a wet one, and no one had ventured out except Sir James Cooper. Accustomed to the Scotch mists, this rain seemed a genial shower, and Sir James was enjoying it accordingly. It was a warm, close day, in spite of the rain; and the large fire in the grate made the room oppressive, so that they were glad to throw the windows open.

Lying on a sofa near the fire was the invalid boy. By merely looking at him you might see that he would never rally, though he fluctuated much. To-day he was, comparatively speaking, well. Little Maude was threading beads; and the two others, much younger, stood looking on— Reginald and Anne. Lady Margaret Cooper, having a fellow-feeling for an invalid, sat near the sick boy. Lord Hartledon sat apart at a table reading, and making occasional notes. The dowager, more cumbersome than ever, dozed on the other side of the hearth. She was falling into the habit of taking a nap after luncheon as well as after dinner. Lady Laura was in danger of convulsions every time she looked at the dowager. Never in all her life had she seen so queer an old figure. She and Anne stood together at an open window, the one eagerly asking questions, the other answering, all in undertones. Lady Laura had been away from her own home and kindred some twelve years, and it seemed to her half a lifetime.

"Anne, how *was* it?" she exclaimed. "It was a thing that always puzzled me, and I never came to the bottom of it. My husband said at the time I used to talk of it in my sleep."

"What do you mean?"

"About you and Val. You were engaged to each other; you loved him, and he loved you. How came that other marriage about?"

"Well, I can hardly tell you. I was at Cannes with mamma, and he fell into the meshes. We knew nothing about it until they were married. Never mind all that now; I don't care to recall it, and it is a very sore point with Val. The blame, I believe, lay chiefly with *her*."

Anne glanced at the dowager, to indicate whom she meant. Lady Laura's eyes followed the same direction, and she laughed.

"A painted old guy! She looks like one who would do it. Why doesn't some one put her under a glass case and take her to the British Museum? When news of the marriage came out to India I was thunderstruck. I wrote off at once to Val, asking all sorts of questions, and received quite a savage reply, telling me to mind my own business. That letter alone would have told me how Val repented; it was so unlike him. Do you know what I did?"

"What did you do?"

"Sent him another letter by return mail with only two words in it—'Elster's Folly.' Poor Val! She died of heart-disease, did she not?"

"Yes. But she seemed to have been ailing for some time. She was greatly changed."

"Val is changed. There are threads of silver in his hair; and he is so much quieter than I thought he ever would be. I wonder you took him, Anne, after all; and I wonder still more that Dr. Ashton allowed it."

A blush tinged Lady Hartledon's face as she looked out at the soft rain, and a half-smile parted her lips.

"I see, Anne. Love once, love ever; and I suppose it was the same with Val, in spite of his folly. I should have taken out my revenge by marrying the first eligible man that offered himself. Talking of that—is poor Mr. Graves married yet?"

"Yes, at last," said Anne, laughing. "A grand match too for him, poor timid man: his wife's a lord's daughter, and as tall as a house."

"If ever man worshipped woman he worshipped you, though you were only a girl."

"Nonsense, Laura."

"Anne, you knew it quite well; and so did Val. Did he ever screw his courage up to the point of proposing?"

Anne laughed. "If he ever did, I was too vexed to answer him. He will be very happy, Laura. His wife is a meek, amiable woman, in spite of her formidable height."

"And now I want you to tell me one thing—How was it that Edward could not be saved?"

For a moment Lady Hartledon did not understand, and turned her eyes on the boy.

"I mean my brother, Anne. When news came out to India that he had died in that shocking manner, following upon poor George—I don't care now to recall how I felt. Was there *no* one at hand to save him?"

"No one. A sad fatality seemed to attend it altogether. Val regrets his brother bitterly to this day."

"And that poor Willy Gum was killed at sea, after all!"

"Yes," said Anne, shortly. "When you spoke of Edward," returning to the other subject, "I thought you meant the boy."

Lady Laura shook her head. "He will never get well, Anne. Death is written on his face."

"You would say so, if you saw him some days. He is excitable, and your coming has roused him. I never saw any one fluctuate so; one day dying, the next better again. For myself I have very little hope, and Mr. Hillary has none; but I dare not say so to Margaret and the dowager."

"Why not?"

"It makes them angry. They cannot bear to hear there's a possibility of his death. Margaret may see the danger, but I don't believe the dowager does."

"Their wishes must blind them," observed Lady Laura. "The dowager seems all fury and folly. She scarcely gave herself time to welcome me this morning, or to inquire how I was after my long voyage; but began descanting on a host of evils, the chief being that her grandson should have had fever."

"She would like him to bear a charmed life. Not for love of him, Laura."

"What then?"

"I do not believe she has a particle of love for him. Don't think me uncharitable; it is the truth; Val will tell you the same. She is not capable of experiencing common affection for any one; every feeling of her nature is merged in self-interest. Had her daughter left another boy she would not be dismayed at the prospect of this one's death; whether he lived or died, it would be all one to her. The grievance is that Reginald should have the chance of succeeding."

"Because he is your son. I understand. A vain, puffed-up old thing! the idea of her still painting her face and wearing false curls! I wonder you tolerate her in your house, Anne! She's always here."

"How can I help myself? She considers, I believe, that she has more right in this house than I have."

"Does she make things uncomfortable?"

"More so than I have ever confessed, even to my husband. From the hour of my marriage she set the two children against me, and against my children when they came; and she never ceases to do so still."

"Why do you submit to it?"

"She is their grandmother, and I cannot well deny her the house. Val might do so, but he does not. Perhaps I should have had courage to attempt it, for the children's own sake, it is so shocking to train them to ill-nature, but that he appears to think as she does. The petty disputes between the children are frequent—for my two elder ones are getting of an age to turn again when put upon—but their father never corrects Edward and Maude, or allows them to be corrected; let them do what wrong they will, he takes their part. I believe that if Edward *killed* one of my children, he would only caress him."

Lady Laura turned her eyes on the speaker's face, on its flush of pain and mortification.

"And Val loved you: and did *not* love Maude! What does it mean, Anne?"

"I cannot tell you. Things altogether are growing more than I can bear."

"Margaret has been with you some time; has she not interfered, or tried to put things upon a right footing?"

Anne shook her head. "She espouses the dowager's side; upholds the two children in their petty tyranny. No one in the house takes my part, or my children's."

"That is just like Margaret. Do you remember how you and I used to dread her domineering spirit when we were girls? It's time I came, I think, to set things right."

"Laura, neither you nor any one else can set things right. They have been wrong too long. The worst is, I cannot see what the evil is, as regards Val. If I ask him he repels me, or laughs at me, and tells me I am fanciful. That he has some secret trouble I have long known: his days are unhappy, his nights restless; often when he thinks me asleep I am listening to his sighs. I am glad you have come home; I have wanted a true friend to confide these troubles to, and I could only speak of them to one of the family."

"It sounds like a romance," cried Laura. "Some secret grief! What can it be?"

They were interrupted by a commotion. Maude had been threading a splendid ring all the colours of the rainbow, and now exhibited it for the benefit of admiring beholders.

"Papa—Aunt Margaret—look at my ring."

Lord Hartledon nodded pleasantly at the child from his distant seat; Lady Margaret appeared not to have heard; and Maude caught up a soft ball and threw it at her aunt.

Unfortunately, it took a wrong direction, and struck the nodding dowager on the nose. She rose up in a fury and some commotion ensued.

"Make me a ring, Maude," little Anne lisped when the dowager had subsided into her chair again. Maude took no notice; her finger was still lifted with the precious ornament.

"Can you see it from your sofa, Edward?"

The boy rose and stretched himself. "Pretty well. You have put it on the wrong finger, Maude. Ladies don't wear rings on the little finger."

"But it won't go on the others," said Maude dolefully: "it's too small." "Make a larger one."

"Make one for me, Maude," again broke in Anne's little voice.

"No, I won't!" returned Maude. "You are big enough to thread beads for yourself."

"No, she's not," said Reginald. "Make her one, Maude."

"No, don't, Maude," said Edward. "Let them do things for themselves."

"You hear!" whispered Lady Hartledon.

"I do hear. And Val sits there and never reproves them; and the old dowager's head and eyes are nodding and twinkling approval."

Lady Laura was an energetic little woman, thin, and pale, and excessively active, with a propensity for setting the world straight, and a tongue as unceremoniously free as the dowager's. In the cause of justice she would have stood up to battle with a giant. Lady Hartledon was about to make some response, but she bade her wait; her attention was absorbed by the children. Perhaps the truth was that she was burning to have a say in the matter herself.

"Maude," she called out, "if that ring is too small for you, it would do for Anne, and be kind of you to give it her."

Maude looked dubious. Left to herself, the child would have been generous enough. She glanced at the dowager.

"May I give it her, grand'ma?"

Grand'ma was conveniently deaf. She would rather have cut the ring in two than it should be given to the hated child: but, on the other hand, she did not care to offend Laura Level, who possessed inconveniently independent opinions, and did not shrink from proclaiming them. Seizing the poker, she stirred the fire, and created a divertissement.

In the midst of it, Edward left his sofa and walked up to the group and their beads. He was very weak, and tottered unintentionally against Anne. The touch destroyed her equilibrium, and she fell into Maude's lap. There was no damage done, but the box of beads was upset on to the carpet. Maude screamed at the loss of her treasures, rose up with anger, and slapped Anne. The child cried out.

"Why d'you hit her?" cried Reginald. "It was Edward's fault; he pushed her."

"What's that!" exclaimed Edward. "My fault! I'll teach you to say that," and he struck Reginald a tingling slap on the cheek.

Of course there was loud crying. The dowager looked on with a red face. Lady Margaret Cooper, who had no children of her own, stopped her ears. Lady Laura laid her hand on her sister-in law's wrist.

"And you can witness these scenes, and not check them! You are changed, indeed, Anne!"

"If I interfere to protect my children, I am checked and prevented," replied Lady Hartledon, with quivering lips. "This scene is nothing to what we have sometimes."

"Who checks you—Val?"

"The dowager. But he does not interpose for me. Where the children are concerned, he tacitly lets her have sway. It is not often anything of this sort takes place in his presence."

The noise continued: all the children seemed to be fighting together. Anne went forward and drew her own two out of the fray.

"Pray send those two screamers to the nursery, Lady Hartledon," cried the dowager.

"I cannot think why they are allowed in the drawing-room at all," said Lady Margaret, addressing no one in particular, unless it was the ceiling. "Edward and Maude would be quiet enough without them."

Anne did not retort: she only glanced at her husband, silent reproach on her pale face, and took up Anne in her arms to carry her from the room. But Lady Laura, impulsive and warm, came forward and stopped the exit.

"Lady Kirton, I am ashamed of you! Margaret, I am ashamed of you! I am ashamed of you all. You are doing the children a lasting injury, and you are guilty of cruel insult to Lady Hartledon. This is the second scene I have been a witness to, when the elder children were encouraged to behave badly to the younger; the first was in the nursery this morning; and I have been here only a few hours. And you, Lord Hartledon, their head and father, responsible for your children's welfare, can tamely sit by, and suffer it, and see your wife insulted! Is this what you married Anne Ashton for?"

Lord Hartledon rose: a strange look of pain on his features. "You are mistaken, Laura. I wish every respect to be shown to my wife; respect from all. Anne knows it."

"Respect!" scornfully retorted Lady Laura. "When you do not give her so much as a voice in her own house; when you allow her children to be trampled on, and beaten—*beaten*, sir—and she dare not interfere! I blush for you, and could never have believed you would so behave to your wife. Who are you, madam," turning again, in her anger, on the countess-dowager, "and who are you, Margaret, that you should dare to encourage Edward and Maude in rebellion against their present mother?"

Taken by surprise, the dowager made no answer. Lady Margaret looked defiance.

"You and Anne have invited me to your house on a lengthened visit, Lord Hartledon," continued Laura; "but I promise you that if this is to continue I will not remain in it; I will not witness insult to my early friend; and I will not see children incited to evil passions. Undress that child, sir," she sharply added, directing Val's attention to Reginald, "and you will see bruises on his back and shoulder. I saw them this morning, and asked the nurse what caused them and was told Lord Elster kicked him."

"It was the little beggar's own fault," interposed Edward, who was standing his ground with equanimity, and seemed to enjoy the scene.

Lady Laura caught him sharply by the arm. "Of whom are you speaking! Who's a little beggar?"

"Regy is."

"Who taught you to call him one?"

"Grand'ma."

"There, go away; go away all of you," cried Lady Laura, turning the two elder ones from the room imperatively, after Anne and her children. "Oh, so you are going also, Val! No wonder you are ashamed to stay here."

He was crossing the room; a curious expression on his drawn lips. Laura watched him from it; then went and stood before the dowager; her back to her sister.

"Has it ever struck you, Lady Kirton, that you may one day have to account for this?"

"It strikes me that you are making a vast deal of unnecessary noise, Madame Laura!"

"If your daughter could look on, from the other world, at earth and its scenes—and some hold a theory that such a state of things is not impossible—what would be her anguish, think you, at the evil you are inculcating in her children? One of them will very soon be with her—"

The dowager interrupted with a sort of howl.

"He will; there is no mistaking it. You who see him constantly may not detect it; but it is evident to a stranger. Were it not beneath me, I might ask on what grounds you tutor him to call Reginald a beggar, considering that your daughter brought my brother nothing but a few debts; whilst Miss Ashton brought him a large fortune?"

"I wouldn't condescend to be mean, Laura," put in Lady Margaret, whilst the dowager fanned her hot face.

They were interrupted by Hedges, showing in visitors. How much more Lady Laura might have said must remain unknown: she was in a mood to say a great deal.

"Mr. and Mrs. Graves."

It was the curate; and the tall, meek woman spoken of by Anne. Laura laughed as she shook hands with the former; whom she had known when a girl, and been given to ridiculing more than was quite polite.

Lord Hartledon had left the room after his wife. She sent the children to the nursery; and he found her alone in her chamber sobbing bitterly.

Certainly he was a contradiction. He fondly took her in his arms, beseeching her to pardon him, if he had unwittingly slighted her, as Laura implied; and his blue eyes were beaming with affection, his voice was low with persuasive tenderness.

"There are times," she sobbed, "when I am tempted to wish myself back in my father's house!"

"I cannot think whence all this discomfort arises!" he weakly exclaimed. "Of one thing, Anne, rest assured: as soon as Edward changes for the better or the worse—and one it must inevitably be—that mischief-making old woman shall quit my house for ever."

"Edward will never change for the better," she said. "For the worse, he may soon: for the better, never."

"I know: Hillary has told me. Bear with things a little longer, and believe that I will remedy them the moment remedy is possible. I am your husband."

Lady Hartledon lifted her eyes to his. "We cannot go on as we are going on now. Tell me what it is you have to bear. You remind me that you are my husband; I now remind you that I am your wife: confide in me. I will be true and loving to you, whatever it may be."

"Not yet; in a little time, perhaps. Bear with me still, my dear wife."

His look was haggard; his voice bore a sound of anguish; he clasped her hand to pain as he left her. Whatever might be his care, Anne could not doubt his love.

And as he went into the drawing-room, a smile on his face, chatting with the curate, laughing with his newly-married wife, both those unsuspicious visitors could have protested when they went forth, that never was a man more free from trouble than that affable servant of her Majesty's the Earl of Hartledon.

# XXXVIII

## Explanations

A change for the worse occurred in the child, Lord Elster; and after two or three weeks' sinking he died, and was buried at Hartledon by the side of his mother. Hartledon's sister quitted Hartledon House for a change; but the countess-dowager was there still, and disturbed its silence with moans and impromptu lamentations, especially when going up and down the staircase and along the corridors.

Mr. Carr, who had come for the funeral, also remained. On the day following it he and Lord Hartledon were taking a quiet walk together, when they met Mrs. Gum. Hartledon stopped and spoke to her in his kindly manner. She was less nervous than she used to be; and she and her husband were once more at peace in their house.

"I would not presume to say a word of sympathy, my lord," she said, curtseying, "but we felt it indeed. Jabez was cut up like anything when he came in yesterday from the funeral."

Val looked at her, a meaning she understood in his earnest eyes. "Yes, it is hard to part with our children: but when grief is over, we live in the consolation that they have only gone before us to a better place, where sin and sorrow are not. We shall join them later."

She went away, tears of joy filling her eyes. *She* had a son up there, waiting for *her*; and she knew Lord Hartledon meant her to think of him when he had so spoken.

"Carr," said Val, "I never told you the finale of that tragedy. George Gordon of the mutiny, did turn up: he lived and died in England."

"No!"

"He died at Calne. It was that poor woman's son."

Mr. Carr looked round for an explanation. He knew her as the wife of clerk Gum, and sister to Hartledon's housekeeper. Val told him all, as the facts had come out to him.

"Pike always puzzled me," he said. "Disguised as he was with his black hair, his face stained with some dark juice, there was a look in him that used to strike some chord in my memory. It lay in the eyes, I think. You'll keep these facts sacred, Carr, for the parents' sake. They are known only to four of us."

"Have you told your wife yet?" questioned Mr. Carr, recurring to a different subject.

"No. I could not, somehow, whilst the child lay dead in the house. She shall know it shortly."

"And what about dismissing the countess-dowager? You will do it?"

"I shall be only too thankful to do it. All my courage has come back to me, thank Heaven!"

The Countess-Dowager of Kirton's reign was indeed over; never would he allow her to disturb the peace of his house again. He might have to pension her off, but that was a light matter. His intention was to speak to her in a few days' time, allowing an interval to elapse after the boy's death; but she forestalled the time herself, as Val was soon to find.

Dinner that evening was a sad meal—sad and silent. The only one who did justice to it was the countess-dowager—in a black gauze dress and white crêpe turban. Let what would betide, Lady Kirton never failed to enjoy her dinner. She had a scheme in her head; it had been working there since the day of her grandson's death; and when the servants withdrew, she judged it expedient to disclose it to Hartledon, hoping to gain her point, now that he was softened by sorrow.

"Hartledon, I want to talk to you," she began, critically tasting her wine; "and I must request that you'll attend to me."

Anne looked up, wondering what was coming. She wore an evening dress of black crêpe, a jet necklace on her fair neck, jet bracelets on her arms: mourning far deeper than the dowager's.

"Are you listening to me, Val?"

"I am quite ready," answered Val.

"I asked you, once before, to let me have Maude's children, and to allow me a fair income with them. Had you done so, this dreadful misfortune would not have overtaken your house: for it stands to reason that if Lord Elster had been living somewhere else with me, he could not have caught scarlet-fever in London."

"We never thought he did catch it," returned Hartledon. "It was not prevalent at the time; and, strange to say, none of the other children took it, nor any one else in the house."

"Then what gave it him?" sharply uttered the dowager.

What Val answered was spoken in a low tone, and she caught one word only, Providence. She gave a growl, and continued.

"At any rate, he's gone; and you have now no pretext for refusing me Maude. I shall take her, and bring her up, and you must make me a liberal allowance for her."

"I shall not part with Maude," said Val, in quiet tones of decision.

"You can't refuse her to me, I say," rejoined the dowager, nodding her head defiantly; "she's my own grandchild."

"And my child. The argument on this point years ago was unsatisfactory, Lady Kirton; I do not feel disposed to renew it. Maude will remain in her own home."

"You are a vile man!" cried the dowager, with an inflamed face. "Pass me the wine."

He filled her glass, and left the decanter with her. She resumed.

"One day, when I was with Maude, in that last illness of hers in London, when we couldn't find out what was the matter with her, poor dear, she wrote you a letter; and I know what was in it, for I read it. You had gone dancing off somewhere for a week."

"To the Isle of Wight, on your account," put in Lord Hartledon, quietly; "on that unhappy business connected with your son who lives there. Well, ma'am?"

"In that letter Maude said she wished me to have charge of her children, if she died; and begged you to take notice that she said it," continued the dowager. "Perhaps you'll say you never had that letter?"

"On the contrary, madam, I admit receiving it," he replied. "I daresay I have it still. Most of Maude's letters lie in my desk undisturbed."

"And, admitting that, you refuse to act up to it?"

"Maude wrote in a moment of pique, when she was angry with me. But—"

"And I have no doubt she had good cause for anger!"

"She had great cause," was his answer, spoken with a strange sadness that surprised both the dowager and Lady Hartledon. Thomas Carr was twirling his wine-glass gently round on the white cloth, neither speaking nor looking.

"Later, my wife fully retracted what she said in that letter," continued Val. "She confessed that she had written it partly at your dictation, Lady Kirton, and said—but I had better not tell you that, perhaps."

"Then you shall tell me, Lord Hartledon; and you are a two-faced man, if you shuffle out of it."

"Very well. Maude said that she would not for the whole world allow her children to be brought up by you; she warned me also not to allow you to obtain too much influence over them."

"It's false!" said the dowager, in no way disconcerted.

"It is perfectly true: and Maude told me you knew what her sentiments were upon the point. Her real wish, as expressed to me, was, that the children should remain with me in any case, in their proper home."

"You say you have that other letter still?" cried the dowager, who was not always very clear in her conversation.

"No doubt."

"Then perhaps you'll look for it: and read over her wishes in black and white."

"To what end? It would make no difference in my decision. I tell you, ma'am, I am consulting Maude's wishes in keeping her child at home."

"I know better," retorted the dowager, completely losing her temper. "I wish your poor dear wife could rise from her grave and confute you. It's all stinginess; because you won't part with a paltry bit of money."

"No," said Val, "it's because I won't part with my child. Understand me, Lady Kirton—had Maude's wishes even been with you in this, I should not carry them out. As to money—I may have something to say to you on that score; but suppose we postpone it to a more fitting opportunity."

"You wouldn't carry them out!" she cried. "But you might be forced to, you mean man! That letter may be as good as a will in the eyes of the law. You daren't produce it; that's what it is."

"I'll give it you with pleasure," said Val, with a smile. "That is, if I have kept it. I am not sure."

She caught up her fan, and sat fanning herself. The reservation had suggested a meaning never intended to her crafty mind; her rebellious son-in-law meant to destroy the letter; and she began wondering how she could outwit him.

A sharp cry outside the door interrupted them. The children were only coming in to dessert now; and Reginald, taking a flying leap down the stairs, took rather too long a one, and came to grief at the bottom. Truth to say, the young gentleman, no longer kept down by poor Edward, was getting high-spirited and venturesome.

"What's that?" asked Anne, as the nurse came in with them, scolding.

"Lord Elster fell down, my lady. He's getting as tiresome as can be. Only to-day, I caught him astride the kitchen banisters, going to slide down them."

"Oh, Regy," said his mother, holding up her reproving finger.

The boy laughed, and came forward rubbing his arm, and ashamed of his tears. Val caught him up and kissed them away, drawing Maude also to his side.

That letter! The dowager was determined to get it, if there was a possibility of doing so. A suspicion that she would not be tolerated much longer in Lady Hartledon's house was upon her, and she knew not where to go. Kirton had married again; and his new wife had fairly turned her out more unceremoniously than the late one did. By hook or by crook, she meant to obtain the guardianship of her granddaughter, because in giving her Maude, Lord Hartledon would have to allow her an income.

She was a woman to stop at nothing; and upon quitting the dining-room she betook herself to the library—a large, magnificent room—the pride of Hartledon. She had come in search of Val's desk; which she found, and proceeded to devise means of opening it. That accomplished, she sat herself down, like a leisurely housebreaker, to examine it, putting on a pair of spectacles, which she kept surreptitiously in a pocket, and would not have worn before any one for the world. She found the letter she was in search of; and she found something else for her pains, which she had not bargained for.

Not just at first. There were many tempting odds and ends of things to dip into. For one thing, she found Val's banking book, and some old cheque-books; they served her for some time. Next she came upon two packets sealed up in white paper, with Val's own seal. On one was written, "Letters of Lady Maude;" on the other, "Letters of my dear Anne." Peering further into the desk, she came upon an obscure inner slide, which had evidently not been opened for years, and she had difficulty in undoing it. A paper was in it, superscribed, "Concerning A.W.;" on opening which she found a letter addressed to Thomas Carr, of the Temple.

Thomas Carr's letters were no more sacred with her than Lord Hartledon's. No woman living was troubled with scruples so little as she. It proved to have been written by a Dr. Mair, in Scotland, and was dated several years back.

But now—did Lord Hartledon really know he had that dangerous letter by him? If so, what could have possessed him to preserve it? Or, did he not rather believe he had returned it to Mr. Carr at the time? The latter, indeed, proved to be the case; and never, to the end of his life, would he, in one sense, forgive his own carelessness.

Who was A.W.? thought the curious old woman, as she drew the light nearer to her, and began the tempting perusal, making the most of the little time left. They could not be at tea yet, and she had told Lady Hartledon she was going to take her nap in her own room. The gratification of rummaging false Val's desk was an ample compensation; and the countess-dowager hugged herself with delight.

But what was this she had come upon—this paper "concerning A. W."? The dowager's mouth fell as she read; and gradually her little eyes opened as if they would start from their sockets, and her face grew white. Have you ever watched the livid pallor of fear struggling to one of these painted faces? She dashed off her spectacles; she got up and wrung her hands; she executed a frantic war-dance; and finally she tore, with the letter, into the drawing-room, where Val and Anne and Thomas Carr were beginning tea and talking quietly.

They rose in consternation as she danced in amongst them, and held out the letter to Lord Hartledon.

He took it from her, gazing in utter bewilderment as he gathered in its contents. Was it a fresh letter, or—his face became whiter than the dowager's. In her reckless passion she avowed what she had done—the letter was secreted in his desk.

"Have you dared to visit my desk?" he gasped—"break my seals? Are you mad?"

"Hark at him!" she cried. "He calls me to account for just lifting the lid of a desk! But what is he? A villain—a thief—a spy—a murderer—and worse than any of them! Ah, ha, my lady!" nodding her false front at Lady Hartledon, who stood as one petrified, "you stare there at me with your open eyes; but you don't know what you are! Ask *him*! What was Maude—Heaven help her—my poor Maude? What was she? And *you* in the plot; you vile Carr! I'll have you all hanged together!"

Lord Hartledon caught his wife's hand.

"Carr, stay here with her and tell her all. No good concealing anything now she has read this letter. Tell her for me, for she would never listen to me."

He drew his wife into an adjoining room, the one where the portrait of George Elster looked down on its guests. The time for disclosing the story to his wife had been somewhat forestalled. He would have given half his life that it had never reached that other woman, miserable old sinner though she was.

"You are trembling, Anne; you need not do so. It is not against you that I have sinned."

Yes, she was trembling very much. And Val, in his honourable, his refined, shrinking nature, would have given his life's other half not to have had the tale to tell.

It is not a pleasant one. You may skip it if you please, and go on to the last page. Val once said he had been more sinned against than sinning: it may be deemed that in that opinion he was too lenient to himself. Anne, his wife, listened with averted face and incredulous ears.

"You have wanted a solution to my conduct, Anne—to the strange preference I seemed to accord the poor boy who is gone; why I could not punish him; why I was more thankful for the boon of his death than I had been for his life. He was my child, but he was not Lord Elster."

She did not understand.

"He had no right to my name; poor little Maude has no right to it. Do you understand me now?"

Not at all; it was as though he were talking Greek to her.

"Their mother, when they were born, was not my wife."

"Their mother was Lady Maude Kirton," she rejoined, in her bewilderment.

"That is exactly where it was," he answered bitterly. "Lady Maude Kirton, not Lady Hartledon."

She could not comprehend the words; her mind was full of consternation and tumult. Back went her thoughts to the past.

"Oh, Val! I remember papa's saying that a marriage in that unused chapel was only three parts legal!"

"It was legal enough, Anne: legal enough. But when that ceremony took place"—his voice dropped to a miserable whisper, "I had—as they tell me—a wife living."

Slowly she admitted the meaning of the words; and would have started from him with a faint cry, but that he held her to him.

"Listen to the whole, Anne, before you judge me. What has been your promise to me, over and over again?—that, if I would tell you my sorrow, *you* would never shrink from me, whatever it might be."

She remembered it, and stood still; terribly rebellious, clasping her fingers to pain, one within the other.

"In that respect, at any rate, I did not willingly sin. When I married Maude I had no suspicion that I was not free as air; free to marry her, or any other woman in the world."

"You speak in enigmas," she said faintly.

"Sit down, Anne, whilst I give you the substance of the tale. Not its details until I am more myself, and that voice"—pointing to the next room—"is not sounding in my ears. You shall hear all later; at least, as much as I know myself; I have never quite believed in it, and it has been to me throughout as a horrible dream."

Indeed Mr. Carr seemed to be having no inconsiderable amount of trouble, to judge by the explosions of wrath on the part of the dowager.

She sat down as he told her, her face turned from him, rebellious at having to listen, but curious yet. Lord Hartledon stood by the mantelpiece and shaded his eyes with his hand.

"Send your thoughts into the past, Anne; you may remember that an accident happened to me in Scotland. It was before you and I were engaged, or it would not have happened. Or, let me say, it might not; for young men are reckless, and I was no better than others. Heaven have mercy on their follies!"

"The accident might not have happened?"

"I do not speak of the accident. I mean what followed. When out shooting I nearly blew off my arm. I was carried to the nearest medical man's, a Dr. Mair's, and remained there; for it was not thought safe to move me; they feared inflammation, and they feared locked-jaw. My father was written to, and came; and when he left after the danger was over he made arrangements with Dr. Mair to keep me on, for he was a skilful man, and wished to perfect the cure. I thought the prolonged stay in the strange, quiet house worse than all the rest. That feeling wore off; we grow reconciled to most conditions; and things became more tolerable as I grew better and joined the household. There was a wild, clever, random young man staying there, the doctor's assistant—George Gordon; and there was also a young girl, Agnes Waterlow. I used to wonder what this Agnes did there, and one day asked the old housekeeper; she said the young lady was there partly that the doctor might watch her health, partly because she was a relative of his late wife's, and had no home."

He paused, as if in thought, but soon continued.

"We grew very intimate; I, Gordon, and Miss Waterlow. Neither of them was the person I should have chosen for an intimacy; but there was, in a sense, no help for it, living together. Agnes was a wild, free, rather coarse-natured girl, and Gordon drank. That she fell in love with me there's no doubt—and I grew to like her quite well enough to talk nonsense to her. Whether any plot was laid between her and Gordon to entrap me, or whether what happened arose in the recklessness of the moment, I cannot decide to this hour. It was on my twenty-first birthday; I was almost well again; we had what the doctor called a dinner, Gordon a jollification, and Agnes a supper. It was late when we sat down to it, eight o'clock; and there was a good deal of feasting and plenty of wine. The doctor was called out afterwards to a patient several miles distant, and George Gordon made some punch; which rendered none of our heads the steadier. At least I can answer for mine: I was weak with the long illness, and not much of a drinker at any time. There was a great deal of nonsense going on, and Gordon pretended to marry me to Agnes. He said or read (I can't tell which, and never knew then) some words mockingly out of the prayer-book, and said we were man and wife. Whilst we were all laughing at the joke, the doctor's old housekeeper came in, to see what the noise was about, and I, by way of keeping it up, took Agnes by the hand, and introduced her as Mrs. Elster. I did not understand the woman's look of astonishment then; unfortunately, I have understood it too well since."

Anne was growing painfully interested.

"Well, after that she threw herself upon me in a manner that—that was extraordinary to me, not having the key to it; and I—lost my head. Don't frown, Anne; ninety-nine men out of a hundred would have lost theirs; and you'll say so if ever I give you the details. Of course blame attached to me; to me, and not to her. Though at the time I mentally gave her, I assure you, her full share, somewhat after the manner of the Pharisee condemning the publican. That also has come home to me: she believed herself to be legally my wife; I never gave a thought to that evening's farce, and should have supposed its bearing any meaning a simple impossibility.

"A short time, and letters summoned me home; my mother was dangerously ill. I remember Agnes asked me to take her with me, and I laughed at her. I arranged to write to her, and promised to go back shortly—which, to tell you the truth, I never meant to do. Having been mistaking her, mistaking her still, I really thought her worthy of very little consideration. Before I had been at home a fortnight I received a letter from Dr. Mair, telling me that Agnes was showing symptoms of insanity, and asking what provision I purposed making for her. My sin was finding me out; I wondered how *he* had found it out; I did not ask, and did not know for years. I wrote back saying I would willingly take all expenses upon myself; and inquired what sum would be required by the asylum—to which he said she must be sent. He mentioned two hundred a-year, and from that time I paid it regularly."

"And was she really insane?" interrupted Lady Hartledon.

"Yes; she had been so once or twice before—and this was what the housekeeper had meant by saying she was with the doctor that her health might be watched. It appeared that when these symptoms came on, after I left, Gordon took upon himself to disclose to the doctor that Agnes was married to me, telling the circumstances as they had occurred. Dr. Mair got frightened: it was no light matter for the son of an English peer to have been deluded into marriage with an obscure and insane girl; and the quarrel that took place between him and Gordon on the occasion resulted in the latter's leaving. I have never understood Gordon's conduct in the matter: very disagreeable thoughts in regard to it come over me sometimes."

"What thoughts?"

"Oh, never mind; they can never be set at rest now. Let me make short work of this story. I heard no more and thought no more; and the years went on, and then came my marriage with Maude. We went to Paris—*you* cannot have forgotten any of the details of that period, Anne; and after our return to London I was surprised by a visit from Dr. Mair. That evening, that visit and its details stamped themselves on my memory for ever in characters of living fire."

He paused for a moment, and something like a shiver seized him. Anne said nothing.

"Maude had gone with some friends to a fête at Chiswick, and Thomas Carr was dining with me. Hedges came in and said a gentleman wanted to see me—*would* see me, and would not be denied. I went to him, and found it was Dr. Mair. In that interview I learnt that by the laws of Scotland Miss Waterlow was my wife."

"And the suspicion that she was so had never occurred to you before?"

"Anne! Should I have been capable of marrying Maude, or any one else, if it had? On my solemn word of honour, before Heaven"—he raised his right hand as if to give effect to his words—"such a thought had never crossed my brain. The evening that the nonsense took place I only regarded it as a jest, a pastime—what you will: had any one told me it was a marriage I should have laughed at them. I knew nothing then of the laws of Scotland, and should have thought it simply impossible that that minute's folly, and my calling her, to keep up the joke, Mrs. Elster, could have constituted a marriage. I think they all played a deep part, even Agnes. Not a soul had so much as hinted at the word 'marriage' to me after that evening; neither Gordon, nor she, nor Dr. Mair in his subsequent correspondence; and in that he always called her 'Agnes.' However—he then told me that she was certainly my legal wife, and that Lady Maude was not.

"At first," continued Val, "I did not believe it; but Dr. Mair persisted he was right, and the horror of the situation grew upon me. I told all to Carr, and took him up to Dr. Mair. They discussed Scottish law and consulted law-books; and the truth, so far, became apparent. Dr. Mair was sorry for me; he saw I had not erred knowingly in marrying Maude. As to myself, I was helpless, prostrated. I asked the doctor, if it were really true, why the fact had been kept from me: he replied that he supposed I knew it, and that delicacy alone had caused him to abstain from alluding to it in his letters. He had been very angry when Gordon told him, he said; grew half frightened as to consequences; feared he should get into trouble for allowing me to be so entrapped in his house; and he and Gordon parted at once. And then Dr. Mair asked a question which I could not very well answer, why, if I did not know she was my wife, I had paid so large a sum for Agnes. He had been burying the affair in silence, as he had assumed I was doing; and it was only the announcement of my marriage with Maude in the newspapers that aroused him. He had thought I was acting this bad part deliberately; and he went off at once to Hartledon in anger; found I had gone abroad; and now came to me on my return, still in anger, saying at first that he should proceed against me, and obtain justice for Agnes. When he found how utterly ignorant of wrong I had been, his tone changed; he was truly grieved and concerned for me. Nothing was decided: except that Dr. Mair, in his compassion towards Lady Maude, promised not to be the first to take legal steps. It seemed that there was only him to fear: George Gordon was reported to have gone to Australia; the old housekeeper was dead; Agnes was deranged. Dr. Mair left, and Carr and I sat on till midnight. Carr took what I thought a harsh view of the matter; he urged me to separate from Maude—"

"I think you should have done so for her sake," came the gentle interruption.

"For her sake! the words Carr used. But, Anne, surely there were two sides to the question. If I disclosed the facts, and put her away from me, what was she? Besides, the law might be against me—Scotland's iniquitous law; but in Heaven's sight *Maude* was my wife, not the other. So I temporized, hoping that time might bring about a relief, for Dr. Mair told me that Miss Waterlow's health was failing. However, she lived on, and—"

Lady Hartledon started up, her face blanching.

"Is she not dead now? Was she living when you married me? Am *I* your wife?"

He could hardly help smiling. His calm touch reassured her.

"Do you think you need ask, Anne? The next year Dr. Mair called upon me again—it was the evening before the boy was christened; he had come to London on business of his own. To my dismay, he told me that a change for the better was appearing in Miss Waterlow's mental condition; and he thought it likely she might be restored to health. Of course, it increased the perplexities and my horror, had that been needed; but the hope or fear, or what you like to call it, was not borne out. Three years later, the doctor came to me for the third and final time, to bring me the news that Agnes was dead."

As the relief had been to him then, so did it almost seem now to Anne. A sigh of infinite pain broke from her. She had not seen where all this was tending.

"Imagine, if you can, what it was for me all those years with the knowledge daily and nightly upon me that the disgraceful truth might at any moment come out to Maude—to her children, to the world! Living in the dread of arrest myself, should the man Gordon show himself on the scene! And now you see what it is that has marred my peace, and broken the happiness of our married life. How could I bear to cross those two deeply-injured children, who were ever rising up in judgment against me? How take our children's part against them, little unconscious things? It seemed that I had always, daily, hourly, some wrong to make up to them. The poor boy was heir to Hartledon in the eyes of the world; but, Anne, your boy was the true heir."

"Why did you not tell me?—all this time!"

"I could not. I dared not. You might not have liked to put Reginald out of his rights."

"Oh, Percival; how can you so misjudge me?" she asked, in tones of pain. "I would have guarded the secret as jealously as you. I must still do it for Maude."

"Poor Maude!" he sighed. "Her mother forgave me before she died—"

"She knew it, then?"

"Yes. She learned—"

Sounds of drumming on the door, and the countess-dowager's voice, stopped Lord Hartledon.

"I had better face her," he said, as he unlocked it. "She will arouse the household."

Wild, intemperate, she met him with a volley of abuse that startled Lady Hartledon. He got her to a sofa, and gently held her down there.

"It's what I've been obliged to do all along," said Thomas Carr; "I don't believe she has heard ten words of my explanation."

"Pray be calm, Lady Kirton," said Hartledon, soothingly; "be calm, as you value your daughter's memory. We shall have the servants at the doors."

"I won't be calm; I will know the worst."

"I wish you to know it; but not others."

"Was Maude your wife?"

"No," he answered, in low tones. "Not—"

"And you are not ashamed to confess it?" she interrupted, not allowing him to continue. But she was a little calmer in manner; and Val stood upright before her with folded arms.

"I am ashamed and grieved to confess it; but I did not knowingly inflict the injury. In Scotland—"

"Don't repeat the shameful tale," she cried; "I have heard from your confederate, Carr, as much as I want to hear. What do you deserve for your treachery to Maude?"

"All I have reaped—and more. But it was not intentional treachery; and Maude forgave me before she died."

"She knew it! You told her? Oh, you cruel monster!"

"I did not tell her. She did as you have just done—interfered in what did not concern her, in direct disobedience to my desire; and she found it out for herself, as you, ma'am, have found it out."

"When?"

"The winter before her death."

"Then the knowledge killed her!"

"No. Something else killed her, as you know. It preyed upon her spirits."

"Lord Hartledon, I can have you up for fraud and forgery, and I'll do it. It will be the consideration of Maude's fame against your punishment, and I'll make a sacrifice to revenge, and prosecute you."

"There is no fraud where an offence is committed unwittingly," returned Lord Hartledon; "and forgery is certainly not amongst my catalogue of sins."

"You are liable for both," suddenly retorted the dowager; "you have stuck up 'Maude, Countess of Hartledon,' on her monument in the church; and what's that but fraud and forgery?"

"It is neither. If Maude did not live Countess of Hartledon, she at least so went to her grave. We were remarried, privately, before she died. Mr. Carr can tell you so."

"It's false!" raved the dowager.

"I arranged it, ma'am," interposed Mr. Carr. "Lord Hartledon and your daughter confided the management to me, and the ceremony was performed in secrecy in London"

The dowager looked from one to the other, as if she were bewildered.

"Married her again! why, that was making bad worse. Two false marriages! Did you do it to impose upon her?"

"I see you do not understand," said Lord Hartledon. "The—my—the person in Scotland was dead then. She was dead, I am thankful to say, before Maude knew anything of the affair."

Up started the dowager. "Then is the woman dead now? was she dead when you married *her*?" laying her hand upon Lady Hartledon's arm. "Are her children different from Maude's?"

"They are. It could not be otherwise."

"Her boy is really Lord Elster?"

She flung Lady Hartledon's arm from her. Her voice rose to a shriek.

"Maude is not Lady Maude?"

Val shook his head sadly.

"And your children are lords and ladies and honourables," darting a look of consternation at Anne, "whilst my daughter's—"

"Peace, Lady Kirton!" sternly interrupted Val. "Let the child, Maude, be Lady Maude still to the world; let your daughter's memory be held sacred. The facts need never come out: I do not fear now that they ever will. I and my wife and Thomas Carr, will guard the secret safely: take you care to do so."

"I wish you had been hung before you married Maude!" responded the aggrieved dowager.

"I wish I had," said he.

"Ugh!" she grunted wrathfully, the ready assent not pleasing her.

"With my poor boy's death the chief difficulty has passed away. How things would have turned out, or what would have been done, had he lived, it has well-nigh worn away my brain to dwell upon. Carr knows that it has nearly killed me: my wife knows it."

"Yes, you could tell her things, and keep the diabolical secret from poor Maude and from me," she returned, rather inconsistently. "I don't doubt you and your wife have exulted enough over it."

"I never knew it until to-night," said Anne, gently turning to the dowager. "It has grieved me deeply. I shall never cease to feel for your daughter's wrongs; and it will only make me more tender and loving to her child. The world will never know that she is not Lady Maude."

"And the other name—Elster—because you know she has no right to it," was the spiteful retort. "I wish to my heart you had been drowned in your brother's place, Lord Hartledon; I wished it at the time."

"I know you did."

"You could not then have made fools of me and my dear daughter; and the darling little cherub in the churchyard would have been the real heir. There'd have been a good riddance of you."

"It might have been better for me in the long run," said he, quietly, passing over the inconsistencies of her speech. "Little peace or happiness have I had in living. Do not let us recriminate, Lady Kirton, or on some scores I might reproach you. Maude loved my brother, and you knew it; I loved Miss Ashton, and you knew that; yet from the very hour the breath was out of my brother's body you laid your plans and began your schemes upon me. I was weak as water in your hands, and fell into the snare. The marriage was your work entirely; and in the fruits it has brought forth there might arise a nice question, Lady Kirton, which of us is most to blame: I, who erred unwittingly, or you who—"

"Will you have done?" she cried.

"I have nearly done. I only wish you to remember that others may have been wrong, as well as myself. Dr. Ashton warned us that night that the marriage might not bring a blessing. Anne, it was a cruel wrong upon you," he added, impulsively turning to her; "you felt it bitterly, I shamefully; but, my dear wife, you have lived to see that it was in reality a mercy in disguise."

The countess-dowager, not finding words strong enough to express her feelings at this, made a grimace at him.

"Let us be friends, Lady Kirton! Let us join together silently in guarding Maude's good name, and in burying the past. In time perhaps even I may live it down. Not a human being knows of it except we who are here and Dr. Mair, who will for his own sake guard the secret. Maude was my wife always in the eyes of the world; and Maude certainly died so: all peace and respect to her memory! As for my share, retribution has held its heavy hand upon me; it is upon me still, Heaven knows. It was for Maude I suffered; for Maude I felt; and if my life could have repaired the wrong upon her, I would willingly have sacrificed it. Let us be friends: it may be to the interest of both."

He held out his hand, and the dowager did not repulse it. She had caught the word "interest."

"*Now* you might allow me Maude and that income!"

"I think I had better allow you the income without Maude."

"Eh? what?" cried the dowager, briskly. "Do you mean it?"

"Indeed I do. I have been thinking for some little time that you would be more comfortable in a home of your own, and I am willing to help you to one. I'll pay the rent of a nice little place in Ireland, and give you six hundred a-year, paid quarterly, and—yes—make you a yearly present of ten dozen of port wine."

Ah, the crafty man! The last item had a golden sound in it.

"Honour bright, Hartledon?"

"Honour bright! You shall never want for anything as long as you live. But you must not"—he seemed to search for his words—"you must undertake not to come here, upsetting and indulging the children."

"I'll undertake it. Good vintage, mind."

"The same that you have here."

The countess-dowager beamed. In the midst of her happiness—and it was what she had not felt for many a long day, for really the poor old creature had been put about sadly—she bethought herself of propriety. Melting into tears, she presently bewailed her exhaustion, and said she should like some tea: perhaps good Mr. Carr would bring her a teaspoonful of brandy to put into it.

They brought her hot tea, and Mr. Carr put the brandy into it, and Anne took it to her on the sofa, and administered it, her own tears overflowing. She was thinking what an awful blow this would have been to her own mother.

"Little Maude shall be very dear to me always, Val," she whispered. "This knowledge will make me doubly tender with her."

He laid his hand fondly upon her, giving her one of his sweet sad smiles in answer. She could at length understand what feelings, in regard to the children, had actuated him. But from henceforth he would be just to all alike; and Maude would receive her share of correction for her own good.

"I always said you did not give me back the letter," observed Mr. Carr, when they were alone together later, and Val sat tearing up the letter into innumerable bits.

"And I said I did, simply because I could not find it. You were right, Carr, as you always are."

"Not always. But I am sorry it came to light in this way."

"Sorry! it is the greatest boon that could have fallen on me. The secret is, so to say, off my mind now, and I can breathe as I have not breathed for years. If ever a heartfelt thanksgiving went up to Heaven one from me will ascend to-night. And the dowager does not feel the past a bit. She cared no more for Maude than for any one else. She can't care for any one. Don't think me harsh, Carr, in saying so."

"I am sure she does not feel it," emphatically assented Mr. Carr. "Had she felt it she would have been less noisy. Thank heaven for your sake, Hartledon, that the miserable past is over."

"And over more happily than I deserved."

A silence ensued, and Lord Hartledon flung the bits of paper carefully into the fire. Presently he looked up, a strange earnestness in his face.

"It is the custom of some of our cottagers here to hang up embossed cards at the foot of their bed, with texts of Scripture written on them. There is one verse I should like to hang before every son of mine, though I had ten of them, that it might meet their eyes last ere the evening's sleeping, in the morning's first awakening. The ninth verse of the eleventh chapter of Ecclesiastes."

"I don't remember," observed Thomas Carr, after a pause of thought.

"'Rejoice, O young man, in thy youth: and let thy heart cheer thee in the days of thy youth, and walk in the ways of thine heart, and in the sight of thine eyes: but know thou, that for all these things God will bring thee into judgment.'"

THE END

# A Note About the Author

Ellen Price (1814–1887) was an English novelist and translator, better known by her penname, Mrs. Henry Wood. Wood lived with her husband, Henry Wood, and four children in Southern France for twenty years, until moving back to England when Henry's business failed. In England, Wood supported her family with her writing, becoming an international bestseller. Wood was praised for her masterful storytelling of middle-class lives, and often advocated for faith and strong morals in her work. Wood's most celebrated work was *East Lynne*, a sensation novel popular for its elaborate plot. In 1867, Wood became the owner and editor of Argosy Magazine, which she continued to publish until her death in 1887. By the end of her career, Wood published over thirty novels, many of which were immensely popular in England, the United States, and in Australia.

# A Note from the Publisher

Spanning many genres, from non-fiction essays to literature classics to children's books and lyric poetry, Mint Edition books showcase the master works of our time in a modern new package. The text is freshly typeset, is clean and easy to read, and features a new note about the author in each volume. Many books also include exclusive new introductory material. Every book boasts a striking new cover, which makes it as appropriate for collecting as it is for gift giving. Mint Edition books are only printed when a reader orders them, so natural resources are not wasted. We're proud that our books are never manufactured in excess and exist only in the exact quantity they need to be read and enjoyed.

# Discover more of your favorite classics with Bookfinity™.

- Track your reading with custom book lists.
- Get great book recommendations for your personalized Reader Type.
- Add reviews for your favorite books.
- AND MUCH MORE!

Visit **bookfinity.com** and take the fun Reader Type quiz to get started.

Enjoy our classic and modern companion pairings!

Printed in the USA
CPSIA information can be obtained
at www.ICGtesting.com
JSHW020020090324
58879JS00004B/45